The Poetry Cure

by Alice Carlton

Copyright © 2022 by Alice Carlton
Kindle Direct Publishing, a division of Amazon

"The Journey" by Mary Oliver
Reprinted by the permission of The Charlotte Sheedy Literary Agency as agent for the author.
Copyright © Mary Oliver 1986, 2017 with permission of Bill Reichblum

ISBN: 979-8-9864054-0-7

Book design by Diana Wade
www.alicecarlton.com

To Dave

Foreword

What I love about novelists is their imagination. And Alice Carlton is no exception. Utilizing her experience as a relationship therapist, she narrates a tale of marriage gone awry, growing through the pain, and new love entering that had been predicted years before by a Ouija Board. That combined with these two people's love of poetry and the healing it provides offers a creative twist that warms the heart.

An added bonus to this love story is the novel's portrayal of good therapy. This art form is not often depicted realistically in books and drama. But *The Poetry Cure* paints a picture of a skilled therapist providing a solid grounding, thus adding depth and wisdom. Readers will cheer for the protagonist, Annie, as she works through her struggles, matures, and learns to love herself enough to love another authentically … a journey most of us find ourselves taking. *The Poetry Cure* blazes the trail in a most distinctive way.

—Linda A Marshall, author of *A Long Awakening to Grace:*
A Memoir of Loss and Discovery

Chapter 1

$\mathcal{A}$ new student joined the class that night. He swam in a quarter-hour late after the early spring storm had dropped on them like a bucket of water upturned. Fortunately, he was dressed for it—in a bright yellow slicker with a hood that made him appear like a giant firefly beaming light in defiance of the angry thunderstorm that had them all hunkered down awaiting the next blow. Lightning struck again and again. He must have had trouble finding them and who could blame him? No other class roved from coffeehouse to coffeehouse every Sunday night. Annie had thought it strange when she signed up. But after that first class, sipping cappuccino while pouring over poems seemed better than sitting in the same cold classroom. This coffeehouse even had a fireplace. Group members had pulled their chairs in a semicircle in front of it, fluttering their pages like moth wings and peeling wet layers as they struggled to warm themselves and dry off.

Their instructor, Ian Bartlett, ever the warm host, pulled another chair into the circle. His black hair and Irish white skin made his blue eyes appear to glow atop his tall frame. "And who might you be, coming in late on such a wet night?" he sang out. "We've only just begun. Please come dry out next to me and the fire."

1

"Sorry, but I couldn't find you," said the newcomer. "It took me forever to find someone at the community arts center who knew where you'd wandered to from last time. And then the storm hit. Ye-ow! What a downpour." He threw back his head and chortled in a way that made all seven of them join in with him.

The stranger began peeling his layers of yellow rubber then maroon jacket down to a red and brown flannel shirt that rang out back-country camper. He set the yellow slicker beside his chair. It stood at attention, a valet in waiting, raindrops flowing down and puddling on the floor. His smile lit up his rugged features. His unwrinkled skin showed him to be in his early thirties. His thick sandy-colored hair waved around his head like a halo. "A name? Yes, indeed. My name's Taffer, George Taffer."

When his name hit her ears, a current ran through her. Annie froze, her slim body folded in her chair, her ankles crossed, her hands holding her notebook in her lap. She stared, but her eyes did not focus on him. Instead, she saw herself years ago, in her college dorm room with her roommate, Nancy, and a few others, sitting on the floor with the Ouija Board between them. They asked it the usual questions: Where will I live? What work will I do? Whom will I marry? They touched the planchette lightly with their fingertips. It moved across the letters on the board as if guided by some invisible hand. They roared at the answers given. The Ouija Board told her she would live in France her last two years of college—well, that never happened. It told her she would become an actress—that never happened. And it told her she would marry a man named G-e-o-r-g-e-T-a-f-f-e-r.

She didn't marry anyone right out of college. She traveled (to

France), then joined the Peace Corps and served in a small town in northeast Brazil for two years and lived in a dirt shack teaching English to the Portuguese-speaking natives, helping with water projects and anything else they needed. Then, lonely and in culture shock back in the US, she married Harry Thomas, a tall, dark, and handsome lawyer, the strong, silent type. Here she was five years later and nearly thirty years old. His silences felt hostile to her. His strength seemed like that of a stone post. She turned to writing poetry, first as an outlet, then as a serious pursuit. Here she was in this poetry class with someone she had thought existed only in the amusement of the Ouija Board. *George Taffer. There really is a George Taffer.*

"Annie, let's do your poem now." Ian's voice shocked her awake. She blinked brown eyes at him, then quickly looked down at the pile of papers in her lap. Her light brown wavy hair fell across her face like a curtain. Ruffling through her pages, she dropped some. They slid out of reach, multiple copies of one short poem, spread like a fan on the floor, within easy reach of George Taffer, who picked them up one by one and passed them out.

"'The World of Spiders.' Is this the poem you want to share, Annie?" George grinned. "What a unique method of distribution." He chuckled.

She looked at him, then felt the corners of her mouth turn up despite herself.

When she opened the kitchen door, she was still smiling. George saw things in her short poem that even she didn't know were there.

Nuances of meaning, depths unplumbed. She couldn't wait to revise it further. Then her eyes caught the kitchen sink. Full of unwashed dishes. The leftover food from dinner still in pots on the stove. She sighed. She had cooked. Harry had promised to clean up so she could get to class on time. Her irritation knotted her stomach. She opened her mouth, then closed it. She envisioned what would happen if she said anything. Nothing. He might not even answer her. Or he might explode at her in a rage that could both bewilder her and knock her against the wall like a hurricane. She felt a headache coming on and just wanted to get the mess cleaned up and go to bed. Which she did. After she dried her hands on the dish towel and stuffed it back in the refrigerator handle, she peeked into the den and greeted Harry. Just as she imagined, he was engrossed in TV. His tightly gelled dark hair had come unglued and bounced atop his head as he leaned his tall, thin frame forward dribbling an imaginary ball on the rug in front of him. He'd found a basketball game. Yes, March Madness had begun. He gave her a dismissive wave as she walked past.

Yet she found she couldn't resist the urge to say, "I thought you were going to do the dishes?"

"Yeah," he replied, leaning towards the screen. "I will. This is almost over."

"Never mind," she whispered to herself as she ascended the stairs.

Later she curled in the far corner of their king-sized bed and pulled out her poem. She reread it and wondered what George and the others had seen in it. To her now it looked flat and empty and very amateurish. She wondered why she bothered anyway. She put away her notebook and pulled the covers over her, but she couldn't get warm. At last she fell asleep and woke only briefly hours later to glance at the clock when Harry climbed in next to her. It was 2 a.m. Fortunately, he lay on his side pointed away from her so his snoring was less likely to keep her awake. She never knew it was possible for one man to snore as loudly as Harry. It had been one of her first disappointments in the marriage. Back in the early days when they still made love before falling asleep curled up together, she found herself shocked out of a languid torpor by his rough sounds. That he grew furious when she poked him to turn over and accused her of lying only added to her frustration. One night she reached her limit and got up quietly to go to the couch, pulling the blanket around her and off the bed, leaving him, she imagined with perverse pleasure, to awaken later cold and alone. That he said nothing to her in the morning just added to her growing belief that he was some sort of mad Neanderthal unworthy of her normal courtesy. Slowly over time she quit trying to talk to him about anything she felt. And he didn't seem to notice. But, every now and then, he rolled onto her late at night when she lay half asleep, and the fact that he could stimulate the same melting she had felt when they had first met just confused her.

Eventually, she turned her attention to her job teaching high school English. When she asked him to share the housework, he grumbled and grew more remote. She insisted, so he agreed to do the vacuuming. But weeks would go by. And then he exploded when she reminded him. After a while, she too become remote and poured what she might have shared with him into her poetry. They lived their separate lives, and she signed up for the coffeehouse poetry seminar.

When she arrived at the next meeting, she found George had made himself the center of attention. As they waited for Ian to show up, he was leading a lively debate about the comparative syntax of T. S. Eliot and Robert Frost. *Who would ever think of comparing those two?* She took her seat across the circle and busied herself selecting the poem she wanted to share, one she felt good about, that could withstand the class microscope. The suggestions were always useful, although sometimes hard to take.

There was a pause as George took a breath, as if on the edge of the high dive ready to take the plunge. He turned towards her, and she instinctively cringed, seeing he was about to take the plunge towards her.

"Annie, let's see what you did with the poem you brought last week." She felt that same current run through her from head to toe as she searched her memory bank to tune into what he was talking about. She felt her face grow hot when she realized it was still on the night stand next to their bed.

"I forgot it," she said, feeling her heart beat faster. She thought of the dirty dishes and Harry's derisive tone and how she'd crawled into bed feeling deflated and had set the poem aside.

"What happened to you?" George continued. His bright eyes enveloped her. She was surprised to see them warm with concern.

"I looked at it again and didn't like it that much. Then I guess I just forgot."

"I liked it," he said. "How about the rest of you?" He turned to the others.

"I loved it," said Peter.

"Me, too," said Claire. "It's the best thing you've ever written."

Ian stood at the edge of the circle smiling wide. "Dynamite poem." He took his seat and took command the way only he could do so gracefully. "You have a real talent, and I want to see you invest in it. No forgetting allowed, you hear me?"

If it was possible, her face grew more hot and red. Her throat closed up tight and she was horrified to feel tears gathering and pooling in her eyes. She always knew Ian to be encouraging, but she never thought he was doing more than what she did every day with her students, what a teacher was supposed to do. She never believed he meant it. But with the group chorus George had conducted, she had the feeling he did. She couldn't possibly live up to it all. Or could she?

"Hmm," said Peter, always the sly quiet one. "Can it be? Yes, I have a copy of your poem I must have stuffed in here from last week." He lifted a page from his briefcase.

And so they began to read it out loud. To marvel at it. To repeat the suggestions they had made the week before. Stunned and silent, she sat there, palms sweating, until she had to speak. "I meant what I said in that line." She didn't realize until all eyes were upon her that she had raised her voice.

"OK, you tell us," said Ian. And she was off the high dive and swimming in the deep end.

When she opened the kitchen door, she saw the pile of dirty dishes, the leftover food still in pots on the stove, and the doorway where she could see Harry crouched before the television set. She marched up the stairs past their bedroom, down the hall to the spare room. The door, having been closed so long, stuck when she pushed. But she put her shoulder to it and forced it open. She stacked the miscellaneous papers scattered from long ago on her desk, made a space, and sat down with pen and poem.

Harry only found she had come home when he came to an empty bed and went searching for her. She looked up briefly, gave him a dismissive wave, and bowed her head once more.

Chapter 2

The next morning Annie barely made it out of bed in time to throw on her clothes and dash off to teach her classes. It had been late when she finally crawled into bed next to Harry, who was snoring like a lumber mill. Somehow his snoring didn't bother her as much. She felt satisfied in a way she had never experienced before, full like after a big meal but calm inside. She liked what she'd written. If she hadn't had to face six classrooms of high school English students, she would have kept writing all night. Instead, she found a good stopping place and had slipped into bed. She lay there a moment dazzled by the new world she saw inside her own imagination, as if a thousand stars were churning into a new galaxy inside her. But soon her weariness rolled over her like strong ocean waves and pulled her under. She didn't dream exactly, but words and phrases and images rolled around inside her all night, like on a circular movie screen inside her head. She never heard Harry get up. Usually she was the first one up making coffee, slicing grapefruit halves, or removing cantaloupe from its rinds. But this time, when she opened her eyes and gasped at the red digits on the clock, she hurled herself up and into the first dress she grabbed and barely got her teeth brushed.

When she reached the kitchen, she was surprised to see that, not only had he cleaned up the dishes from the night before, he had coffee made and a plate of cinnamon toast awaiting her at her place at the table. Harry sat in his usual place across from her behind the newspaper, but this time he lowered the paper enough to greet her. His plate was empty except for cinnamon toast crumbs, his coffee half gone from his cup.

"Running late, eh?" he ventured. He peered at her over his reading glasses. She felt uneasy with such direct eye contact from him and wondered if he was angry she hadn't been up earlier to make breakfast.

"Yes," she responded as she took her seat. "Thanks for the toast and coffee." She spooned some sugar into the brimming cup beside her plate and stirred. She glanced at the clock over the stove. "I guess I'll have to take it with me." She wrapped the toast in a paper napkin, poured her coffee into a travel cup, picked up her stack of books and lesson plans, and headed for the door, only to discover she had no free hand to open it. Harry startled her by laying his paper down and getting up to open the door for her.

"Have a good day," he said, giving her a peck on the cheek.

Instinctively, her body grew tense as if he had hit her. She studied his face. His eyes were warm, and he was smiling.

"Thank you," she mumbled as she hurried to her car. As she drove, she reflected on his strange behavior, solicitous, considerate. Not what she was used to from him but what she longed for. A spark of hope was lit inside her, then dread, then confusion. She tried to blow it out but failed.

At school, although she was tired and sleep-deprived, she felt propelled through the day with a strange new energy. She couldn't present her lessons exactly as planned. New ideas bubbled up as if from some fire lit deep inside her. Even in her toughest classes, she felt inspired. When she got to her senior honors class, she completely abandoned her lesson plan. It was the last class of the day, and she felt like being bold.

"Good afternoon," she began, standing at her desk after they filed in and settled into their seats.

"Good afternoon, Mrs. Thomas," they said, turning their eyes toward her. Unlike some of her classes, these students were bright, self-motivated, and attentive.

"Today, in light of our study of Shakespeare's sonnets, I want you to write your own sonnet." A few faces looked at her in panic, a few frowned. "Think of some issue or situation in your own life, and see what comes." She felt her own energy radiate outward to them. "Use iambic pentameter and a similar rhyme scheme to what he used, but put your editing mind aside and let your words flow. This is an experiment and won't be graded. Except you'll get a zero if you don't try." She smiled and saw a few grimaces in return. "Read a few of his sonnets first if you need a jump start. We'll spend the entire class on this assignment." She hoped to ignite a fire inside them just like the one she felt inside herself.

She watched as some of their faces relaxed and they began to flip through their textbooks. Others continued to show skepticism, but some picked up their pencils right away in "aha" moments, as their imaginations took over and their pencils began to move. Soon she saw all their eyes glaze over as they focused inward and found the words take form on that inner screen. "Leave what you've written on my desk at the end of class." She sat at her desk watching in awe. Then she picked up her own pencil.

When she got home after school, she dropped everything on the coffee table and curled up on the living room couch with their sonnets. She was amazed at how good some of them were. She was onto something, she could feel it. She got so absorbed, she forgot what time it was. After she read and red-penciled her suggestions, she turned to her own sonnet that she had started in class. It seemed impossible to give such an assignment without feeling her own inspiration fill her up and spill over onto her own paper. Before her pen touched paper, George Taffer's face and smile floated into her mind, like a wispy cloud blowing across the sky. She smiled in response. *Who is he? Why is he here? What does this mean?*

She didn't even see Harry when he came in.

"Hello," he said.

She jumped as if shot, papers flying in all directions. She leaned over to pick them up, hands shaking and papers falling every which way.

"Hi," she mumbled, finally getting them into a disorganized pile. She avoided looking at him directly and searched the wall for the clock. "What time is it? You're home already?"

"I'm late," he replied, "by about an hour. Have you been sitting there all afternoon? What's for supper?" He stood in the doorway in silence, having come through the kitchen door where no dinner was waiting. He said nothing but stood there, briefcase hanging down in his hand, tie loosened at his neck, his other hand beginning the contractions that were usually only soothed by the beer she placed in it at the end of each work day. He sat his briefcase down and stepped back into the kitchen where he got his own beer from the fridge, popped it open, and sat down in the wing chair. He lifted the can, took a long swallow, then studied her with his piercing eyes, the kind of look she had always suspected made him such a sharp litigator. He repeated his question, "What's for supper?"

She took a deep breath and raised her eyes to meet his. She trembled as if she had just stepped onto the witness stand and was about to be skewered under cross-examination. Then that inner fire lit the spark she needed. She shrugged and said, "I have no idea. I've been busy."

"That I can see," he said. "Busy with what?" He laid one lanky leg over the other knee and took another long swig of his beer.

Stuff that's none of your business, she thought, *stuff you'd never understand.* But she wasn't that foolish so she said, "Just schoolwork."

"Tell me." His face relaxed, and his eyes softened.

Despite the wariness she felt, she found excitement rising and words spilling out of her. "I tried something new, something different with my senior honors English class today. I threw away my lesson plans and had them write sonnets, Shakespearean sonnets. They really got into it; it was so exciting. There are some good writers in that class." She flushed and smiled and turned inward, remembering, then looked to see his reaction.

Harry drummed the fingers of his free hand on the arm of the chair. "You don't say? What will your principal say about that? Doesn't he have to approve your lesson plans in advance?"

Her smile fell. *I might have known, finding the negative legal point as always.* She decided to let it go and change the subject. "Why don't you fix supper for a change? I am all out of ideas and I'm not very hungry anyway."

"Uh huh, changing the rules all over the place," he continued. He raised the beer to his mouth again.

She felt her stomach tense up. She turned inside to find anything in the "smart-ass comeback" file but found nothing. The silence she usually filled felt like the best alternative she could come up with at the moment.

He moved his leg from his knee and set his foot on the floor. "I guess I could order Chinese. I'm in the mood for sweet and sour pork." He reached for the phone and looked around. From the drawer of the side table next to him, he pulled a stack of take-out menus. He opened the menu for the Nanjing Wok. "What do you want?"

"I'll have an egg roll and some lo mein," she said. "And plenty of duck sauce." She couldn't remember the last time he had even cooked burgers on the grill. It was hopeless.

"Is that all you want? God, you eat like a bird." He shook his head as he scanned the menu.

"I told you I'm not very hungry." She stood up with her rough pile of papers and everything else of hers and headed upstairs to the spare room. "And order some fortune cookies," she threw back at him over her shoulder. When she reached the top of the stairs, she heard him giving their order into the phone. Then curtly, "Forty-five minutes to deliver? Forget it, I'll pick it up." And he stomped out without a word to her. She was just as glad to have the house to herself again.

They ate at the kitchen table in silence. Harry seemed there in body but somewhere else in spirit. He wolfed his sweet and sour pork with his fork, staring off into space. She picked at her lo mein, twirled the noddles around on her chopsticks. She hesitated to do what she usually did—ask him about his day. She glanced at his face. He frowned and moved his eyes around as if in deep conversation with some voice inside his head. When he emptied his plate and left the table, she breathed a sigh of relief. Her thoughts drifted to her sonnet. She felt a pull to return to it. She twirled one last bite onto her chopsticks. In a few minutes, she had the kitchen cleaned up. She saw Harry in his study bent over his desk. She sighed as she padded up the stairs into her writing room.

She opened her notebook. Entering the writing trance, she wrote more, scratched out words, and wrote more. She revised a few times. Then she read it aloud.

When I at end of day behold your face
I long to have you greet me with a smile.
Or reach your hand to mine across the space
Between us that can seem ten thousand miles.
But lately you are here and seem afar
Preoccupied by thoughts you do not share
I might as well remain inside my car
Than face my fear that you no longer care.
Our love that once was bright and shining new
On which I leaned with trust I'd never fall

Has faded as hot sun dispels the dew
My voice reverberates each time I call.
You no longer speak unless it is to curse.
What can I do but soothe my soul in verse?

Chapter 3

As the warm weather came and the days lengthened, the poetry seminar began to meet outside whenever possible. They found a restaurant with a garden patio that, although rather upscale, let them linger while sipping their modest purchase of tea. The patio was surrounded by a tall hedge that held them like the walls of a secret garden. The circular herringbone brickwork paths were lined by elaborate flower beds designed to have plants in bloom in nearly every season one could enjoy being outside. They led to several areas with small and large tables that felt quite private. They found a large round table that could hold their varying group size of five to seven behind a large fig tree and shaded by a flowering apple tree. It seemed such a perfect spot that they abandoned their roving habit and settled there for weeks in a row. The restaurant owners discussed hosting poetry readings whenever they were ready with the unspoken assumption the group would draw hungry art patrons with big wallets to eat the gourmet dinners for which they were famous.

Annie found herself creating a rhythm at home of cloistering herself upstairs every evening after dinner. This well of creativity she had tapped inside showed no signs of drying up. She was anxious to keep the flow going and not get corked up again. Each poem she wrote came from a deeper layer of self. The group bonded and became so safe that poems that once had felt too personal and vulnerable to share slid onto the table almost without a second thought.

Except this evening. Just as she put her hand on the door knob to leave home, Harry said, "I want to talk."

She stood still for a moment facing the door with her back to him in disbelief. "About what?" she asked without turning around.

"I'm sick of you going off every Sunday night. You've gotten so involved in this poetry stuff that it's like you're not even here."

Isn't that what you wanted? she thought but did not say. "Later, Harry, I'm going to be late."

He took her arm and tried to pull her back to the table. "No, now. I said I want to talk." He barked his words like a drill sergeant.

Only then did she turn and look at him. She matched his piercing eyes with her own and stood tall before him in silence. They stood toe to toe and eyeball to eyeball for the space of a breath. "Let me go. We can talk another time."

"You can bet we will. Soon." He released her arm and fell back into his usual silence.

Only outside with the door closed between them did she feel how frightened she was. She had not felt frightened of him before. Although his frame was tall and imposing, he had never touched her like that before. She had no idea how she had extricated herself. She hurried to her car and drove off quickly.

When she pulled her car into the parking spot in front of the entrance to the patio, her hands trembled as she opened the car door. She shook her head to rid herself of the feel of Harry's hand on her arm. The patio had a heavy wooden gate that opened in a break in the high hedge. There was no need to go through the restaurant.

The owners had showed them where the old heavy key was kept in a secret container nestled inside the hedge. The key was gone so she knew she was not the first to arrive. She creaked the gate open and stepped through with trepidation. Her feet followed the meandering path to the corner that held their large table under the apple blossoms. She took slow deep breaths as she walked.

She wasn't yet sure she would share the poem she had brought. She had a backup just in case she chickened out. It revealed so much of her secret inner life that sharing it could feel more disclosing than actually disrobing. Baring her naked soul took infinitely more courage. But why was this poem any different than the others she had dared to share? She wasn't sure, but somehow she felt that sharing it was more than sharing a poem. It was taking a first step towards transforming herself and her life in a profound way. If she opened that door, she might not be able to close it again.

George saw her first and sang out his greeting. "Annie! I've been watching for you. Where you been?"

She glanced at her watch. Fifteen minutes late. How could that be? She was religiously punctual as a rule. She shook her head and smiled at George. "Oh, sorry, the time got away from me."

"You are a lady who is never late," George declared. "My guess is it was something more than time you had to get away from." He winked at her.

An electric current hit her like the first time she heard his name. Annie took a deep breath to disconnect from it. She caught the ball and threw it back to him. "Never say never about this lady." She grinned and sat in the empty seat he pulled out for her between himself and Claire.

"Now that our circle is complete," Ian observed, "let us begin." They all sat up expectantly. Ian often began with a poem from a published poet. His knowledge was wide-ranging, and he dipped his literary ladle into any century. "Guess this poet," he challenged them and began reading.

One day you finally knew
what you had to do, and began,
though the voices around you
kept shouting
their bad advice–
though the whole house
began to tremble
and you felt the old tug
at your ankles.
"Mend my life!"
Each voice cried.
But you didn't stop.

Ian paused and surveyed the group. Peter frowned, puzzled. Claire nodded in pleasure. George sat with his Buddha smile. Annie breathed slowly to keep from visibly shaking.

He continued:

You knew what you had to do,
Though the wind pried
With its stiff fingers
At the very foundations,

Though their melancholy
was terrible.
It was already late
enough, and a wild night,
and the road full of fallen
branches and stones.
But little by little,
as you left their voices behind,
the stars began to burn
through the sheets of clouds,
and there was a new voice
which you slowly
recognized as your own,
that kept you company
as you strode deeper and deeper
into the world,
determined to do
the only thing you could do–
determined to save
the only life you could save.

They sat in silence a moment absorbing it fully as the music of the words echoed around inside their minds. "What's the title?" Peter asked, still frowning, "can we at least have the title?"

Claire beamed. "'The Journey' by Mary Oliver. I'm her biggest fan."

"Ah!" exclaimed Ian. "A winner in the first second. So tell us what you especially like about this poem then."

"Oh, oh," Claire stammered for the words. "It's just so damn true! And it took me too long to know that truth." Claire, sixty-eight, had raised five kids and then found herself tending a chain-smoking husband until emphysema and lung cancer finally took him fifteen years earlier. Her poems were full of her family life—how she finally learned to pull them all off her teats and send them off into the world so she could hear herself think again. And how the hardest one to deal with had been her very old-fashioned husband who expected his dinner on the table at six o'clock sharp every night but refused to listen to her entreaties to stop smoking or make her a young widow. "That journey is mine!" she declared.

Peter nodded in dawning understanding as Claire talked. "I get it," he sighed. "Only a woman could write a poem like that." Peter, at twenty-five and the youngest of the group, came from a family of scientists. He was the youngest of three boys and had not dated much. His parents still hoped he would study science, but he worked for the university communications department in web design and dreamed of going to graduate school in creative writing.

"Not at all," said George. "It transcends gender. I have felt all those feelings." George came from a large Irish family with four younger siblings he helped raise after their father died in a freak accident. His father was cutting down a tree in their back yard when his saw hit a knot; the tree fell towards him before he could get out of the way. He was killed instantly, and George came home from college to help his mother. Several years later he returned to finish his degree.

George went on. "And notice the movement away from those voices in the beginning that demand rescuing, yet into the world at the end."

Annie sat silently taking it all in. She felt the surprise and recognition she had felt when the name invented on her college Ouija Board had come alive that rainy night months before. "That's like my poem," she murmured, not fully realizing she was speaking out loud.

"What, Annie?" asked Ian. "What did you say?"

She blushed. Her heart beat loudly. "I like that poem," she covered herself quickly. It was not her time yet.

"I heard you," offered George. "You said that's like *your* poem. Let's see *your* poem."

She swallowed. *There goes my cover.*

"Are we ready to move on?" inquired Ian. "Any other responses to Mary Oliver at this time?"

"I must say I love the line about 'bad advice' and the wind's stiff fingers and the whole feeling of darkness and danger and the terrible melancholy of those who want you to mend their lives," said Claire. "They could eat you alive, but you can escape and be whole."

"But it feels so difficult," said Annie.

"Nothing worth doing is easy, Annie," Claire assured her.

"Annie, why don't you start," said Ian, closing the Mary Oliver volume and leaning towards her.

"Yes, let's see your poem," George repeated, with a twinkle and a smile.

Annie took a deep breath to calm herself and opened her notebook. She looked at her poem a moment. How could she read it after Ian had read such a fine poem by such a fine poet? Hers seemed so amateurish by comparison. She flipped pages to her backup poem. She closed her notebook.

"Okay, Annie, give it up," demanded George, reaching for her notebook. "There you go underestimating yourself again. Let's hear it!"

She pulled the notebook away from his reach. She met his gaze and felt a spark of confidence. "Hold on, it's my poem, I'll read it." And she began. "You'll recognize the title. It's called 'The Journey.'"

"What a coincidence," said Ian. "I'm all ears."

"So am I," came the chorus from the rest of the group.

Annie cleared her throat with a slight cough. *"The Journey,"* she began.

She is awake now
no doubt about it.
Her feet planted solidly
on her own ground.
Not even these gathering storm winds
can knock her over now.

Her delicate cart—
built for short trips
into town and back—
has finally collapsed,
a suicide of splintered boards
that rattle like bones
in this new wind.
Her heavy stone wagon stands
ready-packed, oiled,
insistent.
She looks behind one last time.
She doesn't know which frightens her more:

the rumbling in the sky
or the rumbling inside,
pushing her to climb on board
as the stone wheels turn.

She laid the notebook open on her lap, her eyes on her poem, and waited. The silence seemed thick and long.

Claire spoke first. "I like it. Very much. I like the contrast between the image of the delicate cart and the heavy stone wagon. I really can relate to it."

"Another woman's poem?" asked Peter, "or do I misspeak again?"

"Not at all," said George. "I can relate to it as well. Let's hear it again."

"Yes," insisted Ian, "read it again."

She raised her eyes finally and looked at her friends. *What do they see here?* she wondered. *Do I dare?* She read it again, warming to it herself as she tried to listen with their ears. She saw a simile that could be better as a metaphor, but mostly she liked it too. Where she was going with it was another question entirely.

When she finished, Ian asked Annie to respond first.

"Good idea," said George.

"Well," she began tentatively. "I like it, I think." She pressed her lips together then smiled. "It really helps to hear your response to it. I'm rewriting it already." She raised her eyes to the group, then back to the page. "I'd change the next to last line in the second stanza to read: "a suicide of splintered boards/bones that rattle/in this new wind.""

"Excellent!" said Ian. "Much stronger to replace simile with metaphor. Responses from others?"

Claire folded her arms over her chest. "It's clear to me. I like it a lot."

"It's a good poem. Weird how like Mary Oliver's poem it is," said Peter. "Had you read her poem before you wrote this one?"

Annie shook her head. "No."

"Yet different, not fully realized," said George. "I think there's another poem to follow."

"Maybe," whispered Annie, turning inward for a brief moment. How she longed to stay here in this very moment with her friends. She had no desire to go home. It didn't feel like her true home anymore, if it ever did. She thought of Harry waiting with his demands. She did not want to deal with him tonight. Or maybe ever.

The rest of the evening, she wrote and rewrote inside her mind, finding inspiration from the other poems shared. How she loved to tinker with words and imagery.

When it was time to go, Annie was the last to stand and push in her chair. The others scattered, but, outside the hedge, she put her notebook into her car and looked around. The restaurant was adjacent to a small park. A shallow creek gurgled from behind some trees. She saw a path into the shadows and hesitated. It was late and Harry would be waiting. A sliver of moon floated through the stars and wispy clouds and peeked at her through the treetops. A cool breeze tickled skin. It was a beautiful night. She decided to walk down the path for just a short time before she went home. Thinking of Harry, she felt turmoil boil up inside. *If he wants me to quit this poetry seminar, I won't, no matter what he says.*

The pine needles on the path felt soft beneath her feet. It curved around a giant oak tree as the sound of the creek grew louder. The sounds washed over her like a caress. She began to relax. *Let what's next take care of itself.*

As the darkness grew, she could hear the music of the creek better than she could see it. She moved slowly and carefully, feeling ahead on the path with her foot before putting her weight on it. She could barely see rocks lining the path that had obviously been well tended. Ahead she saw a rustic wooden bench beside the gurgling stream. She headed towards it. When she saw someone else sitting on the far end of the bench, she inhaled sharply and felt a stab of fear. The dark figure turned in her direction. Like the Cheshire cat, a wide smile was all she could see. Part of her wanted to run but another part thought there was something familiar about this smile. She held her breath and didn't move.

"Annie?"

She gave a big exhale. "George? Is that you?"

"I came to look for the wishing star. Come join me." He waved towards the other end of the bench.

She smiled and sat down facing the stream. "What a beautiful spot. I've never been here before." Her heartbeat accelerated and her hands grew moist. A magnetic force pulled her towards him. *What is going on?* She dared not look at him.

"Oh, I come here after class from time to time. I'm glad you found it. Good to see you."

"I'm certainly glad it was you," she said. "And not what my mind first imagined."

He chuckled. "Yes, a friend not a stranger."

"Even better, a fellow poet." She glanced at him sideways and then returned her gaze to the stream. *A friend, yes.* She felt her face grow warm. The darkness was a blessing.

"I really like your poetry," George said. "And I can tell you have more inside waiting for your words to find them."

"Yes," she replied, "thank you, and I like your poetry too. I believe I do have more. But I don't know what exactly yet."

"It will come," he assured her. "Just listen inside. I've found that's where my own poems are born."

They sat watching the creek. As her eyes adjusted, she saw a leaf, then another, then a small stick float by in the water. They bounced and slid around rocks in the shallow water. Images in her mind flowed by with the leaves: Harry waiting, perhaps impatiently, for her return, her students in her classroom struggling with the language of Shakespeare then breathing in the clear words of Langston Hughes, herself cloistered in her writing room upstairs. *I can't hide in there forever, I must get out where I can breathe*, she mused. She took a deep breath to calm herself, contemplated the mystery of this new friend beside her. Feeling a strong urge to touch him, she clasped her hands tightly together.

"There it is," said George, pointing into the sky. "The wishing star." He sat tall, took a deep breath, and began, "Star light, star bright, first star I see tonight, I wish I may, I wish I might have the wish I wish tonight." He exhaled slowly. "There, I didn't blink. I get my wish." He turned to her in triumph.

"I want to leave my husband." She was shocked to realize those words, which had been inside her mind for so long, she had now spoken aloud. She moved over and looked away from George. A bird flew past her up into the trees. Then the most beautiful birdsong began to ring out. She cocked her head. They both fell into a deep silence for a few moments as they listened. Then the song stopped and the spell was broken. She looked at George, who turned and smiled at her.

"I was married once," he said. "She was beautiful but volatile. I think I was on a rescue mission. I learned you can't make anyone else happy—and you'd better not sacrifice your own happiness trying. I had to leave."

"Yes," she said. She felt suddenly shy.

"I guessed you were unhappy in your marriage," George offered. "I could see hints in your poems. And the one you shared today." He paused, then stammered. "It was clear to me that you . . . " He gathered himself. "I feel confident you'll make the right decision for yourself."

Her eyes widened as she looked at him. She had never seen him anything but perfectly poised.

He began to examine his hands. "I like you. You deserve the best." He studied his shoes.

"Why, thank you, George," she said with a smile. "I've enjoyed getting to know you. I like you too." She felt buoyed up by some invisible hand. She stood up. "Well, I guess I'd better go home. I'm glad to run into you here."

He stood facing her. She could see he had regained his composure. "Good to see you too," he said. "And I look forward to hearing another dynamite poem next week."

The sky had cleared. Above them a billion stars all flickered at once. She felt pulled into them and lost herself for a moment of awe. But as they left the park for the restaurant parking lot, the city lights soon drowned out the brightness of the stars. *OK, back to civilization, back towards home and Harry. To my life, my real life.* She stood a bit straighter, sighed, then got into her car and drove.

Chapter 4

Annie began to rehearse what she might say to Harry. Her hands gripped the steering wheel. As George's image flashed in her mind, she smiled. How nice to run into him. A new friendship. She needed friends more than ever now. She had let so many friendships slip away in the past five years with all that had happened. She drove slowly, dreading the inevitable encounter. She passed an ice cream shop, closed down and dark. A taste of mint chocolate chip would hit the spot about now. She sighed again as she drove ever closer to her destination.

But when she got there, he was not waiting up. The numerals on the kitchen stove clock glowed 10:20. She was shocked it was that late. She knew Harry had to be in court in the morning so she figured he had gone to bed. Surprised she was not a bit sleepy, she put down her purse and notebook on the kitchen table and went into the living room. His legal papers were stacked on the coffee table beside his briefcase. She could picture him in the morning flipping through them one last time, stuffing them neatly inside his brief case, taking coffee in his travel cup, and being out the door before she had poured her first cup. She felt relieved at the thought. She knew she'd have to face him eventually but she thought waiting another day wouldn't hurt. A poem she had written a while back surfaced in her mind. Images and words swirled on her inner screen. She decided to pull it out, look at it, maybe work on it a bit. She retrieved her note-book and tip-toed upstairs. The stairs seemed to creak more loudly than they ever had. She gripped the railing as she ascended. Pausing a moment to remove her shoes, she padded in her bare feet the rest of the way. Much quieter. As she passed their bedroom, she peeked in at Harry on his side sound asleep. No snoring. How strange. She settled down at her desk and pulled it out. As she reread it, she felt shocked to recall the state of deep confusion and insecurity that had inspired it.

The Question

> *She looks too much to others*
> *For an answer to the enigma*
> *Of existence.*
> *She lays herself bare*
> *Hands them the scalpel and the knife*
> *Then despairs later*
> *When she misses her lung or liver.*

> *She takes the knife to herself as well*
> *Cuts a large middle section*
> *Gives it away hopefully.*
> *Surely they must know what it is!*

> *Then why does the hole still ache*
> *And the whole seem incomplete?*

Her eyes widened. The date showed she had written it a few years before she joined the poetry seminar. She winced, remembering. Outside the window, a blanket of darkness covered the trees, the grass. A lone streetlight made deep shadows. The poetry seminar, could she share this poem there? Not yet. But how much she had learned about the craft of poetry, about herself. She smiled to realize how different she now felt. Her eyes glazed over as she turned her attention inward. Something warm began to bubble up inside her, followed by images, words. She picked up her pen and began to write. Words poured onto the page, as if this poem had been lurking just below the surface, waiting. A *found poem* they called it. She sat back to read it over.

The Answer

I am a dry sponge
Soaking up moisture
     growing.

I am a mountain spring
From the source outward
     flowing.

She smiled. It was short, but she felt satisfied. Maybe she could go right to sleep for a change. She quickly brushed her teeth, splashed water on her face, dressed for bed, and slipped in beside him, being careful not to touch him. Within minutes she was asleep on her back.

In the morning they were in the same positions, as if frozen in a game of swing the statue. She remembered playing it as a child, being held by her hand, swung around until dizzy then released, flying off then stopping to pretend to be a statue. Fun game. She blinked once at his back when his alarm went off at 6 a.m., then rolled away from him and fell back to sleep. When she awoke, she heard the shower then drifted off again. When she finally came fully awake, he was nowhere to be seen. She heard the sounds of radio news from downstairs. Did she smell bacon cooking? Harry had never cooked bacon. Suddenly she was wide awake and out of bed. She threw on her robe and had one foot on the top stair before she stopped herself. *If he wants to cook bacon, let him.* She released the impulse to feel guilty or to fear his accusation she was neglecting her wifely duties (as her mother would say), she wasn't sure which, and turned towards the bathroom. She showered and dressed leisurely, hoping he'd be gone when she came down. But he wasn't.

He was sipping coffee and reading the paper. In the middle of the table was a serving dish full of scrambled eggs, bacon, and toast. She couldn't believe it. She stood in the kitchen doorway taking it all in.

Harry raised his head. "Good morning, sweetheart. Are you hungry? I made breakfast."

"I see," she said. "Wow, what's the occasion?"

"You were out so late, I thought you might not be up to cooking," he replied.

"Thank you." She poured her coffee and sat across from him, being careful not to look directly at him. She spooned eggs on her plate. With her fingers she picked up a piece of crisp bacon and bit off a taste. "Umm, good." She reached for part of the paper. Her hands trembled as she spread it next to her plate. She was in very foreign territory and had no idea what to expect. She read a few headlines searching for guidance. Suicide bombings in the Middle East. No help. She turned to her horoscope. *Cancer: Don't take the bull by the horns. An emotional dilemma is best left alone.* OK, that's better. That's exactly what she felt like doing.

She looked at Harry's hair above the top of the sports page, a more familiar sight. She began to relax a bit. She unscrewed the bottle of vitamins and swallowed one with her coffee.

Harry jumped up. "Omigod! Look at the time. Gotta go!" and he was out the door. His chair wobbled on the floor, then settled back on all four legs. He flew out, briefcase in hand, with nary a glance her way as he slammed the door behind him. She looked around the kitchen and saw the mess he had made: egg carton open on the counter, bacon out of its wrapper, frying pan crusted with egg pieces over the burner left on low. She turned it off, put the eggs and bacon in the refrigerator, stacked the dishes, and was soon out the door herself. She'd have to deal with the rest of the mess later.

As she taught classes that day, she felt Harry's unusual behavior rummaging through her mind as background noise. This time she followed her lesson plans exactly. It was boring, but she felt preoccupied. How long had it been since he'd called her "sweetheart?" She couldn't remember. She did remember when he called her mean and hurtful names or when he didn't answer when she asked about his day over dinner. But doing something unsolicited for her? Only when he was courting her. Was he courting her now? Did she want to be courted? She'd been outside the window peering into his life so long, she could barely consider that he had opened it and invited her inside.

35

She frowned and snapped at her students when they didn't pay attention and asked questions they should have known the answers to. She kept glancing at the clock in each class, willing the hands to move faster so she could have time to contemplate undistracted. She forgot the names of students she knew well. For the first time in a long time, she looked forward to her reunion with Harry at the end of the day. Maybe they could talk, take down the wall between them brick by brick, forge new intimacy. Maybe they could go for counseling finally. She had made that suggestion many times over the past few years, after the romantic stage had become a dim memory, after she stopped idolizing him and began to talk to him about her frustrations, hurts, wishes, and fears and grew tired of being told she was too sensitive or just ignored.

"Counseling?" he had roared. "You think I'm crazy? We don't need counseling. You just need to accept me for who I am and quit trying to change me. I have a good job. I don't beat you. You don't know how good you have it, girl!"

Then he'd storm off and not speak to her for three days. She was crushed the first time she suggested it. She had worked up to asking that question for at least six months. She had *tried* to accept him. But then she'd noticed how often she got headaches, how plugged up she felt, how she hid her feelings from him more and more, how lonely she felt, and knew she had to do something. But he had made it clear counseling was out. So poetry was in.

Finally, the last student left her last class, and she packed up and headed home. Eagerly and with trepidation and confusion. She had thought she had decided. But his unusual considerate behavior gave her pause.

On the way home she stopped at the market and got some steaks, fresh asparagus, new potatoes, a baguette, and a bottle of cabernet sauvignon, his favorite. She had dinner ready on the dot of 7:00 p.m., a time he was sure to be home, even if he stayed a bit late. The table was set, candles waiting to be lit. She'd show him how much she appreciated the breakfast he had made for her by making his favorite dinner. She was more a chicken and fish sort of person, but Harry was definitely a meat and potatoes guy.

She poured herself a glass of wine, leaned back in the recliner, and clicked on the news, keeping everything warm in the oven. The news was all bad. More suicide bombings in the Middle East, more floods in the Midwest, more drought in the South. Soon the wine made her sleepy and she drifted off. When she woke, it was 7:45 p.m. and no sign of Harry. She stood up and walked to the front window. Enough light outside to see no car in the driveway. Suddenly she felt very tired. Her mood returned to resignation.

She went into the kitchen and fixed herself a plate. She put it on the table at her usual place, sat down, and began to eat. The steak tasted like leather now, the asparagus limp, the potato mushy. She began to weep but kept chewing in determination till the salt in her tears ruined what taste was left. At last she gave into it, put her head in her hands and let it flow from her, all her hopes and disappointments and wishes and fears until she was spent.

She pushed in her chair, leaving his dinner on the cold stove and her dirty plate by the sink. Just as she was about to head up the stairs, she heard the rumble of a car. She stood still and listened as his key opened the door. He didn't even see her. He didn't seem to see anything. His mind was far away, his mouth in a flat line, his brows in a frown. She watched as he sat his briefcase down by the back door. Then he saw the table with his place set and the plate of food on the stove. He went to get the plate, pulled open the fridge and grabbed a beer, popped it open, and brought both back to the table. She continued to stand at the bottom of the stairs and still he didn't seem to see her. Now he saw the empty wine glass by his place and the bottle of cabernet next to it. Slowly he lifted his eyes to find her by the stairs. He stared silently back at her as if tuning in to the scene for the first time.

"Didn't I tell you I might have to work late tonight?"

She shook her head.

"That damn judge told me I had to present the affidavit at nine o'clock sharp tomorrow or he wouldn't allow it into evidence! Damn him! I hadn't even collected it and the witness was about to leave town for a whole month." He sat at the table and began to cut the steak, grumbling to himself.

She said nothing but continued up the stairs. He hollered after her: "The damn steak is stone cold!" She paused. "Oh, never mind, I'll nuke it myself. I'm sure you'd rather write your drivel than give a damn about my day anyway." He pushed the chair back, knocking it over with a clatter.

She resumed climbing the stairs and imagined bludgeoning his head with an ax. No, maybe she'd wait till he slept and super glue his penis to his leg. She read about a woman doing that once.

Chapter 5

$\mathscr{A}$nnie climbed the stairs wearily. She could hear Harry rustling around downstairs, slinging things in the kitchen. She decided the best thing to do would be to go to bed, leave him to his own bad mood, and sleep on it. She brushed her teeth, got her nightgown on, and settled in bed with a collection of poems from her class. *Drivel.* She was still steaming from hearing him pellet her with that word.

But soon her fatigue and stress overcame her, and she turned out the light and drifted off to dreamland.

She dreamed she was in prison but found a key in her book. She examined it then tried it in the door of her cell and, much to her surprise, it opened. She heard the jailer in another room watching TV with the volume turned high. He was so engrossed in his program that she was able to walk past his doorway and outside where she found a beautiful beach with children playing on the sand, people lounging on blankets and under umbrellas. She felt so happy, so free. She looked behind but saw only dunes and beach grass.

She woke with a start when Harry stomped in and climbed into bed next to her. He was asleep within a moment, snoring loudly. She turned away from him but suddenly felt every nerve and muscle in her body stand at attention. She looked at the clock: 1 a.m. Thank goodness tomorrow was a delayed school opening because she could tell she was never going back to sleep as long as she lay next to him. She threw her covers off and padded down to the spare room. There was a small single bed there made up with sheets and blankets she had used in college. She crawled in and immediately felt more at ease. But sleep would not come. She found herself wide awake with an electric current of anger buzzing through her. With a sigh, she turned on the bedside light and sat up. She had to get this feeling off her or she would never sleep. Could she turn this into a poem? She got her notebook and pen and listened to the crackling inside her. Then she began to write. Not a poem. Yet. First, three pages of ventilation and then a page of sadness. Then an image—herself bent over and slowly, intentionally unbending, straightening, standing taller.

Sleep eventually came.

In the morning she woke late and saw no sign of Harry when she got downstairs, breathless from throwing her clothes on and rushing to get ready for school. Even though school opened two hours late, she still needed to attend the staff meeting. The sun shone through the kitchen window onto the empty kitchen chair. The newspaper was strewn around the table. An open box of cereal sat beside a bowl with half eaten soggy cereal and milk left in it. She had no time to clean up his mess. She grabbed a banana and handful of almonds and was out the door.

This day went faster for her. The staff meeting was boring as usual, but she sat through it, giving at least the appearance of paying attention. As the day passed, she felt ever more fired up. Her stomach stayed in a knot. She tolerated no misbehavior in any of her students. And they stayed out of her way. She piled on the homework, oblivious to the groans from the class. She was mad as hell and wasn't going to take it anymore.

She went to the gym on her way home, knowing Harry might not be home for hours. She pounded out her frustrations on the treadmill and lifted extra pounds of weights until she felt purged and limp with fatigue. She showered the sweat off then rewarded herself with time in the sauna and the whirlpool, which was surprisingly empty. She stepped into the hot water as she considered how to get herself ready to face Harry. She leaned against a jet of warm water and felt it massage her back, her arms draped over the top of the pool to keep the force of the water from pushing her off the seat. Inside her mind, she rehearsed over and over. "Harry, I want a divorce. Harry, I'm leaving you. Harry, I've had enough of this loveless marriage. Harry, I'm finished with you."

Then inside she crumpled. Her hands went to her face, and the current pushed her across the pool. Just before she went under, her feet grabbed the firm bottom and she found some modicum of balance. She stood in the waist-high water and thought about their wedding, their vows. They had promised to love each other in sickness and in health, for richer and for poorer, till death do us part. Deep inside, she knew he was a good man. She sat down on the opposite ledge. He just didn't handle stress well. He worked, he didn't hit her. She had fallen in love with him once. *Maybe we should go to counseling. Maybe I shouldn't give up till we've gone to counseling. Maybe we can work it out if we get counseling.* The waters stilled as the timer on the jets turned off. She got out. It was time to go home.

She stopped by Bettie's Pizza for a couple slices of pepperoni and reflected further. She revised her speech. "Harry, I'm unhappy in this marriage. I don't feel close to you anymore. I can't live this way anymore. I want us to go to counseling." She bought a small pizza to take home to Harry.

When she got home, it was nearly 7 p.m. He was watching TV in the living room.

Immediately, he was in her face in the kitchen. "Where the hell have you been?" he roared. "I got home an hour ago!"

She handed him the box of pizza. He took it, examined it, then tossed it on the table. "Tell me, where have you been?"

She felt her resolve quiver and tremble and some small part of her run for cover. She examined her hands closely, turned them over, then slowly raised her gaze to meet his. "I went to the gym."

"And forgot I'd be home from court exhausted and wanting to eat? You should know what kind of day I had. It was hell. And there you are, traipsing off to the gym!"

"Harry, I have something to say."

"Oh, you do, do you?"

Her voice felt dry and scratchy. She cleared her throat. He sat at the kitchen table, opened the box, and bit into a big slice of pizza.

"Well, say it. I'm listening," he said, looking at the paper on the table.

She couldn't look him in the eye so she looked at his hairline. The dark, thick unruly hair that could not be tamed. Tonight he didn't have the usual slicked-back hair with lots of gel that he wore to court. It sprung from his head in all directions.

"I'm not happy," she whispered.

"What? Speak up!" He picked up a second slice of pizza.

"I'm not happy in this marriage. I want us to go to counseling."

He sat shaking his head in silence, tossing her words from his ears like water after swimming. He looked around the room then down at the floor then back at her. "Counseling."

She felt the color drain from her face. His voice sounded, well, she wasn't sure how it sounded.

He began to laugh. "Counseling? You want us to go to counseling?"

A lightning strike ran through her and ignited something she didn't know she had. "Yes, either we go to counseling or we separate." Then she raised her voice. "I can't, I won't live this way anymore. You decide!"

She turned towards the stairs. He got in front, towering over her. His eyes pierced her like laser beams. Her heart began to beat out of her chest. She ran around him up the stairs and shut the bedroom door. She trembled, unsure what to do next. She realized she was holding her breath. *Breathe, I need to breathe.* Some slow deep breaths helped calm her as she sat. She held her hands in her lap, palms up, and waited. Usually he was the one who left the room and refused to talk. Usually she followed him, pleading to talk it through, whatever it was. This was new for her.

She stretched out on the bed, her arms stiff beside her body, her fists clinched. He would refuse counseling as he had every time before. What if they did separate? A teacher's salary wasn't much. The details of what could lie ahead tumbled around inside her. Rolling into a fetal position, she gave herself what comfort she could. No sound came from downstairs. Unfurling, she stood tall. In the spare room, she began to pour it all out into her journal. When she had begun to paint a picture, to fit the pieces of the puzzle together, she felt somehow satisfied or at least purged. She crawled under the covers in the spare room and was soon asleep.

In the morning she woke early, surprisingly well rested. In their bedroom, their bed was untouched. She dressed for work and went downstairs. On the couch was a pile of blankets. She smelled coffee brewing. Swatting butterflies inside, she ventured into the kitchen, drawn there by the smell of bacon. Harry was standing at the counter filling his coffee cup.

"Good morning," he said, handing her a plate with toast and bacon and motioning for her to sit down. He did not smile nor did he frown. She recognized the inscrutable look he must use in court.

"Good morning," she replied, taking her seat, her stomach in knots. "Thank you for making breakfast."

"You're welcome." He poured a second cup and handed it to her, then sat down with his cup and plate. The newspaper lay unopened next to his plate. As he ate his toast and bacon, he looked out the window.

She took a bite of bacon and waited. The air felt thick between them. She spread strawberry jam on the toast and ate it. Her lower back started to twinge so she sat up straight and concentrated on her breathing till it relaxed a bit.

His eyes were glued to his plate. He took a sip of coffee then raised his eyes to hers. "I didn't sleep very well. I lay on the couch and thought a lot about what you said. I don't want to go to counseling but, if you insist, I will give it a try." He gave a big sigh. "I don't want to separate."

She gasped. "Really?"

"You'll have to arrange it and find someone who has evening appointments because I can't go any other time. And make sure whoever it is takes my insurance and isn't some twenty-five-year-old just out of school!" Then, wrapping his toast and bacon in a napkin, he was out the door. She reached to give him a hug, suddenly feeling a surge of tenderness rise up inside her. But he and his briefcase were gone.

Chapter 6

$\mathcal{A}$nnie paced the living room, checked her watch, looked out the window, then paced some more. *Where can he be?* she wondered. Harry had promised to meet her at home no later than 5:20 p.m. so they could drive together to their first appointment with the marriage counselor and now it was 5:40 p.m. They would barely make it if they left now. She had called his office but no answer, so he must be on the way, but *Where is he?*

Just then the phone rang. She nearly tripped over the coffee table to get to the phone.

Harry sounded cold and curt. "I got delayed. I'll have to meet you there."

She sighed but decided it would be useless to protest. "I guess so."

"And where is this damn place?" He sounded angry. As usual.

"I told you this morning. It's at 5225 Hamilton Street."

"Oh, no, I know that building. Barnes & Stern have their offices there. What's the suite number?"

"It's on the ground floor: Number 102."

"Oh, good, Barnes & Stern are on the fifth floor. I'll meet you there in fifteen minutes." He hung up.

She threw her bag over her shoulder and headed for the car.

As she backed out of the driveway, her heartbeat started to accelerate and her hands grew damp on the steering wheel. She had never consulted a therapist and, other than taking Psychology 101 in college, knew very little of what to expect. Harry certainly knew less, even though, in her opinion, needed help more. She didn't realize until she had been living with him for several months how easily angered he could be and over such small issues. Once she was so harried trying to get dinner made before she had to return to school for a PTA open house, she didn't leave the not-quite-thawed left-over pizza in the toaster oven long enough and it was stone cold when they ate it. Harry blew up and talked about it for weeks. As if she had committed a capital crime. She never understood what the big deal was. Her stomach twisted as she remembered. She was so grateful to have a counselor to help her learn how to deal with him. Or learn if their marriage was hopeless.

It sure felt hopeless to her at the moment. In the days since he had agreed to go to counseling, he had withdrawn even more. The chasm between them was already wide and now it seemed wider. She had worked so hard to find a marriage counselor who fit his requirements. She had called the local Mental Health Association for a referral. She had thought of asking Claire from her poetry group who seemed so wise and had lived here a long time, but she knew Harry would be furious if she told anyone. If his office colleagues found out, he would deny it and quit therapy immediately. "They'll think I'm crazy," he had said. Fortunately, the man at the Mental Health Association sounded calm and sympathetic and had a long list of names of experienced therapists and a few who even specialized in couples. She called the first three, but only Amanda Murphy's office called her back and did so promptly.

She pulled into the parking lot. No sign of Harry's car. Tears filled her eyes. She got out and looked around. Very few cars parked. Then she saw Harry walking up.

She surreptitiously wiped her eyes with her fingers. "Where did you park?"

"The next street over."

"So no one will see you?"

"Of course." He stared at her hard.

Am I on trial? She wondered but led the way inside. He followed, his lips pressed in a firm line.

Inside, Natalie looked up from her desk. "Are you the Thomases?"

Harry stepped in front of Annie who moved back to avoid being knocked over. "We have an appointment."

Natalie smiled and handed him a clipboard. "Please fill out the intake form and I'll let Ms. Murphy know you are here."

Harry turned around and sat in a chair by the door. Annie sat next to him and watched as he wrote, then pulled out his insurance card and wrote some more. She leaned over to read what he was writing, but he turned his shoulder to her. So she sat with her hands in her lap and looked around. There was a bulletin board with fliers on one wall, a painting of the beach with rolling waves and seagulls flying on another wall. Looking at the beach, she began to realize her shoulders were hunched and tense. She relaxed them a bit and took a deep breath. A closed door held a sign that read "Amanda Murphy, LCSW."

Chapter 7

When Amanda Murphy opened her office door, she saw a very anxious couple turn to look in her direction. "Anne and Harry Thomas? I'm Amanda Murphy, please come in."

Harry got up, straightening his frame to his full height, and headed toward the open door. Annie padded a few paces behind him. Amanda watched their body language closely as they entered her office. She followed and waved them towards two chairs. "Have a seat. Welcome." She sat opposite them in a larger chair on rollers. Natalie stepped in briefly to hand her the intake form then closed the door.

Amanda noticed Annie holding her hands, sweaty, trembling, and gazing around the room. Her eyes landed first on the wall with a beach scene, of a couple walking along the sand holding hands and smiling at each other. Annie smiled then turned her head to another painting of a mountain waterfall with a lone figure sitting on a rock in front of the falling water in apparent contemplation. She thought she saw Annie take a deep breath and relax a bit as she turned to face Amanda. Harry sat perched on the edge of his chair as if preparing to bolt. His eyes bored into her with a fierce intensity. She glanced at the intake form a brief moment as she prepared to begin the session.

When she raised her eyes to them and began to open her mouth to speak, Harry started talking: "Now I can't come to too many of these sessions. I have a demanding job. And I must know that it's all confidential or I will leave right now."

Amanda nodded and picked up the reins. "I understand. Everything you say in this room stays in this room. I see my first job as to help my clients feel comfortable to open up about what really bothers them. How long you come is totally up to you."

"Okay," said Harry, sitting back in his chair a millimeter.

Amanda smiled. These were common concerns. If he hadn't brought them up, she would have. But what does this tell her about him? She looked forward to finding out. "Let's get started. Today I first want to learn about your frustrations—which I assume you have or you wouldn't be here—and then teach you the intentional dialogue process, which will give you a structured way to talk about your frustrations at home." She paused a moment to see if they were still with her. Annie had her eyes glued on her. Harry frowned but was listening. "Then I want to have an individual session with each of you—to get your life story, hear your goals for therapy, and hear anything you need to tell me that might be easier to say without your partner present. Then that will complete my assessment and we will meet again together and get to work."

Amanda noticed Harry stiffen at the words 'life story' while Annie brightened at hearing 'without your partner present.' She was fascinated. Seeing they both were paying close attention, she continued. "Let me tell you how I usually start the first session with a new couple. I assume most couples want the same thing in a relationship—to feel safe and to feel loved for who you really are, usually in that order. But frustrations get in the way. So I want to hear about your frustrations."

"I'm frustrated Annie insisted we come here," Harry said.

Amanda smiled. "That's makes you the drag-gee and Annie the drag-ger. Most in your position come reluctantly but most are glad they came when it's all over." She smiled to see if Harry would smile back. He did, barely. She then continued. "I want to hear about your frustrations in this way: I want each of you to tell me how you believe the other is frustrated with you."

Harry's mouth dropped open. He inched forward in his chair. Annie sat still and frowned.

"I will ask the one who is listening to give a neutral reflection of what you hear your partner say—we call this a *mirror*—resisting the temptation to say if you agree of not—you'll get to do that later. I do this for two reasons. To find out if you have an accurate understanding of your partner's frustrations and to emphasize the importance of stretching to see things from the other's point of view, to empathize. Questions, comments?" She paused and looked at them both for a moment—they both seemed deep in thought. She went on. "I ask for two frustrations, an arbitrary number, there may be more or less. Then, after you each name two of your partner's frustrations, you will get to speak for yourselves. Finally, I will teach you the intentional dialogue process. Who would like to start?" She waited and turned her gaze from one to the other.

Harry sat back and crossed his arms over his chest. "Annie can start."

"Are you willing to start, Annie?"

"I guess so." Annie gave a wan smile.

"Hmmpf! I can't wait to hear this," said Harry. He pressed his lips together in a tight line.

"Turn your chairs to face each other," Amanda directed.

Annie swiveled her chair and sat up tall. Harry moved his half-way and began to squirm, adjusting his body in the chair with his eyes cast down.

"Annie, name one way you believe Harry may be frustrated with you." She waved at the white board in the corner. "Please complete the sentence stem on the board."

Annie looked at the board, cleared her throat, and looked directly at Harry. "I believe you may be frustrated with me because . . . I've been spending so much time writing poetry lately."

Harry stared at Annie's feet, shook his head and started to open his mouth as if to interrogate the dust mites in the rug. Amanda quickly spoke: "Harry, just mirror her. 'What I hear you saying is . . . '"

He turned his eyes to the window, sighed, and began: "What I hear you saying is you think I'm frustrated with you because you spend more time writing your . . . uh . . . driv . . . uh . . . poetry than doing what I want you to do." His eyes cast white bolts at Amanda.

Annie looked stricken.

"Harry, mirror her exact words, please. No editorializing," said Amanda firmly. That he almost said "drivel" was clear to her.

In a sing song tone, his eyes now riveted on the ceiling, "What I hear you say is you believe I am frustrated because you neglect me to write your whatever you write."

"Better but no cigar," smiled Amanda. "Her exact words, Harry. One more try."

" . . . because you spend so much time writing *your* poetry lately." *His tone made poetry writing sound like a criminal act,* thought Amanda. She noticed how distressed Annie looked.

"Better," said Amanda. "Next frustration, Annie."

Annie looked at Amanda, then at Harry's feet. "And you're frustrated because I want you to help with the housework, wash the dishes when I cook."

Amanda nodded at Harry. "Mirror that, please."

"And you're frustrated because I want you to help with the housework, wash the dishes when I cook." He looked at Amanda. "See, I did her exact words."

Amanda let out a big exhale. *This guy is going to be a pain,* she thought. To Harry, she said, "Mirror from her point of view, Harry. Try one more time: 'I'm frustrated because *you* want me . . . and so on.'"

"Yes, ma'am," said Harry, with a grimace. "OK, I'm frustrated because *she* wants *me* to help with the housework, which I don't have time for with my job!" He raised his voice.

Amanda wanted to scream back but instead she smiled. "You'll get a chance to speak for yourself in a moment, Harry, but that first part was close enough." Out of the corner of her eye, she watched Annie's shoulders drop and her face soften a bit.

Amanda turned to Harry. "Your turn, Harry. You name one of Annie's frustrations next."

Harry arched his eyebrows and clenched his jaw.

"Yes, you take a turn." Amanda waved toward the white board and the sentence stem.

Harry regarded it suspiciously, looked at Amanda who nodded, then closed his eyes pensively.

"Well, she's frustrated with me because I don't have time to do the housework and she's frustrated with me because I don't like her going off all the time to her damn poetry club."

"One at a time, one more time please," said Amanda.

Harry sighed. "Yes, ma'am."

Amanda leaned towards him smiling.

Harry smiled back. "I believe she is frustrated with me because I don't do the house work in a timely fashion." He sat back and crossed his arms.

Amanda smiled. "Better." She turned to Annie. "Now your turn to mirror, Annie."

Annie faced Harry and looked him straight in the face. "You believe I am frustrated with you because you don't do the housework in a timely fashion." She smiled and looked at Amanda.

"Good." She turned towards him. "Harry?"

He shook his head at the dust mites. "And I believe she's frustrated with me because I don't like her spending so much time at her poetry club."

Amanda smiled. "Much better."

Annie was ready. "What I hear you saying is you believe I am frustrated with you because you don't like me spending so much time at my poetry club."

"Good. Now you get to speak for yourselves."

Harry gave a wide grin. "Finally!"

Amanda had been taking notes. "Harry, Annie believes you are frustrated because she has been spending so much time writing poetry lately. Is that true?"

"Yes, yes," he said. "That's all she ever wants to do anymore. It's a big waste of time. She forgets to pick up my shirts from the cleaners, she runs off to that club leaving me to clean up the dinner dishes. I have more important things to do!"

Amanda nodded, mirrored, and looked at her notes. "And she believes you are frustrated that she wants you to help with the housework. Is that true?"

"Damn right it is!" He scooted to the front of his seat. "But no, she insisted on having a job teaching which wears her out so then she wants me to do housework. That's not the way it's supposed to be!" He sat back and crossed his arms again.

Amanda took a deep breath. *I wonder how late the gym is open tonight?* She smiled, mirrored him, and kept going. "Are there other frustrations she didn't mention you'd like to put on the table today?"

Harry frowned. "Like I said, I'm frustrated she made me come here. I don't like spending time discussing my personal matters in public." He glared at her. "Even if you claim it's confidential."

Amanda nodded. *He's sealed up tight like a drum and scared of exposure.* She mirrored him. She noted a slight, ever so slight softening in his expression. *People so want to be listened to and heard,* she mused. "Another frustration she didn't mention?"

"Sometimes she won't sleep with me, because she says I snore. But I don't!" He raised his pointer finger and stabbed the air. Then he put his hands in his lap and bowed his head, looking a tiny bit more relaxed.

Again Amanda mirrored him and made a mental note to inquire later if he'd ever been tested for sleep apnea. "Any more?"

"No, I don't have time to list them all! That's all for now." He frowned.

Amanda repeated the process with Annie, then asked her if she had more frustrations to add.

"He's always so angry," she said in a whisper. "I do everything I know not to provoke him, but he still gets so angry." Her mouth turned down, and she looked at her hands.

Amanda mirrored her, keeping an eye on Harry.

Harry shook his head and muttered almost to himself. "She just doesn't understand, she just doesn't understand."

Amanda made a few more notes, then looked at them both. "Now I want to teach you the intentional dialogue process."

Harry looked at his watch.

"This won't take long," said Amanda. "You already know the first step, mirroring. One of you will be the sender who shares a frustration, the other the receiver who will mirror what you heard, ask 'Is that right?' then, if it was, ask 'Is there more?' You go back and forth sending and mirroring until the sender says 'That's all for now.' Then the receiver summarizes, validates, and empathizes. Then you switch. Does this make sense so far?"

Harry frowned and sighed. "I guess so."

Annie nodded but had her face scrunched up looking confused.

"I know it sounds like a lot, but I'll walk you through it and then send you home with a handout," said Amanda. "Harry, why don't you begin this time? I don't care what issue you pick, I just want you to experience it so you can do it at home."

Harry sighed and closed his eyes a moment. He looked at Amanda. "It can be something simple?"

Amanda nodded.

He turned towards Annie and began. "I'm frustrated you didn't remember to pick up my shirts from the cleaners this week. You know I have to look good for work."

He sat back in silence and looked at Annie.

Amanda noticed Harry was finally making eye contact with

Annie. "Annie, mirror that."

"You're frustrated I forgot to pick up your shirts because you need to look good at work. Is that right?" She looked at Harry who nodded. "Is there more?"

"Yes," said Harry. "You know I have ambitions, and you will benefit from them. If I succeed like I want to, you won't have to work anymore. And then it will be easier for you to remember to pick up my shirts." He sat taller and looked quite proud of himself.

Amanda nodded to Annie who picked up the cue. "You have ambitions that I will benefit from and then I won't have to work and then I won't forget your shirts. Is that right?" she asked Harry. Annie frowned.

Amanda chuckled to herself. *I think she doesn't want to quit work and pick up shirts.*

"Yes, that's right," said Harry.

"Is there more?" asked Annie, keeping her face studiously neutral, which was not lost on Amanda.

"That's all," said Harry, smiling and sitting back in his chair.

"Now in your own words, summarize what Harry said as briefly as you can," Amanda instructed Annie.

Annie took a deep breath and sighed. "You're frustrated that I forgot your shirts, you have ambitions which will mean I won't have to work and can pick up your shirts." She raised her eyes to Harry then Amanda.

"Is that a good summary, Harry?" asked Amanda. He nodded. She turned back to Annie, whose shoulders slumped as if under a huge boulder. "Now validate. Validation does not mean agreement." Annie lifted a tiny bit. "It means you understand Harry's train of thought. If you do, say something like 'I understand. You make sense.'"

Annie sat up with a wry smile. "I totally understand what you're saying, Harry. You make perfect sense."

I wonder if Annie feels safe enough to say how she really feels when she gets her turn, thought Amanda. "Now empathize, Annie. 'I imagine you are feeling...'"

Annie sighed. "I imagine you are feeling frustrated. And ambitious." She looked at Amanda.

Amanda smiled and then turned to Harry. "Is that how you feel, Harry?"

"Yes, that's exactly how I feel." Harry smiled and visibly relaxed in his chair, as if he had just won his closing argument.

"Ready to listen to Annie?" Amanda asked.

"Sure."

"Annie, it's your turn to be the sender. You've done a good job mirroring. Just say whatever has been coming up for you as you listened to Harry."

Annie trembled as she gathered her thoughts. After a few moments, she raised her eyes to Harry. "I'm sorry I forgot your shirts. I actually thought you would pick them up as it's on your way home from work." She paused.

"Now you mirror Annie," said Amanda. She noticed his frown. "Just mirror."

Harry closed his mouth, squinted his eyes, and took a deep breath. "You're sorry you forgot my shirts and you *actually* thought *I* would pick them up? You think it's on my way home?"

"Remember, Harry, it's a neutral mirror," said Amanda. She noticed the color had drained from Annie's face. *She's scared of him.*

Harry said nothing. Annie said nothing.

"Ask her, 'Is that right?' Harry," said Amanda. "And use a neutral tone."

Harry sighed and complied. "Is that right?"

Annie nodded.

"Is there more?"

Annie nodded again.

"Better," said Amanda.

Now Annie's face was flushed. "I like my job. I want to work," she said.

"Neutral mirror, Harry," interjected Amanda before he could speak.

He sighed. "You like your job. You want to work," he said quietly.

"Good," said Amanda. "Continue, Harry."

"Is that right? Is there more?"

"Yes. No," whispered Annie.

"Okay, Harry, summarize, validate, empathize."

"You're sorry you forgot my shirts, you thought I would get them, you like your job." He sat back and looked at Amanda as if to say, "Are you happy now?"

"Is that a good summary, Annie?"

Annie nodded numbly.

"Do you understand what she said, Harry? How do you think she feels?" said Amanda.

"Yes, I understand."

"And I imagine she feels . . ."

"I imagine she feels sorry. And happy in her job." Harry sighed and shifted in his seat.

The torture is almost over, Harry. "You did a good job for your first time," she said to them. She handed them each a sheet of paper. "Here is a handout describing the intentional dialogue we just did. I recommend you practice it thirty minutes a day." *I'll believe it when I hear it,* she thought.

Annie nodded and turned her head to Harry. He gave his inscrutable look.

She faced them. "I see our time is about up for today. I have at least a beginning picture of what you all are dealing with. The issues are normal, common issues for couples. How you spend your time, how you divide up chores, time together versus time apart. Using the dialogue will help you talk about these issues constructively. Harry, will this time work for you next week?" She looked at him.

Harry looked shocked. "Next week?" He pulled out his phone and consulted his calendar.

"Next week this time works for me," Annie quickly offered.

Harry shook his head. "I can come next week." He huddled over his device and began typing.

"Can you come the week after, Annie?" asked Amanda. "This is for your individual session."

"Sure," said Annie, smiling. "Thanks."

"Happy dialoguing," Amanda said as she showed them out.

Harry headed down the street. "I've got to go back to the office." He threw his words over his shoulder as he disappeared. "Do what you want for dinner."

Despite herself, Annie felt her eyes tear up. By the time she drove home, however, she was grateful to have the house to herself. She heated up some leftovers and then she poured everything out in her journal. She fell asleep before Harry got home.

Chapter 8

$\mathcal{I}$an stood in front of the fireplace, now empty of wood and ash, in the coffeehouse where they had first met. "As you know, tonight is the last class." It was mid-May. Floor to ceiling windows stood on either side of the fireplace, giving an expansive view of budding fruit trees, manicured shrubs, and the sun moving towards the horizon. A dark brown couch flanked by matching chairs held the class in a semi-circle facing him, supplemented by folding chairs. On the walls were large paintings by local artists. "Then we're off for the summer. But you all get first crack at signing up for next fall where we'll use the same format."

Claire spread her long legs ahead of her as she leaned back on the couch. "Sign me up."

Peter sat upright on a stuffed chair next to the couch. "Me too."

"Me three!" said George from the opposite chair, "I wouldn't miss it. I hope everyone will return." He passed his smile around the circle, then stopped with Annie, on the couch next to Claire, who appeared deep in thought.

There was a chorus of yeses from three more. "So we have six and room for one more." Ian smiled broadly at Annie. "Anyone else?"

Annie had been studying the floor, biting her bottom lip. She looked up. "I want to. I'm not sure right now. When is the deadline to sign up?"

"You have one more week to decide before the Community Arts Center catalog hits the presses and anyone else can sign up. We do have a waiting list so don't take too long to decide."

Annie nodded. She was worried about money, although the class was inexpensive. She knew she might soon be on a tight budget as a newly separated woman. Annie wasn't sure Harry would stick with couples therapy. They were supposed to practice the intentional dialogue process at home, but Harry had refused every time she had suggested it and was silent or angry the rare times he was at home. This poetry class had been a breath of fresh air for her. She wasn't sure how she'd make it through the next few months without it.

Annie looked around the circle of these people who were now such close friends. This room felt to her so cozy and comfortable. Her second home. Her eyes rested on George's face. His eyes opened wide as he smiled and nodded at her. She took a deep breath. "Oh, go ahead, sign me up. I will have to find a way to get back here." She gave a wan smile to Ian.

"Great! I'm so glad, Annie. I'd hate for you to stop now," Ian said.

The rest of the class applauded. "You go, girl!" cried Peter. Claire draped her arm over Annie's shoulder in a half hug and whispered in her ear: "So happy. Let's get together for lunch or something this summer. I don't want to miss seeing you." Annie met her gaze and nodded, surprised to feel her eyes tear up. She needed a friendship with a warm older woman like Claire especially now.

"Now that that's decided, let's get to work!" Ian handed out copies of the chapbook of the poems he had selected as examples of their best work to be printed and shared. It was black in color, the size of a small notebook, with a photo on the front of a white cup full to the brim with coffee spilling over onto its saucer. "Tonight we'll have a poetry reading!" He looked around the group. "Who would like to begin?"

For a moment, no one spoke. After much squirming and eyes cast around the room, George held up his hand. "I'll break the ice." He grinned and shook his head. "At least get it over with."

Ian had him stand in front of the group with instructions to read each poem twice to allow full absorption by the audience. Ian sat in George's now empty chair. They all turned their eyes on George. He opened the chapbook and thumbed through the pages to his poem. He cleared his throat, forced a smile, and began.

Watch Your Step

The bark on a dogwood tree
leads your eyes high above
where a dense canopy reaches
to shade its white blossoms.
You stand and gaze a moment until
your boot slips on the wet moss
covering these sharp rocks.
Watch your step here, I say.
Be attentive as you make your way.
Remember how long it took
to pull those thorn vines free.

George paused and ran his eyes over the faces of his friends. He cleared his throat again then continued.

Her tangles pierced deep,
even drew blood.
Nothing to do then but flee,
leaving a hunk of flesh on the tree.
Watch your step here I say.
Beware the edge,
thorns on the ledge.
Don't lose your way again,
It's too high a price to pay.

George lowered his page and waited.

Ian beamed at him. "Again," he prompted. "Slower." George read it again, letting each word roll off his tongue like a gum ball into their waiting ears. When he had finished, he kept his eyes on the page and waited. Annie noticed a tremble in his hands.

"I like what you've done with it," said Peter as he raised his hands and clapped. Claire wiped away a tear. "Oh, yes, it is complete now," she said and clapped also. Annie smiled and clapped as everyone joined the applause. She remembered when he first presented this poem in class. How curious she was to know what had given birth to it. Then they had their walk and talk in the starlight and now she thought maybe she knew.

As the others took their turns, Annie sat with rapt attention. She felt her spirits lift as she listened. She had no words for the joy she felt. For a moment, she forgot she would have to take her turn. Finally she realized everyone had read but her. Ian nodded to her and gestured towards the front. Immediately, her heart started beating faster and for a moment she felt faint. *How can I feel so nervous in front of these dear people?* she wondered as she stood up. She took a deep breath to calm herself and cast her eyes around the circle. There was Peter with his eyes glued to her face, Claire with a big smile, George with a twinkle in his eyes, Ian looking proud. She looked down at her poem and began.

The World of Spiders

The world is held together
by the million tiny filaments
of spiders. Spiders weaving
through winter branches
a tapestry invisible
except to the quiet eye
for whom they shine—

She paused and raised her eyes a moment. Peter was nodding, Claire had closed her eyes. George held her face with his eyes, his cheeks soft and relaxed as he listened. She cleared her throat and continued.

tiny angel's hairs
covering the world
as far as the eye can see.
Fragile, they bend in the wind,
and some break.
But the spiders spin them again
and again—the spiders never give up.

Ian nodded and his smile grew wider.

They know, if they do,
the world will surely
fall apart.

She lowered the chapbook and raised her eyes to them. She remembered when she had presented the first version of this poem, the first class George had attended. How she had almost given up on it, but they hadn't let her. They sat in silence a moment, then she read it again. When she finished, they all began to clap. She flushed and trembled.

"Fantastic!" declared Peter.

"My favorite!" said Claire.

"I love it!" grinned George.

Ian stood up. "Never give up writing, Annie, never give up."

"Thank you, thank you all. I won't give up, I promise." She stuttered and flushed and nearly tripped as she took her seat next to Claire, who grasped her hand and squeezed it.

"Now let's celebrate!" Ian opened a bottle of champagne with a pop and began passing around plastic stem-wear full of bubbly. Inside, Annie felt warmth rise up and spread over her. Whatever happened to her marriage, to her life, she would remember this moment. Poetry and friendship, with a bit of bubbly. Just then, George leaned over with a sly grin and passed her an open box of chocolates. She picked a dark piece, wondering what she'd find inside, and passed the box to Claire.

Chapter 9

"Mr. Thomas is here." Amanda heard Natalie's voice through the intercom as she sat at her desk.

Amanda opened her office door into the waiting area. Harry held a magazine he appeared riveted by. His thick black hair was gelled securely into place; his suit and tie showed little sign he'd been working all day, crisp and unwrinkled. He didn't look up when she stepped into the room, but she couldn't help but notice his right leg began to jiggle and shake up and down. "Hello, Harry, welcome," Amanda smiled. Harry stood but did not smile. He nodded and sat in his usual chair, his head down. He reminded her of a child sent to the principal's office. Amanda followed and took her seat.

"I knew I'd be late. I called to cancel."

"You're my last appointment today. We can take as much time as we need."

"I see." Harry rolled his eyes, and the corners of his mouth turned down.

"Tonight I'd like to hear your life story." Harry grimaced. Amanda went on. "Why don't you start by telling me where and when you were born." She held her pen and clipboard and waited.

"My childhood was fine. My parents are gone, I live far away from my siblings. What does this have to do with me and Annie?"

69

Amanda smiled. She often got this question. Especially from those who weren't psychologically minded, which she suspected might be true of Harry. "It helps me understand better where you're coming from, what kind of early experiences shaped you, that kind of stuff."

Harry sat up tall. "I shaped myself," he said.

"You shaped yourself. Tell me about your family. Start with where and when you were born, please."

Harry sighed. "If I must. Forty years ago this past March outside Washington, DC. My father was with the government."

"How would you describe your father? His personality?"

"How would I . . . ?" Harry paused, thinking, then continued, "He was a good provider. We had everything we needed. He worked hard." Harry sat back, and smiled smugly.

"Good. But what was he like as a father?" she pressed on.

"Honestly?" Amanda nodded. "How would I know? He was never there. Chief counsel to the head of whatever. He traveled, he worked late, I hardly knew him."

"He was more like a stranger who occasionally visited than a dad?"

Harry nodded. "You got it." He sat back in his seat.

"And he was a lawyer too?"

"Yes," said Harry.

"What's your relationship with him like now?"

"He's dead." He closed his eyes a moment then opened them to the rug.

"I'm so sorry. Yes, you did say your parents were gone. When did he die?" she asked gently.

"Fifteen years ago. Age fifty-eight. Dropped dead of a heart attack."

"Did you get closer to him before he died?"

"How could I? He worked all the time. But, like I said, he did what he was supposed to do, he was a good provider."

"But what a loss for you," she offered.

"Not really," he said. "Like I said, he was never there."

"How about your mother? Did she work outside the home?"

"My mother? No, she was home. She had three kids in five years, she was busy." Harry sat back.

Amanda realized his story was not going to flow as it often does with some people. This was a man with a high wall around his heart. Which usually hides a lot of pain and trauma. What was Harry's? And how could she help him feel safe enough to reveal it to her? She tried again. "Tell me more about your mother, please."

"More? What more do you want? She was my mother."

"How would you describe her personality?"

Harry laughed. "Her personality? She had none. She was a drunk." His voice dripped with contempt.

Now we're getting somewhere. No wonder he doesn't want to talk about it. "She had a drinking problem? Tell me more."

Harry showed tension all over his face. His leg began to jiggle again. She wondered if he had ever talked about any of this childhood trauma. She felt for him. She knew she'd have to be patient. She waited.

Harry sighed. "I can't remember much, just she was always drinking. My grandparents drank. She drank. My uncles drank. Holidays were really something, more whiskey than turkey. But I couldn't blame her, she had three kids. My dad was never home. And we were a wild bunch, just normal kids, mind you, but we were full of energy. Mother couldn't do much with us—maybe we drove her to drink. It got so she was always drunk and passed out after school. Then my older sister took over and bossed us all. And she was mean!"

"How old was your sister when she took charge?"

"Oh, eight, ten, around then. And she was a tyrant. I hated her."

Eight or ten years old and filling the empty space of the parents, a parental child. Horrible. Her heart softened.

"And which one were you in the line-up?"

"My brother was one year older than me and a few years younger than my sister. He tried to be boss too but that just meant he beat me up."

"Oh, how tough for you. How did you deal with that, Harry?"

"I fought back, what would you do?" He challenged her. She knew he didn't really want to hear her answer. She waited in silence. "I might have been younger but I was strong and sometimes I did beat him up." Harry sat taller in his seat.

"So you learned to fight your way through life," she said.

"Yeah, it's a jungle out there!"

"But how awful for that young boy, no functional parents, no one to take care of you, guide you as you grew." Now she had a hint of the origins of his rigidity, his anger. She knew she needed to tread carefully here. She didn't want to trigger the volcano that could be simmering underneath. She wondered if he would be able to let Annie love him. So many unknowns this early in the process.

Harry seemed in a daze, as if miles away. Then she watched him draw himself up and return. He looked at her. "Like I said, I shaped myself. I had to."

"And obviously you survived and made something of yourself. How did you choose law as a profession?" Amanda decided to move to the present and perhaps safer territory. She had had previous clients who opened up too many painful memories early in therapy and fled or, worse, fell apart. She had no way of knowing how Harry would react, especially if her hunch was correct that he had never talked about his past before.

"I don't know. I felt drawn to it. And when Dad was home, that's all he talked about. I took a course or two as an undergrad at the University and found I was good at it. So I applied, got into the University Law School, and the rest is history." He looked up as if the interview must be over. He looked at the clock. "Are we done now?"

"Not quite. I'd like to know what you hope to accomplish by coming to these sessions with Annie." Amanda smiled and again she waited.

Harry looked incredulous. "What? It wasn't my idea to come here! I really don't have time for all this touchy-feely crap!"

Steel-plated defenses, but far from the worst I've heard. Her memory flashed to the man who put a hole in her wall with his fist on his way out the door. *This one's not that bad.* "But you're here so there must be some reason you came and something you want," Amanda persisted.

"Humph! Annie gave me an ultimatum—either we come or we separate. I had no choice!"

Just like when he was a child. "So you want to stay married?" she asked.

"Sure I want to stay married! Of course! I just wish she wouldn't spend so much time with her stupid poetry writing crap. She's gone all the time."

"Yes, it's hard to have a relationship with someone who is never there. Like your father."

Harry looked shocked. "Huh? What?" he stuttered. Then he recovered and raised his voice. "But he was working, he had to work, it wasn't a stupid hobby that kept him gone. A man has to work. A wife is different. I want her to stop that poetry crap. I want her to have dinner ready when I get home." He leaned forward, shifted his weight to his feet and began to rise.

Amanda remained seated. "It sounds like you might feel a bit neglected. Could that be?" Harry sat back. She studied his demeanor to see if he would let his armor crack.

Harry grunted. His body softened. "Maybe. I don't know. I just want my wife at home cooking dinner when I get home."

"At home cooking dinner? Doesn't Annie also work?"

"Sure, you know, she's a teacher. That's okay, taking care of kids."

Amanda's feminist tendencies rose up inside her. She held them in check and parked her inner judge at the curb with some difficulty. There was another important question she needed to ask. "Does Annie drink? Like your mother?" She looked at him carefully.

"No, Annie hardly drinks at all." His raised his eyebrows. "I would never have married someone who drinks a lot. That can kill you." He frowned.

Okay, here we go. "Did drinking kill your mother, Harry?"

He winced as if he'd been stabbed. "I guess you could say that." He lowered his gaze, rolled his fingers into fists in his lap.

Amanda watched, concerned his mother's death was too painful for him to talk about. Such deep traumatic wounds. "What a tragedy. I'm so sorry," she said quietly. He raised his eyes to her. They were moist. She saw a glimpse of vulnerability she had not yet seen. He unfurled his hands and put his palms down on his thighs.

She moved to validate and soothe him. "You were smart to choose a wife who didn't drink. It's not easy growing up with an alcoholic mother and an absent father. You must have seen something else in Annie, something that made you sense with her things could be different. And I assume as a teacher she gets home before you do. And sober. An improvement from childhood with your mother," she said.

The moment of vulnerability closed with a clink. He turned to steel. "Like I said, my mother was a drunk and I've told you already that I don't want to talk about her anymore. I just want you to make my wife be how a wife is supposed to be." He stared at her as he stood up.

"I understand." Amanda was aware she had hit a nerve by referencing his mother a second time. He was like a crustacean, hard on the outside but soft on the inside. She decided it was time to close the session for today. "Let me see if I can summarize your main message. You want to stay married and you want Annie more available to you." She raised her eyes to him.

Harry sat.

"We're almost done." She felt her own eyes moisten as she went on. "If you can hang in here with me, I'll do my best to help you and Annie create a close, loving relationship."

Harry met her eyes, tilted his head and squinted. For a moment he was speechless. He looked down at his hands cradling each other in his lap. Amanda waited. Then his face softened and, in barely a whisper, he said, "Um, thank you."

"Anything else you want?"

He stiffened visibly and glared at her. "Yeah, I want to stop talking about all this old stuff. It's past. It's gone. It doesn't matter anymore. I've got to get back to the office." His voice began softly then rose in crescendo as he spoke.

"I take it you don't enjoy talking about your childhood. Have you ever talked about it before?"

"Why would I want to talk about it?"

"To make sense of it, learn from it, so you can let it go and move on."

Harry narrowed his eyes as she spoke as if what she said was all new to him. "Otherwise, it operates like an undertow that can suck you down when you least expect it." She watched him carefully. She saw a spark, maybe of curiosity, in his face, then in a flash it was gone. "I know it's painful to remember, but, trust me, it does get easier. And it helps me learn how to help you. Thank you for telling me. I understand you better now."

Harry gave her a wan smile. "Can we stop now?"

Amanda smiled. "We certainly can. Our time is up."

She stood up. Harry stood up. She savored the moment of seeing moisture in his eyes. Would she see it again? She couldn't be sure. For now, she extended her hand. He grasped it hard, then released it quickly and moved away towards the door.

"I'll see you in two weeks after I have my individual session with Annie. Have a good two weeks, Harry."

"Yeah, you too," he muttered and was out the door.

Amanda closed her door and stretched out in her chair with the tall back. She slipped off her shoes and put her feet on the hassock. *What a sad and angry man. I wonder if he'll stick with therapy. He seems to have done his best to become just like his father, a workaholic lawyer. So glad it looks like Annie isn't much like his mother. So far.* She tucked her hair behind her ear and began to picture her home and the couch and a glass of red wine. It was Bill's night to cook. She looked forward to getting home and unwinding in the shelter of her family. She felt so lucky to have married Bill. She would have to show him how much she appreciated him. Maybe after a good night's sleep first. When they were both off work. Maybe Saturday.

Chapter 10

*H*arry staggered outside Amanda's office onto the street, feeling disoriented at first. As he headed down the street and around the corner, he felt a volcano simmering slowly up inside him that began to overflow. *Damn her and all her questions, damn Annie for making me do this therapy crap.* Sweat rolled down his sides underneath his shirt. Tears sprang up in his eyes. His stomach churned with acid. He stomped on, trying to tamp down those feelings, those images, those memories that pelleted him inside like machine gun fire. When he reached his car, he gunned the engine without checking first to see if the coast was clear. A car coming up from behind narrowly missed him as it swerved around him, blasting its horn. He gripped the steering wheel, cursed, but slowed down a bit. He drove around a few blocks and then onto the freeway to calm himself before returning to the office. He switched on the radio, hoping to hear loud rock and roll music to drown the fury inside him, but instead it was the 7:30 p.m. local news. *Seven-thirty! Jeez, it's getting late.* He punched buttons until he found the University student station with some wailing hip hop or rap or whatever they confuse for music these days. He found listening to it soothing—he'd stumbled onto a jazz show—it reminded him of his more carefree undergraduate days. When he pulled into the parking lot by his office twenty minutes later, he had burned it off on the freeway enough so he thought he could concentrate on the piles of work waiting for him.

He took the elevator to the tenth floor and stepped onto the plush carpet in the hall. He breathed in the smell of polished mahogany tables next to cushioned arm chairs, smiled with satisfaction at the art on the walls depicting scenes of grandeur and opulence. This was his world, he had made it, and he luxuriated in it. He headed down the hall to his office in the back corner. The wall of windows peered down to a brick patio with a gurgling fountain. He sat in the large desk chair that swiveled and reclined and looked out the window. The sun was about to set, casting beams of light through the tall trees of the nearby park. He opened his desk drawer and pulled out a bottle of Scotch and a glass. As he sipped, he ran over the "to do" list inside his head. He breathed a sigh of relief to be home here in his office.

But he couldn't entirely stop the images that leaked in beneath the door in his mind. He saw himself as a young boy. "Clean up that mess!" Sara screamed, raising the broom high above her head. He was busy on the living room rug building with blocks and cars and doing his best to ignore her. He had the couch cushions down and the rug rolled up over them to make mountains. He was having so much fun! But she kept screaming and coming closer and now that broom. *Swat!* She hit him on the back, sweeping him up like a piece of trash.

"Hey!" he cried. "Stop that! You can't tell me what to do! You're not my mother!"

"No, but I'm the oldest and I'm in charge and you better clean up your mess and come get your homework done! Momma said!"

Then his brother was on him pushing and yelling an echo of her. "You better do what Sara says or I'm gonna smack you." Buddy was only a year older but a head taller and mean as sin. Harry instinctively flinched and covered his head just before Buddy's fists hit. Then Harry grabbed those fists and jumped up, flipping Buddy onto his back with a surprised look of disbelief on his face. Harry smacked him across the face with his hand and didn't see the broom Sara wielded until he felt the wooden handle hit him on the back of his head, sprawling him on top of Buddy in a tangle of arms and legs. Harry somehow extricated himself and ran up the stairs in tears hollering, "I'm gonna tell Momma!" and ran smack into the closed door of her bedroom. He pushed it open and saw her lying on the bed. Moving closer, he saw her eyes were closed and her arms and legs spread wide. He stopped in wonder and tip-toed to the edge of the bed. "Momma?" he whispered. "Momma?" But she didn't move or open her eyes or show any sign she was aware of his presence. He tapped her arm. Her hand hung off the bed holding a glass she dropped onto the carpet. He took the glass and set it on the bedside table. Then he noticed the almost empty bottle there and the smell of what he was too young to recognize as whiskey.

He turned and saw both his brother and sister standing silent in the doorway, in shocking contrast to their earlier volume. He looked at Sara. "What's wrong with Momma?" he asked. His eyes pleaded and tears welled up and rolled down his face.

Sara softened a tiny bit, then drew herself up tall and gathered her authority around her. "She's passed out from drinking that whiskey." He looked at the bottle, then back at her. She nodded. "She told me to make you guys clean up and do your homework and fix supper. We're having frozen fish sticks and French fries and maybe frozen peas. Come on." She turned and headed back downstairs. Buddy said, "Yeah, come on," and followed her. Harry wiped his eyes with the heels of both hands, turned his back on his mother, and followed.

They did indeed have fish sticks, only burned not frozen. Sara did better on the French fries, at least they weren't burned. He and Buddy joined forces to talk her out of the peas. They found the ketchup and had lots, making another mess to clean up. She forgot about the homework or making them brush their teeth. She even let them watch television before bed, something they were never allowed to do before, except tonight there was a show on she liked. They laughed at the television. Harry fell asleep on the couch, staggered upstairs when Buddy poked him and pulled him up. That effort got him awake enough to crawl into bed in the room he and Buddy shared. He lay awake pondering it all. He'd never seen his Momma like that, but then he'd never gone past her closed door before. He grabbed his stuffed dog and used it to rub the tears from his cheeks as his eyelids grew heavy and he fell asleep.

Looking out his office window, Harry saw the last sliver of light disappear and the sky turn pink and purple and then the darkness fall like a heavy curtain. Slowly the stars appeared. He switched on his desk lamp. The light shown over the pile of papers on his desk he had not touched. The clock chimed nine times. He shook his head to get the fog of memories to leave him alone. *Momma's dead now. Buddy too after he joined the army and got blown up in Iraq. I can't remember the last time I saw Sara, probably at our brother's funeral.* He thought of Annie, her wavy brown hair, her long eyelashes, her impeccable style and courtesy. He had thought she'd make a good lawyer's wife, not drag him to some shrink where he'd have to remember all this old stuff. He pressed his lips together. He should have called her to say he'd be home late but he was too angry at her to bother. He promised himself he would never go there again. Never dredge up those dark memories. It wasn't worth it. He picked up the top stack of papers. He sighed. He'd have a late night tonight for sure.

He plowed through for some time, feeling the tension inside him decrease to a hum as he reconnected with his work. Depositions, research, preparation for a hearing next week, endless. But satisfying. He knew he was good at it. He had worked hard ever since he joined this firm right out of law school. In record time, he made partner. He had more billable hours than any of the other partners and more money than he knew what to do with. He should be enjoying life. But after he and Annie married, he soon had learned that her time in that shack in Brazil had ruined her for the life of opulence he desired. She was too focused on helping the poor, increasing their donations to all those stupid charities. He refused. How did he end up with such a bleeding heart do-gooder? And now she was making him bare his soul to a stranger. He ground his teeth.

Then he heard a door open and close. Was someone else here this late? He heard a tap on his office door.

"Yes?"

It opened slowly and there stood Gloria Benjamin. Gorgeous Gloria, the paralegals called her behind her back. Yes, she was gorgeous and a damn good litigator. Tall and stately with long lustrous blond hair that just touched her shoulders. She knew how to dress too. Tonight she wore a gray Armani suit that fit her like a glove. Gorgeous and she knew it. She stood in the doorway a moment regarding him with a quizzical smile. "Hello, Mr. Thomas," she purred. "Working late tonight, aren't you?"

Harry chuckled. "I work late every night. And that's why I'm partner and you're not."

"Oh, yeah?" she grinned. "Well, that may be about to change, you never know. You may be about to see me here late more often."

"Oh? What you working on tonight? Need supervision from a partner?" Harry had kept his distance from her in the year she'd been at the firm. She seemed a bit too flirty and also seemed a bit too aggressive, although female lawyers had to be aggressive to make it in law these days. But in this moment he decided to throw caution to the winds. He felt his anger melt away. He gestured toward the chair facing his desk. She sauntered in, a file tucked under her arm, and, instead of the chair, sat on the couch against the wall, leaving plenty of space for him to join her. Smiling, she waved him towards the place on the couch next to her. "It's that MacDonald case. I think we need a new strategy if we're going to win it." She set the folder on the coffee table.

Harry leaned his chair forward and set his feet on the floor, then stood up. "Let me see what you got. That's a tough case, I agree."

For nearly an hour they sat close to each other on the couch and leaned over the papers, studying all the evidence collected in the case. He didn't touch her, but, with each breath, he inhaled her scent, even at the end of the day filled with the fragrance of rich cologne. She was smart and her ideas for a new strategy ran along the same lines his instincts led him. He watched the inch of space between their thighs diminish as she narrowed it. He forced himself to focus on the case and move to widen the distance between them. *Remember, Harry, you're supposed to be trying to save, not sabotage, your marriage,* he lectured himself. *You and Gloria are here to talk about work, only work.* He succeeded, barely. Soon they had outlined a bold incisive new strategy he was sure the other partners would think was brilliant. How had he never noticed her fine legal mind before tonight? Her seductive manner had made him dismiss her. He sat back and looked at her just as the clock chimed ten times. *Her mind, Harry, it's her mind you need,* he reminded himself.

"Good work, Ms. Benjamin. I think we're on to something." He nodded towards his bottle of Scotch where he had left it on the corner of his desk. "Have a drink to celebrate?"

She smiled. "Sure, but no need to be so formal. Call me Glo." She leaned back and crossed her legs, causing her skirt to shift higher on her thigh. *And she knows it,* he mused as he got up to bring the bottle and two glasses to the coffee table. "May I call you Harry?" she asked.

"Certainly," he said as he smiled and poured their drinks.

Chapter 11

$\mathcal{A}$manda saw Annie come in looking relieved. She wore a short-sleeved white blouse over a long flowing skirt of gauzy turquoise. A turquoise and black scarf draped around her neck. Amanda couldn't help but notice wrinkles on her forehead that vanished as she entered. As Annie took her place, Amanda saw a spark of hope in Annie's eyes.

"Tonight I'd like to hear your life story," Amanda began.

"I've been been thinking about it." Annie frowned. "I'm not sure where to start." She pressed her lips together and looked at Amanda for guidance.

Amanda smiled and said: "Why don't you begin by telling me where and when you were born, Annie."

Annie chuckled. "Sure, right at the beginning. I was born July 21, 1982, in Atlanta, Georgia."

"So that makes you thirty this July and a Southern girl."

"Yes. My mother was a homemaker, my dad was a reporter for the *Atlanta Journal-Constitution*."

Amanda relaxed. Annie's story flowed easily.

"How would you describe your mother's personality?"

"She was smart and organized, always had dinner on the table when Daddy got home. She gardened and drove me to youth group at church, the usual homemaker stuff. I confided in her. She told me stories about when she was a girl. I was about the only one of my friends who didn't hate her mother. I was lucky."

"That's wonderful. But I'm sure there were some challenges. What was hardest about having her for a mother?"

"She was glamorous and had quite the fashion sense. I felt I could never meet her standard." Annie put her hands to her scarf, adjusted it, and pulled her skirt up an inch off the rug.

"Nice outfit," said Amanda.

Annie's eyes widened and she blushed. "I got this skirt and scarf on sale from my favorite store. Mayo's. Do you know it?"

"Oh yes, I love that store. But back to your mother."

Annie closed her eyes briefly then opened them with a sigh. "In a way, she was a bit too devoted. When I became a teenager, I felt she was living through me. She had to know where I was going and when I'd be back. And if I was late, oh boy, she'd get really upset."

"Hmm," said Amanda, "the pattern of vicarious living, perhaps."

"Is that what you call it? Well, sometimes I felt like my job was to make her happy. I don't think she was very happy with my father."

"Tell me what you noticed."

"Well, he was gone a lot covering his stories. He'd go off after dinner when he had a deadline and sometimes they'd argue." Annie paused. Amanda watched Annie's eyes glaze over. She seemed to be opening a door inside herself that creaked loudly, a door onto a scene she hesitated to remember. Annie looked away and closed her eyes.

"What are you thinking, Annie?" she asked gently.

Annie opened her eyes and gazed out the window. "There was one time when I was maybe nine or ten when they woke me in the middle of the night arguing loudly. I couldn't hear exactly what they were saying, but my mother sounded hysterical, and my dad kept saying: 'Mabel, Mabel, please calm down.'" Annie turned her head towards Amanda. "I was terrified. I figured they must be talking divorce. I thought I heard something about another woman but I couldn't be sure. Then in the morning at breakfast, they acted like nothing had happened. I kind of knew if it was in the night I wasn't supposed to know so I said nothing."

"That must have been very scary, and then to feel you couldn't ask about it, very difficult for you," said Amanda. "What happened after that time?"

"I started to get scared anytime they would go out and leave me with a babysitter. When they got home, I'd be awake crying, 'Don't leave me, don't leave me.' I started getting stomach aches and head-aches whenever they'd go out. Mother took me to the doctor think-ing I must have an ulcer or something—my dad had had ulcers—but the doctor found nothing."

"You were probably scared of being abandoned."

"Yes, you're right," Annie said. Her eyes widened in surprise.

I must have hit the bulls-eye, poor thing. "Did you have friends you could confide in?"

"I tried to tell one friend. I asked if she'd ever awakened in the night and heard her parents arguing. She said 'No' so I didn't say anything else."

"Oh, too bad. I wish they had known to take you to a counselor so you could have had someone to talk to. Did you tell your doctor about that night?"

"No, the doctor just examined me, said there was nothing physically wrong with me, and sent me home. He didn't really spend much time with me." She thought a moment. "I wish they had taken me to a counselor."

"Well, they probably did the best they knew how. But I imagine that was a hard time for you."

Amanda saw Annie relax, as if she had just wrapped her in a warm blanket. She saw tears in her eyes and wondered if she would let them out.

"They stayed together, and I never heard another argument so I guess it all worked out. But I don't know. Mother never . . . well, I don't know."

"She never what?"

"She didn't seem completely happy. She had a quick temper. Daddy deferred to her about things, everything really, as if he was tip-toeing around her. And once she complained, 'I'm just someone's mother and someone's wife.' As if she was nobody on her own. I was horrified. I hope I'll never feel that way."

"I hope you don't either, Annie. How do you think all this has affected you as an adult?"

Annie tilted her head and thought a moment. "I think it first made me want to get far away from home, to be independent. That's why I joined the Peace Corps. And it made me want to have a career and be more than a wife and mother. And then I think it made me want to get married to have someone to hold on to. And you see how that has turned out!" She threw out her hands and let them land in her lap with a plop. Now her tears began to fall. She plucked a tissue from the box next to her chair and dabbed at her eyes. "I'm sorry."

"No need to apologize for tears. It's quite okay to cry in here.

That's why I have so many boxes of tissues."

Annie looked around and saw a box next to her, another by the other chair, and several on the book case. She smiled. "I bet you hear lots of sad stories, Amanda."

"Yes, and yours is not the worst. Tell me . . . " and Amanda had her tell it all, school, friends, being an only child and how she met Harry and decided to marry him.

"Oh, that was too quick I see now. When I got home from Brazil, I had real culture shock. I left Atlanta. The only teaching job I could find was in Roxboro, about an hour from here. I hardly knew anyone there and I felt so lost. Then I met Harry through the personals. He was a handsome lawyer with a law practice here but drove up to see me every weekend. We got engaged a month after we met."

Amanda listened carefully. A lot of young people Annie's age got involved in a romantic relationship quickly hoping to solve all sorts of problems. Not many got married. But hearing about Annie's mother helped her understand why Annie would. Her mother would expect her to marry rather than live with someone, and Annie didn't seem free yet from wanting to please her mother.

Annie looked up and paused. Amanda nodded to let her know she was with her.

Annie continued. "I liked coming to see him here. He took me to plays and concerts and fancy restaurants and showed me what I thought would be a great life. So, after knowing him three months, we married. Then I found out I hardly knew him at all. But we were married so there we were."

"And here we are," added Amanda. None of this surprised Amanda at all. "Tell me about the early part of your marriage."

Annie cleared her throat, looked down, and tucked herself deeper into her chair. "We got married in the spring and had a wonderful honeymoon in France during my spring break. We went on a cruise on the Rhone River, had lots of wonderful French food, then went all through Provence tasting lots of wonderful wine. I thought I'd died and gone to heaven. Harry was so attentive and loving. But not long after we got home, I found out my mother had cancer." She gave a big sigh and looked up at Amanda.

"Oh, I'm so sorry."

"It was horrible. The next few months became a blur. I spent as much time with her in Atlanta as I could." She paused to wipe a tear off her cheek with a tissue. "I felt bad for leaving Harry but he urged me to go be with her." Her voice caught. "She died just a few months later." Tears rolled down Annie's face, then she pressed her lips together and continued. "Then just after the funeral—my mother's grave was not even cold—" she punched her words, "my father hooked up with Hilda. A few months later, he married her and moved to Arizona to be near her family." Annie shook her head, then, barely audible, she whispered, "The bastard."

Amanda shook her head. "So in less than a year, you married and essentially lost both parents."

Annie sniffed into her tissue, blew her nose, and sighed. "That about covers it."

"Tell me how you handled all that. How you and Harry handled it."

"I have no idea really. I went numb and walked around in a fog for I don't know how long. I cried on Harry's shoulder a lot and then we'd make love. Then he got busy with work and wasn't around as much. I think he got tired of my eternal grief. Finally, I came back to life and wanted to connect with him, and he just seemed so busy and so preoccupied. Well, I got busy teaching—I got a job in the high school here. I wrote a lot in my journal and started writing poetry and somehow the years went past." She gave Amanda a weak smile. "And here we are."

"Yes, here we are," said Amanda. "It sounds like a very difficult time. You and Harry were barely bonded when you had these tremendous losses. What do you most hope to accomplish by coming to these sessions, Annie?"

Annie took a deep breath. "Really, I want to find out if there is any hope." She looked imploringly at Amanda. "If I can make a marriage with him. I just don't feel close to him . . . or even safe with him. Ever since his session with you, he has become more and more distant. And he seems angry all the time."

Amanda nodded and had her lips drawn into a tight line. "Has he ever hit you?" asked Amanda, frowning.

"Not really."

Chapter 12

*O*n a sunny June morning, Annie woke up and stretched her arms high above her head. She ran her fingers through her wavy brown hair, untangling the knots from sleep. The clock by her bed read 10:15. *Time to get up.*

After the poetry seminar had ended, she had had a whirlwind few weeks with exams. She was too busy to do much more than charge to the finish line of the school year. Harry continued to spend more and more time with his work, claiming he had no choice. He warned her not to expect to see him much during this time, so she didn't. He was seldom home for dinner, but she was consumed with exams and grading papers every evening so didn't mind a bit cooking for herself. They had had one more couples therapy session with Amanda when they had gotten more practice with the intentional dialogue process. But it didn't seem to go very far. Annie sensed Harry was unwilling to discuss much of any depth. After that one session, he had insisted he couldn't do the weekly couples therapy sessions for the foreseeable future. He still avoided practicing the dialogue at home as Amanda had encouraged them to do. Annie felt frustrated but didn't know what else to do but focus on her teaching. When he was home, he seemed silent and angry, a caged animal ready to spring if she got too close. She left him alone.

When the school year had finally ended, she had slept late for three days in a row, more often in the spare room just because she slept better without Harry's snoring. He didn't say much except the day he told her his big case had come to a successful conclusion and he'd be out late with his staff celebrating. In the past, she had been invited but not this time. This puzzled her, but she found, a bit to her surprise, that she didn't really care that much. She just felt relieved he seemed calmer.

As she brushed her teeth, she considered the day ahead. She recalled Claire suggesting they have lunch sometime. She had a break before summer school started. She wished she could take off the whole summer but, with her worries about finances in light of the uncertain state of their marriage, she decided she'd better do it. Caught up on her rest and on all the household chores that had been left undone, she had time to do what she wanted to do. Get back to writing, of course. Get back to exercise. Well, she and Claire could have dinner, for Harry was hardly ever home for dinner anymore. Yes, she'd have to call Claire. She rinsed her mouth and returned to the spare room to rustle in the papers on her desk looking for the poetry class roster. Just then the phone rang from the extension in the upstairs hall. She got there on the third ring.

"Hi, Annie, it's Claire!" came a cheery voice. "I called to see if you were free to plan a visit with me. Am I right?"

"Right as rain! I'd love to. I've got two weeks off until summer school starts."

"Want to try that place out off the highway? Kimbers, I think it's called. It's been there a long time, but they're having a grand reopening. I've never been there. Can you get away for dinner some night soon?"

"Sure, how about tonight? I've heard of that place but I haven't been there either."

"Are you sure Harry won't be home to have dinner with you?"

"Harry has been working late so often, I've given up on eating dinner with him."

"Oh?" Claire sounded puzzled but then recovered: "It's a date! I'll meet you there at 6 p.m. if that works for you."

"Great! See you then." Annie hung up and smiled. How fun. A ladies night out. She hadn't done that in too long. Her stomach began to growl, so she headed downstairs to the kitchen. Harry's empty coffee mug sat at his place. Other than that sign, you'd think she lived here alone. She decided to treat herself to a big breakfast of bacon and eggs and toast and see if she could last until dinner. Thinking of Claire made her think of poetry. Maybe she'd spend the afternoon writing some, then go to the gym in time to get to the restaurant by 6 p.m. *Sounds like a plan,* she thought, excitement bubbling up inside her.

Annie drove west holding a slip of paper with the address of Kimbers. The trees closed in around her. The road grew rutted. She found the rustic old building with Claire on the front porch waiting for her. Claire greeted her with a big hug and led her inside a dimly lit room. The tall, slender hostess in a black sheath seated them in a cozy booth in a far corner and set large menus in front of them, then quickly returned with water.

Annie looked around. Walls of rough hewn logs gave the feel of being inside a very large cabin. There were open beams on the ceiling and dark cedar posts at regular points around the open room. Paintings on the walls showed pastoral scenes. "What a fascinating place!"

Soon they were sipping bubbly over steaming plates of delicious Asian fusion gourmet fare, inhaling scents of soy sauce and ginger and cedar from the walls, and talking nonstop. Annie learned all about Claire's long traditional marriage that began before she'd hardly had time to have a thought of her own, then she got pregnant on the honeymoon and gave birth to the first of five children. They came close together, just as the previous baby was barely out of diapers. "I nearly drowned in dirty diapers!" Claire chuckled. "And my husband was the old-fashioned type who expected me to stay home with the babies and be available to him, if you know what I mean. And this good Catholic girl found *legal loving* was awesome!" Claire winked.

Annie smiled—she got it—but she couldn't help but wonder at the contrast with Harry who hadn't touched her in longer than she could remember.

"So that's how we got so many so fast. Then I finally learned to say 'no' and got on birth control—we had left the church behind by that time. Tim was a good provider and I guess by today's standards I was lucky to be able to stay home with them, but I don't think I slept through the night until the oldest was ten."

Annie saw a plump woman wrangling four children under ten across the room and wondered how Claire, in contrast, had kept herself slim. "Did you mean to get married so young and have so many kids?"

"Hell, no! I met Tim senior year and fell madly in love. Our wedding was practically the day after graduation. I was young and starry-eyed. All I knew was that he was handsome, sexy, and could make me laugh. I think we did nothing but laugh until the first baby was born. Even then he had a way of using humor that made even sick kids and no money a laughing matter. But he didn't take care of himself, smoked like a chimney, ate like a horse."

"Your good cooking I bet. And how come you didn't get fat like that woman over there with all those kids?" Annie nodded towards the table full of kids, now behaving properly, seated between their two parents.

Claire smiled. "I loved to cook—it was my only creative outlet for a long time. And I guess chasing them around kept my figure. We did do a lot of camping and hiking when they were growing up. Do you like to hike?" Claire's eyebrows flew up like wings.

"Yes, but Harry doesn't. I miss it." She sighed.

"We'll have to do it sometime. Yes?" Claire nodded a question mark.

"Sure," said Annie. "But keep going with your story."

"Anyway, when he died—now fifteen years ago—I fell apart. Once the last child graduated college, he just up and died. No chance for us to enjoy life without kids. I don't know what I would have done if I hadn't discovered poetry."

"Me neither," said Annie. "I can't believe we haven't done this before. I'm having a great time."

"Me too," smiled Claire. "I thought about it but figured with teaching all day and taking care of Harry at night, you were too busy."

"Not lately. He's gone all the time. Workaholic lawyer, just like the stereotype."

"Yeah, Tim worked a lot too, but I was so busy tending to children I hardly noticed. But he was always home for dinner with the family.

And he loved playing with the kids at night to give me a break. They'd wrestle on the rug, rearrange furniture, all that." She paused and sighed, remembering. "And we always had date night once a week."

"Sounds lovely. A happy marriage." Annie gave a wistful smile, then the corners of her mouth turned down.

Claire noticed. "So Harry works late every night?"

Annie nodded. "It seems that way." She wasn't sure how much to share, but Claire was so open.

"That must be lonely for you," said Claire.

"Especially now that school is over. That's why it's so fun to have a ladies night out with you tonight. During the school year, it seemed I was always grading papers, making lesson plans, I don't know. I haven't made much time for female friends." And before she knew it, the cork was out of the bottle and she was pouring out all her hurt and pain and uncertainty. Claire sat quietly and listened, nodding from time to time. Annie felt she was dumping on her but each time she looked up, Claire seemed spellbound so she kept talking.

"When are you going back to see the counselor?" Claire prodded. "From what you're saying, I doubt Harry will go again unless you insist."

"I'm not even sure he's there when we're there." She looked away and sighed.

"What do you want?" Claire sounded strong and sure.

"I want him to be that man I fell in love with."

"And if he doesn't or won't, what are you going to do then?" Claire was pushing, and Annie wasn't sure she liked it but she wasn't sure she didn't either. She thought of that Mary Oliver poem. She smiled and looked up at Claire.

"*One day you finally knew/what you had to do, and began.*"

Claire smiled. "*And there was a new voice/which you slowly/ recognized as your own . . .* "

It felt like ping-pong between them. "*That kept you company/as you strode deeper and deeper/into the world.*"

Claire finished it for her: "*Determined to do/the only thing you could do—/determined to save/the only life you could save.*"

They sat in silence a moment grinning at each other, knowing they both knew the truth in that poem. Claire had already realized it. Annie was building her courage to do it.

Annie studied Claire. She wasn't tall but she was wiry. Her short dark hair was sprinkled with gray, and there were lines around her eyes and mouth. She was no longer young but she was alive and full of herself, her true self, Annie suspected.

Claire spoke first. "When Tim died, I thought for a long time I was going to die. What was there to live for? My whole life had been about him and the kids. But I was only fifty-three, I knew I had years left in me. I went off to a five-day silent meditation retreat. I'd never done anything like that before. When I came back, I knew I was going to create a new life."

Annie sat in awe. *Five days of silence? A whole new life?* Her mouth hung open.

Claire gave a big belly laugh. "Close your mouth, Annie! There might be flies in here!"

Annie closed her mouth and giggled. "Maybe I like flies! Extra protein!"

The short, plump waitress who looked like an Italian Mama appeared and removed their empty plates. "Can I interest you ladies in some dessert?" she asked as she refilled their champagne flutes.

"What do you have with chocolate?" Claire asked.

"We have a decadent black bottom pie." Annie imagined the waitress had had more than her share.

Claire turned to Annie. "One piece or two? We must have chocolate with the last of our champagne. It's a rule!"

Annie giggled again. "Two of course. This is one rule I intend to keep."

The black bottom pie was indeed decadent. They did not leave a crumb. Nor a drop of champagne. Claire grabbed the check before Annie could. "My treat this time. Yours next time."

"Yes, let's have a next time very soon." Annie couldn't believe she didn't feel a bit tipsy after sharing a bottle of champagne. But all that food must have helped. And the company, nourishing and sobering both. She felt a warm glow fill her as they headed towards the door. She looked around the room. She wanted to remember everything about this place.

Then she stopped. Claire bumped into her and followed her gaze. In a dark and shadowy far corner a couple was being seated in the booth they had just vacated. A tall, willowy blond woman with a tall, dark handsome man with thick dark hair slicked back with gel. As she watched, he leaned over towards the woman who smiled in return. She whispered to Claire: "That's my husband."

Chapter 13

Claire took Annie by the hand and led her outside the restaurant. They stood on the porch a moment as Annie trembled and wept. The sky where the sun had just set was pink and violet slowly turning to darker blue as night fell. The wind blew the leaves of the trees back and forth as the evening star shone through the trees. Claire fumbled in her pocketbook and found an unused tissue to hand to Annie who took it and gripped it in her fist, then dabbed her wet cheeks.

"I don't know what to do!" she cried, casting her eyes about as if the answer lay somewhere just out of sight.

"Come home with me for tonight. Let him wonder where you are." Claire sounded firm, even angry. Annie nodded. Together they walked towards their cars. Annie leaned against Claire, grateful. "I'll follow you to your house where you can get what you need to spend the night, then I'll take you home with me."

Annie was only too glad to follow orders in that moment. The evening was warm, but she felt cold. The image of Harry bending over the table towards that glamorous blond would not leave her mind. She felt so shabby by comparison, plain, not glamorous at all. She looked at her skirt and saw wrinkles. No wonder.

How she was able to drive she wasn't sure. But within a short time, she was snuggled on Claire's couch with a cup of tea, her overnight bag on the floor beside her. The night air and drive had cleared her head a bit. Claire was in a big stuffed chair next to the couch and waiting to listen. Annie gathered her thoughts, frowning.

"I guess now I know what he's been doing all those late nights."

"Did you recognize the woman he was with?"

"I think she's a lawyer in his firm." Annie recalled the last party of his firm she had attended. It must have been a holiday party. Harry had introduced her to so many people, but wasn't there a tall blond? "She just joined the firm last year. I think." She frowned and wrinkled her nose trying to remember. Then she looked at Claire. "Thanks for taking over and bringing me home with you. I had no idea you lived so close to us."

"You seemed in such shock. I wasn't sure you needed to go home alone and wait for Harry to arrive at some late hour. I'm just glad you could drive."

"Yes, barely." She looked around. There was a warm feeling here. Over the stone fireplace was what must be a family portrait. It showed Claire, looking younger, a man next to her who must be Tim, and five children, dressed in their finest, of various ages. Beside the couch opposite the chair where Claire sat was a love seat in a blue color that matched Claire's chair. The couch where Annie sat was a pattern of maroon, blue, beige, and green stripes. "Is this where you raised your kids and lived with your husband?"

"It sure is. I have four bedrooms so plenty of room for you. Do you want to talk a bit or are you ready to go to bed?"

Annie held the steaming cup of tea in both hands and inhaled the smell. "What is this tea? I smell cinnamon."

"Yes, it's Constant Comment."

"Oh, my mother used to have it. I love it. I think I'll finish my tea first. But I don't want to keep you up."

"You won't, I'm a night owl." Claire tucked her legs under her on the soft cushions and sipped her own cup of tea. "My daughter married a man who beat her. We had never liked him but that was the last straw. I remember sitting up with her the night she finally told us. I'm so glad she kicked him to the curb."

"Did she divorce him?"

"Oh, yes, once she dried her eyes, she saw a lawyer the next day and changed the locks on their house while he was at work."

Annie's eyes widened. "Really? I wonder if that's what I'll end up doing." She looked into her teacup as if it held the answer. "Or maybe I should make another appointment with Amanda for the two of us." She looked up at Claire. "Honestly, I'm scared to talk to him about what I saw tonight."

"Has he ever hit you?" Claire asked, frowning.

"No, not really, but he has been so angry and distant, I've just been avoiding him these last few weeks. He's had a big case, I thought he was busy working as well."

"Well, he may have been working with that scuzzy looking blond. We couldn't really see much in that dark place, but he sure looked like he was enjoying her company."

Annie sighed, "I didn't know Harry very long before we married. We had a whirlwind three month courtship then my mother's idea of a high fashion wedding. Living together brought lots of surprises." Annie took a big swallow of her tea. "Now I wonder *what was I thinking?*" She gave a big sigh and felt all the energy drain out of her. Her eyes grew heavy. "Okay, show me which room, I'm exhausted."

Annie fell to sleep immediately but woke four hours later, confused and not sure where she was. Like an electric current, it all ran through her, images of Harry, the beautiful woman. Tears filled her eyes. Then she became aware how full her bladder was. She got up and staggered across the hall, hearing the floorboards squeak as she went. The bathroom door creaked as she closed it. She sat on the toilet, then was soon back in bed, hoping she hadn't disturbed Claire. She heard a clock strike three. Claire's house seemed so quiet, like hers might be soon. Quiet and empty. She felt suddenly bereft, and tears spilled from her eyes. She saw the lonely years stretch out endlessly ahead of her, as if her fate was already sealed. She rolled over on her right side into the fetal position. The various choices lying ahead of her began to jump through her mind, but it wasn't like counting sheep. Instead, she felt more and more awake.

She tried to imagine confronting Harry but couldn't. Too scary. Call a lawyer? But who? The only lawyers she knew were in Harry's firm. Talk to him in front of Amanda Murphy? That sounded scary too but better than any other possibility. She rolled over onto her left side, then to her back. She heard the clock strike four. She purposefully lay very still and focused on her body sensations, tried to close down her mind. It struck five. Then the next she knew, sunlight was peeking between the slats of the Venetian blinds. She must have finally fallen asleep. She looked at her watch: nearly eight o'clock. Was that bacon and coffee she smelled?

She got up, pulled on her robe, and padded down the hall. There were family photographs lining the walls. She paused to look. A faded wedding photo with a young woman and man, then several with a slightly older looking couple with small children tucked in around them. Then a high school graduation photo and another wedding photo, only this time Annie could recognize Claire as she was now with other family members around a beaming young couple. Claire's whole life was on this wall. She blinked back tears and wondered what her photos would show someday. She headed into the kitchen.

Claire stood before the stove, spatula in hand, lifting pieces of bacon and laying them on paper towels. She turned and grinned at Annie. "I don't know if you like coffee, but there it is," she gestured towards the coffee pot on the counter. "I confess I love a hot breakfast, bacon, eggs, toast, the whole bit."

"Sounds wonderful. I haven't had breakfast before ten or eleven a.m. lately. I've been making a big hot breakfast myself."

"And for yourself alone, I bet."

"Yes, I'm afraid so."

Claire turned and pointed towards the table with two place mats. "Pick your spot. Eggs coming right up!"

Annie picked a mug sitting conveniently next to the coffee pot, filled it and sat down. She admired the homey table setting. A round table with round mats with blue flowers. Blue flowers in a vase. Solid blue cloth napkins by each place. "You must like blue."

"My favorite color, haven't you noticed?"

Annie remembered now that Claire often had worn some shade of blue to their poetry seminar. Long flowing blue dresses and skirts with blue shawls in various patterns. Now Claire stood before her in a blue bathrobe.

Claire set a plate with scrambled eggs, toast, and bacon before her, then sat opposite her with her own plate. "I started wearing blue after my husband died. Better than black I figured, and I just kept on." She took a bite, then looked Annie over carefully. "How did you sleep? Did you come to any conclusions?"

"I think the next step is to get an appointment with our counselor and see if Harry will come. I feel safer discussing things there." She took a big bite of eggs. It fairly melted in her mouth.

Claire nodded.

"And I don't know any lawyers . . . "

"Well, I do." She looked around, riffled through some papers on the bookcase next to the table. "It's here somewhere. Oh, this is a poem I wrote." She lifted a paper from near the top of the pile and set it aside. "I'll find it later." She turned back to Annie who saw the piles of paper that she now realized were on every surface in every room she'd seen. "But you may be right to start with your counselor."

"Yes, I'll call her this morning."

After stuffing themselves with Claire's good cooking, Annie and Claire sat around the table talking for a good two hours. They could have kept talking all day, but finally in the late morning, Claire dropped Annie back in front of her house. "Call me and let me know what happens," Claire ordered as Annie opened the car door. "And remember you can come stay at my place anytime." She blew Annie a kiss.

Annie blew a kiss back and smiled. "A million thanks, Claire. You've surely been a friend when I needed one. See you soon." She closed the car door, threw her overnight bag over her shoulder and faced the front door. The sidewalk was lined with monkey grass she had planted when they moved in five years before. Now it formed a thick mat of thin leaves going every which way. On either side of the front door were boxwood and holly bushes that were long overdue being trimmed. Annie lifted her shoulders, took a deep breath, and marched forward.

Chapter 14

When Annie unlocked the door and stepped inside, her feet slid on the mail that had fallen through the slot in the door. She set down her bag and picked it up, flipping through the stack of envelopes quickly for anything that needed immediate attention. It seemed to be mostly yesterday's junk mail. The mailman usually came early afternoon. Had Harry been home? Though it would be just like him to leave the mail on the floor. She shook her head as she dropped it in a basket on the small table just inside the door.

She passed through the living room, pausing to admire the matching sofa and wing chairs she had chosen with their colorful rose and bluebird pattern, and the mahogany coffee table Harry had insisted on over her rustic pine selection. He did love an upscale look. In the kitchen, the morning paper was open and scattered over the kitchen table. A used coffee mug sat beside it alongside a bowl and a box of Cheerios. Ah, he had been home. She set the bowl and mug in the sink, folded up the newspaper and set it neatly down before she could ask herself, *Why bother?* Peals of grief rang inside her. Chaos and disruption probably ahead. Still, she liked a tidy house. It gave her the feeling her life was in order. An illusion maybe. Like the illusion of a faithful husband. Tidy on the surface but hiding other things underneath.

Then she saw the white board on the refrigerator with something written on it. This was no grocery list. She stepped closer to read it.

"Annie, Where are you? Late meeting again last night. Call me!! I'm worried! Love, Harry."

Annie read it again and again, shaking her head. The image of him in the restaurant flashed in her mind. *Yeah, Harry, a late meeting. Is that what you call it?* Hot lava surged up inside her. She stomped over to the counter next to the fridge, grabbed a paper towel, and wiped the message board clean. She felt like taking his mug and smashing it. Instead, she got her overnight bag from the living room and went upstairs. As the stairs creaked under her feet, her anger softened. *Is he really worried about me?* She resisted the urge to call him. In their bedroom she saw the unmade bed and his robe thrown across the covers. *Oh, yeah, I'm still the maid. Has he ever even once pulled up the covers?* Clenching her teeth, she unpacked her bag, hung up his robe on the hook behind the door, and made the bed, smoothing the bedspread exactly as she did every morning. It was a dark brown and maroon paisley pattern. Now it looked gloomy to her. She thought of Claire's bright blue kitchen table mats. Maybe she'd get something brighter someday. For herself.

Looking around, she saw the laundry basket in the corner full to overflowing, his shirts on top for her to take to the dry cleaners. Should she check for lipstick on his collars? She laid the shirts on the bed and headed down the hall with the basket where the washer and dryer were in a closet. When she had the first load started, she looked down the hall. Their wedding photo stood on a chest in a cozy nook next to a small chair. Seeing it now stabbed her. It used to make her smile. She turned towards the spare room. She had put a small armless stuffed chair in there. It had belonged to her grandmother, and she loved it.

She decided to sit and meditate. She had been thinking of starting a regular meditation practice, had read a few books about it, so why not start now? Lighting a candle on her desk, she exhaled into the chair. With eyes closed, she began to focus on breathing slow and deep. Her first awareness was how tight her shoulders felt. She rolled them around and returned her attention to her breath. She sensed her belly rise and fall with her breath. Her mind jumped around from one worry to the next. She was surprised to find some tenderness for her husband just there behind her heart. Then fear raised its ugly head. Then sorrow. She tried to do what the books said, to let each thought and feeling pass as leaves floating on a stream or clouds blowing across the sky and return her attention to her breath. Slowly, as she took more slow, deep breaths, she felt a tiny warm glow inside grow bigger. A quiet confidence rose and the words "you can do it" came right behind. *I can do it*, she thought, *I can do it, whatever 'it' may be.* When she opened her eyes, she was surprised to see twenty minutes had passed.

She blew out the candle and sat a moment, casting her gaze around this small room. Next to her was a day bed in deep blue velvet with big pillows that made it comfortable as a couch. It had a trundle bed underneath that could be pulled out and raised to make a double bed. She had picked this soft fabric a while ago, not realizing this room would become her writing room. And sometimes where she now slept. Her desk stood under the window across from the day bed. When she sat there, she could see the trees and shrubs in the back yard. On the walls were a few of her special things. A painting her Aunt Elizabeth had done of a small child holding a fuzzy duck, one a college boyfriend had painted for her in splatter-paint style. He had claimed it was a portrait of her, but she had trouble seeing herself in it. She could see herself more easily (even though it held no picture of her) in a poster of the recent Full Moon Poetry Festival, the first one she had ever attended. Oh, the poems and people there, a whole new world opening up. And this room—she doubted Harry had ever set foot in here—this room was her sanctuary.

Downstairs she got the newspaper, made herself a cup of tea, then stretched out on the living room couch. She started with the comics and the horoscope, avoiding the bad news of the front section. The new movie at the Azalea Cinema sounded interesting. Soon she dozed off.

"There you are!" She woke with a start, rubbed her eyes, and sat up. "I thought you might have had a wreck. Where were you?" Harry stood in the kitchen doorway, his hands strangely empty without his briefcase, then he sat in the living room wing chair, leaned towards her with his arms on his knees, and waited.

Annie was shocked to see him home. "What are you doing here at this hour? What time is it?" She looked at the wall clock and saw it was 12:30 p.m.

"It's lunch time. I came home to make sure you're okay." He wrinkled up his forehead and clasped his hands. Then before she could answer, he got up and sat at the other end of the couch. He laid his arm over the top and patted her shoulder. "Tell me."

Annie blinked and sat in silence a moment, gathering her thoughts. She turned her head to look at him. "You look worried" was all she could manage.

"I almost called the hospital but then I figured they would have called me. Where were you?" he asked again.

Annie paused. "I went out to dinner." The scene in the restaurant rose up inside her mind, him leaning across the table towards that glamorous blond woman. She looked at him and saw his eyes had glazed over. She said nothing else.

"I had a late meeting," he said. "The Parkwood case is not over yet." He gave a big sigh. He lifted his focus to her again. "But you didn't come home last night."

Annie took the plunge. "I met Claire at the Kimbers Restaurant for dinner." She waited.

He said nothing.

"We left just as you and whoever got there."

He was dumbfounded. She watched the wheels turn in his mind. His eyes rolled up then down. He blinked, then cleared his throat and turned his eyes to hers. He sat up straight. His words shot out rapid fire. "Gloria. She's my assistant on this damn Parkwood case. She's busting her balls trying to get me to recommend her for partner. She's dreaming. She's just been with the firm eighteen months." His mouth fell open. "Why didn't you come over? You met Gloria at the holiday party. Who's Claire?"

"She's in my poetry seminar." Despite herself, Annie felt tears fill her eyes and spill over. "After we saw you, I was so upset she took me home with her. I spent the night there." Now she was weeping. She

115

put her face in her hands.

Harry drew her into his arms and held her. "Oh, Annie, no. It's not what you think. We were working, I promise. Working over dinner." She leaned into his shoulder and wet his shirt with her tears. "Sweetheart, no, I know I've been a bear lately, but it's just this awful case. Millions of dollars are on the line. If we win, we'll be on easy street." He stroked her hair.

She couldn't remember the last time he had held her, had been anything but distant and angry. Now he was gentle and tender. She remembered this man, barely. This was the man she had fallen in love with. Was he back? She pulled back from his embrace and lifted her head to meet his gaze. She felt so tired. She gathered her courage. "I'd like us to make another appointment with Amanda Murphy." She watched him, feeling her stomach tighten.

Harry stiffened visibly, exhaled, and pulled his arms from around her. "If we must." He looked at the clock. "I'd better grab something and go."

Annie felt she had just turned a switch off inside him. Was going to therapy torture for him? At least he had agreed to go. As he stood and turned to leave, she began to see him differently, less scary and more scared. Something soft inside made her say, "I'll make you a sandwich."

He smiled. "That would be great."

In the kitchen she made a turkey and Swiss sandwich and put it in a plastic bag with an apple. She smiled as she handed it to him.

He gave her a quick kiss on the cheek and was gone.

She sat down at the kitchen table with her sandwich, found Amanda Murphy's phone number, and reached for the phone. Her fingers trembled as she dialed. A whirlwind of emotions tumbled inside her. She thought of what Claire had said of her marriage to Tim. A deep longing rose up inside her. A single tear rolled down the side of her face and wet her ear. The phone rang and rang. *Oh please, please answer. I need help. I need it now.*

Chapter 15

Amanda opened the Thomas file on her desk and leaned over it, propping her head in her hand. She hadn't seen them in a few weeks, but they were scheduled next. Something must have happened. Annie seemed eager to open up and make use of the therapy process, but Harry was another story. She'd seen other men men with a lot of unprocessed childhood trauma. Some had stiff-upper-lipped it so long that they knew no other way to be. They were taught "boys don't cry" and, at four or five years old, they got cut off from their emotions. They put all their passion into work and thought that's all they had to do. They usually didn't show up in her office unless brought there by a woman longing for emotional closeness. She was glad Harry was coming back, even if Annie was dragging him.

Annie was easier but not without her issues. Amanda had a hunch Annie had unresolved issues about her father. That she married a man ten years older was one clue. That she didn't think her mother was happy with her father was another. And her father seemed to be the same workaholic type as Harry.

Just then the intercom buzzed. She closed the file and stepped into the waiting room where Annie and Harry stood. Harry looked stone-faced as ever but maybe even more so. He had his briefcase in his left hand as if it were attached. Annie's face looked tense and maybe tear-stained. She clutched her purse in front of her like a shield. But her face lit up when she saw Amanda. Harry seemed to hang his head just slightly at the same time.

Amanda extended her hand to Harry and gave him a warm smile. "I'm glad to see you both." Harry's hand felt cold. He gripped her hand firmly then dropped it quickly. Annie's hand was warm and limp. These small behaviors gave Amanda clues that she'd found invaluable over the years. She waved them towards her open door.

Harry stepped back to let Annie go first, looking back towards the entrance door for a second as if planning his escape. Then he followed, sat next to Annie in his usual seat, and clasped his hands in his lap, regarding the rug with intense interest. Annie watched his every move, then turned her attention to Amanda.

Amanda smiled, then began. "Let's take a moment to gather together. Please close your eyes and take a few deep breaths. Check in with yourselves and see what's important. Consider your intention for this session. Take as much time as you need." Amanda sat back and watched. Annie closed her eyes immediately. Her shoulders went down. She placed her right hand in her left and laid them in her lap. Her chest and abdomen began to rise and fall slowly. Harry stared at Amanda initially, then at Annie, then looked around the room. His brow furrowed, but he said nothing. Then he too closed his eyes and took a big heaving breath. His hands remained clasped tightly but slowly unfurled just the slightest bit.

Amanda took a few deep breaths. She had learned this opening method in a workshop years ago. She didn't use it every time but she used it especially when she hadn't seen a couple in a while and when the tension between them was palpable. Without it, she had found some couples would offer her a shouting match in the first moments, probably one that had started in the car on their way over. Shouting matches they could do on their own time. "When you are clear where you want to start, open your eyes. But take your time."

Harry's eyes flew open. He shook his head. He looked at Annie who seemed to be waking up, opening her eyes, then lifting her head to smile at Amanda.

"Who would like to start?" Amanda looked from one to the other.

"What was that all about?" Harry demanded.

Amanda smiled. This was not the first time she'd had this question. "I like to help my clients transition from the often hectic pace of the world outside my office. I find a few moments of guided meditation can help."

Annie sat up taller in her chair. "I liked it. A lot."

"Hectic pace is right," whispered Harry.

"Harry, would you like to start?" Amanda asked. She was most concerned to check in with his mood and mental state.

He looked startled. "All this was her idea." He pointed at Annie. "I've been under the gun with this big case at work, hardly having time to sleep." His suit seemed to rumple as he spoke.

"So you are very stressed with work right now?" reflected Amanda, wrinkling her forehead in concern. "No time to sleep?"

"Yes, and it's not going to let up anytime soon. She wanted to come because I had a late meeting with a colleague."

"At Kimbers Restaurant. A female colleague," Annie burst in.

Amanda nodded, glanced at Annie, but returned her eyes to Harry. "She saw me and totally misunderstood, thought I was having an affair!" He threw up his hands, looked at Annie and kept going. "This young associate has lofty ambitions, wants to prove herself a rainmaker for the firm so she can make partner. She talked me into letting her do second chair on this big case that is going to trial next week. So we have to meet every night to form our strategy. This one night I was so tired of skipping meals and eating at 9 p.m., I suggested we talk over dinner. She picked Kimbers. I'd never been there before. I had no idea it was one of those dark romantic places. And I had no idea Annie would be there that night."

"What an awful awkward scene that must have been."

"I didn't even know Annie was there. I never saw her. We didn't get there until nearly 8 p.m. Annie never goes out to eat and never eats that late." He sat back. "But when I got home after 10 p.m. she wasn't even home. Her car was there but not her. I didn't know where she was!" His face got red.

"So you never saw Annie?"

"No! If I had, I would have reintroduced her to Gloria. They'd met at the holiday party. It wasn't like I'd picked up some slut in a bar. I was working. I wasn't doing anything wrong." He turned to address Annie. "It wasn't what you thought."

Annie bit her lips and shifted in her chair, crossing then uncrossing her legs. She stared silently back at Harry, then looked away.

"Tell me your experience, Annie." Amanda leaned towards her.

After Annie explained what transpired that night, Harry looked at Amanda imploringly as if she were the judge and this was a courtroom. She could hear him thinking: *I'm innocent, believe me, I'm innocent!* But she really hadn't formed an opinion about what really happened, and it wasn't her job to do so. Her job was to help them talk it out. She suspected that they had not had a thorough dialogue yet.

She addressed them both. "I think I get the picture. Harry, from your point of view, you were working late over dinner, not engaging in any infidelity, and you very much want Annie to believe you." Harry nodded emphatically. "Annie, Harry has been working late so much that you haven't felt very connected to him, and what you saw in the restaurant, while unclear, really upset you. Is that right?"

Annie nodded tearfully.

Harry looked visibly relieved. Amanda imagined he had expected her to automatically take Annie's side. He sat back in his chair and looked at Annie who kept her eyes locked on Amanda.

She turned to Harry. "Let's move into the dialogue process. Harry, tell Amanda what you really want her to know and understand." She looked at Annie. "And Annie, you listen and mirror."

They both nodded. Harry rolled his chair towards Annie and began, his eyes on his hands. "Annie, I want you to know what incredible stress I've been under with my current case. It's very important to my career. If we win, it could, well, we'd have a lot more money." He raised his gaze to Annie.

Annie nodded and mirrored his exact words. "Is this right? Is there more?"

Amanda smiled. "Very good. Keep going."

"I've been working with Gloria on this case every night. Just working." He paused and again Annie mirrored.

"I am not, I repeat, NOT, having an affair with her. She's a good lawyer but she pushed herself on me to work on this case. She's actually kind of a pain." Harry screwed up his face. Annie's eyes got big, then she squinted, but she contained herself and mirrored accurately.

"Please believe me." Harry begged. "That's all."

Amanda waited to see if Annie would remember what to do next.

"So, to summarize, you are under a lot of stress and having to work late on this very important case. You are not having an affair with Gloria and you want me to believe you."

"Yes!" cried Harry.

"I understand what you're saying and I imagine you feel stressed, worn out, and . . . " Annie paused. "Scared I won't believe you? . . . And you really want me to believe you?"

"Yes!" Harry nearly floated off his chair.

Amanda smiled at them both. "Excellent. Now Annie your turn to speak, and Harry your turn to mirror."

Annie put her fingers together, pressed them to her lips, and sat quietly for a moment. She raised her head and began. "Harry, I have hardly seen you at all these last few weeks. You've stopped calling to say you'll be late. You work all weekend. Of course I've also been busy with exams until just recently. Then I had time to realize how lonely I feel, how abandoned." She paused.

"I've been gone all the time and not calling and you've been busy too but now you feel lonely. And abandoned," reflected Harry.

Annie nodded. "Close enough. And there's more."

"I was about to ask, 'Is there more?'" Harry smiled. Annie looked at him, frowned, then smiled back.

Amanda could feel a shift in the space between them. Amazing how powerful being heard could feel. She studied each one, her eyes flowing from one to the other.

"I feel like a law widow," Annie continued. "I can barely remember when we used to laugh and have fun together. I get that you're stressed. All you do is work work work and, if you're home, you seem angry and far away."

Harry frowned and pressed his lips together. He took a deep breath and leaned forward, his elbows on his knees. He exhaled a hum. He sat up. "But . . . " he began, then stopped himself and mirrored her exact words. Amanda saw Annie soften in response just slightly.

"Seeing you in that restaurant with that beautiful woman—" She began to get choked up. She stopped, reached for a Kleenex, calmed herself and continued, "I'm not so glamorous. I wasn't sure what I saw, I just wasn't expecting to see you there with a beautiful woman. What else could I think?" She raised her head toward him and waited.

Amanda watched Harry closely. His eyes held Annie's, while his hands lay open on his lap. His breathing slowed a tiny bit. Annie kept her eyes on his face and sat still. *She wants to believe him, I think she's going to,"* Amanda thought as she watched them both.

Harry's right hand twitched as if he wanted to touch Annie but he didn't. Instead, he diligently mirrored her every word then added, "I think you're plenty glamorous."

Tears streamed down Annie's face. "You do?" He raised his eyebrows and nodded. "That's all," said Annie, releasing a big exhale.

Without any prompting, Harry summarized Annie's message, then added his validation and empathy. "I understand everything you said and I imagine you were feeling terrible. And I'm so sorry." This time he did reach his hand and took hers in both of his. Annie crumpled like she wanted to crawl into his lap. Harry smiled at her, and Annie lifted her head with a smile of her own.

Amanda decided it was time to teach them the "Holding Exercise." They took to it naturally, Annie draped across his lap, her head on his shoulder and his arms around her holding her tight. "No need to talk. Just take a few moments." Amanda sat back and savored this moment in silence. They had talked about one of the touchiest topics couples ever discuss. They used the dialogue process like experts. And they connected. She loved this work, when it worked.

Harry broke the silence by whispering in Annie's ear. "I think I'll take the evening off. Will you go to dinner with me?" He kissed her hair just above her ear.

Annie lifted her head and nodded. "But let's not go to Kimbers."

"Yes, let's not. You pick any other place you want, sweetheart."

They went to *Le Vigneron*, a French restaurant, and sat on the patio by a gurgling fountain with a statue of an elf-like figure holding a shell out of which flowed water. They had *escargot,* which Harry had taught Annie to like, *coq au vin* and *mousse au chocolat* and lots of freshly baked baguette washed down with a bottle of chardonnay. As they ate, Harry told her his dreams for making a fortune working on this case with its promise of many more if he won the lawsuit, traveling to exotic locations, buying a bigger house. She didn't really share this dream, but she listened patiently. At home they made love for the first time in months, then fell asleep curled together. She fell into a dead sleep, exhausted. If he snored, she didn't hear it.

The next morning, half asleep, she turned towards him. But all she found was his pillow. The clock showed 8 a.m., so she wasn't surprised. She turned over and went back to sleep.

Chapter 16

$\mathcal{A}$nnie slept until nearly ten. When she finally opened her eyes, she lay there a while savoring the memory from the night before. Was the Harry she had fallen in love with really back? *Oh, please, let it be so.* She got up, made the bed, threw on her robe, and headed downstairs. When she found an almost empty bowl of soggy cereal in the sink beside an empty coffee mug, she smiled. *At least he got it this far.* She made herself a fresh pot, cooked herself some eggs and toast, and sat down to consider the day ahead.

The phone rang. It was Claire. "I haven't heard from you since that awful night, Annie. Just wondered how you're doing."

"Much better."

"Oh?"

"Our couples session really helped, Claire. Harry explained everything. He was just working late. He's under so much stress, I really understand now. It wasn't what it looked like."

"Oh?" asked Claire again, clearly skeptical. "Well, good, I hope you're right."

"Oh, I'm sure I'm right," said Annie.

"I called to let you know I heard from George and Peter and they want us all to meet for dinner next week. Sort of a mid-break reunion. What do you say?"

"That sounds fabulous. When and where?"

"Andre's Bistro, you know, the one with the coffee house where we first met as a group? They suggested Wednesday."

"Perfect! And maybe the weather will cooperate better this time. Now I know what I want to do this afternoon—write!"

"Yes, we're supposed to bring our latest poems. Shall I pick you up at 6:30 that day?"

"That would be wonderful. And how about a walk in the woods some afternoon before that, just you and me?"

"It's a deal. Talk to you soon! Bye."

Annie hung up, finished her breakfast, stuck all the dishes in the dishwasher, and headed to her study to gather her supplies for writing. Maybe this time she'd sit on the screen porch where she could see the trees and flowers in the back yard.

Chapter 17

When Harry got to work that day, he found Gloria in his office, sitting in his chair looking out the window. He cleared his throat. She swung the chair around. Her long blond hair was up in a French twist. A few tendrils framed her face. She wore a dark blue business suit with the top few buttons of her cream-colored blouse unbuttoned, showing her cleavage provocatively. His body began to respond before his mind could engage. *God, she's gorgeous,* he thought. He lowered his gaze to the rug while he tried to collect himself. *Down boy*, he said to an errant part of his anatomy.

She grinned when she saw him. "Hello," she crooned.

He set his briefcase down on the desk. "What are you doing here so early?" he asked. "And that's my chair."

"I couldn't wait to see you and discuss the case," she said, lowering her lids flirtatiously.

Harry didn't move. He stared at her and waited. The errant part of him rebelled. He stilled himself to regain control.

"Want to have our meeting now?" She stood and moved around the desk towards Harry, who moved around the opposite side of the desk towards his chair.

"Perhaps later?" she asked, running her eyes over his frame.

He felt moisture spring out under his shirt. "Yes." He looked at his desk, frozen.

"I'll let you go," she smiled. "If you're interested, someone just made a fresh pot of coffee, I believe."

"Thank you," he said and exhaled. "Come back in an hour and we'll meet." Harry nodded towards the door, then took his seat in his chair. Gloria glided slowly towards the door, paused in the doorway, then winked at him as she left. Harry shook his head. His body relaxed. Finally. She was too much. He wasn't surprised Annie thought there was something between them. Gloria seemed ready, willing, and able if he gave her the opportunity. It could be fun, but also risky. He didn't want to be like his father. But his mother was such a drunk, he couldn't really blame him. He had once asked his dad why he had put up with her drinking. This was shortly before she died. His dad had only sighed deeply and said, "Marriage is for life, son, for life." The way he said it made it sound like a prison sentence. As it turned out, it was shortly before his father died as well.

His mind drifted back in time, and he saw himself as he stood in the line with his fellow law students, all clad in their long black robes, waiting to walk across the stage, get their diplomas and toss their caps into the air. The stadium grass was bright green, the sky blue with a few wisps of puffy clouds drifting across it. As the graduates jostled each other and the line moved slowly towards the stage, Harry scanned the stands for any sign of his family. His dad had promised him faithfully to get them all there.

His dad had shone with pride at the prospect. "My son, a lawyer just like his old man!" he had chortled that morning over breakfast. When he saw his parents making their way up the stairs to the third row, his father had a firm grip on his mother's arm. Then he saw her stumble and he knew. Anger rose up inside him like machine gun fire. Just one day, his day, couldn't she stay off the sauce for one day? He turned his head away, then looked again. Now his father was sitting down, his mother standing and waving her arms wildly overhead.

"Harry! Harry! Harry!" she cried.

His dad pulled on her jacket in a vain attempt to pull her down to her seat. His older sister and brother had come home especially for this occasion. And his mother was making a scene. He shook his head and walked forward as the line progressed.

That afternoon his mother had collapsed and been rushed to the hospital. Their graduation celebration took place in the hospital cafeteria. She died a week later. Her liver finally couldn't take it anymore. A week after that, his father dropped dead. Apparently, he couldn't live without his wife, his drunken wife. As soon as Harry passed the bar exam and got hired by this firm, he was out of there.

Now looking over the pile on his desk, Harry picked the top folder and opened it. He felt a flash of anger at Annie. *Her and her damn poetry class!* Deliberately, he turned his thoughts to their sweet evening the night before. And their couples session hadn't been too bad. At least Annie believed him. He was a good guy. He smiled, thinking maybe she knew that now. Sure, he had a temper, but who wouldn't with all the stress of his work? And, thank goodness, Annie was nothing like his mother. Hell, she hardly drank at all. She did like a clean house, sort of like his tyrant older sister, and they did argue about it. His anger flared again. He trembled and gripped his hands into fists.

He turned his mind to his work. Once he won this case, his reputation as a tough litigator would be sealed. The dam would open, releasing an unstoppable flow of cases. He would win them all. They could sell their first home and buy a bigger one. Shaking these fantasies out of his brain, he took a deep breath and started reading the papers in his hands. Wrongful death, what a joke! The company he represented hadn't let the child drown. The parents had left their child unsupervised. His anger found its home.

Annie looked out the window for Harry's car. She had a plan for dinner—broiled salmon with new potatoes and grilled asparagus—but hadn't started cooking yet. After their romantic evening the night before, she had her hopes up he might find a way to come home for dinner. But here it was 7:00 p.m. and no sign of him and no call. This was too familiar. Tired of waiting around for him, she picked up the phone and dialed his office. It rang and rang and rang. Finally "Hello?" in a soft female voice. She asked for Harry and soon he answered in a gruff voice. "I'm trapped here. Too much to do. You go ahead and eat." He hung up without hello or good-bye.

Despite herself, she felt her eyes well up. *Here we go again,* she thought, putting her head in her hands. And that female voice? Was it Gloria? Her stomach knotted. She didn't feel hungry anymore. She picked up the remote and clicked on the evening news. Then she made herself a plate of cheese and crackers in the kitchen, grabbed an apple and a glass of red wine, and sat back down. After the news, she watched several reruns of old shows that blurred together.

She was determined to wait up until he got home. She wanted

to tell him about the special meal she had planned and see if maybe tomorrow night . . . but maybe she shouldn't even bother. She picked up the phone and called Claire.

"Hi Annie! How are you?"

"Okay I guess. Just sitting here all alone..."

"Harry working late again?"

"I'm afraid so." Annie choked back tears. "I was hoping after last night and given it's Friday night. But he has this big case." She couldn't help but defend him. She wiped her eyes and suddenly felt angry. "What are you doing tomorrow? It's supposed to be warm and sunny and not too hot. Want to go walk in the woods, maybe even take a picnic?"

"That's the spirit, Annie! Let me bring the picnic. I had the family over last night for dinner and have lots of fried chicken and potato salad left over." Claire's son and wife lived in town and had triplet boys five years old. Annie could imagine the noise and the fun.

"I'll come get you around 11 a.m., okay?"

"Sounds like a plan!"

Harry got home at 9:30 p.m. Annie had just turned off the TV to go to bed. He came busting in the kitchen door, dropped his briefcase beside the table, and got out a beer. Annie stood in the doorway between the kitchen and the living room.

"Hi," she said.

"God, what a day!" he grumbled, snapping open a can of Bud. He took a long swallow and looked at her.

This was her chance. "I missed you. I planned a salmon dinner. Last night was so nice, I was hoping we could spend some more time together." She smiled at him and waited.

He said nothing but just stood there sipping his beer. "Sorry, but I'm so tired." He shook his head. "Spare me the guilt trip. I'm going to bed." He pushed past her and stomped up the stairs. She felt slapped.

She sat down at the kitchen table in a fog. A whirlwind of emotions swirled inside her. A confusing tapestry of hurt, discouragement, frustration, and longing. She just wanted someone she could talk to, just some companionship and communication and caring. Was that too much to ask? Was she wrong to tell him how she felt? She didn't think so, but then he sure didn't want to hear it. Maybe her timing was off. Maybe she should go back to not bothering to try. But that was no way to live. All he did was work. Life was more than work, wasn't it? But that was her. Maybe Harry was different.

As Annie sat, words began to form inside her, phrases. She thought of a poem she had started some time ago but never finished. She went upstairs to her writing desk to see if she could find it. As she sifted through the papers of poem scraps in her desk drawer, more words began to come. She found the paper, pulled it out and scribbled. Her eyes glazed over as she went into her poetry trance. She lost track of time. It was coming out almost whole and it felt good. Short but good. She booted up her laptop and opened her poetry file. She scratched out and rewrote on the paper. Ah, this is it! She typed it into her laptop.

These are moments to be lived through
What you work out in silence that I put words to.
So I learn to suckle the memory of your open face
Behind the sharp shoulder you show me now.
Curse our differences anyhow.

She hit 'save' and smiled. She'd worry about a title later. Now she could go to bed. She couldn't imagine crawling in next to Harry. She'd sleep here tonight, in her poetry room.

Chapter 18

The weather turned out to be perfect on Saturday. Sunny, high of 80, not a cloud in the sky. Annie pulled her hiking clothes out of the closet. Dark blue pants that zipped off into shorts, matching t-shirt, bandanna a friend had given her when she turned twenty-one with a story from the Lakota tribe. As the story went, a woman who had proven herself brave enough to be a warrior was awarded by the woman's circle a bandanna to wear around her forehead. The woman's circle met weekly to share their challenges and support each other. If a woman came in one week discussing a problem, the group listened, asked questions, and offered support. If she came in the next week with the same problem, they did the same. If she came in a third week with the same problem, they all got up wordlessly and walked away. A warrior woman was expected to do something about a problem, not just whine helplessly. Annie tied the bandanna around her neck, not quite sure she qualified yet to wear it around her forehead. Downstairs, she filled her water bottle and pulled on her hiking hat.

Toot toot! Claire blew the horn. Annie skipped out the door and soon they were headed down the road.

"Have you ever been out Whitfield Road to the University Forest?" asked Claire.

"I don't think so."

Claire chuckled. "Well, today I'm going to take you to the Magic Forest."

"Magic Forest?"

"It's a place special to me. It takes a while to hike in to it, but then it's like you're in the wilds far away from civilization. There's a rocky bluff, a gurgling stream. You'll see."

"I sure could use some magic about now."

Claire had her hands on the wheel and a big grin on her face. Her short dark hair with streaks of silver was tucked under a canvas hat with mesh vents. She, too, wore a bandanna tied around her neck, a purple t-shirt with big orange letters "Outrageous Older Woman," and well-worn blue jeans. She turned to Annie, then back to the road. "We all need some magic from time to time. Just remember, you make your own." Claire gave a big belly laugh. "I remember when my youngest was finally in college. I had looked forward to having time with my husband. I had visions of us hiking the Grand Canyon, biking through France, you know. But after smoking all his life, he got emphysema and could barely walk across the room. I was so frustrated! So I took care of him but also sometimes I went hiking without him. Ha!" She beat a rhythm on the steering wheel and began singing: "Ain't gonna keep me down, no way, sister!"

Annie smiled. Claire sure was wearing the right shirt. She didn't know the song but she began to clap in rhythm and hum along. She stomped her feet also. Before she knew it, they were miles out of town and winding down a road with thick woods on both sides. Then they were parked beside a trail and hiking into the woods. A hush fell on them both as they walked. There was no other human in sight. Pine trees, oak, and a few dogwood stretched as far as they could see. Squirrels scurried up trunks and leaped from branch to branch. Birds zipped in and out while an occasional tapping signaled a woodpecker at work. The sun's rays shone through the leaves, leaving dappled shadows on the ground. A cool breeze ruffled their hair. A quiet peacefulness began to rise up inside Annie as she soaked in the smells of pine and fresh air and the companionship of the woman beside her.

The trail took them up a hill and then down again. The sound of rushing water became slowly more audible. "We're almost there," whispered Claire, touching Annie on the arm. "Just around the next corner."

Around the bend Annie saw tall trees and behind them even taller trees, and then could make out a rocky bluff holding them that reached to the sky. Beneath the bluff, the creek bounced and jumped and flowed over rocks of all sizes. The trail continued beside the creek. Claire led the way slowly, as the trail was full of stones and roots, to a wide flat rock with a clear view across the stream to the further rocky shore with the bluff rising above it. Claire set down her backpack and pulled out a blanket she spread on the smooth rock. She motioned to Annie to sit and then sat down beside her. Annie felt spellbound as she listened to the singing of the water, felt the warm sun on her shoulders, and saw the majestic bluff reaching high above. She lifted her water bottle and took a long drink. She had worked up a bit of a sweat, but just enough to feel good. The water tasted especially delicious. She rested her hands on her knees and leaned against the rock behind her.

Claire watched Annie for her reaction. "See what I mean, Annie?

This is a magic place."

Annie nodded. "It sure is."

"Hungry?" Claire asked as she rooted through her pack.

"Starving," said Annie. "I used to love to hike. But Harry never has time for it—he's really not the outdoorsy type—so I haven't done it in a long time. Too long."

Claire handed a plastic plate and fork and a paper napkin to Annie, then pulled out a container filled with fried chicken and another filled with potato salad. They began to feast.

Annie took a bite off a big drumstick. "What gives this chicken such an unusual flavor? It's delicious."

"Cinnamon. Just a pinch of cinnamon makes it taste so good. It lowers your cholesterol too."

"Really? Well, I haven't worried about that yet."

"Just wait. You'll get your turn."

Next came a fruit salad of watermelon, pineapple, blueberries, and grapes.

"Wow. Thanks for such a great picnic, Claire."

"You are so welcome, but we're not done yet." Claire pulled out one more container with homemade chocolate chip walnut cookies.

Annie gasped and squinted her eyes at Claire. "Did you know I'm a cookie monster?"

Claire smiled. "Aren't we all?"

Stuffed and content, they both lay back, rolling up sweatshirts as pillows, and rested. Annie felt so happy, so far away from her troubles, so relaxed. She dozed off.

Claire poked Annie with her elbow. "Look!"

Annie opened her eyes and followed Claire's finger. Across the creek and about half-way up the bluff there was a wide flat ledge. It was far enough away that she could not really tell what Claire saw but it was sloped just enough to let her see something on it. "What?" she asked.

"On that shelf, what do you see?"

Annie looked again and something began to come into focus. "Is someone lying there?"

This particular ledge was in full sun. "I believe so." Then out of Claire's seemingly bottomless pack, she pulled a pair of binoculars and looked again. "I do believe there is a naked man sunbathing over there, take a look!" She handed the binoculars to Annie who lifted them to her eyes. He seemed to be asleep on a mound of clothes.

"And a handsome man at that," said Annie as she peered through the binoculars.

Claire reached for the binoculars. "Let me get another look. It has been a while since I've had the pleasure." She gave a long look, then a big sigh.

Annie grabbed her hand. "Do you think he could be dangerous?"

"Naw. There are two of us, remember. And we are surrounded by rocks that can be weaponized." She gave a big grin. "We are not helpless females, Annie."

"It's just so weird. I've never seen a man naked in the forest before." She thought of all Harry's warnings. To him, the world was full of criminals and rapists. She looked up the bluff at the man and over at Claire who had the binoculars to her eyes again, obviously enjoying the view. She relaxed a bit and shook her head, marveling at Claire.

Claire patted Annie's back. "He's just a man outside with nothing left to hide." She laughed.

Annie smiled and laughed herself, in relief that there were more ways to see the world than Harry's. Claire's world was full of wonders, full of beauty, of adventures to be enjoyed. Annie's giggles of relief turned into overwhelming hilarity. Claire let the binoculars tumble as she shook with laughter. Annie grabbed them before they rolled into the stream. Claire hugged her and laughed soundlessly, her abdomen jiggling. To Annie it was infectious. She began to shake with her own silent laughter. Tears rolled down both their cheeks. When they were finally quiet and spent, they looked at each other then started again. Soon they were gasping and lying back, not daring to look at each other till they could quiet themselves. They both took deep breaths and lay quiet for a few minutes.

"I feel like a kid again," said Claire. Then she looked back up without the binoculars and pointed. The man was now wearing shorts, t-shirt, and hiking boots and was making his way slowly down the bluff. Claire quickly stuffed the binoculars back into the pack. He had sandy-colored hair, rugged features, and a water bottle in his hand. As he came closer, his face lit up.

Claire broke the spell. "George? Is that you, George Taffer?"

Annie's jaw dropped.

"Claire? Annie?" George's booming bass voice rang out. Then he threw back his head and laughed. "Having a picnic? Got any food left? I'm starving." And he began scrambling down the trail on the other side to a place where the rocks were close enough to cross.

Fortunately, Claire had plenty of food left but not for long. "You came out here without anything to eat, no snacks even?" She handed him a plate full of chicken, potato salad, and fruit salad.

"I didn't expect to be out here that long." He chuckled, chomping down on a piece of chicken, then wiping his mouth with a napkin. "But then the sun was so warm on that high ledge over there, and I didn't see another soul. I lay down, made myself comfortable, and fell asleep." He reached for the last cookie as Claire opened the container.

Claire turned to Annie and winked. "I bet you were very comfortable. Did you hear us coming?"

"No, didn't hear a twig crack. Not till I got myself up." He paused as something clicked. "Did you see me up there?" His face grew red.

"Nah, "said Claire.

"No, we didn't see you at all," said Annie, stifling a giggle. "We would need binoculars."

George exhaled, visibly relieved. "I just love these woods. I come out here all the time. So glad I found them. Do you gals like to hike, too?"

"I love it," exclaimed Annie. "I haven't done it in a while."

Claire put her arm over Annie's shoulders and squeezed. "Me too. Glad I found a good hiking partner in Annie."

"I need to get out in the woods. It just renews my soul, especially after a hard work week."

"What do you do, George?" asked Claire. "You've never said."

"When I first moved down here, not much. I'd had a bad divorce and needed some time to regroup. Then I started a construction business. It took a while, but it's getting going now, and I'm busy all week."

"Is that what you did up north?" asked Annie.

"Yeah, but I worked for someone and that got old. Now I'm

working for myself and I love it, especially now that I have a lot of work." He laughed and picked up a small flat rock and tossed it into the creek. It skipped over the surface once then twice before it sank with a plop. "But when Saturday comes, I sure do need a break, and coming out here is the best thing for me."

"I'm so glad Claire brought me here. Once long ago I went backpacking a few days on the Appalachian Trail in college. That was rugged but exhilarating." She grew quiet, remembering. "We had great weather mostly but then one day a real downpour—that was a test of something. But we got to a shelter and changed into dry clothes, so it wasn't so bad."

"The AT," George mused. "I hiked some of it in Maine but never got far south. I might have to try it again." He lifted his water bottle to his mouth and drained it.

"I could just see us," Claire said, "hiking along, making up verse as we go. What fun that would be."

"Let's get our poetry group to plan a hike. What do you think?" cried George.

"I'm game," said Claire.

"Me too," said Annie.

George looked at his watch. "I'm afraid I have to leave you lovely ladies. I've got to give a guy an estimate on a job for next week." He stood up. "Thanks for feeding me. I guess I'll see you both when we meet for dinner next week."

They sat a while after he left. "I really like George." Claire repacked her backpack, watching Annie's face as she did.

"So do I," said Annie, wistfully.

Claire looked across the creek and up. "Want to scale the bluff,

Annie? Maybe take a sunbath? It's only 3 p.m."

Annie laughed, "Sure, why not, I'm game. I've got no place I'd rather be."

Chapter 19

When Annie got home, Harry's car was gone. But her day in the woods had filled her with such peace, such fun, she just couldn't worry about things in quite the same way. Claire had certainly had her share of disappointments and hard times in life yet she hadn't been destroyed by any of them. She still loved to hike and cook and write poetry. Annie felt lucky to have her as a friend.

Annie stood inside her front door in a trance, the sounds and smells of the forest vivid inside her. After her day in the fresh air, the house felt stuffy. She opened the windows upstairs and down and started filling the tub for a long soak, adding some Epsom salts to ease her tired muscles. She unpacked her backpack, unpeeled her clothes from her sticky skin, and, holding her nose, dropped them into the laundry basket. As she slipped into the warm water, she began to relax and even feel a bit sleepy. Scrubbing with her pink bath puff, she watched the bubbles pile up on her arms and abdomen. She was surprised to notice the first pangs of hunger. After eating Claire's food in the woods, how could she be hungry? She smiled as she remembered the wild caught salmon she had not yet cooked. Expecting to be home alone most of the evening, she decided to cook herself the gourmet dinner she had hoped to share with Harry. But when she rinsed off all the bubbles and dried herself with the fluffy pink towel, she felt a nap might be next. Slipping into her pale blue silk robe with pink embroidered flowers, she stretched out on the bed and drifted off.

She woke to hear sounds from downstairs, clattering and foot-steps. The red numerals on the bedside clock showed she had slept nearly an hour. Now she really was hungry. She sat up, tilted her head to one side, and listened. Remembering she had opened all the windows, she felt her heartbeat accelerate. Harry always warned her not to leave windows open, told her tales of intruders, robbery, rape, murder. Immediately, she was sucked back into his world view, as if it inhabited the walls of their home. Wrapping her robe tightly around her body, she tip-toed down the stairs. The sounds were coming from the kitchen. She peeked her head around the kitchen door to see a figure leaning into the open refrigerator and rooting around. It was Harry.

"Harry?" she asked.

He turned around, a bottle of wine in his hand. "You woke up. I came home alarmed to find all the windows wide open for any burglar or mugger to come right in. You were so sound asleep, I thought you'd be out until morning. Had a busy day?"

"I went hiking out in the University Forest." She noticed the oven door open, and the broiler on.

"Alone?" He shook his head.

"With Claire. We hardly saw another soul. We were quite safe. We had a wonderful time . . ."

He cut her off. "Well, you were lucky."

Luckier than you can imagine, thought Annie. "I see you're cooking."

"Yes. I'm starving. This case is gonna kill me. I couldn't keep working. I'm broiling up that salmon. Have you eaten?"

She shook her head, hardly believing her ears. Then she noticed a pot boiling and asparagus spears grilling in a pan. "You got the potatoes on too? And asparagus. It smells delicious. Yes, I worked up an appetite in the woods. What can I do?"

"Sit down and I'll serve you." He nodded towards the table where she saw two places set.

She sat at her place and watched him. He had on his apron from Harrington's of London, an oven mitt on one hand and a fork in another. He pulled out the oven shelf and poked the salmon with the fork. "Just about ready." He turned towards her. "How about a glass of pinot grigio? Is that still your favorite?"

She nodded and watched him fill first her glass, then his with the cold liquid. Words left her. He removed her plate, smiling at her with a twinkle in his eye, filled it with salmon, new potatoes, and grilled asparagus, then did the same with his own and sat across from her. He lifted his glass. "To the successful conclusion of my case and the beginning of our life of luxury!" He tapped her lifted glass with his. "Can you drink to that?"

"To successful conclusions and new beginnings." She wasn't sure she wanted a life of luxury but she sure wanted things to change.

"Dig in," he said as he picked up a big hunk of salmon on his fork. "Good, if I do say so myself."

She took a taste herself. "Delicious, Harry. Remember how you used to cook for me when we first met?"

"I did, didn't I? I hope to have more time to cook again soon." He launched into telling her his elaborate dreams for future fame and fortune.

Her mind drifted back to when they first dated. They met through an online dating site in January, just after she had spent a lonely New Year's Eve watching videos in her apartment and had finally decided to sign up with Findamate.com, having run out of other ideas and at the urging of several girlfriends. He was the first man she met that way. On their first date he had taken her dancing, twirled her around the dance floor with such skill that she wanted to sing "I could have danced all night" and didn't really mind that the music was too loud to talk. When he dropped her off at her apartment, he kissed her tenderly on her forehead, and, taking her hands in his, looked directly into her eyes and said, "I've had a wonderful evening. I hope you have too. Can I see you again soon? Tomorrow night?"

And so began their whirlwind romance. He had been so attentive, showering her with flowers, fancy restaurant dinners, tickets to Broadway on Tour, things she couldn't afford on her teacher's salary. The chemistry between them was intense, but he didn't push her. They saw each other all weekend and at least one night during the week. He called her every day but did no more than kiss her the first week. Three weeks later as he dropped her off on a Friday night, she invited him to stay. The next day he proposed. Their courtship had been a bright light in the sadness that followed. When her mother had died, Harry had been her shoulder to cry on, her rock, during her grief.

She smiled at him across the table as he droned on. "If this company likes my work on this case, they will surely give me many more in the future. And they need good legal representation. They are a magnet for lawsuits. And they don't deserve to be." He folded his napkin and replaced it beside his empty plate. "I am so sure we'll win this case, and then we'll be on easy street!" He grinned at her.

"I hope then you'll be home more and so will that man I fell in love with. I wonder whatever happened to him?" Annie looked at Harry with a smile and waited.

"I know I've been distracted and grumpy lately, Annie, but I've been under so much pressure, and this is the case of a lifetime!" He glowed with anticipation of his success.

"I didn't marry a bear, I married a handsome, attentive, loving man. Someone I hope to have a family with."

"I don't know about that. I've never wanted kids really."

"Oh," said Annie, shocked. Then she realized they had never discussed children. She had just assumed.

"But once we win this case and the world knows I'm a tough litigator, there'll be more big cases in the pipeline, and you can have a Mercedes and a bigger house and everything you've ever dreamed about."

She stared at him and opened her mouth to speak. "You don't want kids?"

He stood up and stacked the plates. "I'll clean up. You rest."

Annie's eyes got big. "Thank you," she said. "But . . ." she began again, before her dream of one day holding a baby of her own slipped away.

"You go on to bed. I'm afraid I've just thought of one more work thing I have to do tonight. I'll be up soon."

She could tell he was gone now. "Okay, we can talk later." She moved slowly, stunned by his comment about not wanting kids and about more cases. She felt a burning inside. She shook her head as she pulled herself up the stairs with her hand on the banister. *Do we even want the same life? Am I to be a childless law widow forever? Will we ever get a chance to talk about all this?* But, just in case, she got into the marital bed to read and wait. It was 10:15. Soon, however, her eyes grew heavy. She put down her book, rolled onto her side, and fell asleep. She was only vaguely aware when Harry joined her much later.

Chapter 20

When the night for the poetry group reunion came around, Annie wished she had thought to invite her friends to her house. But the distance between her and Harry made her hesitate. She ignored him mostly except to inquire about further sessions with Amanda Murphy. He waved her off, saying he couldn't do anything until this case was over, so she let it go. She couldn't imagine he would like her having friends over.

Still she had cleaned her house to sparkling, rearranged the living room to her satisfaction, cataloged her poetry into notebooks according to when written, and even planted some day lilies in the front yard. Her life might be in disarray, but her house wouldn't be.

Claire was right on time picking her up at 6:30. "Do you think George ever figured out that we saw him sunbathing last Saturday," asked Claire, giggling.

"I hope not. But if you lie naked out in the forest, you take the risk of being seen."

"That's right. Have you been writing much? I brought a few things, but I had my grandkids here a lot lately, and they keep me busy."

"Yes, I've had plenty of time. Harry is buried under this big case that he promises will give us a 'life of luxury,' so I've had nothing else to do until summer session starts next week."

"Life of luxury, eh? Is that what he wants?"

"Apparently, but I couldn't care less. I just want enough to pay my bills and keep a roof over my head and have some friends to share poetry and to hike with."

"Well, you already have that, don't you?" Claire downshifted as she turned into the parking lot by Andres Bistro.

"Yes, and I intend to spend more time with them. I'm tired of waiting around for Harry."

"Atta girl!" said Claire. "Life is too short to waste waiting for those who can't keep up." She grinned. "Hey, I like that line. I think I'll steal it!"

"From yourself?" Annie laughed.

Up ahead they saw George and Peter on the porch at a table talking and waving their arms around.

"Hi guys!" shouted Claire. "Your dreams have come true, we have arrived."

They jumped up and hugs were shared all around.

"We thought, on a nice night like this, a table on the porch would be just right, what do you ladies say?" said Peter. His lanky frame towered over her, his bright blue eyes mirrored the blue sky above them. He leaned over the chair he had pulled out from the table for her across from George. He winked at her and then at George. Annie wasn't sure what to make of that gesture so she ignored it.

"Thank you, Peter, you are such a gentleman." Annie sat down. "I love dining 'al fresco.'"

Annie looked at George standing across from her. He was impeccably dressed, with pressed tan trousers and a light blue short sleeve shirt. A stark contrast to when Annie had last seen him in the forest. She found her eyes taking him in, his shaggy hair, clearly just combed, his rugged features. He returned her look and blushed. Seeing this, her heartbeat accelerated. She realized she had been staring and turned her gaze away, blushing herself.

"I'm sorry," said George, collecting himself. He chuckled. "Al Fresco couldn't come tonight. Neither could anyone else. You're stuck with us two guys, I'm afraid."

"I'm shaking in my boots," said Claire as she sat down in the chair George held out for her.

"Whatever happened to Al, anyway?" said Peter with a big grin. "I thought he was a bit too 'fresco' but he went inside in the winter."

Annie chuckled. "Oh, you guys are too funny!" She picked up the menu and started checking the specials. "It's so good to be here. I spent all day cleaning and organizing at home. I'm ready for a break."

"Hey, Wednesday night is half-price on bottles of wine," said Claire. "Shall we get one?"

"Only if we get four glasses," said George.

"Only if my glass is a double," said Peter.

Soon Ryan, their server, returned with the wine and poured them each a glass.

"Here's to us, none like us, damn few, and they're all dead, more's the pity!" said George lifting his glass. More laughter with the toasts.

"Where did that come from?" asked Claire.

"Old Scottish toast," said George. "My maternal grandfather was William Mackay from Scourie. Someday I'm going to go visit."

"He lives in Scotland?" asked Annie.

"He did and his grave is there so, to be precise, that's what I intend to visit. But also the clan headquarters is there I hear."

"Sounds like a fun trip," said Annie.

"Want to come?" George raised his eyebrows and leaned towards her.

Annie said nothing.

"Why not?" said Claire. "Let's all go, make it a class field trip! But after we hike the Appalachian Trail."

"Appalachian Trail?" asked Peter.

"It's an idea we came up with in the woods last Saturday," said Claire. "You should have been there. We were all there taking a sunbath."

Annie put her head in her hands.

"A sunbath?" said Peter. "All three of you. Together?"

George's eyes had grown big and his face turned red. "Not together! I saw you ladies and you were *not* taking a sunbath."

Claire was giggling so hard she could hardly speak so Annie explained to Peter.

Peter listened and nodded.

Claire took a deep inhale and contained herself. "After George left, Annie and I talked about taking a sunbath."

Annie bent towards Claire with a frown. "But we didn't."

Peter shook his head. "Ah, shucks, and I missed it." He raised his eyebrows. "But what about the Appalachian Trail?"

"Annie and I had both hiked some of it," said George. "In the past."

Claire clapped her hands and grinned. "And I said let's all do it together!"

"Claire, it seems you are the group organizer," said Peter.

Annie shook her finger at Claire. "Or trouble maker."

Claire smiled. "This trouble maker did not suggest this reunion, it was you guys."

Peter pointed at George. "Blame him." He inclined his head towards Annie, then winked at George. "He couldn't bear to be away from you lovely ladies another day."

"That's right," said George. His smile lingered on Annie a few extra seconds.

Ryan appeared with a tray of plates and soon they were enjoying their meals. As Annie sipped her wine and chewed her calamari, she felt waves of well-being roll over her as they laughed and talked and eventually got down to sharing some newly minted poetry. This is what she wanted her life to be like. Good friends, good food, good verse. Why she had deferred to Harry for her entire social life was now beyond her comprehension. She remembered how scared she had been to sign up for the poetry seminar, imagining harsh criticism and finding out she had no talent. But the absolute opposite had happened. Plus she made some wonderful new friends.

Her reverie was interrupted by Peter. "Who wants to go first?" he asked. "Did everyone bring a poem to share? How do you want to do this?"

"Let's just read and enjoy," said Claire.

"I agree, no critiquing tonight. This is just for fun," said George.

Annie flipped through her notebook to a poem she'd written years ago when she'd first arrived in South America. She'd never shared it with anyone. Maybe this was the time.

"I have one," she said. "It might be the first poem I ever wrote. From my time in Brazil."

Peter emptied his water glass, then signaled the waiter. "Brazil? Cool. What was it like?"

"Don't tell us, just read your poem," said George.

Annie looked up from her well of memory. She nodded to the waiter who refilled her water glass and all the others.

"Let me just say this was when I first got there and didn't yet know much of the language. I named it after the village."

Afogados, Pernambuco, Brazil

A long journey to arrive there—
four hours by plane from Rio,
seven more by car into the interior,
then by jeep bouncing on roads carved
and sliced by the rains that had come
five years overdue—
to small half-open brick houses,
with the look of fresh white-wash,
encircling a dusty field.
Children peer at us from doorways.
We wait in the one-room school house,
admire its colorful maps and picture books.
Around the walls, wooden desks fill up
as men and women with children
wander in after their day in the fields.
A kerosene lamp is lit and hung from the rafters.
The room buzzes with greetings and chatter—
then quiets as the meeting begins.

I do not understand Portuguese
but I feel the warmth, the searching
for a way to come together,
to lift each other up,
to resist the onslaughts
of the world outside:
my world.

Yet the path is rough and rutted.
The next day our jeep hits a trough
even four-wheel drive cannot conquer.
Our spinning wheels dig us in deeper
as dirt and water from the recent rains
make an expanding sea of mud.
My mind grasps at the familiar technological
solutions, then realize no other vehicle
with chains to pull us out
is anywhere nearby: we are stuck.
We climb out and stand helpless,
not noticing the girl-child watching with wonder
who runs home to tell the news—
and returns in her own hands a shovel
and two men behind—plenty of muscle.

Before it's done, upwards of twenty people come
with six harnessed oxen and rope
and every tool to till the land.
Children laugh and splash through puddles.

An old woman attacks the clay and mud
with pick and shovel.
When the jeep at last leaps free,
a woman with leather face
and grey straw hair
exclaims with such delight
I cannot miss her message
ringing through her unknown tongue:
"When we all pull together,
*   just see what we can do!"*

She read it twice, then felt a sudden shyness and cast her eyes into her lap. When she felt brave enough, she lifted her eyes to their faces. She saw Claire nodding, Peter smiling, and George with a far-away look in his eyes before he pulled himself back and spoke.

"Lovely. Vivid. How long were you there in, is it, Afogados?"

"Yes, that's right, Afogados. A tiny place. I was there two years. I taught English in that one-room school house. And did anything else needed in the village."

"Your first poem," said Peter. "I like it."

"I like it too," said Claire. "Like George said, vivid. And clear. I can almost see that schoolhouse. I bet you not only taught, but learned a lot."

"I sure did. I did eventually learn to speak Portuguese. And I learned about real community, that having friends is what counts, not whether or not you have a fancy house or make a lot of money." She turned her gaze to each one with a warm smile. "Real friends. Who enjoy poetry."

When she got home that night, she didn't even care where Harry was. He was actually home, leaning back in the recliner snoring with the baseball game blaring. She found the remote on the coffee table in front of his chair and muted the sound so she could sleep. How he could sleep with that noise was beyond her, but she knew she couldn't. She set the remote back down and began to walk softly around him.

He jerked and sat up, his eyes opening and darting around the room. His shook his head, coming fully awake, and slowly focused on her. "What the hell? What are you doing?" He tipped the recliner forward, gripped the arms, and stood up.

She took a step back, judging the space between him and the stairs. He blocked the way.

"I said what are you doing, damn it!" He took a step towards her.

"You were asleep. I turned down the volume."

"Don't you dare," he bellowed. "I was watching that."

You were snoring, she thought and dared not say. She began to inch around him, one eye on the stairs, one on him.

"Turn the volume back up and give me the damn remote," said Harry through gritted teeth, his face leaning towards her.

She nodded towards the coffee table where the remote lay atop a magazine. His eyes held her face. With a trembling hand, she picked it up and pressed the mute button. The ballgame roared back at full volume.

He sat back down, arms on his knees, his hands clasped. Just as suddenly, his focus shifted as he leaned towards the screen. "Don't ever do that again." He punched each word but at a lower decibel. She went silently past him and up to bed.

Chapter 21

The following Monday morning, Annie was surprised to see Harry at breakfast. She was up early herself for the start of the summer session, so they were together for a change. As she started the coffee and began to warm the pan for frying eggs, he appeared in his crisply tailored dark go-to-court suit with his hair gelled into place and wearing a dark turquoise tie with matching handkerchief in his pocket. He had the air of someone about to be awarded the Nobel Prize who hadn't quite finished his acceptance speech. He set his briefcase, full to overflowing, by the kitchen door, walked over to her, gave her a kiss on the cheek, and looked at the pan. She reached for a second egg, cracked it into the pan, and put two slices of toast in the toaster oven.

"Today's the day," he said. He sounded giddy as he stood beside her.

"Oh?"

"Yes, the trial begins today and today begins our way to a life of luxury."

"I hope it goes well," she said, lifting her head to him and smiling.

After a moment, he frowned, then looked at her. She wore a blue sleeveless shirtwaist dress with a pattern of white flowers, her shoulder-length wavy brown hair carefully styled. "What are you doing up?" He poured himself a cup of coffee.

"Summer session starts today."

"It might be your last time to teach summer session if this case goes the way I think it will." He set the cups at the usual places and sat down.

Annie lifted eggs and toast onto two plates and joined him at the table. She added some sugar and milk to her cup and busied herself eating.

Harry took a big forkful of egg and a bite of toast and looked off into space. "We are ready. I have an excellent legal team working with me." He shoveled more egg and toast into his mouth.

Oh, yes, Gloria, she thought. "Well, good luck," she said. She gave a big exhale and spread strawberry jam on her toast.

"I don't know what time I'll be home tonight. I'm sure we'll have to work tonight to prepare for tomorrow."

"Yes, I'm sure you will." Annie nodded. She was long past being disappointed at hearing this.

The closing door behind him left a slight breeze as she took her last bite of toast.

Chapter 22

The courthouse was a tall red brick building with stately columns built around the turn of the last century and recently remodeled to suit today's technology standards. The day was already warm and promised to be a scorcher by afternoon. Gloria was waiting for him on the steps in the shade of the building, her blond hair pulled back with a few wisps of hair curling around her face. She wore a dark turquoise Armani suit with a short strand of pearls hugging her neck. She held a leather briefcase in her left hand. When she saw him, she pressed her moist lips together and opened them to a big smile.

"I see you are following the color code," she said.

"What color code?" he asked, shaking his head. Not that he hadn't been looking at her and feeling waves of approval, even desire, rise up inside him at her appearance.

"Look at your tie and handkerchief, Boss, we match perfectly."

He looked with approval at his attire, smiled, then looked up at her with bright eyes. "Ready for our big day?"

"I believe so. I think we may be over-prepared."

"Can't be too prepared with a case like this. But I think we have a good jury." Last week they had spent four days in jury selection. Their firm had hired a jury consultant to do background checks and assure a jury that understood the limits of business liability. "And the other counselors do not have anywhere near the experience I have."

She caught his eye, her eyebrows raised.

"Or such a good legal team," he added with a smile. "Shall we?" He nodded towards the door and strode up the steps with Gloria at his elbow.

Inside they walked down the hall past portraits of justices, governors, and other state officials in ornate gold frames and paused in front of double doors of carved mahogany. Harry took a deep breath and opened the door. Tall windows graced the side walls shining light on the gold carpet, dark walls and tables in front. The US, state, and town flags stood at attention framing the judge's bench. The jury box sat on the right with two levels of chairs inside its gated enclosure. They marched past rows filled with spectators to their appointed table on the left. Harry removed his pile of folders from his briefcase, fluttering them down on the table in front of his chair, nodding at the opposing counsel at the table on their right. He noted their bulging briefcases and piles of paper already on the table and felt a twinge of anxiety.

"All rise," said the courtroom deputy at the front. A tall wiry man with short gray hair in a black robe appeared from a door up front and stepped to his chair behind the bench as a shuffle of chairs and feet rippled throughout the room. He nodded and sat down. As he took his seat, the jury filed in. Twelve men and women of different backgrounds, all looking serious as they too sat down. Again there was a ruffle of feet and chairs as everyone sat down. Judge Robert Sexton rapped his gavel and called the court to order.

The deputy read from a list. "The case before the court today is John and Sheila Matthews v. the Parkwood Company." He handed papers to the judge and stepped back. Judge Sexton pulled his wire-rimmed glasses lower on his nose, tilted his head down to see over them, and began reading.

"The Matthews family accuses the Parkwood Company of negligence in the death of their daughter, Candace. Who represents the Matthews family?" He looked towards the table on his left.

A dark man in a dark navy suit and a short woman with short brown hair stood. "Justin Jones and co-counsel Barbara Shore, Your Honor."

The judge nodded and cast his eyes to Harry's table. "And who represents the Parkwood Company?"

Harry and Gloria both stood. "Harry Thomas and co-counsel Gloria Benjamin," said Harry.

The judge nodded them down and turned back to Justin Jones. "You may proceed."

Justin Jones stood tall and spoke loudly. "Your Honor, we intend to show that the preponderance of the evidence will prove that the Parkwood Company was negligent in the drowning death of Mr. and Mrs. Matthews' eight-year-old daughter, Candace, due to a faulty filter system in the swimming pool they built and installed on the Matthews' property, that the company knew about this faulty filter system and did not address and repair it, and that, therefore, created a suction entrapment causing their daughter to be pulled under the water and drown. And the court to award the Matthews family punitive damages."

At the end of the table where he stood, a woman with curly brown hair dressed in a beige suit with coral blouse dabbed at her eyes with a tissue while the man next to her leaned towards her and placed his arm around her shoulder, touching his head to hers.

Gloria leaned towards Harry and whispered, "The parents look very sympathetic."

"Don't worry, I've got it," Harry replied. Then he sat up straight as the judge nodded to him. He stood and spoke in a soft but penetrating tone. "Your Honor, it is always tragic when parents lose a child." He cast his eyes towards the jury, then back to the judge. "But we intend to demonstrate that the preponderance of the evidence clearly shows that, sadly, any negligence here belongs to the parents for failure to adequately supervise their child, and that the Parkwood Company was not negligent in this matter. The filter system in question was not in fact faulty at all and this case against the Parkwood Company should therefore be dismissed." He sat down, drawing his lips into a firm line.

"Mr. Jones, call your first witness," said the judge. He put a finger to the bridge of his glasses to push them up his nose.

"We call Jonathan Smithers to the stand."

A tall, uniformed brown-skinned man whose belly protruded over his belt stepped forward. When Mr. Smithers was sworn in and seated on the witness stand, Mr. Jones approached. "Please state your name and occupation, Mr. Smithers."

"My name is Jonathan Smithers. I work for the State Recreational Equipment Inspection Office." He sat erect and bore a half-smile, his hands in his lap.

"And what is your position at the State Recreational Equipment Inspection Office, Mr. Smithers?"

"I inspect playgrounds, water parks, swimming pools, any equipment people use for recreational purposes."

"And how long have you had this position, Mr. Smithers?'

"Twenty-two years next month, to be precise."

"And have you inspected swimming pools built and installed by the Parkwood Company?"

"Yes, sir, lots of them."

"And have you found any problems with their swimming pools?"

"Yes, sir, I have often had to reject their filter systems for safety violations."

"Thank you. No further questions."

"Mr. Thomas, you may cross examine," said the judge.

Harry winked at Gloria and stood up. He walked a few steps towards the witness, glanced at the legal pad in his hand, then smiled broadly at the witness. "I understand you to say, Mr. Smithers, that the Parkwood Company has had problems with their filter systems."

"Yes, sir."

"And when you have rejected them for safety violations, what have they done?"

"Well, sir, they have to fix them or I can't pass them on the next inspection."

"Did you examine the filter system in this particular swimming pool?"

"Not me personally but one of my workers did, sir."

"You yourself did not examine this filter system?"

"Correct."

"Judge, I propose this testimony be stricken from the record as the witness did not examine this filter system." Harry looked at the judge.

"So move," said the judge. "The witness may be dismissed." He addressed Mr. Jones. "If you have a witness who did examine this particular filter system, bring them in. Counselor, you know better."

Mr. Jones consulted his co-counsel. "Yes, sir, we do."

Harry stepped aside to let Mr. Smithers exit the courtroom.

Harry sat down and gave Gloria a subtle smile. Across the aisle, Mr. Jones and Ms. Shore leaned their heads together and spoke quietly. Mr. and Mrs. Matthews squeezed their hands together and hung their heads. Mrs. Matthews reached for a tissue and gripped it tightly against her lips, sniffling quietly.

"Next witness," said the judge.

Ms. Shore stood. "Doreen Balsam."

A young woman, twenty-something, with brown hair pulled back in a ponytail and a slim, muscular body came from the first row behind the Matthews' attorneys. She wore a simple short-sleeved dress in light green. Her arms were muscled and tan.

"Please state your name and occupation," said Ms. Shore when the witness was seated.

"I'm Doreen Balsam, swimming instructor."

"And where do you teach?"

"I teach at the YMCA and give private lessons." She looked at the Matthews and smiled.

"And did you teach the Matthews' daughter to swim?"

"Yes, Candace was one of my favorite students. She was a very strong swimmer. I even recommended her for the Lakeside Swim Team."

"And how long did you give her lessons?"

"Oh, I started with her when she was six, two now maybe three years ago. She had no fear of the water. She was like a water baby."

The young woman paused and looked down.

Ms. Shore looked at the yellow legal pad in her hand. "Knowing her swimming ability so well, Ms. Balsam, can you imagine any way she would drown without something or someone holding her under water?"

"Objection!" Harry was on his feet. "Leading the witness!"

"Objection sustained," said the judge. "Counsel, re-frame your question.

"Yes, Your Honor." She turned to Doreen Balsam. "Did you have any concerns about Candace Matthews' safety when swimming?"

"None at all. She was an excellent swimmer."

"No further questions." Ms. Shore sat back in her seat and exhaled deeply.

Harry turned to Gloria. "You take this one." Gloria lit up and jumped to her feet.

Gloria walked up to the witness box and leaned her elbow on the top of the partition. "Hello, Ms. Balsam," she said with a warm smile.

"Hello," said Ms. Balsam. She did not return the smile.

"So you say that Candace was a strong swimmer."

"Yes, ma'am."

"What did you teach her?"

"Just about everything."

"Describe your swimming curriculum, please."

"Objection! Relevance!" Mr. Jones shot to his feet.

Harry stood quickly himself. "Your Honor, we're discussing a drowning. Of course it's relevant."

"I'll allow it," said the judge, frowning and pulling his brows together.

The witness continued. "I am a Red Cross certified swimming instructor and follow the Red Cross swimming curriculum. This includes water safety and the various swim strokes. She got it immediately. Like I said, she was a water baby." She crossed her arms.

"Very good. Did you teach her to dive?"

"Oh, yes, she loved to dive." She returned her arms to her lap, then raised her right hand to gesture. "I would throw something to the bottom, you know, those plastic rods, and she could dive down in the deep end and bring them back. I've never seen such a young child do so well." Ms. Balsam shook her head. "Amazing."

"And did she ever take risks while diving?"

"Well, I thought it risky for such a young child to dive to the bottom of the deep end—it's 9 feet at the end of the pool—but I taught her to kick off from the bottom to get back up quickly if she needed air, and she did it every time."

"And how often did you give her lessons, how often were you there to teach and supervise her?"

Gloria glanced at Harry who gave a slight nod.

"I came twice a week at first but then only once a week."

"And was that year round?"

"Oh, no, only in the summer when it's hot," Ms. Balsam laughed. "I don't recommend my students swim when it's cold."

"You were there once a week for her lesson but only in the summer."

"That's right."

"So obviously you don't know what happened when you weren't there. She could have taken excessive risks when you weren't there, and you wouldn't know."

"Well, of course, I only know what I saw when I was there." Ms. Balsam squinted.

"Thank you, Ms. Balsam. No further questions." When Gloria turned to take her seat, Harry met her eyes and nodded.

Across the aisle, Mr. Jones and Ms. Shore both frowned and ruffled through their stacks of papers. Mrs. and Mr. Matthews sighed in unison.

During the lunch recess, Harry and Gloria huddled over their notes in their office conference room. They munched on sandwiches from the deli as they sat at the table. The pungent odor of spicy mustard filled the air. Their laps were draped in large brown napkins. Occasionally, Gloria wiped mustard from the corner of her mouth.

"Good job on questioning the swimming instructor," Harry said.

"Thanks. I believe we can prove that the child took risks diving, did so when her parents weren't there or weren't watching, and that's how she drowned. Tragic, but not the company's fault. You did a good job with the inspector." Gloria leaned towards Harry, brushing her breast on his arm.

His heartbeat accelerated, and he lost his focus momentarily. With a shake of his head, he took a big bite of his pastrami on rye and leaned closer to his notes from that morning. "I wish we could wrap this up today and get a dismissal but I don't see Judge Sexton doing that. I've been in his courtroom before, and he likes to let things play out even if it seems like a waste of time. We'll be here awhile, I'm afraid. And we have to tread lightly and not seem to be too hard on the parents in their grief or we'll lose the jury," he said.

"Who is the next witness?"

"The police officer called to the scene."

"Will the parents testify?"

"Not sure. I'll question the officer. You watch closely."

"Yes, sir, boss." She took the last bite of her chicken salad croissant, tossed the wrapping in the trash, and stood. While Harry finished his sandwich and returned his papers to his briefcase, she put her hands on his shoulders and began to give him a shoulder rub.

He closed his eyes a moment and took a deep breath. "We'd better go." He shook her off and stood up. "I sure could use a massage. But not now." His smile faded. He nodded in the direction of the door.

She raised her eyebrows with a smile and a wink and followed him out the door.

Back in the courtroom, Officer Bud Wilson took the stand. He was a burly round white man with a clean-shaven face and bushy dark eyebrows over piercing eyes. Mr. Jones began to question him. "You were the first on the scene after the child drowned?"

"Yes, sir, me and the EMT guy."

"Please describe what you saw."

"The mother answered the door and brought us through the house to the pool outside in back. The father was leaning over the child who was lying next to the deep end. He appeared to be giving CPR."

"Then what happened?"

"The EMT guy took over from the father, tried to revive the child, which didn't work. Then they loaded her body on a gurney. They had to pull the mother away, she was getting hysterical. Her husband held her while the EMT exited with the body. Then I attempted to interview the parents."

"Attempted?"

"They were of course very distraught so it was difficult.

"What did the mother say?"

"Not much. She was crying and eager to follow the ambulance to the hospital. So I made my interview brief and let them go."

"Did you get an opportunity to examine the pool?'

"Yes, later that day when I returned in my swimming suit to dive into the pool."

"And explain your qualifications as a diver."

"I have certification as a deep sea diver. It's a hobby."

"So what did you find when you dove into the pool?"

"I felt a huge suction from the filter system. The clamps that hold the cover in place appeared to have broken so the cover was missing. I felt my hand could be sucked in if I didn't resurface quickly. So I pushed off from the bottom and came up."

"Thank you. No further questions."

"You may cross-examine," said Judge Sexton to Harry.

"Thank you, Your Honor." Harry approached the officer and smiled. "Good afternoon, Officer."

"Good afternoon," said the officer. He didn't smile.

"What a difficult call that was."

"Yes, but it's my job."

"Yes, and we're grateful to you first responders for the service you provide." Harry smiled.

"Thank you," said the officer.

"And what did you find in the pool when you examined it?"

"Lots of plastic toys, the kind that sink to the bottom for diving, maybe a half dozen, and the filter cover on the bottom of the pool about five feet away."

"And where were those plastic toys?"

"On the bottom of the pool of course."

"Here is the police report." Harry handed a sheet of paper to the officer. "Read the line that is highlighted in yellow." He pointed.

The officer leaned over the paper, located the highlighted line, and read: "One plastic toy in the shape of a starfish was found lodged inside the filter."

"Did you personally find that starfish?"

"Yes, when I dove down to examine the filter. I tried to pull out the starfish but it was lodged so securely I ran out of air before I could. I didn't dive with an oxygen tank."

"Is it possible that Candace stayed down too long trying to dislodge her toy and drowned?"

"Objection!" Mr. Jones was on his feet with his finger pointing. "Calls for speculation."

"Objection sustained," said the judge.

"I'll re-frame," said Harry. "Tell us what you observed when you dove to the filter."

The officer's eyes drilled into Harry and his eyebrows went up. "I observed the plastic starfish lodged inside the filter, the filter cover gone, and a huge suction from the filter. Like I said."

"Thank you. No further questions." Harry sat down next to

Gloria. Under the table, she leaned her leg against his. He kept his eyes on his notes.

After court, they ordered Chinese delivery and collapsed on the couch in Harry's office. "We planted the seed, that's all we could do." He poured them each a glass of Jack Daniels and took a long swallow. "Were you watching the jury?" He turned to her.

"Yes, very closely." She took a sip of her drink. "Got any ginger ale?" Then she spied it on the bar, got up long enough to dilute her bourbon, and sat back down. "Hard to tell. Some sat there stony-faced but some seemed to sit up and look surprised when you made your suggestion Candace may have stayed under water too long trying to get her toy. It sure could have happened that way. I wish I were a mind reader. We've already established she loved to dive so I think it might work."

She leaned against the back of the couch and kicked off her shoes. She lifted her glass to her lips and watched him over it as she sipped. He returned her look and took another long swallow. Feeling the bourbon, he began to relax. Gloria set down her glass and reached over to loosen his tie. He let her and began to feel, well, he wasn't sure what, exhaustion, desire, some mix of the two? He draped his arm over the back of the couch. She moved into his arm and turned her face up to his. Their eyes met. *She wants me to kiss her now. It's tempting.* He sat up straight.

"We've got work to do, Gloria. And I'm hungry." He opened the bag of Chinese take-out and began to set the containers on the coffee table. Taking the hint, she brought the paper plates from the cabinet underneath the bar and began to fill her plate. She opened one pair of paper-wrapped chop sticks and handed him the other. She grasped a small piece of sesame chicken with them, holding it delicately in her teeth, letting her full lips close around the thick, fragrant sauce, and sat up straight.

"Well, boss, what's our strategy for tomorrow?"

Harry felt both relieved and disappointed she took the hint so easily. He turned his thoughts to the case. What *was* his strategy for tomorrow? Jones and Shore may be less experienced, but they were better litigators than he had anticipated. This case was definitely not turning out to be a slam dunk. His stomach knotted. He clenched his fists. He could not lose this case.

The trial went on for another week. The plaintiff's attorneys brought in Mr. Smithers' worker who had examined that particular filter system. He testified that the drain covers were not securely fastened with screws but with plastic prongs that had broken. In addition, the cover did not have the required embossed warning in the plastic that covers must be secured with metal screws. The child's father testified that the parents had gone inside for at most five minutes. He used the bathroom and his wife answered the phone, and they quickly returned to find their daughter under the water. When he dove into the pool, his daughter seemed stuck at the bottom of the pool in a suction at the filter. Others testified to children who had drowned or been eviscerated when they got caught in the vortex created when the drain cover came off. Harry had his own expert witnesses whose refutations to these testimonies were weak. He scrambled to find others and to educate himself on all aspects of pool safety.

The last witness called to the stand was the medical examiner, Dr. Joy Tillis, who had been called to examine the body due to the suspicious nature of the child's death. A trim, fit woman, her gray hair and lined faced attributed to her years of experience. When Dr. Tillis was sworn in, Mr. Jones began the questioning.

"How long have you been the medical examiner in this county, Dr. Tillis?"

"Fifteen years."

"Please describe your findings in the tragic death of Candace Matthews." He glanced towards Mr. and Mrs. Matthews who huddled together watching the proceedings closely.

"There were scrapes on the child's right hand and arm."

"What do you suspect caused those scrapes?"

"Most likely they occurred when the child reached inside the open drain to retrieve her toy. They extend to her elbow, which would be consistent with her arm being pulled deep into the drain by the suction. The water in her lungs is consistent with death by drowning."

"So, to sum up, you found scrapes on her hand and arm extending to her elbow and water in her lungs showing death by drowning."

"Yes, that is correct."

"Thank you, Dr. Tillis."

Mr. Jones took his seat. Harry stood up and took a few steps towards the witness stand.

"Dr. Tillis, how many similar situations have you encountered in your fifteen years as medical examiner?"

"Quite a few."

"How many exactly?"

Dr. Tillis frowned. "I can't recall the precise number."

"So you are not very experienced in judging swimming pool accidents?"

Dr. Tillis frowned and sat up. "I have seen many scrapes and quite a few bodies that drowned. I am confident my conclusions are accurate, if that's what you're implying."

"Could it be possible that the child dove to the bottom and drowned and it had nothing to do with the drain? And that her death was due to her own inexperience as a swimmer, her parents' negligence in watching her, and not due to suction from the drain?" Harry's face grew red and his voice rose. "Could it be you don't know what you're talking about?"

"Objection!" cried both Mr. Jones and Ms. Shore in unison, on their feet in an instant. Ms. Shore sat down and Mr. Jones said: "Badgering the witness!"

Judge Sexton rapped his gavel. "Objection sustained. Mr. Thomas, that's enough."

"I'll withdraw the question, Your Honor," said Harry. "Dr. Tillis, are you certain your findings are correct?"

"Yes. I. Am," said Dr. Tillis through clenched teeth.

"No further questions," said Harry. He hung his head, feeling the room swimming and himself drowning. He sat down and put his head in his hands. Gloria touched his arm and leaned closer.

The jury took less than a day to deliberate. Their verdict: the Parkwood Company was guilty of negligence. The Matthews family would receive $15 million in punitive damages. As Mr. and Mrs. Matthews and their attorneys hugged and cried, Harry sat immobile, starring straight ahead. Gloria took his arm and helped him to his feet. He said not a word as she led him through the milling crowd, outside, across the street, and back to his office.

Kicking the door to close it, she poured him a glass of Jack Daniels. Without a word, he drank it down in one swallow, then held his glass out for more. Gloria refilled it and watched as he downed it. She loosened his tie and refilled his glass, which he emptied again. He took off his jacket and leaned against the back of the couch. He looked at Gloria.

"Do you want to talk about it?" she asked.

"No." Head spinning from the whiskey, he pulled her to him and pressed his mouth to hers. She kissed him back and began to unbutton his shirt.

"Hey, big boy, let me help you forget about it," she purred, unfastening his belt and then his pants. She hiked up her skirt and straddled him. He lay back and pulled her on top of him, pulling off her suit jacket and unzipping her skirt. Soon they were down to bare skin and lost in each other. He sank, then resurfaced over and over in waves of pleasure as she rode him hard, growing wilder with each thrust. Their bodies undulated in their own choreography until they were both spent and Harry had passed out. They slept that way for hours, long past when darkness fell outside and the building emptied. At some point Gloria pulled the afghan over them and tucked the couch pillows under their heads. They lay there that way, still as stones, as the blackness outside deepened.

Chapter 23

$\mathcal{A}$nnie didn't usually go to Harry's office, but this evening she made an exception. She had seen him briefly that morning, rushing, red-faced, and ignoring her. In his hurry, he had spilled the entire contents of his briefcase on the floor, cursed and growled as he grabbed folders and ran out. She had lifted her eyes from her plate and kept her distance as he zoomed past.

When she came into the kitchen to warm up leftovers for dinner that night, her foot slid on something on the floor. She leaned over and saw a file under the table. She hesitated to look inside but wondered if it was important. The file was labeled "Parkwood Case Final Strategy." She shrugged, then ate her dinner. But the file buzzed at her like a mosquito and wouldn't leave her alone. When she finished eating, she dialed his office. By now it was 8 p.m. so she wasn't surprised there was no answer. She left a message about the file left at home. Sipping a glass of white wine, she felt that mosquito buzzing more. So she dialed his cell phone. Still no answer. She left a similar message.

At 8:30 p.m. she decided to take the file over there. He and Gloria were undoubtedly working on their strategy for the next day and too engrossed to answer any phones. This file could be crucial. She had no idea. He hadn't told her anything about the progress of the case. And she sure didn't want to see what Harry would be like if he lost the case. She shuddered to think. Then she remembered. The building was locked after hours and admittance was only obtained by swiping a special card. Which she didn't have. She went into Harry's study and rooted around in the middle drawer of the desk. She remembered long ago Harry had told her he kept an extra swipe card there. Under many layers of papers, her fingers felt something slick. She lifted the papers and there it was—the extra swipe card. She put it in her pocket and headed out with the file.

As she drove toward his office, butterflies began to rise up inside her stomach. She exhaled forcefully to blow them off, but they remained. She had only been to his office a time or two and only when he had invited her for some social occasion. *What am I doing? Invading his sacred space? Surely it's against the rules. Maybe I should just go home.* She shook her head, and the butterflies quieted a bit. There was an errand she wanted to do near his office. The Walgreen's a block over had the best journals in just the right size and she needed one. She drove on.

At Walgreen's she walked slowly through the aisles, her stomach tightening. She got the journal. Turquoise leather—probably fake leather—with a ribbon to hold the place and a magnet tab to close it. She could go home and curl up with it and write. She tossed it in the back seat and sat a moment, feeling oddly intimidated. What was the worst thing that could happen? He'd be annoyed and bark that he didn't need the file. She gave herself a nudge and soon pulled into the parking lot of Harry's office. Using the swipe card was new to her. She stood in front of the outside door a moment, casting her eyes about. There it was, on the wall to the left of the door. She swiped it one way. Nothing. Then she turned it over and swiped it the other way. There was a loud click. She pushed on the door handle, and it easily swung open. Stepping into the first floor, as always she felt stunned by the opulence of wall to ceiling windows, large planters with palm trees swaying against the ceiling, shiny marble floor tiles. The elevator opened the moment she touched the button. Stepping inside, she pressed the number for Harry's floor. As it swooshed up, the butterflies started up again. *Well, I tried to call,* she thought, *I'm just being a good wife.*

The elevator doors opened. Harry's firm had the whole floor. She walked down to his office and saw the door was a tiny bit ajar. She stood a moment listening for voices, but there were none. She tapped the door, and it swung open without a sound. She stood still as stone as she saw what lay before her on his couch. A tangle of arms and legs barely covered by an afghan, frozen. The only movement was bellows rising and falling as two figures breathed. Her heart thudded inside her, and her breath stopped. Perspiration burst from her pores, and nausea rose up inside her. She dropped the file and ran down the hall to the bathroom, barely making it to the toilet before retching again and again, vomiting every last bit of her dinner. She staggered to the sink, wet a paper towel and wiped her mouth. Then, leaning against the walls, she walked back down the hall. Something made her pause a moment in Harry's doorway. Yes, that is what she had seen. She took out her cell phone and snapped a photo, then proceeded to the elevator and pressed the down button. She sat in her car trembling for long enough to reassure herself that she could drive. She called Amanda Murphy's office and left a message for the next available appointment. Then she called Claire and told her she was on her way. Claire had a cup of tea and a bear hug waiting for her.

Amanda unlocked the door to her office waiting room and stepped inside. It was 9 p.m. Wednesday evening. She had just come from the gym, her black t-shirt and black leggings glued to her body with sweat. She couldn't wait to get home and into the shower. But she was thirsty and she had lost her water bottle. Again. She cast her eyes around looking for it. She found it in her office, shook her head, picked it up from the floor beside her chair and emptied half of what was left down her throat. Then she saw a red blinking light on her desk phone. She sat down and dialed into her voice mail where she heard a familiar voice. Annie Thomas, her words clipped and her voice tense, asking for the next available appointment for her and Harry. Automatically, Amanda pulled their file from the drawer in her desk. She hadn't seen them in a while and hoped their usual time of 6 p.m. Thursday was open. It was. She dialed their home number, but no one answered. Something in the tone of Annie's voice made her hesitate to leave a message. She then saw on her Caller ID that Annie had called from her cell phone number. Dialing it, she heard it ring three times.

"Hello?" said Annie.

"Hello, Annie, this is Amanda Murphy. I just got your message. It sounded urgent."

"Oh, thank goodness."

"I can see you all at 6 p.m. tomorrow." Annie didn't speak but

Amanda could hear her choke up and begin crying. "Ooooo," hummed Amanda, "must not be good. Want to talk about it?"

"I found Harry . . ." She began sobbing. "I'm scared . . ."

"Has Harry hurt you?"

"No, not physically, but I'm scared to talk to him without you there."

"Will you be safe until we can meet?" Her mind flashed on other clients, other situations when she had forgotten to ask these questions and regretted it later.

"Yes, I'm at Claire's house tonight. I won't see him until we see you tomorrow. I'll be safe until then," she snuffled.

"Good. Anything else you want to say before we meet?"

She began to cry again, then pulled herself together. "I guess not."

"Okay, tomorrow will be here before you know it. Take care, Annie, and at 6 p.m. tomorrow you all can tell me all about it."

Chapter 24

$\mathcal{H}$arry didn't open his eyes until awakened by the light of the rising sun through the wall of windows. As he untangled himself from the afghan and sat up, he felt a bolt of lightning crack his head. He bent over, clutching his forehead. He had never felt such pain. Then he remembered the lost case, the bourbon, and the bodies. Feeling around, he found he was alone. His lids grew heavy and pulled him back down. A moment or an hour later, snoring woke him up. His own snoring. A dense fog slipped slowly from his mind and, as it did, his headache returned with a vengeance. Hand to his head, he looked up to see Gloria dressed and handing him a cup of coffee, thick with creamer and sugar, and two aspirin. He sat up.

"Here, take these, big guy."

"Where did you get these?" He downed half the coffee and all the aspirin in one gulp.

"No one's here this early so I went down to the lounge and made a pot, figured we'd need at least one. Found aspirin there too." She smiled broadly as she caressed him with her eyes. "Looking good, boss."

It wasn't until then that he realized he was naked. He scanned around him for his boxers, trousers, and shirt. While he pulled them on, Gloria stood and watched while she sipped her own coffee. She

189

picked up a file from the floor and put it on the coffee table in front of Harry. His eyes swam into focus as he saw what it was. He passed his gaze around the room and to the door, now closed, as a scene materialized inside his imagination. Annie standing in the doorway, seeing him, seeing them, seeing everything.

"Shit," he said. He shook his head. "It couldn't be." He turned to Gloria. "Where did you find this?"

"On the floor inside the doorway. The door was open when I went to make coffee."

"Oh, fuck." He saw himself standing before the judge, head hung low. When he raised his head, the judge was Annie, her dark eyes shooting bullets at him, pointing her finger. "Oh, fuck."

"Yes, we did," said Gloria, stroking his hair as she stood next to him.

He could barely get her in focus when he put his eyes to her face. "Gloria. What the hell time is it?"

"Six thirty."

He stood up, smoothed his rumpled clothes with his hands, when his nose caught a whiff of her scent. Remembering more now, he turned his eyes to her. She raised her gaze and smiled. He grabbed her around the waist and pulled her close. "God, what a wild woman you are." He felt his body respond. He pressed her tight against him as his tongue went inside her mouth. She slid her arms around his neck, her fingers into his hair, as she kissed him back. Then the lightning bolt hit again, and he pulled his head back. "Oh my god, what a hangover!" He stepped back, running his hands down her back and squeezing her buns. They heard the elevator door open and footsteps down the hall. He stepped back and dropped his arms.

"The peasants are arriving," she said. "But I'll take a rain check, big guy. Not sure we want anyone else around here to know anything just yet."

"Hell, no." He grinned at her and tapped the tip of her nose with his finger. Then he frowned. "We lost the case, didn't we?"

"Yes, I'm afraid so. But remember, there will be others."

"God, there had better be, or I'm ruined." He shook his head and gazed out the window.

"You're not ruined. I'll help you." She laid her hand on his arm and smiled.

"You were a big help." He stroked her cheek with his fingers. "Especially afterwards."

"Partners with benefits," she said.

He gave her a long look. "If we can win the next big case, you just might make partner. But now I have to ask, how can your clothes look like you just got them out of the closet?"

"Permanent press," she said, laughing.

He saw his reflection in the full-sized mirror on the back of the door. "My clothes look like I slept in them. And I know I didn't." He turned his eyes to her and blew her a kiss. "I'd better go home and change before everyone gets here." *And what the hell am I going to tell Annie?* He felt his stomach knot and his head throb as he walked towards the door. Before he opened it, he turned towards her. "I'll be back."

"See you later, Boss."

He trudged down the hall to face whatever came next. He'd had his dance and now he would have to pay the piper.

Chapter 25

*W*hen he drove into the driveway, he felt relieved to see Annie's car was gone. Inside, he checked the clock on the stove and saw it was nearly 7:00. Then he noticed the blinking red light on the answer machine indicating a voice mail. He hit play and was surprised to hear Annie's voice, icy and tense.

"Harry, we have an appointment with Amanda Murphy at 6 p.m. Thursday night. Let me know if you can't make it. Otherwise, I'll see you there."

A funeral march played inside his throbbing head. *What does she know? What had she seen?* His stomach growled, and he realized he was starving. He filled a bowl with Cheerios and milk and sat at the table, shoveling it in. Then he put two slices of raisin bread in the toaster oven and looked around for coffee. The pot was empty. *How strange, it's like she hasn't been here.* He brewed a fresh pot, buttered the raisin bread toast and ate. Upstairs, he decided he'd better shower and get Gloria's scent off him. *Plausible deniability. Maybe she didn't see anything. Maybe he had dropped the file in the doorway in his stupor after court. It could be.* He paused in the bedroom to check his cell phone and saw he had a message from the night before. He listened, drawing his lips into a firm line. Shaking his head, he cursed and sighed. *Oh, Annie, what a good wife you are.* He undressed, feeling resignation fill his pores, and walked into the shower with his head hung low. As the warm water relaxed him, he began arguing his defense in his mind. *Maybe Annie is just sick of me being gone with this case and wants to chew me out in front of Amanda Murphy. Maybe it will be okay.* He stepped out of the shower and grabbed a big towel as another voice inside him punctured his fantasy. *You are really screwed now, buddy, and you know it.*

Yes, I am in deep shit, he answered, rubbing the towel over his chest and legs. Then, drying his genitals, he smiled to himself. *Then I'll just have to let Gloria comfort me again.* In the bedroom, he picked a gray summer suit with a light blue shirt and navy tie. He stood before the mirror as he tied his tie. *For such a bad day in court and a wild night, you look pretty good, Harry,* he thought. Then he headed out the door.

Amanda opened her office door and saw Annie in her waiting room alone. One leg was jiggling up and down as she stared at a magazine Amanda could tell she wasn't reading. Amanda stepped softly over to where she was sitting and put a hand on her shoulder. Annie lifted her head from her magazine. Amanda could see her eyes were red and puffy. She smiled in hopes to calm and welcome her.

"Is Harry coming?"

"I really don't know. He should know about it. I haven't seen him or talked to him." She looked at Amanda as tears began to fill her eyes. "I left him a voice mail."

"I'm glad you're here. I haven't seen you guys in a while."

Amanda draped her arm over Annie's shoulders as they walked into her office. Then to Natalie, "When Harry gets here, let me know." Natalie nodded, and Amanda closed the door.

Annie sat down, pulled a tissue from the box on the end table, and dabbed her eyes. Amanda sat and waited, her hands in her lap. Annie studied her own hands, shook her head, then raised her head to Amanda and opened her mouth. "Harry . . . I saw . . ." then she was crying again and couldn't talk.

Just then her intercom buzzed. Amanda opened the door and there stood Harry. Taking in the scene before him, he visibly stiffened and remained standing.

"Hello, Harry," said Amanda. "We just sat down. Please join us." She smiled and waved towards the other chair. Harry sat and gripped the arms of the chair. "Do you want to begin, Annie?"

Annie looked at Harry, then at Amanda.

"I lost my case," said Harry to no one.

Annie startled and turned her head towards him. "You lost your case, your big case?"

"Yes," said Harry, staring straight ahead.

"Is that why you haven't been in lately?" asked Amanda.

"Yes, I've been working night and day for weeks. I was sure we would win. We went to court Monday three weeks ago and by Wednesday night it was over. We lost." He hung his head.

Looking pitiful, thought Amanda. *A bit too pitiful.* She watched Annie closely. *Obviously, this was news to her. Yet Annie was not responding much to this news. Something else must have happened.*

"How disappointing," said Amanda to Harry. Then to Annie, "Is this the first you're hearing this?"

Annie nodded her head, her eyes wide. The rest of her still as stone.

"What were you about to tell me just before Harry arrived?" she asked Annie. Amanda felt Harry stiffen. *Ah, he knows, and now I have two frozen statues.* She turned to Annie, tilted her head, and waited. Tears began to well up again in Annie's eyes. "Take your time," said Amanda.

That seemed to pull out the cork, and it all came tumbling out. "I saw him last night—with Gloria all tangled up together on the couch naked. There was a bottle. They were asleep or passed out or something." As she poured it all out, Amanda saw the pain and anguish and finally the anger. Annie looked hard at Harry. "You lied to me! You are fucking her, aren't you?"

Harry exploded to his feet, fists clinched. "No no no no!" a rising crescendo. Harry took a step towards Annie, his fists raised. Annie shrunk back instinctively. In a flash, Amanda had her hand on his arm.

"Harry, let's go for a walk," said Amanda. She took his elbow and moved him towards the door. He turned to her, stunned. "I feel like going for a walk. Let's walk." She led him out the door, and he went with her, through the waiting room, out the door and under a nearby grove of pine trees.

Outside, Amanda spoke in soft soothing tones to Harry. "Take a few deep breaths, Harry. I know you're upset, but you need to calm down."

Harry walked like a ghost, murmuring over and over, "I didn't do it, I'm innocent." After about ten minutes, Amanda led him back inside.

Annie sat still as Harry took his seat again. To both of them, Amanda said, "This is very difficult to talk about. We will use the dialogue. If you have difficulty talking to each other, talk to me and I'll mirror you." To Harry: "I want you to share your point of view, Harry, but you must contain your reactivity. Do you think you can do that?"

Harry reddened. "I'll try. But I'm innocent, I didn't do it!" he said, raising his voice.

Amanda rolled her chair forward and touched her hand to his arm. "Take a deep breath, please." He closed his eyes and inhaled deeply. Then she turned to Annie, concerned to see she looked about ready to explode herself. Annie had her cell phone in her hand, pointing the screen towards Harry. "You liar! I took a picture, see!"

Harry looked hard at the phone. Then he leaped to his feet, knocked the phone out of Annie's hand and screamed a wail to raise the dead. "You spied on me!" He stomped out and slammed the door. This time Amanda let him go. They heard the outside door open and slam. Amanda turned to Annie to find her on her knees retrieving the cell phone from the corner. Annie sat back down and got the picture open again. This time she held it up to Amanda. Amanda scooted her chair close enough to get a good look, then pressed her lips together and shook her head.

"He did do it," whispered Annie.

Amanda could only nod. "Yes, he did."

They both sat in silence for a few moments. Amanda doubted Harry would return. Men like Harry seemed to live in a place of grandiosity as a defense against where he surely was now. Toxic shame. Losing his case must have been a huge narcissistic wound.

Whether or not he and Gloria had been involved earlier Amanda didn't know for certain, but they certainly were now. She wondered how being caught on camera would affect his fragile state of mind. Could he decompensate? She wasn't sure.

She broke her reverie and turned towards the other half of this duo. Annie had her head bowed over the cell phone. When she felt the soft breeze of Amanda's attention, she looked up. "What do I do now?"

"First, tell me how you're doing."

"I don't know. He really scared me. I'm glad he's gone."

"Yes. Frankly, if you both hadn't been able to calm down, I would have had to do something, talk to you separately, end the session." She took a deep breath. "But he left, and you're here so let's talk about you."

Tears ran down her cheeks. "The past few weeks, he has been so consumed with work. So tense. If I asked anything of him, even help with the smallest chore, he'd blow up." Her eyes glazed over as she played scenes on the screen of her mind. "I've been getting more and more scared of him."

"That does sound difficult. And a scary way to live. How have you stayed safe?"

"I avoided him." She looked up at Amanda. "He has seemed like a caged animal ready to attack at the slightest thing. I just tried to stay out of the line of fire. But he wasn't home much so that wasn't very hard. I've been lonely, but that's what I've felt in this marriage for a while. Lonely." She took a deep breath and exhaled a long sigh. She turned to her hands in her lap and the twisted tissue they held. Amanda saw something shift in her demeanor. Annie lifted her eyes.

"I think it's over now. Maybe it's been over, but now it really is over. This is a deal breaker for me."

Amanda nodded. "That makes perfect sense. Tell me more."

"I spent the night with my friend Claire last night—she's in my poetry group. She told me I could come back tonight if I wanted. I want to go home, but I'm scared."

"Safety first. Has Harry hit you or been violent lately?"

Annie shook her head. "Not really. There have been plenty of times he almost did or I thought he would. Mostly he just yells." She paused. "But I've never seen him like this. I don't know."

"Where would you feel safe tonight?" Amanda reviewed a list in her mind. If he did decompensate, he could become dangerously out of control. Just the sight of Annie could trigger him to violence.

Annie sat a few moments thinking. "I have to teach tomorrow, so I have to get my materials. But if Harry's car is at home, I think I'll go straight to Claire's. "

"Sounds good."

"If I figure out there are materials I need, I will ask Claire to go home with me."

"Also good." Amanda uncrossed her legs and set her feet next to each other on the rug. "I don't know if Harry will calm down and decide to return to therapy, but you are certainly welcome to continue with me individually."

"Oh yes, thank you, what a relief. I know I'm going to need help to get through whatever comes next." Annie sighed and let her shoulders drop.

"Is there more?"

Annie thought for a minute. "Well, that takes care of tonight. I wonder if I need to consult a lawyer soon?"

"That might be a good idea. Do you know any other lawyers?"

"Other than Harry and his partners? No, I've never needed one before." Annie gave a big sigh. "And of course Harry is a lawyer, so I don't know what that will mean."

"I would guess it means you'd better get an experienced lawyer who can handle anything. My husband is a lawyer. I could double check with him to recommend the best one for you in these circumstances."

"That would be wonderful, thank you."

"Anything else you want to discuss tonight?"

"I don't think so."

"Do you want to come at this time next week?"

"Yes, although I could come earlier if you have something open. I'm teaching summer school but could get here by 3 p.m. or 4 p.m."

Amanda checked her calendar. "I see I have 3 p.m. open. Want to come then?"

"Yes, thank you."

"Well, see you next week." Amanda stood as did Annie. They paused, then Amanda opened her arms, and Annie came into them for a long hug. When Annie finally let go, Amanda kept her hands on Annie's arms and smiled at her. "You'll get through this."

Annie eyes welled up. "I hope so."

"And I'll help you," said Amanda.

"Thank God," said Annie, standing just a bit taller.

Chapter 26

When Annie got home that night, the house was dark and Harry's car was missing. Inside she paced the rooms looking for signs of whether he'd been there at all as she tried to decide what to do. Perspiration gathered under her arms. She brushed a stray wisp of hair off her face with her fingers as she checked kitchen, living room, study and paused to listen for any sounds of him from upstairs. None. She longed for the comfort of home, to sleep in her own bed and wake to her own kitchen, but she trembled at the thought of encountering Harry. She had never thought he would be unfaithful. She had never seen him as angry as she had in Amanda's office. Who was this man? She wondered what he was capable of.

She sat on the couch and smoothed her long white skirt into a flat place. She opened the bag with the burger she'd gotten on her way home. The burger was still warm and, surprisingly, smelled of the backyard cookouts of her childhood. With her first bite, ketchup oozed onto her lips. She wiped the corner of her mouth with the brown paper napkin provided. As she ate, she thought back to her early years with Harry. He had certainly been the strong, silent type. When they were first married, she was surprised at his long silences over meals, his aloofness outside the bedroom. Then her mother died and her father remarried so quickly and moved far away and all she remembered about that time was her fog of grief. He had been her rock. But always a silent rock. Maybe she didn't know him.

When she finished her burger, she put the wrapping back in the bag and crumpled it up. As she sat, she realized how tired she felt. Her muscles turned to lead, her eyelids began to droop. She wondered if she could even make it upstairs to bed. But she did and even got her teeth brushed. She decided to sleep in her writing room just in case Harry came home. To feel safe, she locked the door. She was asleep before she could even open a book.

After Harry left Amanda's office, he roared off in his black BMW, got on the interstate and was in the next county before the roar inside his mind subsided at all. He clenched his teeth as his hands gripped the steering wheel. His tie felt like a noose around his neck. He swerved as he took one hand off the wheel and grabbed the knot in his tie to loosen it. Returning his hand to the wheel, he sighed a deep sigh and straightened the car into the middle of the right lane. Then he realized he was starving and pulled off at the next exit, following the sign for Libby Hill Seafood. He'd never been there, but it looked good enough to fill the hole inside him. The number of truckers in the parking lot was a good advertisement. He pulled into an empty parking spot in the front row. A smiling waitress led him to a booth in the back. He ordered the fried seafood platter and practically inhaled it along with a gallon of sweet tea. He sure could've used a scotch but didn't even see beer on the menu here.

As he chewed, he thought back over the past few days. How

things change. Three weeks ago Monday he thought he was going to win and become this company's personal attorney with many more lucrative cases in his future and Wednesday he had lost the case and rung a death knell on his marriage by fucking Gloria. But despite his regrets, when he thought of Gloria, he felt his desire rise and his body respond. He gripped his fork, speared a long hush puppy and put it in his mouth. He was just glad Gloria wasn't here now or he could do it again. *God, is she ever hot!* With his fingers, he dipped a small French fry in the last of the tartar sauce and sucked it into his mouth. She knew just what he needed after that crushing defeat. And maybe she was what he needed now. She was more into the lifestyle he wanted than Annie would ever be. And Annie would *never* forgive him. He was certain. And she took a picture! He shook his head, incredulous.

He pictured them in court, getting a divorce, her showing that picture as evidence. His face turned red. Now he wished he had looked at the picture more closely to see if he could even be identified. He'd better get prepared for battle. He washed the last bite of flounder down with half a glass of their incredible sweet tea. He'd have to come here again. Maybe bring Gloria. He set his glass down and smiled. His father had been too stupid to divorce his drunken mother. He knew his dad had had something going with his secretary at work who put up with never being more than the office wife. He was smarter than that. He pressed his lips together. He knew Gloria would never accept being just his mistress. He paid his check and headed out, turning his car back towards his office. Then he felt vibrations in his shirt pocket just over his heart. Was he having palpitations again? He stopped the car in a parking space next to the restaurant exit. Ah, of course, his cell phone. He pulled it out and checked the number. He sure didn't want to talk to Annie right now. But it was another number, a familiar one. He smiled.

"Hello?"

"Hey, big boy, how's it going?"

"Not so great."

"Oh? What happened?"

"Annie knows about us. And, if you can believe this, she took a damn photo!"

"A photo?"

"Yes, you know. Of us. Together." His heart rate accelerated and skipped a beat. *Oh my God, maybe I do have heart disease . . . like my father!* He wiped his damp hands on his trousers and nearly disconnected their call before he got the phone back to his ear.

"Hello? Harry, are you there?" Gloria asked. "You got quiet all of a sudden. You aren't driving are you?"

"No, no, I'm in the car but parked. I'm fine." He took a deep breath. "It's just been a hell of a day."

"I get that. I just wondered if you need a stiff drink, maybe a scotch?" Then she purred: "Come over and I'll take your mind off your troubles."

He chuckled. "Are you a mind reader? That's exactly what I need." He felt his heartbeat ease into a smooth rhythm. "What's your address?"

"Pinewood Estates, number 25."

"I'll be right there." He smiled and felt his pulse quicken in a good way as he pointed the car towards the highway and accelerated.

Annie woke with a start the next morning, realizing she had to teach and was not ready. The clock by the narrow bed showed 5:30. Just about enough time. Her right foot hung off the bed, her left was tangled in the sheet and blanket. It took her a moment to untangle herself and come fully awake. *Where is Harry?* The question pierced her like a knife. She got up, threw her long silk robe over her pale pink gown, and checked the master bedroom. No sign of occupancy. She breathed a sigh of relief and yet still felt nervous. Where did Harry spend the night? She could guess. Then she went to the bathroom to take a quick shower. She couldn't think about him now, she had kids to teach. Soon she was in one of her crisp teaching dresses—no cleavage, knees covered, with the slight fragrance of laundry soap— and was spreading papers over the kitchen table with a cup of freshly brewed coffee in her hand. Summer school was just one class but it went all morning. By 7 a.m. she had found the materials she needed and gotten her final preparation for her lesson clear in her mind. Class started at 8 a.m. so she had time for at least a bowl of cereal. By 7:30 she was in the car and on her way.

At exactly 7:55 a.m., Harry pulled into the driveway. He saw he had timed it perfectly. He took his time at home, hung his rumpled suit in the closet and changed into casual khakis and an orange short-sleeve pull-over knit shirt. He lingered a moment in front of the bathroom mirror, combed his hair and added just a touch of gel.

Looking good, Harry, he told himself. He packed a suitcase, and wrote a note to Annie explaining he had a legal conference next week and would be flying out that day. He didn't tell her that he and Gloria had decided to take a trip to Antigua. It was sort of a legal conference, he reasoned. Gloria was also a lawyer, and they were certainly going to confer. She seemed to like to talk law just as much as he did and had some ideas for their work together that could indeed turn out to be quite profitable. He was very interested in those ideas. She had suggested they go somewhere for a week to recover from this last defeat and relax, as if she had forgotten he was married. In truth, he wasn't sure he still was married, or would be for long. He could avoid Annie for a while but not forever. With some chagrin, he had remembered the time-share week he had thought he would surprise Annie with. He doubted he would ever go there with Annie, but a week in Antigua now with Gloria was just what the doctor ordered. He left the note propped against the salt shaker on the kitchen table and headed out. He also planned to ask Dennis Stacey, the top-notch family lawyer in his firm, to represent him in the inevitable divorce proceedings. Dennis was a bulldog and just what Harry imagined he needed to keep that picture from being shown. He had to protect his reputation.

When Annie got home from school and set her things down on the kitchen table, she saw the flashing red light on the phone indicating a voice mail. Soon she heard a familiar voice: "Hi Annie, Amanda here. I asked my husband to recommend an attorney in a divorce from an attorney. He recommended Jan Stone, says she's experienced and tough when needed. Good luck and see you next week." Annie grabbed the pencil by the phone and wrote the name down. She considered calling right then but then saw an envelope leaning against the salt shaker on the kitchen table with her name on it. In Harry's handwriting. Her heart began to beat faster and her fingers trembled as she stood and picked it up. When did he leave it? She had no idea but it had to be while she was at school. She opened the envelope and pulled out the paper inside.

"Annie—I have a legal conference next week followed by a golf tournament. I'm leaving today and will be gone ten days. Harry"

A legal conference? A golf tournament? She read the note again. It didn't say where. Usually he told her where and gave the hotel he would be staying in. And the one he usually went to she thought was usually in October. And this was the July 4 holiday week. She pressed her lips together. How convenient. She set the note down and sat a minute, drumming her fingers on the table.

Then she looked up Jan Stone's phone number and dialed. "Hello, Jan Stone's office, Mary speaking. How may I help you?"

"I'd like to make an appointment as soon as possible," said Annie. She wasn't sure how much to say but she added: "I am newly separated and facing divorce." She figured she was almost separated, at least for the next ten days.

"Oh, I'm sorry," said Mary. "Let me see, is Monday at 4 p.m. soon enough?"

"Oh, yes, thank you!" Annie exhaled. She couldn't believe she didn't have to wait two weeks. Mary took down her name and other information.

"Okay, we'll see you then."

Annie hung up the phone and sat still. Her heart beat loud enough she thought the neighbors could hear. Butterflies bounced around inside her stomach. *So it's really happening. A lawyer, separation, divorce. It's come to this.*

When the phone rang, Annie jumped. It rang three times before she could calm her trembling hand enough to pick up the receiver.

"Hello?"

"Annie! Oh my god, how are you? I haven't heard a word since you left my house yesterday morning. Are you okay?"

"Oh, Claire, I'm so sorry. I was so exhausted last night I fell asleep before I could think to call you. I'm okay."

"And your session?"

"Harry stormed out. Now he's left town for ten days for a legal conference."

"A legal conference?" Claire sneered and snorted through the phone. "With Gloria?"

"I have no idea, he didn't say. But I have an appointment with a lawyer for Monday. It seems like the next step."

"And you're right about that. How lucky to get an appointment so soon."

"Yes, I guess so."

"I know so! And what are you doing tonight? Come over and have dinner with me and you can tell me all about it."

"Oh, Claire, that would be wonderful. What time?"

"Anytime, honey. We'll eat at 6 p.m., but come anytime."

"I'll be over as soon as I can."

"Sounds great. See you then."

Annie hung up and smiled. Claire was such a godsend. She really had no one else to turn to. Her father had virtually disappeared from her life once he married Hilda and moved to Arizona. A wave of sadness washed over her as she remembered. She propped her elbows on the table and rested her chin in her hands. She shook her head and sighed. She figured she had Harry and he was her family. She laughed. What a joke. After her fog of grief had lifted, she had looked around for Harry but found a large log. She had tried to light a fire with him again but she failed. Apparently, she wasn't enough kindling to get the log burning and there was no way to crack it open. She even wrote a poem about it.

She went upstairs to her writing room and riffled through her notebooks. She finally found it and many others, chronicling the story of a relationship. She sat at her desk and read, starting with one entitled "Trying."

Trying to keep the fire going,
I stuff branches and twigs
under this large log
again and again yet it's almost out.
This log will not catch the gold
flames thrown by these eager sticks.
They dance around him,
lick him on all sides
while he just lies there.
What more does he want?
The spark sleeps inside him.

She looked at the date she had written this poem. It was a year and half after their wedding, a year after her mother had died, when she was coming back to life again. A lifetime ago. She flipped through the pages and kept reading, marveling at her verse. It was all here, her love, her loss, her disappointment, her hurt, her persistence. Then she was surprised to find the one she'd written just a few months ago. It had the same image. She had written this poem sometime after she had given up trying to reach Harry, after she had started the poetry seminar, after that creative spark had been lit inside her. She had entitled it "Light Your Fire."

Such a large log,
hard to ignite,
lies stubborn on
the metal grate
inside the fireplace.
The flammable pulp
waits soft inside
the many layers of hardwood,
a ring for each pain
inflicted as you grew.
Kindling flames, I
dance around you,
lick, tickle, slap, probe,
searching for a tiny crack
to enter and to light.

She touched her lips with her fingers, thinking back. Images from the last five years flashed across her mind. She saw their courtship, wedding, her mother's funeral, her father's quick marriage and departure, her grief that pulled her under for what felt like such a long time, her reawakening to life again, to find Harry preoccupied and emotionally distant. And now this. She looked at the clock, surprised at how much time had gone by. She knew what she was going to do this weekend. She was going to find and read all the poems she had written during her marriage to Harry, let them help her reflect back. She had journals she could reread as well. She wanted to understand how she had fallen so in love with him and how it had come to this—consulting a therapist and a lawyer. Tonight she'd visit with Claire. Then she'd be back with all her questions and her poems to partake of their nourishment and hopefully find some answers and maybe some wisdom. She closed her notebooks and stood up.

Chapter 27

$\mathcal{A}$ small bungalow stood before her, simple but well-tended. Huge oaks surrounded and shaded it. A front porch with rocking chairs and hanging baskets of petunias of all colors brought to mind her college summers singing along with guitar and banjo while sipping beer, teaching herself to like it when she really preferred fresh-squeezed lemonade. The house was painted bright yellow with black shutters. You couldn't miss it. It had five steps leading from the sidewalk onto the porch. Above the steps hung a simple wooden sign that read, "Jan Stone, Counselor at Law." This neighborhood was a few blocks from the center of town and stood as a contrast to the new mixed-use development springing up near the university. Annie imagined this house had once housed students or even professors. Her heart beat hard against her ribs as she stepped inside to find Mary, the woman she had spoken to on the phone, behind a desk to the left.

Mary had long, straight black hair parted in the middle and tucked behind her ears. She wore a long flowing dress of green and turquoise. Large hoop earrings made her look like a gypsy or fortune teller. Her wide smile made Annie feel a tiny bit less nervous.

Mary waved Annie across a small hall into an open room with a couch and several stuffed chairs. End tables full of magazines flanked the couch. She was surprised how calm she now felt. Her visit with

Claire Friday night had felt like being wrapped in a soft blanket. Her weekend rereading her journals and poetry had been even more valuable. It grounded her to her present reality. She saw signs she had missed, recorded in her journals and poems but ignored. The first eruption of his temper, the endless withdrawals and refusals to talk things out, his tendency to work long hours even on weekends. She suspected her grief over her mother's death had blinded her as well as her desire to fulfill her marriage vows. She picked up a copy of *The Sun Magazine* and began thumbing through it. She liked this magazine but hadn't taken time to read it often. She especially liked the Viktor Frankl quotation under the name: *What is to give light must endure burning.* She hoped she could find a way to her own light. Right now she felt pretty burned.

A tall, athletic woman with short dark hair in a gray pantsuit stood before her with her right hand extended. Annie stood and shook her hand, looking into sky blue eyes in a face with just enough lines to reassure Annie that she was a seasoned professional. "Come with me." Jan Stone led her down the hall into a room lined with bookshelves filled with all sorts of books, not just law books, with a long conference table that filled the room. Jan sat at the head of the table and motioned to the nearest chair for Annie. Annie sat, realizing she had been stunned to silence by this woman's presence. Jan Stone exuded strength and intelligence and something more. Power.

Annie felt in awe.

Jan opened her pen and rested her arm near her pad of legal paper. "So tell me your story and how I might help you."

Annie cleared her throat and began, feeling tears gather in her eyes. "I went by my husband's office to bring him a file he'd left at home." She began to choke with her tears and found herself unable to talk. Instead, she opened her phone to the picture she had taken and held it up to Jan.

Jan leaned forward to look. She took the phone from Annie, pushed a box of Kleenex towards her, and examined the picture closely. "Do you know who this woman is?"

Dabbing her eyes with a Kleenex, Annie nodded. "Gloria Benjamin, another lawyer in his firm. I had suspected something was going on—I had even seen them together in a restaurant—but he had said they were just working late on their case. The case they just lost apparently."

"And you're now separated and contemplating legal separation and divorce?"

"He has gone away for ten days to a legal conference, but he hasn't moved out."

"Has he agreed to move out?"

"No."

"First let me get a bit of information from you, such as how long you've been married, when and where you married, and all that." Jan lifted her pen over her pad.

So Annie told her the story, pouring it out in much more detail than she had expected. Jan sat still and calm, her warm blue eyes hardly leaving Annie's face. Jan listened without asking questions. She let Annie tell it her way, only making a few notes, which somehow she did without seeming to look down.

When Annie finished, Jan shook her head. "The bastard," she whispered. Then she tilted her head. "I know this is hard on you, but how are you doing?"

She shifted in her chair and drew herself up straighter. "As well as I can be under the circumstances." She reflected on the new insights she had gotten over the weekend. "I think our marriage has been getting worse for a long time. I never thought it would come to this and I really don't know what I need to do next. I'm hoping you can guide me."

"That's what I'm here for." Jan nodded and smiled. "How long until he gets back?"

"His note said ten days so I'm guessing a week from today."

"Here's what we can do. I will file a decree for 'divorce from bed and board.' Since he has committed adultery, the law considers him at fault. Once a judge approves this decree, you and he are legally separated, and he must live elsewhere. The sheriff will deliver notice to him at his workplace. Get a locksmith to change all the locks on the house while he's gone. If he tries to come home when he returns, do not let him in. If you forgive him or let him stay for just a night, it nulls the decree. Send me a copy of that photo also. How does this sound?"

"You mean it's this simple? Harry is a lawyer. He will be so angry. I am scared what he'll do, especially after seeing him blow up in our session." Annie trembled and clutched her hands on top of the table to stop them from shaking.

"Has he ever hit you?" Jan frowned and held her pen ready to write.

"Not really." Annie closed her eyes briefly and reviewed her memories.

"Not really?" asked Jan, tilting her head.

Annie opened her eyes. "Well, once he grabbed me to try to stop me from leaving. But that was a while ago." She took a deep breath. "But I've never seen him like he was when he stormed out of our session last Thursday. I really don't know what to expect now."

"If he threatens you, we will file a restraining order. Then he can't come near you. Don't worry, I've dealt with men like him before, even lawyers. Open your own bank account. You are legally entitled to take half from any joint accounts and put them in your name. Do you have joint credit cards?"

"Yes, they're all joint."

"Well, call the credit card companies and see if you can get your name off and open a separate account. Separate your finances as much as you can. Same with the utilities or anything else."

"Mortgage?"

"Is it jointly held?"

"Yes."

"Don't worry about that now. I'll file for him to be required to pay the mortgage. Fill out these forms." She handed Annie a stack of paper. "These are financial disclosure forms. I need to know the details of all your assets and liabilities."

Annie smiled and nodded. Jan was taking charge. She felt a warm glow of relief blow over her. Annie had had no clue what she needed to do when she'd stepped into this room. She looked at the stack of paper and saw the top page was a list of all the things Jan had just advised her to do.

"Now if there's any chance he will come home, promise it's over between him and Gloria in such a convincing way that you'll believe him, let me know now and I won't proceed." Jan kept her eyes on Annie and dropped her pen.

Annie burst out laughing and shook her head. "I imagine he and Gloria have gone to this supposed legal conference together. It's over. I now see it. It's over."

"Okay, I will work on this decree tonight and file it in the morning. It should be in effect well before he returns. When you complete the financial disclosure forms, drop them by. I'll examine them and let you know when we need to meet again. Unless you have something else you think I need to know, I think we're done for today."

Then Annie's face fell. "How much do I owe you for today?"

Jan chuckled. "Not a thing. Harry will pay for all your legal fees."

Annie's eyebrows flew up. "Really?"

"Really," said Jan as she stood up. "Don't you worry about a thing."

Annie took a deep breath and exhaled. She extended her right hand. "Thank you so so much."

Jan gripped Annie's hand. She held it a moment and covered it with her other hand. "You'll get through this. And I'll help you." She released Annie's hands and gave her a wide smile. "Believe me, I've dealt with worse situations."

Annie walked out in a daze. She couldn't wait to call Claire.

Chapter 28

*H*arry lifted his scotch to his lips and took a sip. "I wonder how the firm survived without us." He and Gloria were 30,000 feet up in the air on their flight home. Harry felt he was slowly waking up from the hedonistic dream he had been in with her in Antigua. Sun, sand, sex, surf, gourmet food, then strategy sessions about their future rich clients and the buckets of money they would earn. He'd been amazed at Gloria's stamina on all fronts. He really had forgotten about the trauma that had happened before they had left. Until now. His stomach twisted into knots as he thought of Annie and wondered what she would do to him when they finally saw each other and talked. In just a few hours, he imagined. He looked at Gloria and pushed those thoughts away.

"I bet they missed us and have a pile of work waiting for us." She took a sip of her whiskey sour. At his suggestion, they were in first class. He saw by the grin on her face that she loved it. She slipped off her shoe and rubbed her foot against his leg. "Did you check in at all?"

Harry chortled. "When would I have done that? You wouldn't let me get out of bed." He grinned at her.

"Oh, I wouldn't? I thought it was the other way around, big boy." She leaned over and offered him a kiss. They lingered a moment, lips and tongues touching, then sat back.

"Actually, I did check my email once or twice," he said. "Not much happening. Others took the week off too. And, as we agreed, I made sure no one knew we were off together."

"Good. Let's keep this our little secret for now." She winked at him.

"For sure, our little secret." He stroked her hair. "Something delivered for me but I don't know what. I had to sign for it so they sent it back."

"Probably a notice that you won the Publisher's Clearing House sweepstakes."

"I would have had to enter it first."

"Well, I enjoyed the week but I'm ready to get back in the saddle again."

"Yes, you were a great distraction. Do you really have a connection to the Becton Company and do they really want to change attorneys?"

"Yes, I do. Big bucks are coming our way. I could land them if I were made partner." She looked at him with a half smile.

"Oh, you could, eh? Well, you've got my vote." Harry raised her hand to his lips and kissed it.

Just then the captain came on the intercom to say they were approaching their destination. It was nearly noon. He dropped Gloria off at her condo then headed home to drop his suitcase before going to the office.

When he pulled into the driveway, he noticed Annie's car was missing so he figured she had not come home from teaching yet. He drove around back, as he usually did, to enter by the kitchen door.

What a relief that he didn't have to face her quite yet. She was sure to be furious, but, as he thought about it, he realized he had never seen her lose her temper. Not once. But then nothing this bad had ever happened before. Most women would have a big reaction. But sweet Annie? He had no idea what to expect. He pulled out his house key and began to insert it in the lock. Usually it went in easily but not today. He set down his bag and briefcase and tried again. No luck. He shook his head, then looked more closely at the lock. What was different about it? He bent down and brought his head in front of the lock. Then he spied a tiny bit of sawdust on the door sill and it hit him. A new lock. His stomach knotted and his heart started racing. He left his things and ran around to the front door. No luck with it either. Another new lock.

"Damn! What has she done?" Incredulous, he sat down on the front steps. What could he do now? Sit here and wait until Annie returned? But he had no idea how long that would be. If she changed the locks, she might not come back right away for fear of running into him. He felt his temper rise. He smashed his fist into his palm. He sighed. Just then his cell phone rang. "Yes?"

"There's someone here for you. I think you'd better come on over." It was his secretary. "I heard you were back already."

"Who?"

"Gloria told me."

"No, damn it, who is waiting for me?" Harry stomped his foot.

"Somebody from the sheriff's office. He tried to come Friday and said he had to deliver this today."

Harry sighed again, gritting his teeth without realizing it. "I'll be there in ten minutes."

"Don't speed. The sheriff might stop you and give you a ticket."

"Very funny."

He sped down the road and pulled into his office parking lot in 9.5 minutes, then ran to the elevator, which of course was on the top floor so he had to wait for it to descend to the lobby. Then it had to stop four times to let people on and off. He was drenched in sweat when he got to their floor. When he stepped to his receptionist's desk, a uniformed man stood there waiting.

"Are you Harry Thomas?"

"Yes, I am."

"Please sign." He handed the package to Harry and indicated a line on the top sheet. Harry took the pen he offered, signed, ripped off the top copy and gave it to the man who gave a polished smile. "Thank you. Have a nice day," said the man, as he walked off.

Harry opened his office door—at least this key worked—and sat on the couch, dropping his briefcase in the doorway. He ripped open the large manila envelope and began reading. Reading the documents through once, he got up, moved his briefcase, closed the door, and locked it. He read them again. Signed by the judge. Completely legal. He read further, looking for a lawyer's name. Jan Stone. *Jan Stone! That ball-busting man-hating...*he thought of every epithet he could name. *How did Annie find out about Jan Stone? I am doomed now, doomed.* He sat back and stared out the window. Then he kicked the coffee table. *And Jan fucking Stone has probably seen that damn picture Annie took.*

He stood up and began pacing the room. What could he do now? Minimize the damage somehow. He wondered if Dennis Stacy was free right now? Now he needed to hire him—officially—to handle this inevitable divorce. But first he needed a place to stay. He considered going to Gloria's—he'd spent a couple nights there—but that would not look good if he had any hope of disputing the charge of adultery. His reputation was at stake. He sat down at his desk and looked up the name of the real estate agent he had used when buying their house.

He found the agent's cell phone number and dialed. Miraculously, he got him. "Hello, Duncan? Harry Thomas here. No, we're not selling . . . yet. Don't you all handle rentals? I need one today, and a nice one . . . you'll work on it and call me right back? Great! Call my cell. Thanks." He hung up and thought a minute. Jeez, he needed his clothes at least. He rung Dennis's office. It went straight to voice mail. So he decided to walk down the hall and interrupt him.

The door to Dennis's office was ajar so Harry pushed it open. He saw Dennis leaning back in his chair, his socked feet on the desk with his phone held between his ear and his shoulder. When he saw the look on Harry's face, he sat up, put his feet on the floor and said: "I'll do my best to get to at least the last half of his game, honey. I've got to go. See you there. Love you. Bye." Then he hung up. "Have a seat." He waved to the chair in front of his desk.

Harry sat, put his head in his hands briefly, then looked up, took a deep breath, and began. "Dennis, I need your help. Annie has kicked me out. I'm a desperate man. Can you take me on?"

"Oh my god, Harry, I'm so sorry. Tell me what happened." Dennis leaned forward, his brow wrinkled in sympathy.

Harry said nothing but handed him the documents. Dennis read them quickly, his eyes widening, then looked up. "Adultery? Divorce from bed and board? Harry, you have to be totally honest with me.

I'm now the priest and this is confession." Dennis walked around the desk and closed his door, then returned to his chair.

Harry studied the rug beneath his shoes. It had a pattern of waves of different colors, very attractive, very modern. He looked left, he looked right, he crossed his legs, he uncrossed his legs. Dennis watched him and waited, smiling a half-smile. Harry knew Dennis had been doing family law for over twenty years. Undoubtedly, he had seen and heard it all. Harry could not tell him anything that would shock him. He was strict about observing attorney-client privilege and everyone knew it. He was imminently trustworthy. Dennis remained silent. His thoughts whirled inside like a funnel cloud. He wasn't Catholic but somehow this did feel like confession. He feared Dennis's judgment. From what he knew Dennis had a happy marriage. How could he understand?

Harry lifted his head and met Dennis's gaze. He stood on the edge of the cliff and looked down. He saw the rocks below. He'd always liked Dennis. He saw something in his eyes now: kindness. He jumped.

"Annie has been distant for a long time. I guess we've drifted apart. She's been taking a writing class, poetry writing, and spending a lot of time writing. I've been working on that . . ." He couldn't say the words. ". . . that case we just lost." He closed his eyes, feeling for a moment the huge boulder of that defeat crushing him again. He sighed and opened his eyes. Dennis nodded, giving him his full attention. "Gloria was my co-counsel." He looked at Dennis, who continued to listen and wait. "There's a picture. Annie took a picture."

Dennis drew his brows together and tilted his head, asking. He exhaled and dropped his head. He told it all, every last bit until it was all out and he felt like a limp, wet dishrag. With sad puppy eyes, he raised his head in dread to hear Dennis's next words.

"Have you seen the picture?"

Emitting a big sigh of relief, he turned his thoughts to the photo. "I got a quick glance at it in our horrible last counseling session." A jolt of memory shot through him. His face reddened in shame. "It was on Annie's phone. I didn't get to look at it closely." Harry shook his head. "Jan Stone is her attorney. I don't know how Annie found her but she did."

"She's tough." Dennis raked his hand through his tight blond curls. "You know office romantic liaisons are frowned upon by the firm management, don't you?"

"Yes," said Harry, frowning. "I also know it happens. Remember two years ago?"

"I sure do." Dennis shook his head. "I hope you're not as stupid as they were."

"I have no intention of flaunting anything." Irritation flashed inside him, and he felt his temper begin to boil. "Dennis, I need to know: will you help me?" Harry held the shattered pieces of his ego and his pride together just barely.

"Yes, I will help you."

Harry's shoulders lowered visibly. He leaned back against the chair.

"I'll call Jan and make arrangements for you to get your clothes and whatever else you need. For the time being, you'll need to find another place to stay of course." Dennis opened a drawer and pulled out some forms he handed to Harry. "Fill out these financial disclosure forms."

Harry nodded as he grasped them with his sweaty fingers.

"Any chance you and Annie can reconcile? Go to counseling? If you can, I urge you to try. Divorce is messy and not fun."

"Like I said, we went to counseling. It didn't work. I'm not going back."

"Okay, then. Let's sit down first thing tomorrow and plan your defense. We'll see if we can find fault on the other side." Dennis pressed his lips together and squinted.

Harry smiled, and the cogs started turning inside his mind.

Harry's cell phone rang. He checked the number. "It's my real estate agent. See you tomorrow."

Dennis nodded and waved him out.

Chapter 29

*A*nnie sat in the one-person hammock on Claire's screen porch with a glass of fresh-squeezed lemonade in her hand. She pushed her foot on the floor to keep the hammock rocking. Somehow this calmed her nerves. Claire sat on the couch nearby with her own glass of lemonade and a book in her hand. Annie had a book also but she couldn't seem to concentrate on it. Claire had invited her to come over right after school just to hang out and wait in a safe place to see what would happen when Harry got home and found the locks had been changed. This afternoon they'd been reading and talking. But as time passed, Annie got more and more nervous. She knew the ten days Harry's note had said he'd be gone were up today. But she had no idea exactly when he'd return.

Claire looked up from her book. "You're not reading."

"I can't concentrate. I'm just imagining the explosion when Harry found out his key wouldn't work. I don't know what he'll do."

"I know. You're welcome to stay here tonight."

"Oh, Claire, thank you. I have to face him eventually but I'm just scared." She ran the fingers of one hand through her brown wavy locks, then touched them to her lips. "I don't know if the legal papers have been delivered yet. Jan Stone said they would definitely deliver them today, and she'd call me when she heard anything. God, I wish she'd call."

"She will." Claire put her book face down in her lap and gave Annie her full attention.

Annie fidgeted in her seat. She took a sip of lemonade. "This is delicious." She smiled at Claire. "Thanks for being here, Claire, really. I'd hate to go through this alone."

"I make fresh-squeezed lemonade for all hard times." She smiled and shook her head. "I remember so well when I sat here with my daughter after she had kicked that bastard to the curb. I wanted to do something but there was nothing I could do but make lemonade and sit as she swung and paced and waited for another lawyer's phone call."

"Well, having you be here feels like a lot."

As if on cue, Annie's cell phone rang. "It's Jan!" She opened her eyes wide and answered. "Hello."

"Hi, Annie. The papers were served, and I just heard from a Dennis Stacy who claims to be Harry's lawyer. He wants to arrange a time for Harry to come get his clothes and personal items. You can be there if you like but you do not have to. He has agreed that Harry will not take any furniture at this time, just his clothes. If you like, give me a key and I'll meet him. Or if you want to be there, someone from the sheriff's department can also be there for no fee. It's up to you."

Annie's heart began to race and her stomach twist in knots. She imagined all options and just got confused. She wasn't sure she was ready to see Harry, she wasn't sure she wasn't. An image of their wedding flashed on her mental screen. Tears began to fill her eyes and a wave of sadness crashed over her. "I just don't know. I know he needs his clothes but I don't know if I can handle seeing him either."

"Another option is to take a friend with you," said Jan.

"A friend?" Annie repeated as she looked at Claire.

"I'll come," whispered Claire.

"Claire will come with me," she told Jan.

"Would five o'clock be a good time to offer? And remember, if he confronts you or asks you any questions, tell him to have his lawyer contact me."

"How long do I have to wait if he's late?" Annie had to ask, knowing only one time she could remember that he was on time.

"Give him fifteen minutes I guess, then go do whatever you want. Any other questions?"

"Do you know where he's staying?" Annie's stomach churned as she waited for Jan's answer.

"His lawyer didn't say. But if he moves in with Gloria, we will find out and throw the book at him for adultery, and I'll get you alimony. But he's a lawyer and knows that, so I'd be willing to bet he got his own place."

Annie took a deep breath and exhaled slowly.

"I'll be in touch. And if you have any trouble with him, you call me."

Annie hung up and put her feet on the floor to stop rocking. A volcano of anxiety erupted inside her. She pressed her lips together and turned her head to look outside to the oak and pine trees and the well-tended gardens of begonias, impatiens, and irises. She felt she had swallowed a grenade that ticked inside her and was about to explode. She turned back to Claire.

"Ready?" Claire asked. "You might want time to box up his clothes and put them on the street." She grinned.

Claire's humorous suggestion took root in Annie's mind. She went upstairs, Claire trailing behind her, pulled Harry's big suitcase from the closet, set it on the bed, and began opening his drawers.

"That-a-girl!" exclaimed Claire. Then she started singing. "I'm gonna wash that man right out a my hair."

"I haven't heard that one in along time. My mother used to play all those old songs." Annie joined in, singing at the top of her voice: "I'm gonna wash that man right out a my hair, I'm gonna wash that man right out a my hair . . . and send him on his way!" They pulled out shirts, socks, and underwear and threw them into the suitcase. Soon the drawers were empty. Annie found a hanging bag for carrying suits and began emptying the closet.

"He must have taken his carry-on bag because it's not here. This big suitcase is usually for long vacations. Although I can't remember the last time we went away together on a vacation of any length." She shrugged her shoulders, sighed, and kept working.

When they had the closet and drawers empty, they went into the bathroom. Not much there. He had surely taken his shaving kit on the trip. Annie did find a couple of big bottles of Head & Shoulders Shampoo and another of gel for his unruly mop of hair. She threw them into a grocery bag she retrieved from the kitchen.

"I'm feeling charitable now," she joked as she threw in an unopened tube of toothpaste.

They dragged them all downstairs and set them just inside the kitchen door. "This is the door he always comes in." Annie glanced at the clock. It was ten before five. She sat at the kitchen table and scanned the room. Claire sat across from her.

"Anything else you see?"

Annie thought a minute, then opened a cabinet and grabbed a coffee mug. It had a picture of weighing scales and the words "Talk is cheap until you have to talk to a lawyer." She set it on the table and sat back down.

"That's Harry's mug?"

"I gave it to him as a joke when we were first married. But he liked it. Who knew his goal was to make a lot of money? I sure didn't."

"He never told you?"

Annie thought a moment, wrinkling her brow and frowning. "You know, he may have but not in so many words. Money never motivated me, so maybe I just assumed he was like me." She sighed and turned her face to Claire. "Blind. How could I be so stupid?"

"Smoke gets in your eyes," said Claire with a twinkle and began to hum.

Annie joined her and sang: "When a lovely flame dies . . ."

Then in unison: "Smoke gets in your eyes!"

They laughed together a moment. Annie let out a long sigh. "Another song my mother taught me." She thought a moment. "But the line from a song that's been running through my mind is "Freedom's just another word for nothing left to lose."

"You may feel that way now, but I bet you won't forever, Annie." Claire squeezed her arm.

Just then the clock chimed five times. "Anytime now," said Annie.

"Yes, soon he and his stuff will be gone."

They sat in silence as the clock ticked on. Annie tapped her feet and drummed her fingers on the table. She stood up and looked out the window, then sat back down. "Late as usual," she said.

"He's not the punctual sort?" asked Claire.

"Not at all. Once he was an entire hour late for dinner. I had even called to ask when he'd be home so I could time my cooking just right. He said he was leaving right then. When he finally got home and I complained about how late he was, he exploded. That was a fun evening." She leaned back in her chair. "I can barely remember the last time he got home on time." She looked at the kitchen clock. Ten minutes past five. "Or the last time I cared." She sighed.

Claire clucked in sympathy. Then she tilted her head. "Do I hear a car?"

Annie walked into the living room and looked through the picture window. A butterfly convention began in her stomach. She watched him drive into the driveway and stop before driving around back. Harry got out and began to walk towards the front door.

"Oh, no, he's coming to the front door." Alarm bells went off inside her head.

"It's okay, Annie, relax. Want me to let him in?" She got up from the table.

Annie paused. Then she pulled herself up tall and said, "No, I'll do it," and stepped up to the front door. She waited until Harry rang the door bell, then opened the door and faced him. He looked at her for a silent moment. Annie broke the ice. "Hello, Harry."

"Hello, Annie," he said just as Claire appeared behind her.

"Hello, Harry. I'm Claire."

Harry nodded and stepped inside. He walked past them into the kitchen and saw the suitcases and bags by the back door. Then he walked upstairs. They heard him walk into the bedroom and bathroom and come back down. He said nothing but got another grocery bag and headed to his study just off the living room.

Annie stood by the living room couch, shifting her weight from leg to leg. Claire sat down. "I forgot about his study."

"Do you want to watch what he takes?" whispered Claire.

"No, it's all his stuff. I don't have anything in there at all."

Harry soon appeared with the bag full of papers and a box of books from the shelves. He walked in silence past them and back out the front door. They heard him open the trunk of his car. He soon returned and took the suitcases and bags from the kitchen to his car. Then he returned to stand in the front door. Annie gripped her hands together as she stood at a distance in the middle of the living room. Claire joined her.

He walked past them and made one more pass through all the rooms. Coming back through the kitchen, he paused, smiled, and picked up the coffee mug. He stopped in the front door, then turned around briefly. "I guess that's it for now," said Harry. He gave a cold smile. "See you in court." And he left, closing the door behind him.

They sat down on the couch and looked at each other. For a few minutes neither said a word.

Claire examined Annie closely.

"How are you doing?" she asked.

"I'm not sure. 'See you in court'? Oh, I dread that day," said Annie, trembling. She shook her head. "But at least one small part is done." She gave a thin smile. "I sure could use a drink. Maybe a glass of wine." She inclined her head towards Claire.

"Sounds good to me," Claire grinned back. "Let's toast to your newfound freedom."

"Ha, you think I'm free? I don't feel a bit free. Matter of fact, I feel like getting drunk. I think I'll skip the wine and go to the real stuff." She retrieved two glasses with two ice cubes in each and a bottle of Jameson from the kitchen and sat back on the couch. "Join me?" she nodded at Claire.

"Ah, Irish whiskey, that is the real stuff. You're serious. I'll have one ounce only, thank you," said Claire. "You live here, so have as much as you want. I'm my own designated driver."

Annie took a big swallow and stared off into space. She felt it travel down and begin to warm her insides. A small tear rolled down the side of her face.

Claire patted her hand. "Maybe we should order a pizza, eh? Not good to get drunk on an empty stomach."

Annie focused on Claire in silence. Then she smiled. "Good idea. Let's order one with everything. Except anchovies."

"As the Buddha said, make me one with everything," said Claire with a wink.

Annie laughed.

Chapter 30

$\mathcal{A}$t promptly 3 p.m. the following Thursday, Annie smiled as she wrapped the warm cloak of Amanda's presence around her in the sanctuary of her office. "Am I glad to be here."

"Rough week?"

"Well, a lot has happened. I got the locks changed, Harry hired a lawyer. Thanks to you, I have a lawyer, so I guess we'll soon be in the lion's den."

Amanda nodded. "Wow. How are you holding up?"

"Okay I guess. Although I wake up in the middle of the night and lie there worrying for a while."

"I'm not surprised. That's not unusual. Do you eventually get back to sleep?"

"It takes an hour or more, but, yes." Annie paused, studied her left hand with its diamond engagement ring and matching gold band, still in place. She sighed, then raised her eyes to Amanda. "Have you heard from Harry?"

"No." Amanda had expected Annie to ask. She had followed Annie's gaze to her rings. She knew it would take time for Annie to take them off, but it seemed that was the direction she was headed. "I did give him a call just to check on him, but he never called me back," said Amanda. She had not expected to hear back from him, but she wanted to make the effort in case he was in emotional trouble and open to some help. He had seemed in such emphatic denial that she wondered if he had lost his hold on reality. But more likely, he was feeling such shame at being found out and at his outburst in their session that he would just stay away. When he didn't respond to her message, she assumed it was the latter. In her years of practice, she had had to learn to let go. She couldn't help everyone.

"I was worried he'd want to come see you by himself," Annie sighed.

"Don't worry about that. It would be unethical for me to see him individually now that I'm seeing you. If you all decided to resume couples therapy, that's the only way I could see him again."

Annie leaned back in her chair. "What a relief. I think he made it clear he's done with couples therapy. Was he ever angry. I hate to think of how he's bad-mouthing me all over town now."

"I doubt that really," said Amanda, smiling. "He probably only does that with his lawyer."

"You're probably right. He's so into good appearances." Annie sighed. "How did I get here anyway? I was once head over heels in love with him." She shook her head and looked away.

Amanda sat in silence for a while to let Annie collect her thoughts. Annie had a long road ahead to process all that had happened and make sense of it so she could move on. If she didn't, it would be there like an undertow. She'd seen quite a few clients over the years who rushed from one relationship into another without taking time to reflect and learn. Usually they repeated the same patterns. She wanted to create a safe space for Annie for just such deep reflection.

Annie turned her head back to Amanda. "I didn't really know

him when we married. He proposed so soon. And no one had ever proposed to me before. I was dazzled."

"That sounds like the proverbial whirlwind romance," said Amanda.

Annie nodded and pressed her lips together. "That was my big mistake. I didn't know who I was saying yes to or what or anything. My mother had a fit when I told her. She hadn't even met him and here I was calling to tell her we were engaged." Annie's eyes flew wide open and her mouth dropped.

"What are you thinking?" asked Amanda.

"I'm thinking about how upset she was. And a few months later, she got cancer."

"I doubt there's a connection if that's what you're thinking. But tell me more about your mother's cancer; when did you find out?" asked Amanda.

"Not long after we got home from our honeymoon." Annie paused and remembered. "But she looked so happy at our wedding. I've never seen her look so happy." She smiled. "My mother thought Harry was quite a catch. Her daughter, marrying a lawyer, a handsome lawyer. There were plenty other causes of stress in her life. Once she met him, I'm sure me marrying him wasn't one of them."

Amanda was glad Annie had answered her own question. She believed the mind-body connection could be powerful but knew there was no way to know for sure why and how someone got cancer. But she wondered what other stress Annie was referring to. She waited.

"Just a few years earlier, my mother's sister, my Aunt Elizabeth, had surgery for a tumor in her inner ear that had given her vertigo," said Annie, now on a roll. "The surgeon found the tumor wrapped around a major blood vessel and severed it trying to get the tumor. There was nothing they could do then. Aunt Elizabeth survived the blood loss and complications but just barely. It was horrible. She had major brain damage. She couldn't talk or do anything but lie there."

"How awful." Amanda frowned and shook her head. "Was your mother close to her sister?"

"Oh yes, it was the worst time. My dad loved Aunt Elizabeth too. The last time he went to see her in the hospital, he stayed only a minute. Then I found him outside in the hall, his head against the wall. He was weeping. I had never seen my dad cry. He told me he was going to get a cyanide ring and made me promise to never let him be in such a condition."

"Oh, how sad," said Amanda. "So all this happened in the few years before you met Harry?"

Annie nodded.

"Did your aunt linger a long time in that condition?"

"Years, nearly three years, that's what really devastated my mother. Aunt Elizabeth and I were also very close. I considered not going into the overseas job but my mother insisted I get on with my life. But it was doubly hard to be so far away. And there was no way to know how long she would survive. Aunt Elizabeth finally died just before I met Harry. I came back and got to see her one last time."

"How difficult for you. You must have wanted someone to hold on to."

"I guess so. And picked the first one I found. I had no idea what I was getting into." Annie looked at her feet.

"What was it like at first when you got married and started living together?"

Annie paused to reflect. "He could be very aloof. And sometimes when he got home from work, he just seemed in such a bad mood. We'd sit at dinner, and I'd ask about his day, and he mostly said nothing. If I asked again, pushed a little, he'd get angry and say he didn't always take his emotional temperature. And he never asked me about my day. At first I'd tell him anyway—I was looking for a different teaching job closer to home and not having much luck."

"That must have been tough," said Amanda.

"Yes, it was. I was frustrated. He was working all the time and home late. He'd listen but not say much. But then my mother got diagnosed with cancer, and I started spending time in Atlanta every weekend to be with her. He seemed very supportive at first. He went with me a few times, but then his work picked up and he couldn't. So we were apart a lot. Then she died." Annie's eyes filled up. She dabbed her eyes with a tissue. "And my dad went crazy. Harry was my rock. I leaned on him a lot. But I just shut down with my grief. Now that I think of it, I don't know if he really was supportive or if I just thought he was because I was such a mess." She looked up at Amanda. "Does that make sense?"

"It makes perfect sense. You were dealing with a lot: a new husband, the huge losses of losing your aunt, then your mother, and your father, as you said, 'going crazy.' That's a lot. You probably weren't seeing much clearly."

"I sure wasn't." She paused and her eyes glazed over.

"Tell me about your father," prompted Amanda.

"Oh, first he called me every night, crying. Then suddenly he quit calling about a month or two after my mother died. Next I found out he was with Hilda. I couldn't believe it!"

"Yes, that seems quick. Too quick for you I imagine."

"I felt so betrayed by my father." Annie bit her lip. "He didn't even want to talk about Mother around Hilda. And Hilda was always around! She'd finish his sentences. It was awful."

"How long after he met Hilda did they marry and move far away?"

"A matter of months. This is the man who always preached to me: 'Marry in haste, repent in leisure.' He was gone just before Christmas."

"That must have been a hard Christmas."

"I barely remember it. I think I just went numb. And that seemed to suit Harry just fine. As long as we had sex once a week, he was happy."

"And you?"

"I was miserable. When I woke up from my fog of grief and reached for Harry, he wasn't there. Or it didn't seem like he was there. That's when I started writing poetry." She laughed. "It was poetry therapy."

"Poetry therapy is good," said Amanda. "Perhaps it can help you chart your course. When a marriage ends, it's like a new life begins. Now, going forward, you get to create the new life that you want."

Amanda watched Annie closely as she inhaled what Amanda had just said, planting a new seed. Annie's brow furrowed and her eyes narrowed. Her face turned pale, then flushed. She reminded Amanda of a fledgling bird about to try its wings for the first time.

Annie tilted her head. "Oh. And I feel like my life is over. Hmm, a new life." She shook her head and blinked her eyes. "I never thought of it that way."

"It will come to you if you keep your canoe in the stream and keep paddling. You don't have to figure it out all at once."

"That's good because I just feel like curling up in a ball and crying sometimes."

"Of course, and that's important. Crying is part of grieving your losses. I'd worry about you if you didn't cry."

"Really?" Annie looked surprised.

"Really," said Amanda. "And grieving comes in waves. Don't hurry it. Just be with it."

"I'm not sure I know how."

"You know more than you know that you know. And I'll help you."

Annie sat quietly for a while. Tears slowly rolled down her cheeks. "I just feel so sad."

"I know." Amanda was glad to see Annie opening up the well of emotion she knew was there.

"And I don't know what I'm doing next, what I'm supposed to do next." She dabbed her eyes with a tissue.

"What do you want to do next?" asked Amanda with a smile.

Annie pursed her lips. "Go home and ponder it all. Maybe take a hot bath."

"That sounds like a plan," said Amanda. "Let's pick it up there next time. I'm afraid our time is up."

Annie looked shocked. "There's so much more to tell."

"I'm sure there is. Does this time work as a regular time?" asked Amanda, looking at her calendar.

"Yes, believe me, I need this. I feel so much better just pouring it all out." Annie turned toward the door. "A new life. Hmm." Amanda watched her turn inward as if beginning to compose her next poem.

Chapter 31

"Have a seat, Harry," said Dennis Stacy. He waved towards the couch rather than the chair in front of his large mahogany desk. He sat at one end of the couch with his legal pad and his pen ready.

Harry sat at the other end of the couch, his briefcase on the floor at his feet. "I'm sorry we couldn't meet Tuesday but I had to take that day to move, buy furniture, and get my living quarters set up. And, as it turned out, I had to meet with a couple of new clients so I can pay for it all."

"That's fine. I leave Friday mornings open usually for unexpected meetings. How are your new digs?"

"Very good, actually. My real estate agent found me a condo on Westwood Lake that I can rent and even consider buying. It's on the end and has lots of oaks shading it. Even has a fireplace and a balcony. And of course the lake is good for boating. I might even get a canoe or kayak. Or maybe even a Jet Ski."

"Sounds good. Well, I've been thinking about your case a lot and want to see if there is any fault we can find on the other side. Get them to drop the adultery charge and agree to settle on a no-fault divorce. Is there any way you can claim Annie pushed you into having an affair? Did she neglect you or refuse her *wifely duties* or anything along those lines?"

"You mean did she refuse to have sex with me? She was gone a lot once she started that poetry class, either at the class or barricaded up in her room writing." He paused and looked away as he reflected. He could see her stirring her homemade spaghetti sauce clad in her green apron, then pouring hot noodles through the colander over the sink as he sat at the table waiting to be served, a glass of his favorite Merlot in front of him. She was a good cook. But she always wanted to talk over dinner and he liked to eat quietly. Then the tension would start. She'd ask him to clean up, he'd grumble but agree. Then she took to eating without talking herself and retreating into her writing room after dinner. So long ago now he could barely remember.

"Harry, I'm over here," said Dennis. "Where'd you go, buddy?"

Harry startled and turned toward Dennis. "Just remembering." His face fell as waves of sadness swept over him.

"Having trouble with the question?"

Harry looked puzzled. "You'd better repeat it."

"We're looking for *connivance*, remember? You've been accused of adultery and Annie has been given a *divorce from bed and board* because of it. Any way she pushed you into it?" Dennis lifted his pen over the legal pad.

Harry pressed his lips together. "Yes." He sat up and leaned towards Dennis. "Listen, Dennis, my biggest concern is that that photo not get released. How can we prevent that?"

"The photo I haven't yet seen? Did she push you into it?" He looked straight at Harry. "Answer the question, please."

Harry squinted and frowned. "She just withdrew once she started her poetry class. But before that we used to argue a lot. She was always on me to do more housework. Usually when I had a ton of work to bring home or just at the beginning of the playoffs. I hate housework. Someday I'm going to have a housekeeper and cook to do it all."

"Did she withdraw from you sexually?"

"Maybe, but I got so turned off with the nagging over stupid stuff like washing dishes that I guess I withdrew as well. I quit initiating except when I couldn't stand it anymore. If I could catch her awake, I could get some satisfaction. She didn't like it when I tried to wake her up in the middle of the night on a weeknight but sometimes I got so horny . . ."

"Any chance she was also having an affair?" Dennis put the top of his pen to his chin.

"Well, if she did, it would have had to be someone in her poetry class. Or a fellow teacher maybe." He paused and scratched his chin. "But she's been teaching a few years and most of the staff there are female. Things started to change after she joined that class. The only one I ever met was Claire. Ha ha, one thing I know for sure, Annie is not a lesbian." He laughed nervously. "But what do I know?"

"Any men in that class?"

"Sure, I guess, I really don't know."

"We could have a private investigator follow her. I have one I work with when needed. Any idea if that would turn up anything?"

Harry considered that question a minute. He imagined some handsome guy poet in her poetry group being attracted to her, getting to know her, liking her. But that's all he could see. "I doubt it. I could be wrong but I think Annie is just not the type." He paused. "You know, we'd become like strangers. I can't be sure of anything really."

"Well, if you want to, we could hire my guy to tail her for a few days and see what we find."

"How much would that cost?"

"He charges about what they all charge these days, but he's good."

"Jeez." He thought about that photo she took. He never thought she'd do something like that. His face reddened as anger erupted inside him. He clinched his fists and turned to Dennis. "Hell, why not? Who knows what she's been up to."

"I'll get him on it today, let him follow her over the weekend and see what she does. I'll have him report back Monday and stop if he doesn't find anything. How does that sound?"

"I'll be surprised if he finds anything. But who knows? Yes, let's find out." He thought back to his parents. "My mother was such a drunk. I think my dad had someone at his office. Now, she did drive him to it, and I couldn't blame him. I swore I wouldn't be like them. But then we lost that case and Gloria . . ." His eyes glazed over as he remembered and his body remembered.

"So are you still involved with Gloria?"

He jumped, scarcely aware he had spoken his thoughts out loud, sat up, and looked straight at Dennis. "Yes, I sure am, and it's keeping me sane." He paused, looked down, placed his own legal pad across his lap strategically, then back at Dennis. "I'll spare you the details."

"As your lawyer, I advise you not to see Gloria at all until this case is settled. You know if you don't want that photo released, you and Gloria have to be seen as strictly colleagues."

"Yes, I know, I know, we are. I haven't had a moment to see her this week except here with moving and meeting with new clients. But what can we do about that photo? If it gets out, I'll be ruined!"

Harry began biting the nails of his right hand.

"We'll work on that, don't worry. Maybe we can get a photo on Annie."

Harry snorted. "Unlikely." Then he began to stare off into space, and his eyes again glazed over. "But wouldn't that be great."

Dennis laughed. "Stranger things have happened. But now let's talk about the financial disclosure form. I see you made a recent purchase of a time share."

"Yes, and I just visited it last week, which was when Annie had the locks changed. I was going to surprise her with it when I won my case but then . . ."

"So Annie doesn't know about it?"

"No, I didn't tell her."

"And does she know you went there with Gloria last week?"

Harry's eyes grew big. "How'd you know I took Gloria?"

"I'm making an assumption, an easy one. You did, didn't you?"

"Yes, I did, what the hell, I did. And we had a great time. She has a fine legal mind. I'm going to recommend her for partner."

Dennis laughed. "Fine legal mind, eh? You do that, but realize that if I made that assumption correctly, Jan Stone will make it also."

Harry hung his head and plopped himself against the back of the couch. "I'm screwed, aren't I? Really screwed?"

"Right now the only one who has screwed you is Gloria but that appears to be fully consensual. Just stay away from Gloria for a while. If you can't give me more to work on regarding Annie, we aren't going to have any pushback on their complaint. See if anything comes to you. We'll see what my PI finds. Let's stop for today. Let me know if you come up with anything."

When Harry got back to his office, Gloria was sitting in his chair, swinging it right and left. He closed the door behind him when he entered.

"Hey, big boy," she said with a big grin. "I haven't seen you all week. How are you doing?"

Harry shook his head. "We have to keep a low profile, Gloria. I was just with Dennis and that's his advice."

"Sure, I understand," she said. "After you called me Monday night to tell me she changed the locks and hired Jan Stone . . . I knew you were in for a rough ride. That's why you haven't seen me."

"I appreciate that. I sure have been thinking about you, I admit. I've just been overwhelmed with moving, buying furniture, setting up my new place." He sat down on the couch and dropped his briefcase. She left his chair and sat at the other end of the couch.

"Want me to put on a disguise tonight and stop by? I'll bring a bottle of champagne and we can celebrate your new home." She leaned over, giving him a good view of her cleavage. She wore a proper grey business suit with a low-cut blouse underneath.

Harry licked his lips and grinned at her. "That's a great idea. Do you really have a disguise?"

"I sure do. Will a black wig and trench coat be enough? Or should I wear my man's suit and come in drag?"

Harry belly laughed. "Just make sure you can't be recognized. Who knows, that Jan Stone could have me under surveillance."

"I'll need to know your new address, big boy."

"Of course, I'm at 1414 Westwood Lake Road. The one on the end."

"Ooo, fancy."

He opened his briefcase and pulled out a folder. "Now let's have a look at a new case I want your help with. This one could make us rich." He winked at her. "You are an excellent litigator."

She scooted over next to him so their thighs were touching and leaned over to look at the folder. He pretended not to notice the effect her proximity had on him, but a certain part of his anatomy saluted her. His mind flashed on the evening to come and he felt twenty-five again. A young buck in springtime. He paused, verified that his office door was securely closed, and leaned over for a slow, sensual kiss. He pulled back and looked at her closely. "On second thought, you'd better dress as a man tonight."

"You got it, boss," she said, grinning and wetting her full lips.

Then, with some difficulty, he forced himself to refocus on their new client and get to work. At that moment, it was her legal mind he most needed.

Chapter 32

He walked through a thick fog. He felt it caress his skin in a moist embrace. He wore only shorts and could barely see his feet, barefoot on the path, so he set one down, felt with the other for the next step before setting it down. The dirt was so full of rocks and roots, he could easily fall. Then he was lying on moss and felt a woman's embrace, soft yet firm. He turned to look into her face, to see through this mist, to see who held him so tenderly. So out of focus, but a strong feeling of warmth and affection. His own longing rose inside him, his body rose to meet hers. He reached to pull her closer to him, but, as he did, she faded. His outstretched arms were empty. Waves of grief washed over him until he could not move, held down by a boulder of sadness. A ray of sunlight pierced the fog, landing on his eyes, blinding him. He turned his head and burst into tears. Then he awoke to find himself in a tangle of sheets in his own bed, alone. The sun shone through the slit between the two curtains onto his pillow. George felt his grief subside as consciousness came. He wiped the tears from his cheeks and stayed with the dream images. Who was that woman? She felt so familiar. Not his ex-wife. He seldom dreamed about her anymore. And since he'd moved to North Carolina so many months ago, he had hardly dated anyone. After the trauma of his divorce the year before, he didn't dare. His ex had fallen apart when he left, even called him nonstop with vague threats of suicide. Even when their divorce was final, she wouldn't quit stalking him. He had had to move 600 miles south to get free of her. He had wanted nothing to do with any more beautiful, volatile women.

But the dream did remind him how lonely he was now. His self-imposed celibacy had its limits. The feel of that dream woman was so damn good. Maybe he was getting ready to go out there again, into that wilderness of dating. But with that thought, he felt suddenly nauseous. He hated dating. It felt like returning to high school, and he had never been so happy as the day he graduated high school and could leave the classmates who were so fake, the whole phony mess of it. He had hated it. Why couldn't he just meet this dream woman in waking life?

He glanced at the clock on his bedside table: 7:15 Saturday morning. Another Saturday alone. How fun. But he reminded himself to be grateful his construction company was doing so well. He had a crew of four guys and, since he had no social life to speak of, he had worked late the night before finishing up a remodeling job. Just the last details to please the folks so they could move back in today. And by some miracle, the inspector was able to come at 7 p.m. and approve it for occupancy. They had been so grateful. They had a new baby and a four-year-old so he was glad to help.

He threw off his sheets and got up. He heard the gurgle of his coffee pot, which he had programmed the night before to start brewing at 7:15 a.m. Ah, technology! He found his robe and slippers and padded into his kitchen. He realized he was ravenous. Soon he had bacon in the microwave, toast in the toaster oven, and a couple eggs in the frying pan. And soon he was sitting at his kitchen table feasting on it all. As he sipped his coffee, he considered the day ahead. He could complete the estimate for the next possible job. He could take the day off and hike in the University Forest. Annie's image popped up in his mind. Maybe she and Claire would be out there hiking again. Not likely. He spread strawberry jam on his toast and took a bite. He could drive by her house and see if her husband's car was gone.

You idiot, you don't even know what his car looks like! And then what would you do? Go knock on the door? Totally embarrass yourself? She may have said once that she wanted to leave her husband, but you of all people should know it is not that easy to do. And she probably hasn't done it. They are probably deep in couples therapy and making it all better. What is wrong with you? He shook his head. His inner critic might be harsh but so far had kept him out of a lot of trouble.

You're lonely, answered another voice inside. *You need to start dating again, that's all. Once you meet someone new, you'll feel better. There are lots of women out there who are available and looking to meet guys. Just go online and check them out.*

George liked this voice better. He called it the Problem-Solver. He ate the last bite, stood up, rinsed his plate, utensils and mug and put them into the dishwasher. He put the bacon and egg carton back inside the refrigerator and wiped off the counter. Then, on second thought, he retrieved his mug and refilled it. If he was going to face the wilderness of findamate.com, he'd need a lot more caffeine.

Sitting at his desk in his small office off the kitchen, he booted up his laptop and found the dating site. He logged in and was reminded that he hadn't been there in over three months. "Welcome back, LumberjackMan! You have five winks!"

Dutifully, he clicked on the first wink, from early April. A wink was barely more than nothing. Not an email, just a "you might be interesting." Up popped a grainy photo of a woman standing by a file cabinet. He couldn't really see her face, just that she wore a navy business suit. Her profile said she worked in IT, was forty-two, divorced with two kids at home. *No thanks,* said the Problem-Solver voice.

He clicked on the next wink, from mid-May. Up popped a glossy head shot of a dark curly-haired woman with a big smile who looked like she'd been to Glamour Photo that day. He took a long slug of coffee and read on. She lived forty miles away, was newly divorced, thirty-five, and eager to have kids as soon as possible. George was thirty-three and wanted a family but wanted procreation to come naturally over time after he'd found his best friend and knew her well. He consulted the Problem-Solver voice. The consensus was clear: *No thanks.*

George continued on for another hour with the same result. He sat back and gave a big sigh. I *had a crazy wife: strike one. I found no one on the internet: strike two. What's next? The bar scene? That would be strike three. Is something wrong with me?* Then he heard another voice. *Don't worry about it, George, keep your heart open and love will come again.* This voice was new to him. He kept listening. *Just do something nice for yourself today, be your own best friend.* He really liked this voice. He decided to call this voice his Guardian Angel voice.

"Thank you," he said aloud. Well, he would begin by making up his bed and taking a shower. Soon he was singing in the shower, scrubbing himself down with soap, luxuriating in the warm water as it flowed over his body. Once dressed, he scurried around picking up and straightening. He even scrubbed the toilet and wiped out the bathroom sink. Then he sat in his big brown recliner in his living room with pen and paper to make a grocery list. He would make himself a gourmet meal that evening—something like chicken with curried fruit. He wrote down chicken breast, cashews, curry powder, dried pineapple, raisins—wait, he had raisins. He scratched off raisins. He checked his Netflix queue to find what he could watch streaming. Lots of choices. *How do you like that, Guardian Angel?* he asked.

Very good, George, now count your blessings and enjoy the day.

George looked around his living room. He had a big leather couch with matching chair that went well with his brown corduroy recliner. Red and green and blue plaid curtains. A coffee table made from rough-hewn pine. A braided rug with colors to match the curtains. And a forty-two-inch TV screen for watching sports and movies. And across the street, a big park. He looked out the picture window and rested his eyes on the large oak in front of his little house. He saw squirrels scurrying up and down and bluebirds flying from the bluebird house he had on a pole just far enough from the tree so the squirrels couldn't get to it. This was far from his dream house, the one he would build himself someday, but it was just the right size for a guy living alone. It was one floor, with a master bedroom and bath, a small den he used as an office off the eat-in kitchen, and a good-sized living room. Then one more bedroom and a bathroom. It wasn't fancy but it was home.

He eased into reverie and thought about a poem he might write. "It's not fancy but it's home," he wrote on his tablet. He noticed the way the natural light caressed the rug, the coffee table. He jotted a few more notes, then decided to let it incubate until later. He smiled at the paper and set it down. It would keep and maybe come out even better later.

Gathering his grocery bags, he picked up his wallet and his list. It was almost noon. He'd go to Tom's Community Market with its expanse of lawn and tables under the trees selling locally grown produce, free-range chicken, and grass-fed beef. He'd have a sandwich on the lawn, watch the kids and dogs run around, then get his groceries and come home. Just in time for a nap. Or maybe turn on a baseball game. Or maybe a walk in the park. The day was his and life might not be perfect, but it was pretty good.

And love will come again, said his Guardian Angel.

Annie sat on her living room couch, her students' homework papers in a pile on the coffee table in front of her. She held one on a clipboard with her red pen in her hand, reading and correcting it. These students were taking her class because they had flunked English during the school year and, as she read their work, she understood why. They could barely put a sentence together. Yet what they wrote about was heart-wrenching. She had given them writing prompts geared towards their own lives, knowing they had plenty to write about. Some lived in low-income housing, some in affluent areas with workaholic parents who gave them little attention or guidance, and some in between those two extremes. She had been grading papers for two hours now and was ready for a break. She finished the paper in her hand and set it on the pile of papers already corrected.

Then she looked at the pile yet to read. Shorter by a good bit, she was glad to notice. Maybe she'd finish by Monday. Maybe.

Her mind wasn't really on her work. Her life felt in such turmoil. Work was a welcome distraction but only kept her attention for so long. Then the image of Harry leaving with his belongings last Monday popped into her mind. His lips held in a tight line, his eyes narrowed. And his tone of voice so deep and dark when he said, "See you in court." She felt terrified to see him in court. Court was his territory; it was a foreign land to her. If it weren't for Jan Stone, she would be tempted to just give in and be done with it all. She didn't want a big fight. She knew Harry relished just that and could be overpowering. He had roared at her more times than she cared to remember, leaving her wet and trembling. She reminded herself that Jan would be doing the fighting for her if it came to that. Jan seemed tough whereas Annie felt scared and weak. Her thoughts turned to her recent therapy session. Amanda seemed to see strength in her she didn't see. But it felt good to pour it all out. She came away feeling she had pushed the rock a few more feet up the mountain and it hadn't come crashing down on her. Yet.

She shook her head. *Stop it, Annie! Get that guy out of your mind and go do something,* said a voice inside her.

But what? I've got to grade these papers! Annie stared at the pile of ungraded papers and sighed.

Take a break. It's a beautiful sunny day. Look outside.

Annie picked up her head and looked out the window. She stood up and opened the blinds so she could see better. She saw a couple of kids riding by on their bicycles, a couple walking a golden retriever past her house. The thermometer outside the window showed 79 degrees, quite comfortable for July in the Piedmont. Maybe she should take a walk. Or better yet, call Claire and see what she was up to.

Annie sat back on the couch by the phone and dialed. Three rings, four rings, then Claire's voice: "You have reached Claire, leave a message and I'll call you back."

She left a message, then looked at the clock—nearly noon. She could at least get a few groceries, get out of the house a while. Maybe something was happening at Tom's Community Market. Often on Saturday they had something going on: musicians playing or solicitations for a worthy cause or someone with free puppies to give away. She copied her grocery list from the white board on her fridge, got her pocketbook and grocery bags, and headed out.

Brad Schmidt had nearly dozed off when he saw Annie's silver Corolla sedan back out from the driveway and head down the street past his black '82 Volvo. He watched her get to the end of the block, stop at the stop sign, and signal to turn left. Then he sat up, shook his head so his braid fell down his back nearly to his waist, and followed. When Dennis had called with the information he needed, he had found her car easily in the school parking lot. So far this job had been tedious and boring. She drove home and stayed home all evening. He had waited until midnight, then was back at 7 a.m. Here it was nearly noon and finally, this girl was doing something. And she was easy to follow. She drove the speed limit, signaled each turn well in advance, and soon turned into the parking lot at Tom's Community

Market. He watched her circle the parking lot and find an empty place in the last shady spot on the front row. He parked four rows back and watched her gather grocery bags and walk inside before he got out to follow. He pulled a grocery bag from his back seat, grabbed a shopping basket just inside the door and easily found her by the produce. She studied her list, then picked out red and green peppers, green onions, Boston lettuce, and a ripe avocado. He picked out a bunch of bananas and rolled past her to the end of the aisle, circled past the apples, and saw her roll on to the free-range chicken and grass-fed beef. He paused—what goes with bananas?—then put a box of Honeywell's Organic Vanilla Cookies in his cart and looked around for where vanilla pudding mix might be. Then he remembered this wasn't Food Lion and he didn't need pudding anyway. He patted his protruding belly, hoping she'd roll past the beer next.

He looked up and saw her in animated conversation with some dude standing in front of the meat counter. A big guy with wavy dark-blond hair who greeted her with a big hug and bigger smile. And she smiled back. Brad stood with occasional glances at the grapes and figs and took it all in. The dude kept his hand on her arm a moment longer than necessary and the look on his face—to this trained observer—showed a sparkle. Well, the dude is clearly smitten, Brad concluded. But Annie, well, she smiled but now had her arms folded across her chest, nodding as she listened. Brad wasn't quite close enough to hear but got a few snatches when she spoke. The dude must have asked how she was doing because she began to look down and shake her head. He thought he heard "lawyer" and maybe "court" but he couldn't be sure. The dude's face changed dramatically as he listened to her, his brow furrowed, the corners of his mouth turned down, then he patted her arm and gestured outside. She nodded and they walked off together in the direction of the check out line.

Pay dirt! Brad chuckled to himself. He put a bag of green seedless grapes and a container of blueberries into his cart and got into an adjacent line behind someone with a month's worth of groceries. Annie and the dude were through the line in no time, grabbing sandwiches and AriZona iced tea on their way. He tapped his foot as the woman in front of him got her purchases arranged into five canvas bags and placed into her cart. But he could see them through the window find a table under a large oak tree and sit across from each other.

"Oh, Annie, I'm so sorry to hear what you're going through!" said George. He unwrapped his sandwich, then ignored it and sat without moving.

"And I haven't even told you the worst part yet," said Annie. She looked down at the sandwich in its plastic wrapping. George watched her, transfixed. *They wrap these sandwiches so thoroughly,* he thought, he doubted she could open it. His fingers twitched with an urge to help her, but with effort he held them still. Watching her try became fascinating to him. She fingered the plastic to find where it ended and the tape began and began to peel it off. She glanced up at George. His sandwich laid open and untouched in front of him. She smiled. He raised his head and returned her smile. He waited for her to pour it all out but saw that she hesitated. She got the wrapper open and smoothed it on the wooden table with her hands.

"Bon appetit," she said, lifting her sandwich and taking a bite.

George nodded as he chewed and swallowed. "Yes, sometimes it doesn't seem like it could be worse but it's good to focus on anything positive that you can." He patted his mouth with a napkin and continued. "I'm divorced too, I think I told you. I had a good lawyer, a real smart one. He had seen enough to advise me to move away if I really wanted to be free of her. Women can be stalkers too I learned."

"Really?" Annie's eyes grew wide.

"I'm afraid so. But it does get better, believe me. That was a year ago and I have made the beginnings of a real good new life down here. You'll make a new life too, I'm sure."

"I guess. That's what Amanda, my therapist, called it too, a new life. I guess I'll make it." She shook her head and looked down at the last of her sandwich on the plastic wrap. She wiped her mouth with her napkin.

"Of course you will."

"It's so nice to run into you, George. It has been a while."

"Yeah, since that time we all met for dinner."

"Right after Claire and I saw you in the woods." Annie grinned.

George blushed, remembering. *How much did they see?* he still wondered.

Annie took the last bite of her sandwich and folded the plastic wrap. "I'm afraid I'd better get my groceries home." She nodded at the green canvas bag on the bench beside her.

"And I'd better go inside and shop for mine," said George. *What are you doing later?* he thought, then stopped himself from saying it out loud. "Enjoy the rest of your day, Annie." He smiled and pulled his business card from his shirt pocket. "If you need my services or just need a friend to talk to, give me a call."

Annie took the card and read it. "Oh, you do home repairs?"

He nodded.

"Good to know." She smiled and tucked his card into her purse.

He sat a moment after she left, stunned as something barely out of reach in his mind began to come into focus, something just now that felt so familiar. What was it? Then it hit him: his dream—it was Annie. The woman in his dream was Annie. He pressed his lips together, then put his head in his hands. *What the hell do I do now?*

Annie sat in her car a moment. She watched George go back into the store. She felt a tingle as her eyes ran over his muscular frame, saw his long arms untangle a shopping cart from the long row stacked together just inside the door. An image filled her mind of her college dorm room and the Ouija Board on the bed between her and her roommate. *George Taffer. George Taffer is real and was just sitting right across from me,* she thought. The tingle inside grew stronger. She replayed the present scene, saw again his warm body as he sat across from her, saw his eyes on her, waiting for her to tell him. There was so much she hadn't told him that now she wondered if she should have. Then she shook her head and started the ignition.

Chapter 33

*W*hile Jan riffled through her papers, Annie twiddled her fingers in her lap wondering what Jan had to show her and if she would ever find it.

Jan finally handed her documents paper-clipped together, at least ten pages. "Here's the first draft of a proposed separation agreement."

Annie began to read and soon realized it was written in a foreign language. She turned back to Jan.

"North Carolina law requires a year separation before divorce can be filed," said Jan, "but anytime before then you can file a legal separation, which outlines the settlement of everything else— property, debt, and all that. You don't have children so that makes it more simple."

"So can you tell me what it says short of me trying to wade through the legal language?"

Jan smiled. "Sure. Basically, it gives you the house, him any debt, you alimony, you half of his retirement accounts, you one car and him the other. Just the usual stuff."

Annie raised her eyebrows. "It sounds like you're giving me all the good stuff. Why would he agree to this?"

"To avoid the lovely photo you took being shared in court, for one thing." Jan leaned back in her chair, a smile of satisfaction across her face. "If he accepts this agreement, we will file a no-fault divorce in a year."

"And forget that he cheated?" Annie frowned and pressed her lips together.

"Well, yes. To spare you a big court fight. Instead of the current divorce from bed and board for adultery, we will file no-fault. He's in the wrong, sure, but it will be easier on you if we do it this way. If he agrees."

Annie looked away, then up at the ceiling, then down at the papers on the desk in front of her. She shifted in her chair and cleared her throat.

"Something weird happened this weekend."

"Oh?" Jan set her hands on the table and gave Annie her full attention.

"My street is usually pretty quiet, but this weekend I noticed this same car parked across the street, a few houses down, but near enough to get a good view of my place." Annie took a sip of water. "Then I remembered I had seen it there for a couple days. I know all my neighbors, and it's not one of theirs."

Jan sat up and leaned forward. "Can you describe the car?"

"Yes. I also thought I saw it at Tom's Community Market on Saturday. It's a black Volvo, maybe twenty years old."

"Did you see anyone in it?" Jan was taking notes now.

"No, just the car." Annie dug through her purse. "I even took a picture on my phone."

"Ah, very good. You are quick with a camera. Let me see it."

Annie unlocked her phone and scrolled through the gallery. She handed the phone to Jan who studied it carefully for a few minutes.

"Well, I'll be switched, those bastards. I know this car." She lifted her head and looked at Annie. "That car belongs to a private investigator that I have used in the past. They're having you followed."

Annie felt her face grow hot. "What?" she sputtered. "I'm being followed?"

"It appears so. Email me this picture please. Now please tell me everything you did over the weekend, who you saw, where you went. Just to make sure they can't twist something into evidence of connivance."

Annie wrinkled up her nose. "What's that?"

"Oh, it's a legal term to describe something you did wrong to make Harry cheat. To find fault with you to dispute our claim."

Annie's mouth hung open. She began to shake and wrapped her arms around her torso. Tears gathered in her eyes and began to spill over. "What?"

Jan reached a hand to Annie's arm. "It just shows they're trying to play dirty. But that doesn't mean they will succeed. Take a deep breath and tell me all about your weekend."

Annie inhaled, then let her breath out in a long sigh. She took a few more deep breaths, wiped her tears away with her fingers, shook her head, slumped back in the chair. She turned inward as she rewound her weekend. Then she sat up and began.

"I didn't do much really. I stayed home Friday night working on grading papers. I did watch a movie but I fell asleep. I don't think I even went outside."

Jan nodded as she took more notes. "What about Saturday?"

Annie sighed. "My life is so boring right now. I graded more papers until I got sick of it then I went to buy groceries. At Tom's as I said." She closed her eyes as she remembered. Then her eyes flew open. "I ran into a guy from my poetry class, George. I told him a bit of what's going on. He suggested we get sandwiches and sit outside and visit. So we did."

"What is your relationship with George?" asked Jan, looking down at her tablet as she wrote.

"Nothing, I mean, we're just friends. I met him in the poetry class." For a moment, Annie's reverie took her back to college and the Ouija Board and how surprised she'd been to find out in her poetry class that there actually is a George Taffer. She wondered if she should tell Jan. Then decided it was just too weird to share. "He's a really nice guy, but I don't even know him very well."

"Other than Saturday at Tom's Market, have you seen him outside the poetry class?"

"Well, once a bunch of us met for dinner a few weeks ago." Then she remembered and smiled. "And once Claire and I—another poetry class friend—saw him in the University Forest taking a sunbath on a ledge."

"Sunbathing?" asked Jan, lifting her head and raising her eyebrows.

"He was lying on a ledge high up the bluff. With no clothes on. No one was around until we got there." Annie giggled despite herself.

Jan smiled. "So you got to see all of him?"

Annie kept giggling. She put her hand over her mouth and slowly stopped giggling. "Only because we had binoculars . . ." and she giggled and giggled. "I don't know why I'm laughing. I've been so tense. But it feels good."

Jan watched her and smiled. "Did he know you had binoculars?"

Annie wiped tears from her eyes and shook her head. "I don't think so. We sure didn't tell him."

"Did he see you?"

"Yes, he came down fully dressed and hung out with us for a while, ate some of Claire's fried chicken. Then we had that group dinner a night soon after. I didn't see him again until last Saturday."

"Sounds innocent enough. But back to last weekend. When you were with George, did you touch or in any way show affection?"

Annie frowned and felt bumblebees start a convention in her stomach. "Well, he hugged me when we ran into each other." She paused to reflect. "He may have touched my arm once. Why are you asking? Do you think they could make it look like something's going on between us, that we are having an affair?"

"I know that if they can, they will certainly try. Then that lets Harry off the hook."

"Oh, yes, he gets to invent something about me to make me look bad and him look good or not so bad. Just like him." Annie's mouth drew into a stiff line. "I hate this." Her mind flashed on an image of herself in the witness chair, being eviscerated by twisted words making her out to be someone terrible.

"I know. One of the reasons I think it would be good to avoid a court fight."

Annie nodded vigorously in agreement.

"But we have to be prepared for the worst possibilities," Jan continued. "I would say this is not the time to start dating your friend."

"Dating?" Annie's face grew red. "I don't even know how to date anymore."

"And not the time to do anything that could look like dating to a private investigator." Jan lifted her eyes from her legal pad and saw Annie's face. "Sorry, I don't mean to alarm you. Just be careful. What else did you do over the weekend?"

"I saw that Volvo as I loaded my groceries in my car to come home. It looked vaguely familiar. So I started watching for it. It kinda gave me the creeps. I stayed home after that, but late afternoon I saw it sitting across the street. That's when I took that photo. You know my phone camera can zoom?"

"Yes, good. Don't forget to send me the photo. So did he see you?"

"I don't think so. I couldn't see anyone in the car actually."

"Yeah, tinted windows are hard to see through. But we can't be sure he didn't see you."

"I took the photo from inside, through the living room window."

"Oh, well, maybe he didn't see you. What about Sunday?"

Annie grinned. "I had an exciting day of grading papers. I really lead a wild life."

"And let's keep it this way until we get your separation agreement signed, okay? Let's let Harry waste his money spying on you."

"What happens next?"

"If you agree, I send this proposal to Harry's lawyer and we wait for their response. You can keep that copy if you want to read it. Maybe it will be a break from reading your students' papers." She smiled and her eyes twinkled.

"A different kind of writing for sure," said Annie as she folded it up. She nodded at Jan. "Send it to them. Maybe he'll agree and we can get this over with." She sat her purse on the table and stuck the separation agreement in a side pocket. It towered over her head so she had to stand up to find the pocket. Quilted material with a purple cat snuggled up to a black dog on a background of orange, blue, and red.

Jan stood and studied it. "Is that your briefcase? A poet's briefcase? It's beautiful."

Annie laughed. "It holds a lot but it's really just my purse. And I found it at the thrift shop for three dollars."

Jan's eyes got big. "I've got to shop there more often. What a lucky find!"

"If you go there on Tuesdays, you find the stuff newly sorted and put on the shelves."

"Thanks for the tip." She picked up her papers and tablet. "I'll let you know as soon as I hear anything. And next time you see the black Volvo, tell him Jan Stone said 'hi.'"

They walked out together into the waiting room. "I hope he's given up tailing me by now."

Jan patted her on the arm. "I hope so too. Have a good evening. And don't be surprised if you don't hear from me for a while. They may sit on it for a few weeks."

"A few weeks?" Annie shook her head. "Okay, the wheels of justice turn slowly, right?"

"You got it. Call if you have any questions. Bye now."

Annie walked out the front door and down the steps. She paused at the bottom and scanned the area for the black Volvo. None in sight. She pulled out her phone and dialed. After a brief conversation, Annie was in her car and on her way to Claire's house.

Chapter 34

*B*rad Schmidt settled himself into the chair in front of Dennis Stacy's desk, a folder in his hand. At least a day's worth of whiskers covered his face. Wisps of hair had broken free of the brown braid trailing down his back, tickling his neck and cheeks.

"What did you find?" asked Dennis, leaning back in his chair.

"Well, maybe something, maybe nothing." Brad brushed the hair from his face and opened the folder. He read from the first sheet. "Saturday she went to Tom's Community Market and had lunch with a man by the name of George Taffer."

"Oh?" asked Dennis, sitting up over his desk and picking up his pen and pad.

"Yes. George Taffer is a thirty-three-year-old divorced man who runs a fairly new but successful construction business. He was also in the same poetry class that Annie took last spring."

"Oh, you don't say. Well, what did you observe between them? Do you think there's anything going on?"

"I took photos. See what you think."

"Well, he sure looks gah-gah over her. But they're not touching. Not exactly evidence, Brad." Dennis shook his head and handed the photos back to Brad.

"Not those, but I'd be willing to bet there's more. I just picked up

271

a vibe, you know, some energy between them. Let me follow them longer and see if I catch him going into her house or vice versa."

"I don't know, it seems like a long shot. I'll have to ask my client if he's willing. Is this all you found?"

"So far, but I know I'll find more if I keep following them." Brad sat up in his chair and leaned forward, holding the folder up and waving it. "Let me see if I can listen in on phone calls. I can easily hook into her line."

"You know that's illegal. I can't authorize you to do that."

Brad winked at him. "I know you can't and you're not." He handed the glossies back to Dennis.

"Okay, enough for today. Talk to you later, eh?" Dennis winked back.

Annie sat in her usual seat in Amanda's office. Her shoulders lowered as she let the chair support her. Amanda sat opposite her smiling and waiting for Annie to begin. Annie cast her eyes around the room, seeing the heavy tomes on bookshelves, the desk with papers stacked on it, and Amanda's smiling face waiting for her as if saying *Take your time, there's no hurry.*

Annie took a long deep breath, then exhaled and inhaled again.

"I met with my lawyer Monday." Annie clasped her hands together tightly in her lap. "She has prepared a separation agreement. After a year's separation, we'd file for a no-fault divorce. Then we'd drop the accusation of adultery which puts him at fault."

"Okay. Did you agree?"

"Yes. That makes it so much easier. Now we're waiting to see if Harry will sign it. If he does, I'll be very surprised, but I hope he will."

"How are you doing with all this?"

"Okay, I guess. I just want it to be over. I really don't want to have a big court battle. Harry loves stuff like that, but I have hardly spent any time in court. Sometimes I wake up in the middle of the night and start thinking about us in court and I get so nervous I can't go back to sleep for hours. It's awful." Annie shook her head, pulled a tissue from the box next to her, and twisted it up in her lap. "And last weekend, he had someone following me." She raised her eyes to meet Amanda's.

Amanda frowned, "Really? Tell me more."

Annie told Amanda about being followed by a stranger and running into George.

"Do you like him?"

"He really likes my poetry. He's very supportive and encouraging. He's nice looking too. And I think he must be close to my age."

"Are you attracted to him?"

Annie smiled and grew quiet for a moment considering the question. "I don't know, I think so. I haven't thought about anything like that in so long, I've been so, so *married*."

Amanda smiled. "Well, that's about to change, eh?"

"Yes, it sure is." She put her hand to her heart. "Oh, jeez, *dating*, I hate to think about *dating*. Such a bewildering thought."

"So down the road when you're divorced and free to date, what do you want to do differently?"

Annie pressed her lips together and took another look at that inner screen. She saw her first date with Harry, how her heart beat so fast, her palms got so sweaty, the lights so low in the fancy restaurant he took her to so she could barely see him. She lifted her head. "I want to get to know someone really well, just as friends, before getting too involved. That was my big mistake. I don't want to do that again, that's for sure."

"That makes sense," said Amanda. "When you first meet someone who is a potential romantic partner, you can be blinded by attraction and infatuation. We all have a natural longing for connection and that longing gets stirred up in the romantic stage." She saw Annie was all ears so she kept on. "Helen Fisher, a cultural anthropologist, did some research on romantic love. She took people who described themselves as 'madly in love' and looked at their brains in the MRI. You'll never guess what she found."

"What?" asked Annie, spellbound.

"The brains of people in romantic love look a lot like the brains of people on cocaine. It feels intoxicating because it is."

"Wow, that's fascinating. How long does that last?"

"Oh, it can last anywhere from three weeks to three years."

"Well, I must have been intoxicated when I married Harry because I'd known him only three months!"

"Yes, not very long. And that stage is inevitably followed by the second stage, which we call the 'power struggle stage.' When the person of your dreams sometimes seems like the person of your nightmares. You discover your differences, begin to have disagreements, have to learn how to handle conflict. The real work of relationship."

Annie shook her head and sighed. "Boy, I was so naïve back then. I didn't know any of what you're saying. But I can see it now. I didn't know him at all. And when I began to recover from—what did you call it? Romantic intoxication? And my grief over my mother's death and my dad's craziness—and see the real Harry, it did seem sometimes like a nightmare. What a shock it was. I didn't know what to do then . . . except write it all out." She looked up at Amanda. "And to my surprise it turned into poetry."

"And it helped?"

Annie nodded. "Yes, it saved my sanity."

"Good, I'm all for sanity," Amanda grinned.

"Sometimes I feel like I'm barely hanging on." Annie frowned, raised her hand to her mouth, and began chewing on her fingernail, then stopped herself and put her hand back into her lap.

"You told me about your sleep. How's your appetite?"

"Oh, I eat well." She patted her stomach. "Can't you tell?"

"Have you gained weight? You look fine to me."

"Not really. But I do crave chocolate more than ever."

Amanda laughed. "That's not unusual. Chocolate contains phenylethylamine, the same substance your brain releases when you're in romantic love."

"Really? Is that why they always push chocolate for Valentine's Day?"

"Probably. PEA is also in roses and jalapeños."

"Roses and chocolate I understand, but jalapeños?"

"How's your energy level?"

"I'm plenty tired when I get home from teaching but generally about as usual."

"Do you ever get so down you think about harming yourself?"

"Oh, no, never!" Annie's eyes grew wide. "What made you ask that?"

"Just part of screening you for clinical depression. I didn't really think it was an option for you, but I had to ask." Amanda saw Annie sigh and her hands unclench.

"Okay."

"What you are probably experiencing is the normal stress of your situation. If you continue to lose sleep worrying, let me know and we can discuss sleep medication. I expect you'll sleep a lot better once your separation is settled."

"Oh, I hope so."

"Do you have some good friends you can confide in?"

"Claire has been great. We get together often, and she kind of checks up on me if I don't call her. She's old enough to be my mother but she doesn't seem that old—she's quite the adventurer. Now that I think about it, I guess most of my social life comes from that group. Before, I didn't have many friends outside of Harry. And now I realize he wasn't much of a friend."

"Yes, and since you're going through such a major transition, it's a good time to connect with friends. Or make some new friends." Amanda glanced at the clock. "But time's up for today." She nodded at Annie. "See you next week same time?"

"Yes, indeed." Annie stood up and picked up her purse. "I'm so glad I have you to talk to. It's so helpful."

"I'm glad. See you next week." She opened her arms and Annie walked into them. She held on for a moment, then leaned back. "You're going to be okay, Annie."

"I hope you're right." And Annie walked out into her new life.

Annie stood outside the building for a while, savoring the idea of having her troubles behind her and creating a new life, as Amanda called it. Traffic was picking up as rush hour approached. Cars paraded by, knocking the warm blanket of her session with Amanda slowly off her shoulders. When a black car stopped at the red light a car length from her, she shuddered and studied it. A mom with three kids.

She cast her eyes around, landing on each car that passed, wondering. Had she been followed here? As she looked, it seemed the buildings moved a few feet closer, the cars slowed and looked at her. A million eyes watched her. She shrunk inside her body, wishing her dress was a cloak of invisibility. She saw another dark car. Could she get to her car in time? Her stomach knotted and she began to pant. She turned to the parking lot next to Amanda's building and had to stop herself from running to her car. When she found it, she was drenched in sweat. Her fingers shook as she pulled her keys from her purse and shook more as she tried again and again to insert the key in the lock. Time slowed. Finally she got inside the car and locked all the doors. As she backed the car out of the parking place, a dark car pulled up next to her. She didn't look at it. Gripping the steering wheel, she pressed the accelerator and propelled the car into the street. She drove a meandering path, turning right then left then left then right, until she was sure no one was following her. But she knew she couldn't be totally sure. She wasn't sure where to go or what to do. Was this her new life?

Chapter 35

"We've received a proposed separation agreement from Jan Stone," said Dennis, sitting on the couch in his office facing Harry and riffling through a folder on his lap. He handed the document to Harry. "Apparently, they are willing to drop the accusation of adultery and move to a no-fault divorce after a year's separation."

"No kidding," said Harry with a big grin. He opened the agreement and began scanning, turning the pages rapidly. He soon began to frown. Then he laughed and looked at Dennis. "So I'm supposed to give her the entire house and assume all the debt? Including the mortgage? And pay alimony? That's a joke."

"I didn't think you'd like those parts. But from what you've told me, you have some newly acquired other debt, namely the time-share you just bought. Since it is not mentioned in this agreement, maybe they don't know about it. Yet. Jan Stone is very thorough in her research."

"Yes, that's the only other big thing. A bit of credit card debt but not that much." Harry paused as he reflected on the details of the agreement.

"I'm assuming you would rather go the no-fault route."

"Yes, indeed, but with an agreement I can live with, not this one," said Harry. He put a fist to his mouth and closed his eyes a moment.

His eyes shot open. "But wait, what did your investigator find?"

"Not much. Yet. That's something I wanted to discuss. He followed her last weekend. She had lunch at Tom's Market with a guy from her poetry class." Dennis opened his folder, found the glossy photos, and handed them to Harry.

Harry studied them for a few minutes. His face grew hot as a surge passed through him. His right hand closed into a fist. He imagined pummeling this guy. Then his legal mind took control, and he calmed himself. He passed the photos back to Dennis. "I can't tell much from that. I've never seen that guy. They aren't touching. No evidence of anything."

"I agree. But my guy proposes he keep following them and see what he finds. If there's something going on, they surely wouldn't show it in public. His intuition is usually right on."

Harry closed his eyes and followed that path in his imagination. Hot lava bubbled up inside him. But before it could explode out of him, the lawyer voice spoke up. No *evidence means no case. However, there is evidence of your transgression. Calm down. Examine the facts.* He opened his eyes and looked hard at Dennis.

"What if she *is* having an affair? Then it's tit for tat. We both committed adultery."

"Maybe that's why Jan Stone proposes a year's separation and no-fault divorce," said Dennis.

"But no way am I paying the mortgage! She can have the house but then she can assume the mortgage. It's a big house and a big mortgage. Let her have it on her teacher's salary. With no alimony." Harry sat back and grinned.

Dennis looked at him, his face revealing none of his inner

thoughts, then made some notes on his legal pad. "Suppose we say she gets the house and mortgage and you keep the time-share and those payments. Better to disclose it up front."

Harry pressed his lips together, closed his eyes and let his legal mind consider. Then he opened his eyes and sighed. "I guess that's the best we can do on that part. Okay, I agree."

"And no alimony? I want to be clear here."

"No alimony. That's as far as I'm willing to go." Harry crossed his arms over his chest.

"Okay. I'll write up a counter-offer. No alimony. You disclose the time-share, you keep it and she keeps the house and assumes the mortgage. Not completely equivalent, but you have payments on it."

"I may not keep it and of course I may put in an offer on my condo." Then the corners of his mouth turned up. "And I just took on a new case that's sure to bring me millions. If that happens, then maybe I'll keep them both."

"Well, good luck with that. And I recommend we let the investigator, Brad Schmidt, continue in hopes of turning up something."

"Brad Schmidt? I've heard of him. He's been around a long time. Well, it had better be a chest full of diamonds or I'll cancel his services pronto." Harry pounded his fist into the palm of his other hand. "But how satisfying if we can crush Jan Stone." He smiled. "Have you ever faced her in court? Well, I have, and it wasn't pretty, I tell you. She's a tiger."

"She sure is. Been there too." He frowned, then redirected. "Shall we give him another two days? Or a week?" said Dennis, smiling back.

"Give him the weekend. That's enough unless he shows us

something to warrant continuing to pay him." Harry gazed out the window. "I'm not a rich lawyer. But soon . . ."

"I'll tell him to report back Monday and then we can re-evaluate. I think we're done for today, don't you?" Dennis set his legal pad on the coffee table and sat up.

"For today. But you let me know immediately if there's anything else to discuss. I'll be here in a flash." Some inner part of Harry was drooling over what he imagined the PI might find that would take him off the hook. *Maybe she's not who you think she is. Maybe she has a secret life this guy will uncover.*

Annie jumped when she heard the doorbell. She set down the wooden spoon she'd been stirring her sauce with, wiped her hands on her apron, and walked into the living room. She peeked through the sidelights to find a man in a blue uniform holding a clipboard at her front door.

"Hello, ma'am, I'm from AT&T. We've had some service disruptions in your neighborhood. I'd just like to make sure it won't affect you. This will only take a minute and I apologize for the intrusion but I would hate for your phone, Internet, and TV to quit suddenly."

"Service disruption? I haven't noticed anything." Annie took note of the embroidered AT&T logo on his shirt with the name *Travis* underneath. He was clean-shaven and bore a friendly smile. She stepped back to let him come in, noticing a long brown braid hanging down his back. "There's the phone and the TV." She pointed to the small table by the kitchen door where the phone sat. The TV sat across from the couch in the living room. "There's another extension in the study where the computer, router, and modem also are and one upstairs in the hall outside the master bedroom."

"Thank you, ma'am, I need to check all three plus your TV and Internet. I know it's Saturday and you have things to do so again I apologize for interrupting." He paused and turned his nose towards the kitchen. "Something smells really good." He smiled at her.

"Thank you."

"Well, I won't be a minute. From what my nose tells me, he's a lucky guy." He raised his eyebrows and paused.

Then a buzzer sounded. She disappeared into the kitchen.

"That's quite alright. I'll start right here and be quick." He stepped over to the living room phone, picked it up, and set it to his ear. "Dial tone sounds good. I'll just check the others."

Annie barely heard him. Claire was coming over in less than an hour, and Annie was trying a new recipe with lots of steps.

He climbed the stairs. She could hear his footsteps overhead. This bothered her, and she was about to follow him up, even if her sauce burned instead of thickened, when he reappeared. He smiled and waved. "Is this the study?" He pointed towards a door off the living room next to the kitchen door.

"Yes, you'll see everything right there on the desk."

He disappeared into the study and soon reappeared. "All done. I think I may have saved you a service call." He grinned at her as he scribbled on his clipboard, handed it to her to sign, then pulled out the pink middle sheet. "Here's your copy. I'll be off now. Enjoy your evening." And, before she could blink, he was out the front door and out of sight.

Annie looked at the pink sheet in her hand. It looked like a usual work order, but something felt funny. She went to the front window and studied the street. She saw him climb into his white van and drive away. Seeing nothing else unusual, she returned to her culinary activities. The peanut sauce looked about right. She poured olive oil into another skillet. When it just barely sizzled, she added the chopped onion, garlic, and green pepper, gave them a stir, then turned down the heat. She pulled a bowl of boneless chicken breasts from the refrigerator. She chopped them into bite sized pieces and added them to the skillet. Just as she got them the perfect golden brown, the doorbell rang. She wiped her hands on a towel and headed to the front door. Checking the sidelights, she saw it was Claire.

Claire hugged Annie, then plucked from the basket over her arm a cold bottle of pinot grigio and handed it to Annie. "Something smells really good!"

Soon they were in the kitchen working side by side. Claire had brought salad fixings and got busy washing four kinds of lettuce and cutting up a ripe avocado. Annie opened the wine. They sipped as they worked.

"What's that service truck doing outside?" asked Claire.

"Some guy from AT&T stopped by to check something, said there's been disruption in the neighborhood. But I watched him drive away."

"Really? Well, he's back. Or some truck is out there. Have you had problems here?"

"None I have noticed. But then no one calls me but you." Annie smiled as she stirred chicken pieces among the onion, garlic, and peppers, doing her best to squelch the nervous voice inside her. Now it was just a matter of adding the peanut sauce. She turned it down, then got the rice cooker plugged in.

"Do they always work on Saturday? That seems strange." Claire put the salad greens and avocado sections into Annie's large wooden salad bowl, then opened the small jar of salad dressing she had made at home. Just the right amount of olive oil, balsamic vinegar, minced fresh garlic, and fresh basil with a pinch of salt. She poured a tablespoon full onto the salad and tossed it with two forks. She picked up a small piece of coated lettuce and popped it in her mouth. "Just right!" she said.

Annie pressed the button on the rice cooker. "Let's take our wine to the screen porch while the rice cooks." She poured the peanut sauce on the chicken and vegetables and turned down the heat to let it simmer. Her hands trembled with the effort to push away thoughts of the van outside watching.

"How about some chips and salsa while we wait on the rice?" asked Annie.

"Sounds lovely."

Annie gathered up their hors d'oeuvre and led the way through the living room and dining room to the large screen porch on the side of the house. A wicker couch and several wicker chairs with bright red and yellow flowered cushions were gathered around a glass coffee table. Annie set the chips and salsa on the coffee table and sat on one end of the couch. Claire sat on the other end. She had brought the bottle of wine and their glasses, which she refilled. Handing Annie her glass, Claire lifted hers. Annie raised her glass to Claire's and smiled.

Claire grinned and clinked her glass to Annie's glass. Annie smiled.

Claire took a chip and scooped it full of salsa. She popped it in her mouth and looked around. "What a lovely screen porch. I don't believe I've been out here before."

"I love it. We can eat out here too if you want." She waved at the table at the other end of the porch.

"Perfect." Claire looked through the dogwood and maple trees towards the street. She raised her arm shoulder height and pointed. "Then we can keep an eye on that van."

Annie followed Claire's arm. "It's still here? That's weird."

It was indeed, sitting at the curb across the street, half hidden under the branches of an oak tree. The two women sat in silence for a moment staring at it. No sign of life inside. They looked at each other with raised eyebrows.

"Well, it looks like an AT&T van," said Claire.

"I'm just a bit jittery after finding out I've been followed by someone probably hired by Harry and his lawyer," said Annie. She shook her head and tried to drown the tightening in her stomach with a big swallow of her wine. "It just gives me an eerie feeling. What will happen next?"

Claire nodded. "And you live such a wild life, girl! Partying every night, disturbing the neighbors!"

Annie sighed. "Yeah, Claire, I'm a real wild child. Having you over for dinner, really wild."

"Just remember, eventually all this will be behind you. You'll get your divorce and start your new life. I watched my daughter go through this a few years back. She's now doing great. You'll get through it."

"But was she followed by a private investigator?"

"No. Think of it as fuel for writing poetry."

Annie gave a big sigh. "I guess, fuel for something. I have been writing a bit. Want me to show you one?"

"Oh, yes! Bring it out!" Claire sat up and looked around as if there was a poetry stash in front of her. Then there was the sound of a buzzer from inside.

They began to feast, filling their forks, mouths, and stomachs with food instead of talk. Very shortly, though, Claire picked up her head and looked at Annie.

"OK, where's the poem?" She pointed her fork.

Annie closed her eyes and began.

Asshole,
I'd like to see you in a hole,
Your fingers clinging
to the edge
beside my heavy-booted feet.
Heh, heh, heh, I chuckle
while you squirm.
With one swipe,
I could knock you down
Where poisonous snakes
and man-eating Amazons
await to chew you up
and spit you out.
But I won't bother.
I'll just step on your fingers,
once,

hard,
laugh
and walk away.

Annie opened her eyes and looked at Claire. Claire sat with bug eyes a moment, then broke into a big grin and clapped her hands. She took Annie's hands between hers. She shook her head.

"I love that poem. You are a powerful woman, Annie. You have no idea how powerful."

Chapter 36

$\mathcal{B}$rad Schmidt reached for another cigarette from his pack. Finding it empty, he threw it on the floor of his van. He sat in the back with his array of surveillance equipment and checked the monitoring screens. Quiet at Annie's house except for a few gestures from the two women on the porch, the one room he didn't bug. *Damn, and not a guy after all,* he thought. *No phone calls. No nothing.* He exhaled out his mouth, then scratched the stubble on his chin.

But when you decided to hang out your shingle as a PI, you knew you'd be in for a lot of empty hours. He shook his head, then nodded. He wouldn't be sitting here except for the chance he'd get someone to tail. *That would at least be some excitement. Better than empty hours sitting home alone,* he reminded himself. *Yeah, the last few years have been pretty lean. Especially after the bitch left.*

He bit his lips at the thought as memories flooded him. *God, she was hot.* Movement in his jeans accompanied the memories. He pressed his hand against his rising erection. *Down, boy! Yes, she was hot, but remember: you worked night and day and spent all your savings because she just had to go to law school, then what happened? She got greedy, set her sights on big bucks in a big firm and suddenly you were history. And she was a smart lawyer: fucked you one last time, then pushed papers in front of you while you were half-asleep in the afterglow. When you woke up, you found what you'd signed gave you all the law school debt. Her parting gift to you—while you lay there with your mouth hanging open, dumbfounded watching the dust swirl around in her wake. What a bitch!*

Wake up, buddy, and get to work. Three years, let her go.

He scanned the screens. Years of experience had taught him nothing could happen for hours and then all hell could break loose. He smiled recalling how easy it was to set up all his equipment. Those little guys are so tiny now and so easy to install. He patted the embroidery on his pocket. He chuckled. Just for fun, he checked his audio monitor at the guy's house. How easy it had been to set this up—that Taffer guy wasn't even home but had conveniently left a window unlatched. His pulse rate accelerated a moment as he heard heavy breathing and whispered talking. Then gunshots. He turned on the video at the guy's house. A movie. The guy must be watching a movie. He listened and watched a bit longer, then grinned.

"I'm stuffed, can't eat another bite," said Claire, leaning her chair back from the table.

"Don't fall over backwards," said Annie. "Those chairs are really tippy. Harry did that once and cracked his head on the slate floor."

Claire sat her chair on all four legs again, sat up straight, then leaned over carefully to examine the floor. "Maybe that's what happened to him—head injury. That slate looks very hard." She laughed.

"Maybe, or maybe I just didn't know who he really was." Annie sighed, looked down a moment, then shook her head and turned to Claire. "How about some herbal tea?"

"How about another poem?"

"How about you? Do you have one to share?"

"Not from memory unfortunately. I'm working on one. Maybe I'll bring it to class when it starts back if it's ready. I'm so glad I joined that class."

"Me too. I love that class. I have learned so much and I've made such great friends." She patted Claire's hand, which lay on the table.

Claire gave Annie a big smile. "That's entirely mutual." She looked up at the skylight. "Well, how about a walk around the block? I think the moon is almost full and may be above the trees by now."

"Sounds lovely." Annie got up and collected the bowls and plates. Soon they had the table cleared and the kitchen cleaned up.

"You're quick," grinned Annie.

"Had to be with a big family. And I love a clean kitchen."

Claire led the way out the kitchen door and around the side of the house, then stopped. Looking up to find the moon, Annie ran into her. They both stood still.

Claire squinted her eyes and tilted her head towards the street. The moon shone a path on the street as if there were a spotlight. "Annie, that van is still there. What time is it?"

"Nearly ten."

They stood in the shadow of the house without moving. The van was clearly visible in the same place they had seen it earlier. Even under the spreading oak tree, they could see it, a large shadow under the tree with everything else lit up by the moon.

"I have half a mind to go over and knock on the window and ask what's going on!" Annie shook her head. Claire turned back towards the van. "But maybe that's too risky."

Annie was trembling. Claire put her arm around Annie's waist. Annie took one slow deep breath and leaned into Claire's arm. Then she pulled her phone out of her pocket. "So glad this dress has pockets. Maybe I should dial 911, what do you think? Maybe this is the PI who's been following me." She looked up at Claire with question marks in her eyes.

"I wonder that too." Claire narrowed her eyes in thought, nibbling the inside of her cheek, then she looked at the phone. "We could, or we could just take our walk." She looked at Annie, saw she was no longer trembling, and said: "And if we get a good angle..."

Annie smiled. "Maybe I'll just have to snap a photo."

Claire nodded. Annie nodded. And they set out, walking past the van on the far side of the street in the wide path of light cast by the bright orb above them.

Peering closely at his monitors, Brad felt his heartbeat quicken. He saw the two women leave the porch for the kitchen, then come outside. Then he lost them in the shadows. He zoomed in only to see them walk along the street, illuminated clearly by the moon, then down the street past the back of his truck. He studied them until they walked out of sight. They seemed to be smiling and chatting. Did they pay any attention to his truck? He couldn't tell. But he felt his armpits grow damp and perspiration trickle down his sides. Maybe it was time to call it a night. He couldn't see them anyway.

He crawled through the tiny door from the back of the van into the driver's seat. He reached to turn the key in the ignition, then hesitated. If he started the engine and drove away now, he would surely attract their attention. He looked in the side mirror but saw no sign of them. That was strange. They must have crossed over behind the van. Then he slapped the side of his head with his hand. *You idiot!* He crawled back and turned on the camera pointed from the back of the van. Too dark to see them yet. He waited.

Claire and Annie stood ten feet in back of the van in the shadows of the trees that lined the road. Annie opened her phone and snapped a photo of the back of the truck with a clear shot of the license plate.

"Do you need to use the flash?" whispered Claire.

Annie checked the photo she had just taken and examined it. "Maybe."

"Let me see." Claire leaned over. "I'm afraid so. But that will surely draw attention to us."

"What else can we do?"

Claire frowned and wrinkled her nose while she thought. Then her eyes flew open. "Snap it with the flash, then we'll walk away fast and dial 911 if anything happens."

Annie shook her head. "I'll snap it with the flash, then we run fast back to my house, lock all the doors, and then call 911."

"Okay."

Annie turned on the flash. Her insides turned from jelly to steel. The Amazon woman from her poem rose up inside her. She pressed her front foot firmly into the ground, zoomed in, and got a good shot of the license plate. She snapped, the light flashed, and they both ran. In seconds, they were behind Annie's house, through the kitchen door, leaning over clutching their sides and gasping for breath.

Brad saw the flash, then two dark figures running. In seconds, he was back in the driver's seat, turning the key in the ignition, and roaring off.

"Damn!" he shouted as he shifted the gears. "Damn! Damn!"

Chapter 37

When Amanda welcomed Annie into her office on Monday afternoon, she observed her in growing concern. Annie grabbed a tissue the moment she sat down and soon had ripped it to shreds. Then she picked up the blue rubber ball on the side table and squeezed it over and over. She looked at Amanda through tears that filled her eyes and began to spill over.

"Thanks for working me in today." Tears slowly ran down her face as she relaxed her grip on the rubber ball.

Amanda frowned just a bit and examined her closely. "What's going on?"

"I am under surveillance. Constantly. It is freaking me out." She dabbed at her eyes with another tissue. "Harry and his lawyer have this guy following me. I'm guessing now it wasn't the AT&T technician that knocked on my door and went all through my house checking my service last Saturday. It was that damned PI!" She gripped the ball tight and lifted her head to Amanda. "All through my house. How could I be so naive? Then he sat in his truck on my street all evening."

"I'm so sorry. I can see why you're freaked out." Amanda leaned forward. "Is there more?"

"I haven't been able to sleep. Everywhere I go now I'm looking around me." She frowned and paused. Then she laughed. "And I'm really not doing anything worth watching! I don't get it and I'm sick of it!"

"I'll bet you are. It's a real violation." Amanda pressed her lips together and shook her head.

"Well, if they are trying to find something I'm doing that will make his infidelity not so bad, they are going to be sorely disappointed." Annie exhaled a long breath and relaxed her hand on the blue ball. "I even got a photo of the truck's license plate. Boy, I felt great when I did that but then I just kept worrying and worrying . . ."

"Have you told your lawyer?"

"I'm going to see her when I leave here."

"Give yourself credit for having the presence of mind to take that photo. That was a smart move."

"Well, thanks, but I just wish it would stop." Annie gave a big sigh. "I just wish all this would be over and I could get a divorce and be done with Harry."

"You will be. That's what your lawyer will help you with. Now let's see if I can help you calm down."

"I'm for that." Annie let go of the ball and placed her hands open on her thighs.

"First tell me what's in your repertoire of self-soothing methods." Amanda picked up her clipboard and pen.

Annie thought for moment. "Reading a good book, writing poetry sometimes helps. I wish I could say meditation but lately I just can't sit still. So I just do my work, grade papers and all that and then wake up in the middle of the night and start thinking and then I'm done for. No more sleep."

Amanda nodded. "Yes, once your mind wakes up, it's hard to go back to sleep. Let's try something. Let me show you some relaxation exercises." Amanda set her clipboard and pen aside.

Annie tilted her head. "Okay, what?"

"A sort of guided relaxation. Just make yourself comfortable in the chair and close your eyes."

Annie snuggled back in the chair, put her hands in her lap, and closed her eyes.

"Good. Now just take some slow deep breaths. Just focus on your breathing and begin to let go of whatever tensions and worries you've been carrying." Amanda's voice adopted a lilting rhythm as if rocking a cradle. She watched the muscles in Annie's face grow soft and smooth. Annie let go of a big sigh. "Very good. Release them like a handful of helium-filled balloons you take into an open field . . . and release into the air and watch as they rise higher and higher . . . and appear smaller and smaller . . . until they disappear from sight." Annie's shoulders dropped as she sank a tiny bit more into the chair. "Good. Now imagine you are standing in a warm shower of relaxation . . . and as the warm water flows over your body, you let all your muscles relax starting with your face and your jaw." Amanda smiled as she saw Annie's jaw unclench and fall open, her lips lightly touching. Amanda continued her rocking rhythm of speech as she moved down Annie's body to her feet. "I don't know exactly how it is for you . . . And it doesn't really matter . . . All that really matters is that you enjoy as much comfort and relaxation as you would like."

Amanda continued. "Now imagine yourself in a safe place . . . It can be any place at all—a place you haven't been to in a long time, a place you go to often, or a place you've always wanted to go . . . When you find your place and can see it clearly, let me know by nodding your head."

Amanda watched Annie closely until she saw a slight nod. "Very good. Now in a moment I'm going to ask you to describe your safe place . . . You'll find it easy to talk and talking will just take you deeper into this experience . . . So now tell me, where are you?"

There was a long pause, then Annie whispered: "In the mountains by a waterfall, Where we used to go on vacation when I was growing up."

"Lovely. Tell me more."

"I see water falling over rocks, I hear water sounds, there's mist on my face."

"Anyone else there with you?"

"Yes, my parents. We're all just so happy and relaxed."

"And how old are you?"

"Oh, maybe ten, I like to spend time with my parents. Vacations are fun."

"Wonderful. Just continue to enjoy your safe place with your conscious mind while I talk to your subconscious mind, the helper, the part that knows what's best for you . . . It will listen for you and take what you need . . . For your highest good and greatest growth."

Amanda paused and watched Annie enjoying her waterfall. "We all have times when we're scared and we don't know what to do." Finding no change in Annie's face and body posture, she continued. "We all have times when we need to ask for help. Ask and it is given. It's simple really." Amanda saw a slight smile come over Annie's face. "It's okay to ask for help." Amanda decided to reach deeper. "And there are times to be angry, to say 'stop!'" Amanda now saw a firmness in Annie's face, a determination. "A time to gather your allies around you, to face what scares you . . . To find your courage and use it . . . For your own protection . . . For your own growth." Amanda knew Annie had inner strength she had not yet tapped. Harry may be explosive and scary at times, but Annie was more a lion than a mouse. "You are a powerful woman . . . You know what you want . . . You know where your boundaries are . . . Take a moment to savor your inner strength and let it rise inside you." Amanda paused and watched Annie closely. She took a few deep breaths herself. The change was subtle, but Amanda knew how to recognize it. It was time to close the session.

Annie's eyes fluttered, then opened. She looked right at Amanda and smiled. "I feel so much better."

"Good." Then Amanda watched Annie's expression change. She narrowed her eyes and tilted her head.

"Something strange happened towards the end."

"Oh?"

"I felt angry. So unlike the nice Southern girl my mother raised me to be. Like I have a fire inside me. Then it changed and I felt—this feels weird to say—but I felt invincible. Like I had a whip in my hand and was ready to use it." Amanda waited as she followed Annie, saw her close her eyes and go inside, then open them and give Amanda a piercing look. "I wrote a new poem recently, an angry poem. It just poured out of me. Unlike anything I've ever written before. I have only shared it with Claire."

Excitement built inside of Amanda. On the outside, however, she remained placid, merely nodding and continuing to watch.

"I want to share it, I have it memorized," she said as she stood up.

"*Asshole,*" she began.

Amanda listened in awe as Annie punched her words, her voice rising in crescendo then falling to softer tones at the end. When she sat back down, Amanda could only say, "Wow."

Annie laughed. "I feel like I can handle anything, whatever comes."

"After hearing that poem, I'd have to say 'Yes, you can.'" Amanda felt a warm current of pleasure flow through her.

"I think I'm finished for today," said Annie.

"Yes, I agree," said Amanda. "What's next?"

Annie sat up straighter. "Meet with my lawyer and find out how to get this surveillance stopped!"

"Sounds good to me. If anyone knows what to do, Jan Stone does."

"I want to come again Thursday, keep this feeling going."

"The time is yours, Annie."

Annie sat tall at Jan's conference table, her palms on the top of the table. "Thank you for seeing me so promptly."

"I'm glad I had an opening. It sounded urgent." Jan had a legal pad in front of her, her pen in her hand.

"I am sick of being under surveillance. Sick of it. I want it to stop. How can we make it stop?"

"They are still having you followed? This is ridiculous." Jan pressed her lips together.

"Yes, I think they have bugged my house." She told Jan the whole story. "I got a photo of his license plate." She handed the phone to Jan.

"You are on the ball with your photos, Ms. Thomas!" Jan exclaimed as she wrote down the license number. She waved to her assistant at the desk just outside the conference room who came right over. "Mary, look up this license number and see what you find." Jan peeled off the top page of her legal pad and handed it to Mary.

"Sure, back in a jiffy," said Mary as she turned and left.

Jan turned back to Annie. "This is totally illegal. I can have him in big trouble, all of them."

"I want it to stop. I want a divorce. I want to be done with Harry. I have had enough!" Annie hit her fist on the table top.

"I do too, Annie." Jan paused. Her eyes glazed over. Then she also hit her fist on the table top. "I have an idea. If you want, I can write a letter telling them to cease and desist, including a threat to take them to court for illegal wiretapping and even a threat to release the photo of Harry *in flagrant delecto* to the press. I will propose a court date for the final divorce under *divorce from bed and board* so you won't have to wait a year and you can be done with it."

Annie chewed her lips. "Would I have to go to court?"

"I take it you'd like to avoid that." Annie nodded. Jan went on: "Another possibility, if you want to avoid court, is to demand Harry sign the separation agreement we sent them."

"The one that gives me the house, him the mortgage and me alimony?"

"Exactly." Jan watched Annie's face. Annie grimaced.

"Alimony feels like staying attached. I don't know if I even want alimony. Or want to stay in that house. I just want the surveillance to stop."

"Alimony would be paid through the court and go directly into your bank account. You'd never see him. If you sell the house, the proceeds will be yours to do with as you wish, buy another house, whatever. Let me send a cease and desist letter and see what we get back. First priority is to stop the surveillance for sure."

"Okay, that makes sense. Go for it!" Annie nodded and sat back in her chair.

"Is tomorrow soon enough? I can write it tonight and get it in registered mail first thing in the morning."

Mary appeared in the doorway. Jan turned to her with raised eyebrows. "Find anything?"

"You won't believe this. That van belongs to AT&T. It was reported missing and presumed stolen after disappearing on Saturday morning. The police pulled it over late Saturday for speeding and identified it as the stolen van. Brad Schmidt is now cooling his heels in the county jail."

Annie's jaw dropped. Jan looked at Mary. "Wow. You have earned your pay today. Take the rest of the day off!"

Mary laughed. "All five minutes of it? Do you realize it's 4:55 p.m. now?"

Jan looked shocked. "Is it really?" She turned to Annie. "Time flies when you're having fun."

"You call this fun?" asked Annie, shaking her head.

"It is now," said Jan with a big grin. Then she turned back to Mary. "Sleep in tomorrow then. Take the morning off. I'll type this letter up myself."

"Thanks, boss!" said Mary and left.

"Given these new developments, shall we ask the detective on the case of the missing van to send someone over to your house directly to remove any surveillance bugs they find?" Jan grinned.

"They can do that?" asked Annie, frowning.

"Sure, they can bug it, they can remove the bugs. They might find it very interesting. You do want them removed, don't you?"

"When can they come?"

Jan picked up the phone and dialed. "Ben. It's Jan Stone. Hey. I'm great. I hear you've got Brad Schmidt in the tank there. Yeah, I know, it was only a matter of time. But I think he may have left some things in the home of one of my clients. Some very small things. Care to send someone to remove them right away? Yes, someone will be home to let you in."

Jan winked at Annie. "Great. I'll see you there."

"You're coming home with me?" Annie's eyes widened.

"You bet. I wouldn't miss this for the world!" Jan grinned. "Ready to go?"

"I sure am. Lead the way."

Chapter 38

$\mathcal{D}$ennis Stacey sat at his desk first thing Wednesday morning reading the registered letter he had just received. He frowned as he read it once and then a second time. Then he leaned back in his high-back chair and stared at the ceiling. He clenched his jaw and pressed his lips together. Shaking his head, he picked up his phone and pressed the office intercom.

"Yes, boss?" said his receptionist.

"Find Harry Thomas and tell him to get down here immediately."

"Will do."

He slammed the phone down and folded his hands together at his lips. His thoughts tumbled around in his mind like tennis balls in a clothes dryer.

Harry tapped on the door and pushed it open. Seeing Dennis, his face curled into a question mark. Dennis waved him in, shook his head silently, and closed his eyes briefly. When he opened them, Harry had closed the office door and was sitting in the chair in front of him balancing his elbows on his knees and clasping his hands almost in prayer position. His right leg jiggled up and down. "What the hell happened? By the looks of you, it can't be good."

Dennis gave a wan smile. "It could hardly be worse."

He passed the letter to Harry who grabbed it and began reading.

As Harry read, he emitted strange sounds reminiscent of someone panting while being pummeled. "Uhh, ooo, ahh." The sounds soon morphed into curses as his eyes moved down the page. "What the fuck?" He looked up at Dennis. "In jail? Schmidt is in jail? What kind of idiot is he?" He sat back and waited for Dennis's response.

"A pretty big one it would seem," said Dennis again, shaking his head as if trying to get water out of his ears. "Keep reading, it gets worse."

Harry returned his eyes to the paper. His eyes widened and his face flushed. Then he threw down the paper and began pacing the room muttering, "Oh my god, oh my god," in steady acceleration and crescendo until he stood in front of the desk, his voice a full fortissimo. "OH MY GOD! NO! NOT THE PRESS! NO!"

"Yeah, your worst nightmare, eh?" said Dennis, drumming his fingers on the desk.

Harry crumpled back into the chair like a balloon leaking air slowly but steadily. He hung his head, then raised his eyes slowly to Dennis. He retrieved the letter from the floor and returned it to Dennis. "Tell me you have a plan. Please."

Dennis took a big breath and exhaled loudly, relieved that Harry was not taking his frustrations out on him. "I think we'd better get them a generous separation agreement as soon as possible. Give her the house, two years alimony, whatever it takes to extract a promise to delete that photo."

"Jeez, how do we know it's not already on the Internet going viral?" Harry looked like someone who had just fallen into Narcissus's pool and was drowning. He gasped for air. His face grew pale.

"That's driving on the information highway. We don't know."

"What about Schmidt? Have you talked to him?"

"He can go to hell!" Dennis raised his voice for the first time. "He screwed up so badly, I recommend we not pay him a red cent!"

"We hired him. Do we have any liability here?" Harry's face showed sudden terror.

"We didn't hire him to steal a van. I think we can stay out of it. I'll make sure he doesn't work in this town again." Dennis's eyebrows knitted together and his eyes threw lightning bolts.

"Damn right!" Harry shouted. Then he sighed and his eyes glazed over. They both sat in silence for a near eternity. Finally Harry spoke. "Okay, give her the house. I'll pay the mortgage for some reasonable period of time—do you think six months will do it? I'll pay her alimony for two years if you think it will keep that photo from going viral. I want to be done with it." He sat up tall in his chair. "I am done."

Dennis sat tall and picked up his pen. He began making notes on the legal pad in front of him. "I will draw up the agreement as soon as possible. Let's offer to pay the mortgage for twelve months just to be careful or until she sells the house, which is often what happens. Half your retirement, and we'll just split everything else right down the middle according to the law, with two years alimony based on the formula. I'll send you an electronic copy as soon as it's finished so you can approve it. I think that will do it." He looked up at Harry. "Are you agreeable?"

Harry nodded and shook his head. He paused a moment. "Don't forget the part that once the agreement is signed I'm free to associate with whomever I choose."

Dennis smiled. "And of course she'll be free to do that also. I won't forget." He winked at Harry. "I don't suppose you have anyone in mind you'd like to associate with, do you?"

"Life goes on, Dennis, life goes on." Harry stood and turned towards the door. Over his shoulder, he said: "If I could DocuSign it tonight, I would."

"We can send it to them signed and notarized if you want." Dennis leaned back and waited.

Harry brightened. "When can you have it done?"

"Give me two hours."

"You got it!"

Dennis watched Harry walk out the door and close it behind him. He stared at the ceiling just long enough for legal language to begin to flow inside his mind. Then he turned to the computer and keyboard to his left and began typing.

The intercom buzzed and he pressed the button and the speaker phone.

"Brad Schmidt on line two."

"Tell him to go to hell!" shouted Dennis.

Jan sat at the head of her conference table with Annie at her left. Rays from the afternoon sun came through the slits in the blinds onto the table making it look a bit like a zebra. "It's very generous, which tells me we scared them good." With a big grin, she handed it to Annie who held it out of the striped sunlight to skim through it, flipping pages and squinting.

"I think I understand most of it. I get the house. He'll pay the mortgage for an entire year and offers me two years of alimony?"

"Yes, that's right. I know you were reluctant to accept the alimony but I'm glad you decided to take it. It might help ease your transition. It's given now mainly in cases of adultery. Let's just say it's the price he has to pay."

Annie ran her fingers through her hair and thought a minute. She thought of the bills she would have to pay with her teacher's salary, the upkeep on this house, which felt cavernous now that she'd been living in it alone for a while, this house filled with memories of her hopes and dreams for a life with Harry, now shattered. She wasn't even sure she wanted to keep the house. Then she thought of all the repairs required to put the house on the market, repairs she would surely have to hire someone to do. And then finding another house and moving—she'd probably have to hire movers. It all seemed like an awful lot as she listed it in her mind.

"But what if I sell the house?" She turned towards Jan.

"Well, whatever profit there is, you get it all. The alimony will be directly deposited into your bank account so you'll have no dealings with Harry at all." Jan tapped the erasure end of her pencil on the table in the middle of a sunbeam, then held it still, making a thick dark line across the lines of sunbeam and shadow. Then she smiled and looked at Annie.

"I've been thinking of a smaller house." She closed her eyes a moment, then opened them and watched the dark stripe made by Jan's pencil cross the shadow of the blinds. "It feels like a prison, really. That may sound silly but it just feels haunted. I never liked the house that much; it was a bad compromise, but I didn't expect to leave it for a long time, not like this. Now it's empty. I'm bouncing off the walls."

"That makes sense to me," said Jan quietly. "I've heard the same sentiments from other clients going through separation and divorce. A new house for a new life. That can help a lot." She patted Annie's arm.

Annie looked up with a frown.

"So are you ready to sign? That's what's next. If so, I'll call in the troops to witness and notarize it."

Annie sat tall and pressed her lips together. She took a big breath and with her exhale said: "Let's do it."

Soon the conference table was surrounded by several office staff, one bearing the notary seal. Annie signed as directed with the pen Jan gave her, then watched as the witnesses signed and the notary pressed the seal and signed in the appropriate place. It was quick and easy.

"Congratulations, Annie, you are now legally separated," said Jan as the others left. "It was convenient of Harry to have it signed and notarized ahead of time. That let us know he meant it. Running scared I'd say." Jan gave a Cheshire cat grin. "I'll file it and send you a copy." Just then Mary came in and handed her some papers. "Or my clever assistant will have made you one and I can give it to you now." Then to Mary: "I didn't even notice you'd taken it off to copy. You are on the ball, Mary! I'm actually going to let you leave on time today."

Mary laughed. "What a refreshing change of pace. Thanks."

Jan turned to Annie. "Now we delete the photo. Is the one on your phone the only copy you have?"

Annie nodded.

"I will delete the copy you sent me. Do you know how to delete yours?"

In response, Annie opened her phone and scrolled to the photo. She gazed at it one last time—the naked bodies entwined, the clutter of clothes flung off among the empty liquor glasses. It plunged a knife into her heart. She bent over with the blow. Images from their marriage flashed before her mind. She shook them away, then sat up and tapped the delete icon on the screen. When the box asking "Are you sure?" popped up, she did not hesitate but hit "delete." A wave of sadness washed over her. She raised her eyes to Jan, then sighed. "Done."

"And now you are a free woman," said Jan. "Go celebrate. Nothing else to do until a year from now and that will feel like an anticlimax. Probably five minutes before a judge, max."

Annie shook her head in disbelief. "Really?"

"Really," replied Jan, smiling. "The worst is over."

Annie gathered her purse and copy of the agreement and walked out feeling somewhat in a fog. The thought of going home to her big house alone felt daunting. She didn't realize it would be over today. She sat in her car for a while wishing she had made a plan with Claire or someone. She pulled out her phone and called Claire. No answer. She decided to go to Tom's Market and get something special to celebrate. Maybe a small bottle of champagne. For sure some chocolate. Satisfied, she put her car in gear and set out.

In a few minutes, she was parked and walking through the grassy lawn of Tom's Market. The afternoon sun was right ahead of her and still very bright, making it hard to see. Casting her eyes around the tables to find an empty one, she thought she saw a familiar figure sitting at a table under a tree. Her heartbeat quickened. *Ah, George.* Then she moved so the sun was behind a tree and looked again. She saw a young man dressed in blue jeans and T-shirt with a heavy book in front of him. Undoubtedly a student. No one she knew. She was surprised how disappointed she felt. She began to fantasize. What if it were George? Would she go over and sit down? Would he look up and smile, so happy to see her?

She shook the images from her mind and walked into the store. She grabbed a shopping cart and rolled down the aisles. But the image of George stuck and blossomed inside her. There was a specific clause in the agreement saying she was free to associate with whomever she chose without interference from the spouse from whom she was now legally separated. George's tall frame stood in front of her. Or maybe he was sitting home alone. She put a small piece of fresh wild-caught salmon in her cart, then a bunch of broccoli. She moved on to the wine section. They had some half bottles. She picked out a bottle of prosecco. George seemed to be walking beside her now. *How about a small chocolate torte?* Was that his voice? Her dream continued to the bakery section. Right there waiting for her was a small "Love Cake" just right for two. But surely too much for her alone at home tonight. She put it in her cart.

When she unlocked her door at home and brought her groceries inside, she watched her fantasy fade and a great emptiness replace it inside her. She was done with Harry and she was alone. She cooked and ate her salmon and sipped her wine and wondered. She remembered the salmon dinner she had fixed for Harry, the dinner he hadn't come home for. Now he wasn't coming home ever again. She would have to get used to eating alone. Amanda had said she could now create a new life, create the life she wanted. She could cook whatever she wanted. She could stay up late and play her music over and over, something Harry hadn't tolerated. She could clean her house when and how she wanted, not to fulfill some old idea of being a good housekeeper. She could stay in bed on Saturday until noon reading and writing poetry. Who would be part of that new life? Was the long-ago message from the Ouija Board a true one? She smiled remembering sitting with her roommate on the wrinkled sheets of her bed with the board between them as she and Nancy felt the planchette move beneath their fingers.

Chapter 39

Late one Saturday afternoon, Annie sat in her living room to begin the slow process of sorting her belongings and trying to imagine what would fit into the smaller house she had found. George had recommended real estate agents, Steve and Katy Benson, who helped her find it. She felt nervous without someone to help and advise her, but it seemed the perfect house for her new life so she signed on the dotted line. Although she had a mountain to climb before her moving date, she figured she had better get started. How had she accumulated all this stuff? She looked around her living room shaking her head.

Books, lots of books. She could at least put them into some boxes. She had found two boxes in the attic left over from moving to this house. Pulling one next to her, she started pulling books from the bookcase and putting them into the box. College books, others she had gotten over the years, family books, dictionaries. She picked up a fat book. *Robinson Crusoe. Ah, her father's favorite.* Flipping it open, she found a letter stuck between the pages. From her father, in his distinctive scrawl. She picked it up with trembling hands. When had he sent this letter? It was not dated; it was just like him not to leave a date. She looked at the postmark on the envelope. Faded but just legible enough to show it was from a few years ago. Right after he had left with Hilda. Right after they had had a big fight. From Arizona.

She pulled out the folded page and opened it. Had she even read it? She had been so angry then that she could have stuffed it in this book unread. She couldn't remember.

Dear Annie,

I'm so sorry we had cross words. I don't blame you for being angry. I know it's hard for you to understand how an old man feels when he loses his wife, how lost he is, how dependent. But I can't be alone. When your mother died, I thought I would die too. Then I met Hilda. I know it was too quick for you. But I have so little time left, Annie. Hilda was alone too. Now that you have Harry, maybe you will one day understand. Please stay in touch, my dear daughter.

Love, Daddy

At the bottom of the page was a phone number. And an address.

She had thought of calling him. A flash of anger hit her. He was the one that left. She stared off into space as it sunk into her skin, her pores, her stomach, her heart. She did have his number. She could call him. She reread the letter. *Please stay in touch,* he had written. Maybe she did have someone to help her. Maybe. She sat by the phone. She picked up the headset. She put it down. She picked it up. Her palms got sweaty and her stomach knotted. She dialed. The phone rang again and again, then went to voice mail. She heard a woman's voice. "You've reached John and Hilda. Please leave a message." She left her name and number and hung up.

She went back to her sorting, not knowing what to expect and wondering if she should have said more, said what she wanted and needed. Her spirits sank. It had been so long. At least her father must still be alive. But what condition was he in? She had no idea.

The phone rang, the sound striking her like lightning. Picking it up, she heard a shaky voice. "Annie?"

"Daddy?" said Annie, hardly believing her ears. "Dad?"

"Is it really you?" His voice cracked.

"Yes, it's me, Daddy." Annie sat stunned. Tears sprang into her eyes. "How are you?"

"Better now that I hear your voice. I'm okay, how are you?"

"How am I? Oh, Daddy." Her resolve dissolved into the grief and loss underneath, and she began to weep. Hearing his voice after so long just blew her away. She tried but couldn't get a word out so she just kept crying. How could she even begin to answer that question?

"Oh, Annie, my dear little girl, what has happened? Please, please tell me." He began to cry also but he could still talk. "I know you're angry. I know it's all my fault we haven't been in touch, but I just went crazy after your mother died. I missed her so much, but I never stopped thinking about you and missing you."

Annie began to pull herself together. *You need to be honest,* said a voice inside her. *No more Miss Nice Girl. You'd better speak up.* "Daddy?"

"Yes, sweetheart?"

"I have something to tell you."

"Okay, I'm listening."

"I know we had a fight and I know I bear some responsibility in that, but I thought you were gone forever. I thought you didn't care about me. I thought all you cared about was Hilda. I mean, Mother had just died . . ." Annie pulled a tissue from the box on the side table and wiped her tear-stained face. She felt her old grief surface, with shades of anger.

"I know, Annie. I know it seems that way. Your old dad is just a dependent old man who can't get along without a woman. But I do care, I'm just not good at saying it, just old-fashioned that way, I guess. Please forgive me. I thought about you a lot and I should have called you, but I knew you had Harry so I thought you were doing better than I was."

"Oh, Daddy, that's over. Harry ran off with another woman. We're getting a divorce." Annie felt the urge to collapse in tears but instead she found steel in her voice. She wanted her words to hit hard. Her father should have been here for her.

"Oh, no, that bastard! I wish you had told me . . ." He paused. "But I guess I understand why you didn't."

"Daddy, you married Hilda and moved far away. It has not been an easy time."

"Of course it hasn't. I should have been there; I should have tried harder. I never liked him anyway."

Annie leaned her arms on the table, not sure she'd heard correctly. "What? You never liked him?"

"Well, now I can tell you, honey," said her father. "I thought he was too ambitious and not sensitive enough for my little girl."

"You never said anything." Annie sat back in the kitchen chair.

"I know. Your mother was so impressed with him, so I just went along with her. I did that a lot. Yes, he's handsome and has a good career and all that meant everything to your mother. But I just sensed a coldness in him, an anger. I wish I had said something. Should I have?"

Annie thought a minute. "I doubt I would have listened, Daddy. I was too crazy in love to listen to anything back then. But I sure would listen now. Hearing you say that kind of helps me feel better."

"I'm so glad. And I'm so glad to hear your voice, baby." He sniffled into the phone.

"It's good to hear your voice, too, Daddy. How long has it been? I've missed you." Annie felt tears fill her eyes again.

"It has been too long and it's all my fault. Let me come see you. Would you let me? Please? Just me alone. Hilda told me I should and now that I hear what you're going through, I know I should."

"Yes, Daddy, come visit. I have to move. I'm getting my house ready to sell. Today I saw a house I might buy. I'd like to show it to you. I've never done this all by myself."

"I'd love to. Let me check the airlines and get back to you. I'll come as soon as I can. Then maybe you can come visit us. Hilda said she would like to get to know you better. I know it's a long way but it's beautiful in Arizona and we love this retirement community we live in. Of course, I miss the green of the east. It will be good to look at the house with you if I can. Goodbye now. Love you."

"Love you too, Daddy." Annie hung up and sat for some time, so shocked she could hardly move.

"You're not going to believe what happened this week." Annie sat in Amanda's office for her usual Thursday afternoon session.

"What happened?" asked Amanda, curious.

"Well, Friday I signed separation papers. Saturday I called George to help me with repairs. Sunday real estate agents showed me a place I fell in love with, and Monday I put money down on it. And if that weren't enough, Sunday afternoon I called my father." Annie shook her head in disbelief.

Amanda joined her, shaking her head as well. "Wow, you've had a busy week. The first thing on your list I expected would happen eventually, but not the last few."

"Me neither," said Annie. "And tomorrow my father flies in to visit me."

Amanda raised her eyebrows. "That's a lot in a few days. Tell me all about it." Amanda knew Annie had given just the headlines and there was a lot more. She studied Annie's face and demeanor. She looked relaxed, even happy, if also a little nervous.

Annie poured out the entire story of these last few days minute by minute. Amanda listened, only needing to nod occasionally to keep Annie's flow going. "And Daddy told me he never really liked Harry. He just went along with Mother as he always did. He thought Harry was cold and insensitive. And he was right."

"How validating for you," said Amanda.

"Yes. I can't believe he didn't say anything. Well, I can believe it because he's not one to say much anyway, and Mother was so crazy about me marrying a handsome lawyer."

"Well, your father may be quiet, but it's interesting he saw something in Harry neither you nor your mother saw."

"Maybe, but what good did it do me? I never knew it because he never said anything. And he always went along with Mother." Annie paused a moment and studied her hands in her lap, then raised her head and said softly, "I did the same with Harry. I kept quiet and went along."

Amanda smiled. "Tell me more. Sounds like an important

insight on your part."

Annie sat still a moment, then in a low voice said, "Thank you. I never put it together until this very moment."

Amanda remained silent and watched Annie closely. Annie frowned as she reflected on this new awareness, her eyes on her hands in her lap. After a few moments, she raised her head to Amanda.

"After I married Harry, I just did everything he wanted. I thought that was what a wife was supposed to do to make her husband happy. With Harry, I didn't consider what I wanted. Ever. Hardly ever. Until recently." She pressed her lips together and blinked. "I'm new at even asking myself what I really want. It seems foreign, like it's selfish or something."

"Oh?"

"I think I got the message that being nice, being a good girl, meant being sensitive to what other people wanted." Her mouth dropped open. "*Don't rock the boat,* that's what my mother would say to me."

Amanda thought a moment. "Well, there are times it's good not to rock the boat, but there are some boats that need rocking."

Annie smiled. "And there are some boats it's good to get out of. Like the boat of my marriage to Harry."

"Yes, you are out of that boat now."

"I am so glad."

"I'm glad you're starting to feel that way. And now your father has resurfaced in your life. How are you feeling about that?"

Annie's eyes opened wide. "Amazed. Totally amazed. Nervous. I can't remember ever having time alone with my father, at least not as an adult."

"This is a real opportunity." Although it was a familiar pattern to Amanda, it continued to astound her that so many parents undervalued one-on-one time with their children. Her father's reappearance in Annie's life couldn't have come at a more important time.

"I feel such conflicting emotions. Surprise, grief, excitement, anger, confusion."

"I imagine you will have a lot to talk about with him."

Annie paced restlessly in the receiving area of Raleigh-Durham Airport. Her father's plane from Phoenix had been delayed. He'd missed his connection in Houston, and it was now 11:30 p.m. His flight had just landed. As she waited for deplaning passengers to appear, she wondered if she would even recognize him, it had been so long. People began to stream down the hall. She zoned in on every gray-haired man that passed. Toward the end of the swarm, she saw him. Yes, that was her father. He looked thin and gaunt, his tall frame bent slightly and his hair more silver than she remembered. His lined face broke into a wide smile when he saw her, revealing a bit of the handsome man she remembered. The initial awkwardness she felt dissolved as he kissed her cheek and drew her into a big embrace. She could feel the bones in his back beneath her arms. She was shocked at how much he had aged. He looked like he had returned from the dead.

"Oh, Annie, my girl," he said, holding her shoulders in his hands and leaning back to examine her. "You look so beautiful, more beautiful than ever."

"Thank you, Daddy," she said, beaming back at him. "It's good to see you." She took his bag. "Is this all you have?"

He nodded. "I didn't want to waste time waiting for checked baggage. I couldn't wait to get to my girl, I mean, my daughter, the beautiful grown-up woman."

Just then, she heard the sound of a phone ringing. Her father began to stuff his hands into every pocket until he pulled out a cell phone. *My father has a cell phone?* She stared in amazement as he wrinkled his eyes to find the right button to answer.

"Hello, honey. Yes, I got here . . . yes it was a hell of a flight . . . Yes, Annie is standing right here . . . I'm fine, really I'm fine . . . Yes, I'll call you tomorrow . . . Love you, too. Bye." He disconnected the call. "That was Hilda."

"I figured," said Annie, smiling.

"In all the excitement, I forgot to call her to let her know I got here okay and all."

"Well, I'm glad she knows now." She took his arm and led him towards the parking lot.

On the drive to her house, he chattered on about every detail of his flight, as if a cork had been removed from a bottle of bubbly. He seemed delighted to see her but faded quickly once they got home. She was relieved when he went to bed soon after they got there. Too excited to sleep, she sat up late writing in her journal. She got up at dawn, eager to be up before him, started coffee, and began to think about breakfast. After she had it all ready to cook and he wasn't yet downstairs, she began to worry. She positioned herself in the living room with a full view of the stairs, trying and failing to read the morning paper. Checking her watch, she saw it was only 8:15 a.m.

A few minutes later, he finally creaked down the stairs, holding tight to the banister with each step. He saw her waiting and his face lit up. So did hers.

"Hi, Daddy, how did you sleep?"

"I slept just fine." He looked revived and full of vitality.

Trying not to show how reassured she felt, Annie greeted him with a hug and kiss. "Coffee is ready. Are you hungry?"

"Yes, I am. What's for breakfast?" He squeezed her shoulder and followed her into the kitchen.

"How about pancakes? Like you used to make for me when I was growing up. I've got the batter all ready. You used to tell me I'd be making them for you some day." She gave him a wide grin.

"Yes, when I was old. And I am old." He grinned back at her and sat at the kitchen table.

She poured batter onto the griddle and poured him a cup of coffee. "Still like it black?" she asked.

"Well, with a slurp of milk now. My stomach isn't what it used to be." He patted his abdomen. "What's on the docket for today? Am I going to see this house you're interested in?"

"We have an appointment at 11:30 this morning. We'll meet my real estate agent there." She placed a plate full of pancakes and bacon in front of him and soon sat down to join him.

"Now I want you to tell me everything about your life since I last saw you." He filled his mouth with a big bite of syrupy pancakes and sat back to listen.

"It's a long story," Annie said, surprised he was really listening.

"We have time. I want to hear it all."

Later, as they pulled into Willow Lane, Annie watched her father begin his appraisal. His eyes narrowed as he studied the outside of the house and the yard. She felt a growing excitement bubble up inside her.

"Don't you like all the trees, Daddy?" She held his elbow as he got out of the car. She could almost hear his bones creak as he unfolded his tall frame. He straightened himself upright with noticeable difficulty.

"Yes, good shade trees," he said as he tottered.

"And see on the porch, there's a double swing." She held onto him as he slowly gained his balance. He shook her hand off, took a step, then reached for her hand again. "Lean on me, Daddy. Do you usually use a cane? You seem a bit unsteady on your feet."

He grumbled. "Hilda makes me use one, but I don't like it so I didn't bring it on this trip."

She smiled. "Maybe Hilda is right, Daddy. I have a hiking stick you can have while you're here . . . if you want." She thought a minute. "Wait, it's in my car. Let me get it."

"Oh, I guess so," he said. Standing tall, he released her hand and grabbed the top of the car.

She ducked back inside the car and retrieved it from the back seat. "See, you can make it longer." She unscrewed a section and pulled it out to a longer length, then measured it next to him. "This seems about right. What do you think?"

He gripped the handle and felt the ground a step ahead of him. "I hate to admit it, but this is better."

"Well, we wouldn't want you to fall," she said. "I want to send you home to Hilda in one piece."

"I don't want to fall. Look what has happened to me. I used to run marathons and now I can hardly walk on my own. I hate being old." He shook his head and pressed his lips together. He looked at his daughter. "Never get old."

She laughed as she guided him toward the house where Steve was waiting for them. "Hi, Steve, come meet my father."

Steve crossed to meet them and extended his hand. "Steve Benson, nice to meet you," he said with a grin.

Her father shifted the stick to his left hand and grasped Steve's hand firmly with his right. "John Steadman. Thank you for helping my daughter. I'm very grateful."

"My pleasure. Let me show you the house. I think this is just right for her."

"Detail the specs, please," John said as he picked up his pace a bit with the help of Annie's hiking stick.

Steve nodded and began to run down the list as he unlocked the front door and ushered them inside. "You sound like you know something about real estate."

"Some. I thought about going into it at one time and took a course. I ended up a newspaperman. But what I learned came in handy buying my own houses over the years."

"I never knew that, Daddy," said Annie.

"Oh, honey, it was long before you were born, before I met your mother, so a story not worth telling."

They spent a good hour going over every inch of the house. John gradually moved more easily with the hiking stick. Annie hovered, ready to grab him if necessary. But he refused to stop until he had seen everything. Annie suspected he wanted to get down and examine the crawl space when they went outside in the back. "Don't even think about it, Daddy," she said. "The home inspector will do that."

"No rotting wood, Mr. Steadman," said Steve. "Before I got into real estate, I did construction. I did the belly crawl myself. It's good."

"Oh, okay. I just wish I could," he sighed in response. Before either of them could stop him, though, he did squat down and peer in. Getting back to his feet was almost beyond him. Fortunately, Steve was quick to give him a strong hand up. His spine cracked as he again unfolded to an upright position. When they were finished, Annie suggested they sit on the screen porch a moment. The three of them did, enjoying a comfortable silence. She watched her father closely, but decided he just needed a chance to catch his breath and rest.

After a few moments, John spoke. "This is a good house. Old but solidly built. Modernized as well." He turned to his daughter. "I think it's a good investment. I like the neighborhood. I bet you'll be happy here, sweetheart."

"I'm so glad you approve. I was nervous doing this all by myself. I can't believe what a thorough going over you gave it. I'm so glad you're here to help me." She breathed a big sigh and took his bony hand in hers. "Thank you, Daddy."

"You are so welcome, my dear."

"Are you hungry?" she asked.

"Yes. Let's go to lunch. Steve, want to join us?"

"I'd love to but I have another appointment," Steve said. "Thank you, though."

John turned to Annie. "Got any Mexican places around here? That's gotten to be my favorite."

Annie paused to think. "I know one you might like. It's called Marguerita's."

"Yes," said Steve. "Take him there. That's the best one in town."

"I agree," said Annie. "Shall we try it, Daddy?"

Annie and her father sat in a cozy booth across from each other at Marguerita's Mexican Cafe. They'd missed the lunch rush and the place was nearly empty so they could sit as long as they liked. Annie was surprised he had asked for a Mexican restaurant. In her memory, he had always been a steak and potatoes guy. But she guessed that, now that he lived in the southwest, he had developed a taste for spicier food. Or had it been her mother who insisted on standard fare? She couldn't be sure anymore. They had their heads buried in large menus when the waiter approached. He placed a basket of corn chips between them, then two small bowls and a bottle of salsa. "Welcome to Marguerita's," he said in a thick accent.

"*Buenos dias*," said her dad to the young man, lowering his menu to peer over it.

"*Gracias, Señor*," replied the waiter. He was short with dark hair and brown skin and smiled as he pulled his order pad and pen from his apron.

"Um, I mean *buenas tardes*." He looked at Annie. "It's after twelve so it's afternoon."

"*Sí, Señor*," said the waiter with a chuckle.

Annie nodded in amazement. She had no idea he knew any Spanish.

"I'm studying the language," he continued. "Hilda and I take a class at the Senior Center. We hear it all around us so it just makes sense." He grinned and tapped his brow. "And it's good for the aging brain." Then he looked at his menu again. "Do you know what you want, honey?"

Annie studied the menu. "Maybe a taco salad with chicken."

Her father turned to the young man who was patiently waiting. "*Ensalada de taco con pollo,*" he said, pointing at her. "*Chimichanga con pollo,*" pointing at himself.

"*Bueno,*" said the waiter as he wrote on his pad.

Their food arrived quickly. As they ate, Annie felt a surprising contentment inside her. She was still absorbing this new reality: her father was here and helping her and he had listened so attentively at breakfast as she told the whole story of her life since she'd last seen him. Her poetry class, Harry's anger, finding him with Gloria, everything. She had thought she'd just give him a summary, but he was listening so intently that she kept on and on. He seemed so different without her mother. She felt she was getting to know him for the first time. As she studied him, time felt precious. He looked so frail, so weak.

"I didn't tell you this yet, but I think it's time," he said.

"What, Daddy?" She put down her fork and grasped her hands in her lap, suddenly feeling scared.

Chapter 40

"I have good news and bad news, Annie," said her father. "Which do you want first?" He dipped a corn chip in salsa and plopped it into his mouth.

She studied his expression. His lined face appeared relaxed, his demeanor serious but strangely upbeat. "I have no idea, Daddy," she said at first. Then she felt an upsurge of strength. Whatever it was, she knew she could bear it. "Okay, let's get the bad news over with. What is it?"

"I just got diagnosed with Parkinson's Disease. That's what makes me so unsteady on my feet. It's at an early stage, and there is treatment. But no real cure." He gave her a brave smile. "After all, I will be seventy-one before too long. So I knew I'd get something eventually."

Annie reached across to lay her hand on his. "Parkinson's. I don't know much about it."

"I didn't either. Only time will tell how fast it will progress in me. The doctor did say I'm in stage three."

"How many stages are there?" Annie asked.

"Five. I vote for staying in stage three because I can still be physically independent. Mostly. Except for some problems with balance, especially when I get up from sitting down. As you've seen today."

Annie nodded. "This sounds more like a middle stage, not an

early stage. And I don't think you get a vote, Daddy."

"I'm registered to vote in Arizona now. What do you mean I don't get to vote?"

She laughed and shook her head. "You don't get to vote which stage of Parkinson's you're in, silly." Her father the jokester. She didn't feel like joking herself. "You've already been through stages one and two?"

"I know what you're thinking," he said, squinting his eyes at her. "I had symptoms. Just a little tremor on my right side, but I didn't pay it much attention."

"And when did this start?" she asked through narrowed eyes.

"Oh, I think it started, um, let me see, must have been just a short time ago, around when I turned sixty."

"Sixty?" Annie cried out. "That's ten years ago."

"Yes, I guess it is. After a while, well, a long while really, or maybe not so long, I can't remember things like I used to, I felt weak and tired more, too. I figured that's what happens when you get old, so I didn't pay much attention. I never did like to go to the doctor."

Annie sighed. She remembered her mother urging him every year to go get his annual physical. She'd push and he'd resist and they'd argue. And he'd say: "If you want me to go, stop pushing. If you keep pushing, I for sure won't go." Her mother went to the doctor so much that her father called her a hypochondriac. At the first sniffle, she went. She'd take Annie too, usually over her father's objections. Mostly her mother was told to rest until she felt better, which she didn't like hearing and had a hard time doing. But she did and eventually got better. Until she got really sick. She felt a stab of pain as she remembered her mother's illness.

"Would it have made a difference if they'd found it sooner?" she asked.

"Hard to say," her father replied. "It might have slowed it down some. They have medicine but it's not supposed to be effective after a while. Like I said, there's treatment but no cure."

"So what's the prognosis? I know it progresses, but how long does it take . . . " She paused, searching for the right words. ". . . before you can't enjoy a good quality of life?"

He smiled. "Oh, it can take as long as twenty years to get to its worst. But in some people it moves quickly."

"And in you?"

"No way to tell. Just wait and see." He shrugged. "And of course once I got in with the doctor, she had to test me for everything. I like having a woman doctor. I never had one before. Did you know there are lots of women doctors nowadays?"

Annie shook her head and smiled. "Yes, Daddy, women go to medical school, too."

"Wasn't that way when I was coming along. But I guess it's good. I like Dr. Bolin. Rebecca Bolin. She goes by 'Becky' but I can't call her that even though she said I could. She can call me 'John' but she's still Dr. Bolin to me. Guess I'm old-fashioned that way."

"What else did she test you for? Did she find anything else?" Annie squeezed his hand. "Tell me everything, Daddy."

He sighed. "Well, she found out I have prostate cancer."

"Prostate cancer?" Annie frowned, remembering her mother's cancer. Just the word "cancer" spelled doom to her.

"Yes, and she said I'll have it when I die. It's the slow-growing kind so it won't kill me." He grinned. "Apparently lots of old men get it. If you live long enough, you'll get it. Well, not you." He squeezed her hand back.

"So it's not like Mother's cancer?" She held her breath as she waited for his answer.

"Not a bit. Your mother didn't have a prostate." He chuckled.

She released her breath and his hand. She couldn't help but chuckle in response. "I know that women don't have prostates, you old goose. I'm glad you still have your sense of humor." An image of her as a little girl being tickled by him rose up in her mind. And others of him just being a goofball. He had a whoopee cushion he liked to put on his chair at the dinner table. After the meal was over, he'd sit up and smash down onto it, making a loud whooshing sound that always got a rise out of her mother. "This just shows I like your cooking," he'd tease. Other times, he'd poke Annie under the table to signal her before he said something outrageous, like: "I've decided we're moving to Alaska!" She'd giggle when her mother gave the expected outraged, "What?"

"Is there anything else?" Annie asked, wondering if he was teasing her now.

"Well, just a little something with my heart."

"What about your heart?" She raised her voice a few decibels and automatically crossed her hands over her heart.

"I have an irregular heartbeat, just a little bit. They call it *atrial fibrillation*."

Annie sat up taller and leaned forward. "I've heard of that; it can lead to strokes."

"Well, sometimes, but mine is controlled with medication. Most of the time. It's the least of my worries. Well, maybe prostate cancer is the least actually, but a-fib is the second least. And I sure do like Dr. Bolin. She must like me too. She has me coming to see her once a month." He grinned broadly at Annie. "I wonder if Hilda is jealous."

"Daddy, you are a trip!" She laughed. His spirits were good, she'd give him that, the way he strung her along. Trying to pull her strings like he used to do with her mother. He might be joking to distract her, yet her mental inventory of what he'd told her didn't sound good at all. His Parkinson's could get worse anytime. He could have a stroke. What if his prostate cancer wasn't really slow growing? He never had taken his health care seriously.

"I'm not dead yet, Annie," he said. "And I still have good news to tell you."

"Bring it on, I am ready for some good news." She took a big bite of black beans from her taco salad. It felt so good to laugh a bit. She wished she had that whoopee cushion right now. She took another forkful of beans.

"The good news is that I've got more money than I know what to do with. I've always been frugal. And Hilda is frugal just like I am. Now, your mother, that was another story. When I go, you'll get a nice inheritance. We just got our wills updated so there will be no problems when we go. We even set up trusts. Her son will get her money, and you will get mine. Our health care is included in the cost of living in our retirement community. You don't have to worry about me at all."

His words pierced Annie to the heart. She had just gotten him back; she really didn't want to think about losing him. "I'm glad to hear all that, but I am not thinking about my inheritance now. I just want to spend time with you. I am definitely coming to visit."

He reached over and patted her arm. "That would be great. I

didn't mean to say I expect to kick the bucket anytime soon."

"I'm glad to hear that." Annie sat back and gave him a stern look.

"*Carpe diem*, honey," he said. "I think I have many years left, well, quite a few at least. Hmm, I think I'll aim for one hundred."

"A hundred? I hope so."

"I found out from our accountant that I can give you some money tax-free, a yearly gift. He said it could be as much as $13,000."

Annie's eyes opened wide. She sat speechless for a moment. She thought of all the expenses of moving, all on her teacher's salary. She was getting alimony, but it wasn't a huge amount. She was barely separated and had no idea what her budget as a single woman would be like. This felt like a gift from above.

"I know you have a lot of new expenses with moving, getting a divorce, all that," he continued. "I can't be sure I can do this every year but I can this year. I want to do that. I want to watch you enjoy it now."

She felt tears spring up and pool in her eyes. She wiped them away with her napkin and reached both arms across the table. "I want to hug you."

"Well, come on over," he said.

She stood up and scooted next to him in the booth and folded him into a big embrace. She pressed her cheek against his. Then she picked up her phone from the table and set it to take a selfie. "Smile for the camera," she said just before she clicked.

"Is that a selfie?"

"Yes, sir, it sure is," said Annie.

"Well, you learn something new every day," said her father, incredulous. "My first selfie."

A loud commotion from across the dining room drew their attention, so loud it was hard to ignore. Annie saw a woman seated in a booth screaming at a man standing over her. With the man's back to her, Annie couldn't see the woman clearly. Someone official was walking rapidly in their direction. He was probably the manager, but he was tall and built like a linebacker.

"Get away from me," hollered the woman. "We're divorced. I don't care what legal trouble you got yourself into. I certainly will not represent you. What a joke. You can forget that."

"But honey," the man protested, leaning over with his hands on the table, "you left me with nothing. You owe me something, don't you?"

"Don't 'but honey' me. I don't owe you a damn thing." She shoved his hands away and raised her eyes to the manager who was standing behind the man with his mouth open to speak, but she beat him to it. "This man is harassing me; get him out of here."

"Yes, ma'am, I certainly will," replied the man. "Come on, dude, you're out of here." He took the man firmly by the arm and pulled him towards the door, the man's head craning back towards the woman with a beseeching look on his face. She turned her back to him and stuffed notebooks into a briefcase. Turning his head back around towards the door the manager was insistently dragging him towards, his eyes caught Annie's across the room for just a second. He startled, then quickly lowered his gaze and turned away.

Now she saw the woman clearly as well. Her hands clenched into fists on top of the table. She dropped her eyes to her lap.

"Who are those people, honey?" asked her father. "Do you know them?"

Annie nodded, unable to speak for a moment. Her father reached for her fists and laid his open hands over them. She took a few breaths and uncurled her fingers. He enclosed them in his hands but remained silent, waiting. Annie glanced across the room. There was an empty booth where the woman had been sitting.

Annie looked into her father's eyes, saw concern and tenderness. She felt her insides turn to steel. "Remember I told you about the woman Harry had an affair with?"

Her father nodded.

"And the private detective who was following me?"

He nodded as understanding began to dawn on his face.

"That was them. And, apparently, they used to be married."

Chapter 41

*A*nnie sat at her kitchen table at Number Four Willow Lane. The plate that once held eggs, bacon, and toast sat empty in front of her. She was having a second cup of coffee, something she rarely did, but today she had poured another cup in honor of her first morning in her new home. The sun shone on the table. She gazed out the back window to her screen porch and beyond to her small backyard. As she lifted her cup to her lips, she felt her muscles ache in exhaustion from yesterday's move. She sat taller a moment to stretch her lower back, which had lifted far too many boxes and far too much furniture. She couldn't imagine what she would have done without the help of her friends from her poetry class. But they had all come, even Ian, their teacher, and scurried around all day loading and unloading the truck she had rented until it was all here. To thank them, she had ordered lots of large pizzas whose boxes were now stacked high on the trash can beside her. Around 9 p.m., she had collapsed and they had left, but not before Claire had slipped into the master bedroom and made up the bed for her when she wasn't looking. To fall into a freshly made bed had made the boxes yet to be unpacked feel a lot less overwhelming.

She took a deep breath, savoring this quiet Sunday morning after the chaos of the day before. Boxes were still piled in every room, but at least her kitchen was more or less arranged. It had been Claire's suggestion to set up the kitchen first, and Annie was so glad she had taken her advice. Waking up to a kitchen where she could make breakfast this morning had been a big relief. But she couldn't linger at the table forever. Pretty soon she would have to tackle the boxes scattered in every other room. She also had to prepare her lesson plans for teaching on Monday.

Hard to believe she had first seen this house only six weeks earlier. What a surprise having her father visit and examine the house. She felt a warm glow remembering their reunion. His approval of her choice of house had meant a lot. Then getting her old house ready for market was a whirlwind. All done in three weeks thanks to George and his crew. It seemed a miracle that it sold in two weeks. Starting back to teaching in the middle of it all about did her in. Thank goodness George, Steve, and Katy knew what was required. All she had to do was write George a check (she was sure he hadn't charged her enough, but he insisted it was the *poetry* discount and made her promise to write him a poem). Then when her house sold, she took the biggest check she had ever held in her hand to the bank. And right after that, she closed on this house and handed another large check—but significantly smaller than the first one—to the agent, or was it the lawyer? She had been in a fog and all she knew was that Steve and Katy told her what to do and she did it, and in the process traded one set of keys for another. No wonder she felt so exhausted and emotionally wrung out now.

She drained her coffee cup and left her new kitchen shiny clean. Then she walked aimlessly around the rooms of boxes, not sure where to start. Maybe the living room. She opened boxes of books and arranged them on the bookshelves in the corner. Four empty boxes later, the bookcases were full.

She found less to do in her bedroom as she had carried most of her clothes on hangers. But there were suitcases full of clothes. Soon the dresser drawers were full and the suitcases empty. In the master bathroom, she sighed when she found she needed a garbage bag. She had duplicates of bottles of shampoo and hand lotion, some with only a tiny bit in the bottom, and a tiny bathroom cabinet. Why hadn't she sorted through all this when she moved out? Then she remembered the point of near exhaustion she had reached at the end of her move, when she just threw the last things into boxes and hauled them out. Oh well. She made a bag for give-away and a bag to throw away. She took the almost empty bottles into the kitchen and dutifully rinsed them out to recycle.

She stood in the kitchen a moment, wiping perspiration off her forehead with the back of her hand. She felt the urge to fold up like a fan and rest. Her eyes lighted on the porch. It looked surprisingly habitable, and the wicker chair downright irresistible. *Give yourself a break. You deserve it.* She got her journal and pen and soon found herself curled on the soft cushions of the chair gazing trance-like through the screen to the backyard where a swing hung from a big oak tree.

A crow flew down and landed on the seat of the swing. On the branch above sat three more. *A murder of crows*, she mused. *What a strange name to call a flock of birds.* The crow on the swing tilted its head and peered in her direction. *Is he looking at me?* Another flew down and joined the first one. They both appeared to look in her direction. She smiled. *Perhaps they are here to welcome me.* Then she picked up her pen and began to write.

A murder of crows
welcomes me here.
How could I have known
murder could bring needed cheer?

She tilted her head to one side. *How silly*, she thought. Then kept writing.

My old life has died,
marriage and house are both gone.
But the tears that I cried
gave birth to this home

Feeling an inner sparkle, she kept writing.

It's small but it's mine,
My little bungalow find.
The sun beams inside
Where I've no need to hide.

Maybe I'll give this poem to George. She paused and tapped her pen on the arm of her chair. *Maybe not. I may have another poem for George. Ouija Board guy.* She giggled and wrote.

The dark storm has gone.
The air has washed clear.
Now I greet the first dawn
with my crow friends right here.

She nodded and reread it. She took a deep breath, stretched right and left, feeling creaks and crunches in her spine.

Moving a bit more slowly now, she spent another hour unpacking and arranging the spare bedroom and her study. More boxes of books into more bookshelves. She found items that stirred memories of her life with Harry and with them waves of sadness. A photo album from their wedding and honeymoon. Some jewelry he had given her for birthdays and anniversaries. Sitting in her study, she opened the album, not sure doing it was a good idea, but somehow she couldn't stop herself.

Stuck between pages out of order, she found a photo from early in their relationship. With the album open on her lap, she was unprepared for the grief that stopped her in her tracks. She sat by her desk immobilized, leaning her cheek on one hand wearily, holding the photo in the other. In it, they stood on a beach, the waves crashing behind them, frozen in time. Her memory of that day was vivid. He had rented a condo on Emerald Isle and taken her there for the weekend. It had been a very hot July. They'd been in the water and stood together wrapped in big beach towels. Harry had fetched his camera from under their beach umbrella and asked a man passing by to take a photo of them together. The man turned out to be an excellent photographer. He had them look at each other as he snapped the photo. They seemed to be pouring into each other's eyes as if no one else existed. She remembered how happy she had felt that day, newly married, believing them more in love than anyone had ever been or ever would be. She felt tears in her eyes. She closed the album and sat trembling as a few tears rolled down her cheeks. *How could this happen?* She shook her head and stepped out of the pit of despair she now found herself in. But next she felt a volcano vibrating inside her threatening to erupt. Images of Harry silent or angry rose on the screen in her mind. And the ultimate image: him and Gloria naked and passed out on the couch in Harry's office.

Just then she heard Amanda Murphy's voice in her ear, reassuring her, enlightening her. She wiped her tears away with her fingers. *Did he ever really love me? Next time I'll go slow. I'll get to know someone really well before I give my heart away.* She felt a glimpse of inner peace inside, just a glimpse. Then the nesting urge made itself known. *I am going to get this place just the way I like it.* She got up and headed for the next stack of boxes. And the array of framed paintings and pictures leaning against the wall.

Just as she got those boxes emptied, she heard the dim sound of her cell phone ringing. Where had she left it? It was her only phone for now. She followed the sound to the kitchen counter and barely got to it before it stopped ringing.

"Hello?" she panted.

"George here. How's the unpacking going?"

"Oh, George. Pretty well, I think. Slow but steady."

"Wins the race," he laughed. "I'm calling because I believe I left my small toolbox over there. Have you seen it?"

Annie walked through the rooms looking around. "Things are getting a bit more in order, let me see." She walked into the living room. "I see it. Right next to the front door."

"Ah, where I put it so I wouldn't forget to take it with me. Mind if I come get it? Or do you need tools for anything?"

"Sure, come on over. I might get you to help me hang pictures on the walls. I'm just getting to that part."

Annie hung up and noticed her heartbeat had accelerated at the thought of seeing George. *Be still, my heart. He's my friend, just a friend.* She looked around the living room to see if there was even a place to sit yet. Paintings were leaning against the back of the couch. She surveyed the walls to see if she wanted them in the living room. There was a large landscape of a river with sailboats in the distance and cows in the foreground that her grandmother had painted when she was eighteen. She treasured this painting both for its beauty and the family connection. She barely remembered her grandmother who died when Annie was just three years old. Her Aunt Elizabeth had gotten the artistic talent. She had one of Aunt Elizabeth's paintings—a log cabin at the end of a country road. *I'll make my living room a family gallery.*

She stood gazing at the walls and the pictures, imagining exactly where each one would look best. Within ten minutes, she saw George's green truck pull into her driveway. Her hands grew moist and her heart began to flutter. She wiped her hands on her shirt before she opened the door. His wavy, dark blond hair hung down his forehead. He shoved it back with his hand.

"I'm here!" he said with a big grin.

"Yes, you are—that was quick." She smiled as she stepped aside to let him enter.

"Oh, I don't live far from here," he said. "A few blocks, just barely too far to walk. Nothing is far in this town." He ran his eyes around the living room. "Are these the pictures you want help hanging on the walls?"

"Yes, I want this one over the couch." She stepped up to the couch and lifted the large landscape. "My grandmother painted this when she was a young woman. I just love it."

"Wow, so do I," said George, looking at it closely. He picked up a framed photograph. "Is this you as a child with your parents?"

"Yes, it is." She took it from him and looked at it longingly.

"Are they still living?" he asked, seeing her expression.

"My father only." She hesitated, then went on. "My mother died a few years ago. My father remarried right away, too soon for me, and moved to Arizona."

"That must have been hard." George listened with soft eyes.

Annie raised her eyes from the photograph to George. "Yes, it was. But my father recently visited, and we had a wonderful reunion." She sighed. "His health is not good. I keep in touch. I actually taught him to use Skype—oh, you should have seen that, he's so low-tech—but now we can talk regularly, and I can see how he looks. And I'm going to visit as soon as I can. But enough of that."

Thirty minutes later, her family gallery was installed on the walls in her living room. Annie stood and admired them. When she opened the front door, her grandmother's landscape of river and cows drew her eyes into the room. On the adjacent wall, as if just down the road, hung Aunt Elizabeth's log cabin. A framed family photograph hung near it of her grandparents standing with her mother and Elizabeth as children in front of them. Another photograph of her nuclear family—mother, father, herself—hung next to it. A big picture window next to the front door lit up the room, especially as she hadn't yet put up any curtains. But it looked more like it belonged to her. Annie nodded and turned to George.

"Do you like my family gallery?"

"Yes, I do, very much," he said. "You have turned this house into a home in no time at all."

"Yes, a new home for my new life. Thanks for your help. That's one thing it's a lot harder to do by myself." She looked at the clock—1:30 p.m.—and remembered she hadn't had anything to eat since breakfast. "How about something to drink? And a snack? On my screen porch."

"Sure," said George as he followed her into the kitchen. She opened the refrigerator unsure what she would find but, after rooting around a bit, she found two cans of ginger ale, some jalapeno cheese spread, two apples, and, with crackers from the cabinet, enough for a hearty snack. She put them all on a tray and took them to the screen porch, then sat in one wicker chair with the tray on a small table next to her.

He opened his pocket knife and picked up an apple. He sliced it up into eight pieces, then nodded towards the other apple. "Would you like me to slice yours too?"

"Oh, yes, that would be lovely." *Something Harry had never done for me,* she couldn't help but notice. She spread some cheese on a cracker and handed it to him. "I hope you like it spicy."

He popped it into his mouth, then resumed slicing. "I notice you have a lot of empty boxes now. If you like, I can flatten those boxes and carry them to the recycling center in my truck."

"Thank you. That would be great." *He is so thoughtful.* Another contrast with Harry.

He tilted his head towards her and put his hand up as if tipping an imaginary hat. "We aim to please," he said with a grin.

She laughed and took a sip of ginger ale. Then she turned her eyes towards the backyard. "This morning when I took a break and sat out here, I saw a bunch of crows on the swing." She gestured and his eyes followed her hand to the large oak and the swing. "Any idea why they call a bunch of crows a *murder of crows*?"

"Maybe it's because they're scavengers and often circle around battlegrounds and graveyards waiting to find corpses. And farmers hate them for 'murdering' their crops."

"Ah, yes, that's why they put up scarecrows." She took a bite of apple and washed it down with a sip of ginger ale.

"Yes, and there are a lot of colorful names that you, as a poet, might want to know. There's an ostentation of peacocks, a parliament of owls, a knot of frogs, and, my favorite, a skulk of foxes."

Annie laughed. "Those are colorful names. How did you come across them?"

"Here and there. As you might have guessed, I like colorful words. And I like anything to do with the outdoors."

"Me too." She thought of the time she and Claire saw him sunbathing in the forest and smiled.

George took a sip of ginger ale to cool the slight flush he felt as he remembered the time he ran into her and Claire when he was sunbathing in the forest. *I bet they did see me*, he thought. Then he shrugged. He looked at her as she scanned the backyard and noticed the way her hair fell in a wave past her cheek onto her shoulders, a few beads of perspiration on her forehead. *She's been unpacking all day and she still looks beautiful.*

"No crows right now," she said. She leaned forward. "I'd love to see an ostentation of peacocks." She turned and smiled at him.

"Wouldn't that be beautiful?"

Not as beautiful as you look right now, he thought. Instead, he said: "I've heard of folks having them as pets, but I hear they are feisty and don't get along well with other birds. And they prefer a warmer climate."

"George, you are a walking encyclopedia," Annie grinned. "I learn a lot just hanging out with you."

"I like hanging out with you." He smiled at her wistfully. *I wish we could see more of each other.* He had been at her old house working and had seen her nearly every day for a few weeks. He missed that but he just wasn't sure about her, knowing the turmoil he had been in after his separation. He certainly hadn't been ready to date. He liked her too much to rush her and maybe mess things up. He imagined what he would say if she weren't just newly separated: "*Speaking of spending time together, how about you let me take you to dinner some-time, maybe next weekend?*" He felt his palms grow sweaty and his heartbeat accelerate. He took a deep breath and held his cold ginger ale can to his cheek. He closed his eyes and told himself to cool his jets.

"Um, George, hello? Are you okay?" she asked.

He snapped out of his reverie and blinked. "I'm fine. Just remembering when I was where you are, newly separated, feeling lost and confused. Sorry."

"Oh, that's okay."

"I hope you have an easier time of it than I did. How are you doing? Really?"

He watched her eyes glaze over considering his question. She was zoning out too, but he figured it was her turn. She seemed surprisingly comfortable doing it with him sitting next to her and he was glad. He hoped she trusted him enough to confide in him. He wanted to know everything about her. She glanced at him as he waited.

"To be honest with you, I don't really know. The past weeks have been so busy with selling and moving and starting back to teaching in the middle of it all. I'm just catching my breath. Being finally settled feels wonderful, a big relief." She raised her eyebrows and gave a big sigh.

"If you're like me, it will take a while to figure out what's next." He took a sip of his ginger ale. "I was a mess and then had to move away. You seem a lot more functional than I remember myself being."

"Well, I do have my weekly therapy with Amanda to keep me grounded."

"I wish I'd been smart like you and found myself a counselor. It would have helped me a lot, I imagine. It seemed to help you. You sure took charge of all the details fixing up your old house to sell. I just followed your orders."

Annie's mouth dropped. "My orders? I thought I just went along with your suggestions."

George chuckled. "Woman doesn't know her own power. Remember, you picked the paint colors and had an opinion on pretty much everything else."

"Well, I wanted it to look good and sell. Was I being bossy?" She frowned.

"Not at all. I think it's called being assertive. Wouldn't your therapist say that?"

Annie chuckled. "She probably would. Glad you don't think I'm bossy. My mother always told me a woman should never be bossy, even though she was, in a subtle way. 'You catch more flies with honey than vinegar,' she used to say. And I'm quoting."

"And yet why would you want to catch flies? I doubt they taste as good as honey. That old saying has its limits."

Annie giggled. "You don't catch them to eat them, silly."

"You don't?" He feigned a look of shock.

"I think that's called a metaphor, Mr. Poetry Man. Not to be taken literally."

His eyes lit up. "A metaphor? You mean like something you're trying to say without saying it? Like without a megaphone?"

"Similar, like a simile. Like what you just said." Now her belly was jiggling and she was laughing so hard she couldn't speak for a moment. She had to wipe her eyes and gasp for breath before she could gather herself enough to speak. "George, you're a caution!"

"Is that another one of your mother's sayings?" he asked. "I don't even know what that means." He squinched his eyes in mock confusion.

The words were out of her mouth in less than a second. "It means you're funny, you make me laugh, it means I like you." Her eyes grew wide, and she began to blush.

"Well, I'm happy to be a caution then," he grinned, feeling a warm glow inside and wondering if he was also blushing. "I always pay close attention to the caution light."

That night Annie had a vivid dream. She dreamed she was with Harry in their old house. He was stomping around the living room, picking up books and throwing them as he yelled in fury. She felt fear but something stronger: she didn't want to be there with him, she didn't have to be with him anymore. He turned his back and picked up a red vase, one her mother had left her. She saw he was going to hurl it into a million pieces. She got up and in an instant was out the back door, hearing the crash and shattering sound grow ever dimmer as she left.

She got in her car, now full of fury herself, determined to escape. Her car morphed into a horse. She held the reins tightly and, squeezing her legs, urged him into a gallop. Ahead was a field rising to a hill that promised to have a beautiful view. She woke with a start and a racing heart. For a moment she didn't know where she was. Then she felt the sheet covering her and the mattress supporting her and recognized she was in her new bedroom. She saw the red vase on a small table across the room. Relief washed over her as her eyes found it. It was intact.

She took a deep breath and turned over to check the clock on her bedside table. The blue numerals shined almost too brightly, pulsating four-three-five. She lay still, sifting through the dream and the intense feelings it evoked, wondering what it was trying to tell her. It didn't take her long. She turned it over like a gold coin, then tucked it into the back of her mind as she drifted back to sleep.

Chapter 42

$\mathcal{I}$t was Tuesday evening, and Annie was at home alone. Her lesson plans were complete, her dinner eaten and kitchen clean. She sat on her screen porch watching the light fade after sunset. The sky dazzled her with its array of colors: pink, purple, gold against a scattering of puffy clouds floating atop the trees. What had been incubating inside her for a couple days began to surface. A breeze drifted through the screen and caressed her cheek as another strange wind roared into her from the ground into her feet, up her legs, through her torso, and out through the top of her head. She shook her head and imagined the dream she had tucked in the back of her mind. In her imagination, she plucked it out, examined it closely, and tucked it into the wide pocket in the front of her skirt. There she felt her cell phone waiting.

Do I dare? Do I dare to climb the stair? To come in from the cold? To be so bold?

She felt her breathing tighten as her stomach knotted. Her mother's image popped into her mind, frowning, pressing her thin lips together in disapproval. *Not now, Mother. I don't want you here right now, okay?* Her mother disappeared only to be replaced by her father, smiling broadly at her, nodding. *Thanks, Daddy, thanks, I needed that.*

She pulled out her phone, scrolled through the contacts until she found the number she wanted. She waited as it began to dial. One ring, two, three.

"Hello?"

"Hi, George." She smiled and breathed a sigh of relief.

"Annie?" he asked.

Her words, so carefully rehearsed, left her mind. For a moment, she was speechless. Then she laughed. "Yes, it's me, Annie." She shifted in her seat as she listened to herself. "I've been sitting here watching such a beautiful sunset."

"On your screen porch, I bet," said George. "Wish I'd seen it. I've been pouring over estimates for my next job."

"Oh, good, glad you've got another job coming."

"Too many of them, really," he said. "I'd rather be doing what you're doing, watching the sunset."

"I wonder if you'd like to, um, well, I have a poem for you. I think. It's not quite finished but it might be by next weekend." She swallowed and cleared her throat. "Want to get together and do something, go to dinner maybe?" Her hand trembled on the phone. She held her breath a moment before she realized and gave a big exhale.

"A new poem? Sure, I'd love to. Nothing I'd rather do than have dinner with you and hear your poem. Next weekend is completely open for me."

"Oh, great. How about Saturday?"

"Saturday is good."

Annie felt exhilarated. Her heartbeat quickened. She realized she was terrified. "George, I confess, I don't know how to do this. I don't feel I really know what I'm doing."

George chuckled. "You seem like you do. You want to share a

poem with me over dinner. That seems simple enough."

"I've never asked a guy out before." She bit her lip. "I haven't been out with anyone in years. I mean on a date. If that's what it's called now. I have no idea."

"Well, we're already friends so it's not like a blind date. We've spent a good bit of time together already."

"Yes, you're right." She was glad he couldn't see her face. She felt sure she was blushing.

"The most important thing is for you to feel comfortable," said George with authority.

Annie smiled and relaxed a bit. She remained silent a moment, aware of the soothing sound of his voice and how comfortable she did feel, had always felt, around him. She gathered herself. "How about 6 p.m.? I'll think about some place nice to go. My treat. Since I asked you."

"Spending an evening with you and poetry will be a treat for me." Then he added: "We can discuss who pays then."

She imagined him grabbing the check before her. Her mother's frowning face appeared, but she quickly replaced it with her father's grinning one. "No, I insist." She imagined grabbing the check from him. Then she imagined it didn't really matter. What mattered was that she did dare.

Annie sat in her familiar chair across from Amanda on Thursday afternoon. Sunlight shone through the translucent white curtain behind her, warming her back. "It's beginning to feel like home."

Annie gave a big sigh. "Finally."

"Moving is a lot of work," said Amanda. "Separating from a marriage is a lot of work. Big changes."

"You can say that again. I can't believe how much has changed since I first came to see you."

"How does it feel now?"

Annie knitted her brows together and thought a minute. "Slowly better. I'm hoping things will slow down a bit. The past weeks have been like running the rapids. I'm ready for some flat water."

"Sounds good. From where I sit, I'd say you have handled it all really well. Perhaps you're stronger than you realized." Amanda smiled. "Good job."

Annie smiled back. "Thanks." She looked down where she had twisted a tissue into pieces in her hands. "But there are more challenges coming up."

"Oh?"

"Saturday I have the first date I've had in years." A shadow crossed her face and for a moment she looked like a deer caught in the headlights. "With George."

Amanda nodded. "And you're feeling a bit nervous?" She tilted her head.

"Very nervous. The biggest part is—I asked him out." She looked up at Amanda with wide eyes.

"You asked him out?"

"I've never done anything like that before."

"There's always the first time." Amanda smiled. "Women ask men out now. It's quite okay."

"It is? I have no idea." Annie took a deep breath.

"Sounds like it took some courage. Tell me about it."

"First let me tell you about the dream I had last Sunday night."

Amanda's ears perked up. Dreams could be very revealing. She listened closely as Annie relayed her dream. She wasn't at all surprised Annie had had a bad dream about Harry. She was so newly out of that traumatic situation. Yet this dream revealed something beyond that. "Let's go over that dream carefully," she said when Annie had finished. "Tell it to me again, slowly."

Annie began: "I am with Harry in our old house. He's angry. I leave and drive away. Then I'm on horseback galloping through a field up a hill where there might be a beautiful view."

"And what is the mood of the dream?"

"I feel afraid, then angry then . . ." Annie paused. "And then curious, even happy." She smiled at Amanda. "I'm going to a better place."

"Yes, you're taking the reins and urging your horse—and yourself—away from danger."

"Into a new life." Annie grinned. "It was after that dream that I got the idea to call George. Like he was part of what I might see from the top of that hill."

"What you might want to see, perhaps."

"Yes, definitely," said Annie with a smile.

"You called him and he said yes."

"I sat with the idea a few days to make sure it wasn't just a passing thought. But it wasn't and it grew in strength until I felt compelled to call him. And I did."

Inside, Amanda beamed. This was what they'd been working on. "You're taking charge of your life. Good for you."

"There's more," said Annie.

"Of course," said Amanda.

"I told him I was writing him a poem." She raised her hands and let them flop into her lap.

"A poem, eh?"

"Yes, as partial payment for the work he did on my house."

"And how's it going, writing the poem?"

"I think I have writer's block. I'm thinking of telling him how I first heard his name."

"From the Ouija Board?"

"Yes, good memory."

"So you want to put that in your poem?"

"Yes, but for some reason it's making me very nervous. I've written maybe fifteen drafts and torn them up." She pulled another tissue from the box on the small table beside her and began twisting it. Pieces of tissue littered her lap.

"Do you have to write it by Saturday?"

"No, no pressure from him. But I want to."

"So let's look at what's twisting you up inside." Amanda smiled and looked at the tissue in Annie's hands.

Annie followed Amanda's gaze and, as if for the first time, saw the twisted tissue and the pieces littering her lap. She smiled and held her hands still. Her eyes glazed over as she began her soul-searching. Amanda waited and watched the wheels turn. Annie sighed a few deep breaths and studied her hands. Then she inhaled and raised her eyes to Amanda. "I can be such a ninny."

"A ninny?"

"Afraid to go after what I want. When I think about how I let Harry intimidate me . . ." She shook her head and looked away as her voice trailed off.

"Harry could be a scary guy when he got angry."

Annie sighed. "You got that right."

"And you're no longer with him."

"Thank goodness."

Amanda watched Annie's demeanor give a slight shift and her face soften. She knew it would take Annie some time to get Harry's energy, his ghost, to stop haunting her. She thought of it as a million tiny spider's threads that had to be removed one by one. A friendship with George seemed a good thing for Annie. "Let's focus on what you want now."

Annie smiled. "I like George. A lot. I'm scared. I'm not sure I'm ready to like him. I'm not even divorced yet."

Amanda nodded. "I understand. Do you want to go on this date?"

"Oh, yes. Yes, I do." Annie raised her voice. "Very much."

"You're scared," said Amanda. "It's okay to be scared. It makes sense. Dating again after being married is bewildering. Go at your own pace. It's just a date. You don't have to decide anything long term. He's not a stranger. Forget about the poem and the Ouija Board and enjoy being with a man you like."

Annie's face relaxed and she looked like a big weight had been lifted. "You're right. I'm so used to thinking about marriage . . . it's just a date." She chuckled. "Going on one date does not mean I have to marry him."

Amanda chuckled as well. "It doesn't mean that at all. It means hopefully an enjoyable evening getting to know George a little better."

"I like that idea. I like what I know so far. He seems real different from Harry."

"Yes, he does. If your muse brings you a poem," Amanda continued, "write it down. But give yourself a break. Just enjoy."

"Interesting you mention the muse," said Annie. "George mentioned it too. I've been thinking about it, wondering what it means. Do I have a muse? Is it just a figure of speech? I even found a TED talk of Elizabeth Gilbert talking about the creative process. I've started doing daily meditation and have been reflecting on it, even visualizing my muse."

"Maybe that will help with your writer's block," said Amanda. "Although I suspect it's really about this date and your attraction to George. When you are ready to tell him how you first heard his name, perhaps the poem will come. And of course you don't have to tell him now. Or ever."

Annie looked visibly relieved. She rested her hands together in her lap and took in a deep breath. "That makes so much sense, Amanda. Thank you."

That evening, Annie sat on her screen porch. She placed her hands open in her lap, closed her eyes, and settled into stillness. She sent a silent prayer into the air, asked her muse to find her, guide her, help her.

After a while, she picked up her notebook and began to write. This time the words flowed from her pen. She wrote and rewrote and wrote some more. One poem then another. Hours went by. The clock struck eleven times. She startled as if awaking from a dream.

She gathered up her pages, stood and stretched her tired body. She smiled and headed to bed.

Saturday morning Annie awoke to a day with warm temperatures and clear skies. A perfect day for a hike. She decided to make a picnic and invite George to come a bit earlier so they could hike into New Hope Creek in the University Forest. When she called him, he readily agreed. She spent the day cooking spicy chicken pieces, oven-fried potato pieces, and a green salad with miso dressing. She had just the right sized containers to fit snugly in her backpack. As she worked, a blanket of calm settled on her in stark contrast to earlier in the week. Before she had seen Amanda. Before she had found and listened to her muse. Before she had spent two evenings reflecting and writing and rewriting.

George was there at the appointed time. He greeted her with a handful of wild flowers he had picked that day from his yard. Instead of the silk dress she had originally planned to wear, she had on hiking boots, long pants, and a bright tie-dyed T-shirt with a green bandanna at her neck. She found being able to dress casually helped her first date jitters calm down significantly. When she looked at him, she now saw a good friend, a man she liked and looked forward to getting to know better. He also wore hiking gear, although his didn't look like they'd been in the drawer as long as hers. She was glad she had created another chance to use hers. They loaded her picnic-filled backpack, complete with a chilled bottle of pinot grigio, in his truck and headed out of town. When they parked at the trailhead, he insisted on carrying the backpack. She was happy to let him. After a half hour of hiking, they found a flat rock next to the babbling water just right to spread out a blanket.

"It's so beautiful here. What a great idea," said George as he leaned against a boulder and looked around.

"I love it here," said Annie as she unloaded the containers with her camping plates and utensils.

"So do I. And that looks like a gourmet picnic. Yum," said George as he sniffed over the containers and began to fill his plate.

A cozy silence enveloped them as they ate and sipped the wine. George set down his fork, touched her arm, and pointed. Across the creek, almost hidden by some over-hanging branches, was a blue heron slowly wading in the water. Annie held her fork halfway to her mouth, mesmerized. The heron turned its head towards them as they both sat holding their breaths. Then it flew away, spreading its wings wide and quickly disappearing into the trees.

They exhaled in unison. "Ah," said Annie. "I've never seen a blue heron out here."

"It must be our lucky day," George said with a smile. "I know it's my lucky day. What a feast you've prepared. Thank you."

"My pleasure," she said as she opened the last container full of homemade chocolate chip cookies. "That heron must be an omen. I think it's time."

"Time?" asked George, holding a cookie to his lips.

"Poetry time, of course," said Annie with bright eyes.

"Great!" said George, taking a bite, his eyes half-closed in apparent cookie heaven.

"I have two poems to share," she said with a smile.

"Two poems. Wow. I'm impressed," said George. "Delicious cookies." He reached for another.

"Glad you like them. Since this is such a quiet place, I want to share them here, if that's okay with you."

"Certainly," said George. "I'm all ears."

She pulled two sheets of paper from her backpack. She looked at him, paused, then smiled. She took a big sip of wine. "Here's the first one."

George sat back as she began to read slowly.

So the Muse May Come

A winged creature flits
high in the ether.
She seeks someone
open and receptive
who bares an inner field
tilled and free of weeds.

I sit and quiet myself
my silent prayer beseeching.
Hands open on my lap,
I settle into stillness.
I prepare myself to wait
as long as it takes
I know she will not come
to a stressed and burdened place
or to a loud demanding one.

So I empty myself and anticipate
her light touch, seeds like dust
from which I may create.

George looked deep in thought. "I just have to absorb it. Read it again, please."

She did.

"Yes," he said. "Yes, oh yes. I like it a lot. I think my muse is like yours." He laughed. "Although I imagine mine as more a floating wizard than a flying creature. Yours makes me think of Tinkerbell."

"Yes, but mine is more like a fairy godmother. Or maybe now a heron." Annie laughed. "It's just an image I've been playing with. But sitting still seems important, even if, well, especially if I'm full of turmoil."

George chuckled. "You wouldn't believe how much time I spend sitting still staring off into thin air when I feel a poem coming on. And, yes, especially when I'm stirred up. Then the air is thick. I try not to do it in public. The men in the white coats might take me away."

Annie laughed. "It feels so good to talk about poetry with you, George. Most people don't understand." *Or at least Harry didn't.*

"I agree with you there. You write alone but you still need friends." He tilted his head. "Didn't you say you have two poems to share?"

Annie nodded. Dormant butterflies woke up and began to make a ruckus inside her. She took a deep breath. She read it slowly once, then read it again, trying vainly to keep the paper in her hands from trembling. She did not watch him as she read but kept her eyes glued to her page.

Message from the Ouija Board

Idle fingers moved
a heart-shaped wooden
planchette across
a talking board.
College girls
on the board to launch,
full of questions,
as yet no answers.
That wooden heart
spelled a name.

My life grabbed in haste
has now a most bitter taste.
Older by some years,
I pour a new cup,
words spill on the page,
that name hits my ears,
that name has your face,
your smile and your place.
I know my life will never
be the same.

His eyes stood wide open. For a few moments they sat in silence and held each other's gaze. She felt a current running through her a bit as she tried to read his expression, which slowly evolved from shock and surprise into a relaxed, open warm smile.

"Read it again, slowly, please, I need to hear it a third time," said George.

She did, struggling to keep her trembling voice from revealing how nervous she felt.

George cleared his throat and took her hands in his. "Annie," he began. He looked around, searching for words. "Ouija Board. I've never used one. I don't really know much about them. But it spelled *my name*?" He returned his eyes to hers with his question.

"Yes, it spelled G-E-O-R-G-E-T-A-F-F-E-R. I didn't take it seriously then. I had never heard that name. Frankly, I thought I never would. I forgot about it."

"But how does the Ouija Board work?" George asked.

"You ask a question, two or three or more people touch their fingers to the planchette, a heart-shaped piece of wood with short legs, you sit quietly, and it moves across the board—which has the alphabet and numbers. If it pauses over a number or letter, you take note, then keep going."

"What question did you ask?"

Annie paused. Her butterflies buzzed like bees inside her. She closed her eyes, still holding his hands. *Whom will I marry? I can't tell him that.*

George watched her closely. His face crinkled with his own nervousness. "You don't have to tell me if you don't want to."

Annie opened her eyes and smiled in relief. "Maybe some day. I can't tell you how surprised I was. I spilled my papers and you picked them up, remember?"

"Yes, I remember. And I remember liking you immediately. But you were married, so I decided I would think of you as a friend and nothing more."

"I was unhappily married."

He nodded. "As I suspected from hearing your poems. I felt honored you trusted me enough to tell me."

"Yes, from the first moment I trusted you." She laughed. "Maybe because your name was familiar." She shook her head in amazement. "And I confess I liked you immediately too. But I was married." She turned her gaze away for a moment's reflection. She pressed her lips together, then turned to face him with a smile. "And now I'm no longer married. At least, I'm legally separated. And here we are on a date. My first in years. With a guy whose name I heard so long ago. I didn't want it to stay my secret."

He leaned across the blanket, still holding her hands. "I'm glad you did."

They sat in silence a moment. He picked up one hand and kissed it.

She blushed. "I'm having a wonderful time on our first date."

"I'm hoping for a second one." His eyes twinkled. She nodded. "And I sure don't know what to make of your Ouija Board story." He scooted closer and draped his arm over her shoulder. She snuggled in and laid her head on his shoulder. "But I do know one thing that I'm very certain of. My life will also never be the same."

Chapter 43

$\mathscr{A}$ year later, the poetry seminar reconvened in the back room of a coffeehouse with mostly the same participants as the year before. There were stuffed chairs and couches in a semicircle with a coffee table to hold their drinks, just enough room for their small group. Annie fairly glowed with pleasure to be there again. The year had gone by quickly. Her divorce was final. And, just as Jan had predicted, it had been an anticlimactic five minutes before the judge. Since the class had broken for the summer, she had barely seen her friends. Except for Claire, of course, with whom she had become close friends. George and Annie had become more than friends, but she was content to let their relationship evolve slowly over time, a lesson from her failed marriage to Harry that she was determined to employ now. George easily attuned to her pace, which he seemed to share. Ian was back as their teacher and, as he stood in front, announced that he had picked this date because it was the birthday of Jalal ad-Din Muhammad Rumi. There were a few smiles of recognition from the class but more bewildered frowns.

"Rumi is the most popular poet in the US," said Ian, "so I thought we would start with him."

Claire elbowed Annie, who sat next to her on one of the couches. Annie smiled and nodded in response. Claire had introduced her to Rumi's poetry. Some of his poems had fed her during her recent transition. She was already a Rumi fan.

"Rumi was born September 30, 1207. He was a Persian Sunni Muslim poet, jurist, Islamic scholar, and Sufi mystic. His poetry has been widely translated and is appreciated across the world."

"I can't believe I never heard of Rumi," said Peter from his perch next to George. "How much did he write?"

"Oh, volumes and volumes," said Ian. "As a Sufi mystic, he's known as a spiritual poet, and I for one would call his writing spirit-led. Next time we'll look closely at some of his poems. Today, before we get into sharing our own work, let's talk briefly about what spirit-led might mean and perhaps share some about our own writing process."

A deep silence fell in the class and lasted for a time as Ian waited. George, occupying half of a love seat closest to the couch where Annie and Claire sat, was the first to respond.

"I don't consider myself a mystic, but I do sometimes feel when I'm composing a poem that the words are coming from somewhere else. I think of it as from my muse, but maybe I could call it spirit-led."

Peter frowned. "I've never thought of my writing that way."

"I do sometimes write out of a few moments of silence," said Annie. "I don't know where it comes from, but I like the idea it could be spirit-led." She paused as she thought a bit. "Perhaps it's energy from those who came before, like an inheritance, a sort of spiritual inheritance." She thought of her father with all his ailments, surely dying if hopefully very slowly. She already had booked her airline tickets to visit him at Thanksgiving. They talked at least once a week now via Skype, which allowed her to examine him visually as well as talk with him.

"That could be," said Ian.

Claire sat up straight. "Now I know what to call my process. Yes, spirit-led. When I have something incubating, I walk around my house in a daze, maybe for days."

Ian laughed. "Days in a daze."

"Yes. Then, a word or a line comes to me and from there often it flows. It helps that I have a quiet house. I call it my inner voice, but maybe it does come from some sort of spiritual place." Claire sat back.

"Any other responses before we move on?" asked Ian. The three who hadn't yet spoken appeared to be in deep contemplation and remained silent. "Okay, now. Who has a poem to share?" Ian scanned the group.

Annie shifted on the couch as she thought of the poem she had brought. She glanced around the circle, wondering how many others had also brought poems. She hoped she wasn't the only one.

Annie didn't hesitate. "I do."

"Good," said Ian. "Who else is feeling brave tonight?" He raised his eyebrows.

Claire flipped through papers in her lap and frowned. "Maybe."

Peter shook his head.

George studied the page in his hands, pressed his lips together, then shrugged. "I'm thinking about it. Maybe after Annie."

Everyone else sat frozen.

Ian nodded. "We'll start with you, Annie, and then see if anyone else gets inspired to share later."

Annie took her place in front of the class and looked at each person in turn with a smile. "I always loved poetry but never knew I could write it. Well, I won't say more and maybe my poem will say the rest. If you don't mind, I'll give you the copies later." She cleared her throat and began.

Name It

It's there on the horizon
behind the trees,
then above as the road dips,
gigantic and orange.
I follow it home,
watch it silver as it ascends,
glue it to my eyes.

I stand before the class,
face hot with confusion.
Everyone stares and smiles
as I am dissected.
My skin grows too tight
for what I find inside—
it stretches and pops,
slides off easy as butter,
leaving me naked and wet
with new possibilities.

I extend my hand
into the night sky.
Soon my palm will
encircle the shining orb,
a deed once unthinkable,
now mine to name.

"Read it again," said George.

"Yes," came the chorus from the others.

She smiled at them and stood a bit taller. She read it again. When she finished, she raised her eyes to her friends.

"Bravo!" said Ian

"You have come a long way, Annie," said Claire with a grin. "And written some wonderful poetry, too."

"Good poem," said George.

Annie blushed and felt tears pool in her eyes. "Thank you," she said. "But really, I couldn't have done it without you."

"But you did it," said George. His face softened as he kept his eyes on her.

"Yes, I did." And her eyes grew even brighter.

Acknowledgments

Many people supported me on the path to completing this novel. Sybil Wagner first saw the first chapter many years ago. The late Allan Brick, whose writing workshops I attended, read the first three chapters and encouraged me to keep writing. Special mention goes to Jeremy Hawkins who taught the fiction writing classes I took at the Carrboro ArtsCenter and showed me I was a better writer than I thought I was. The writing group that grew out of those classes walked through the story chapter by chapter with me, giving valuable feedback that helped me make it better. Those stalwart friends are Doug Brower, Diana Garcia, Terry Kitson, and Sam Leaman. I thank Eve Porinchak for her expert developmental editing, Diana Wade for her beautiful design work, and Kathy Brown for proofreading. In addition, several friends gave first readings to the completed manuscript: Lori Hoyt, Julian Birnbaum, Laura Marshall, Lois Ann Hobbs, Leslie Bassinger, and Linda A. Marshall. Finally, I thank my husband, Dave Curtin, for his faithful love and devotion and who cheers me on in whatever endeavor I undertake.

About the Author

$\mathcal{D}$uring her forty years as a clinical social worker, Alice Carlton worked with many individuals and couples in distress and gained much insight into human nature and relationship difficulties. Retirement offered her an opportunity to devote herself to creative writing. She is a member of the NC Writers' Network. She has published a story in *Motherscope Magazine* and poetry in *Friends Journal* and in *Iris,* the UNC Journal of Medicine, Literature and Visual Art. She lives in Chapel Hill, NC, with her husband, one dog, and two cats.

Made in the USA
Columbia, SC
21 November 2022

71845196R00228